HELEN HUNT JACKSON

Saxe Holm's Stories, Second Series

The American Short Story Series

VOLUME 62

GARRETT PRESS

512-00363-7

Library of Congress Catalog Card No. 69-11903

*This volume was reprinted from the1878 edition
published by Scribner, Armstrong & Co.*

First Garrett Press Edition published 1969

The American Short Story Series
Volume 62
©1969

Manufactured in the United States of America

GARRETT PRESS, INC.
Publishers

250 West 54th Street, New York, N.Y. 10019

CONTENTS.

A FOUR–LEAVED CLOVER.

PART I.

SERGEANT KARL REUTNER had never found a four-leaved clover. He had often looked for them — at home in Bavaria, in the green meadows at the foot of the giant glacier Watzman, and in America, on the sunny prairies of Illinois. But he had never found one. "It is luck; I shall not have luck before I find the four leaf of clover," he had said, half jesting, many a time, to himself or to gay comrades. And in his secret heart he was not without a shadow of superstition about it It had again and again happened that some one by his side had stooped and picked a four-leaved clover, upon which he was just on the point of treading, while his eyes were searching eagerly for it. It did seem as if Karl could never see the magic little leaf, and why should this not mean something? Whence came the world-wide belief in the spell, if it were merely an idle fancy?

But now Karl Reutner was to find his four-leaved clover. There it was, gently waving in the wind, not two feet away from his eyes. Karl was lying low on the ground. He was not looking for four-leaved clover; he was listening with every faculty sharply concentrated, waiting for a sound which seemed to him inexplicably delayed. He was lying in a trench before Gettysburg, and he was impatient for the order to fire.

The gentle summer breeze stirred the grass blades on the upper edge of the trench, and parting them, showed one tall four-leaved clover. With an exclamation of delight, Karl dropped his musket, picked the clover, fastened it in the band of his cap, and lifting up the cap, imprudently waved it to the right and left, calling down the line : " Good luck, boys ! The four leaf of clover ! "

The next Karl knew, it was night — dark, starless, chilly night. He was alone ; a dreadful silence, broken now and then by more dreadful groans, reigned all around. He was naked ; he could not move ; terrible pains were racking his breast. Something was firmly clutched in his right hand, but he could not lift his arm to see what it was ; neither could he unclasp his hand.

The battle of Gettysburg was over, and Karl was shot through the lungs. "Good luck, boys! The four leaf of clover ! " had been his last words, hardly spoken before the waving cap had proved a mark for a rebel sharp-shooter, and Karl had fallen back apparently dead.

No time then for one comrade to help another. In a few moments more his company had gone, leaving behind many of its brave fellows wounded, dying, dead. In the night Karl had been stripped by rebel prowlers, and left for dead. Only his cap remained ; that was so firmly clutched in his right hand, they could not take it from him. Withered, drooping above the tarnished gilt wreath on the band, hung the four-leaved clover; but Karl could not see it. He remembered it, however, and as he struggled in his feverish half delirium to recall the last moments before he fell, he muttered to himself : " The four leaf of clover brought this of luck ; bad luck to begin."

The feeble sounds caught the ear of a party of rebels, searching for their wounded. As the dark lantern flashed its slender ray of light upon Karl's figure, and the rebel officer saw the United States badge on the cap, he turned away. But at Karl's voice and the broken English : " Water ! For God's love, one water ! " he turned back. The blue eyes and the yellow hair had a spell in them for the dark-haired Southerner. There had been a Gretchen once with whom he had roamed many a moonlight night, in Heidelberg. Her eyes and her hair, and the pretty broken English she had learned from him, were like these.

" Pick him up, boys ; he 'll count for one, damn him ! " were the words under which he hid his sudden sympathy from the angry and resentful men who obeyed his orders. But afterward he went many times secretly to the ambulance to see if that yellow-haired German boy were still alive, and were covered by blankets.

Of the terrible journey to Libby Prison Karl knew nothing. A few days after it he came again, slowly and painfully, to his consciousness, as he had that first night on the battle-field, like one awakening from a frightful and confused dream. He was on the damp dungeon floor ; a pretense of a pallet beneath him. When he tried to speak, a strange, gurgling sound filled his throat.

" Better not try to talk," said the surgeon, who happened to be standing near.

" Am I dying ? " said Karl.

" No, not just yet," laughed the brutal surgeon ; but you won't last long. Our boys have n't left you any lungs."

It was too true. The bullet had gone through both lungs. In one there was a hole into which a man might put his fist. Karl shut his eyes and again the vision of the waving clover leaf floated before them. He fell asleep, and dreamed that he was lying in a field filled with four-leaved clovers, and that a beautiful, dark-haired girl was gathering them and bringing them to him by handfuls. When he waked he saw a kind face bending over him, and felt something pressed between his lips. One of his fellow prisoners was trying to feed him with bread soaked in wine. Ah, the heroes of

Libby Prison! Almost all those who came out alive from that hell of tortures, did so because other men had freely spent their lives for them.

All Karl's fellow prisoners loved him. His fair face, beautiful blue eyes, and golden-brown hair, his broken English, and his pathetic patience, appealed to every heart. Every man saved the soft part of his bread for him; and on this, with occasionally a few drops of wine, he lived — that is, he did not die; but he did not gain; the wound did not heal, and each day his strength grew less and less, long after it had seemed that he could not be weaker and live. But hope never forsook him. The four-leaved clover, folded in a bit of paper, was hid in the lining of his cap. Sometimes he took it out, showed it to the prisoners, and told them the story.

"It has brought to me such bad luck, you see; but I think it shall bring one luck better; it is a true sign; there is time yet."

The men shrugged their shoulders. They thought Karl a little weakened in intellect by his sufferings; but they did not contradict him.

Three months later Karl was again lying on the ground at midnight, alone, helpless. An exchange of prisoners had been arranged, and he, with most of his friends, had been carried to City Point. They arrived there at five in the afternoon. The sun was still high and hot, and Karl being one of the feeblest of the prisoners was laid behind an old hogshead, for shade. Boat load after boat load pushed off from the wharf; but he was not taken. He could not speak except in the faintest whisper; he could not move; there he lay, utterly helpless, hearing all the stir and bustle of the loading of the boats, then the plashing of the oars, then the silence, then the return of the boats, more bustle, more departures, and then the dreadful silence again.

He had been laid in such a position that he could see nothing but the planks of the hogshead. It was old and decayed, and rats were crawling in and out of it. They crawled and ran over Karl, and he could not stir. The sun went down; the twilight deepened into darkness. The last boat had gone; in an agony almost maddening Karl lay listening for the oars, and trying to persuade himself that it was not yet too late for one more boat to come back.

A cold wind blew off the water; he had nothing over him but a bit of ragged carpet; under his head an old army coat rolled up for a pillow.

A rebel soldier came by and tried to take this away. Karl spoke no word, but lifted his eyes and looked him full in the face. The man dropped his hold of the overcoat, and walked away. Eight o'clock, — nine, — ten,— no sound on the deserted wharf except the dull thud of the waves against its sides, and the occasional splash of a fierce rat, swimming away. But Karl heard nothing. He had swooned. The fatigue of the trip, the exposure to the air, the long day without food, and still more the utter loss of hope, had drained his last strength. However, in after days, recalling this terrible night, he always said, " I not once my four leaf of clover forget. I say to myself, it is the luck to go to Heaven that it have bring me ; and yet all the time, I know in my heart that I am not to die ; that I have luck in the over world yet."

Karl was right. By one of those inexplicable but uncontrollable impulses, on which the life and the death of man have so often hung, the young officer, who had had charge of moving the prisoners from the wharf to the transport, was led to return once more to make sure that no man had been left behind.

Karl was not the only one. There were two others who had been laid, as he was, in the shade, and out of sight, and who had been too weak to call for help. It was nearly midnight when these three unconscious and apparently dying men were carried on board the ship. The other two soon revived, but Karl knew nothing until he had been for two days tenderly nursed in one of the Philadelphia hospitals. Even then he had only a half consciousness of himself, or his surroundings. Fever had set in ; he was delirious a great part of the time, for two months ; and when he was not, his broken English, and his frequent reference to the " four leaf of clover," prevented the nurses from believing him fully sane.

At last one blessed Sunday, there came to the hospital a young lady who spoke German. At the first sound of the broken syllables, she went quickly to his bedside, and saying to the nurse, " I can speak to this poor fellow in his own language ; " she said a few words to Karl in German. The effect was magical.

He lifted himself up suddenly in bed, and exclaiming " Ach mein Gott," poured out such a flood of incoherent, grateful, bewildered German that the best of scholars need not have been ashamed at failing to comprehend him. Karl had found a friend. Every day she went to see him, — carried him the food he needed, found out from him the names of his friends, and wrote letters to them in German.

One day he said to her : " You cannot be my girl of the four leaf of clover. You have eyes like the heaven, like mine ; but her eyes were like eyes of a deer that is afraid."

Then he told the story of the clover, and showed her the creased and faded leaf.

It seemed almost a miracle that the fragile, crumbling little thing should not have been lost 'n all these months. But no Roman Catholic devotee ever clung more superstitiously to a relic than did Karl Reutner to his " four leaf of clover."

Often in his delirious attacks he would call for it, and not be pacified until the nurses, who had 'earnt to humor the whim, would put the paper into his hand. Now that he was better, he kept it carefully in the inner compartment of his pocket-book, and rarely took it out. It was enough to look in and see that it was safe.

Karl's only relatives in this country were a brother and sister who lived in Chicago. The brother was a manufacturer of fringes, buttons, and small trimmings, and the sister had married an engraver, also a German. They were industrious working-people, preserving in their new homes all the simple-hearted ways of their life in the old world. When Karl was drafted for the war, they had tried in vain to induce him to let them put their little savings together to buy a substitute for him. "No, no, I will not have it," he said; "my life is no more than another man's life that it should be saved. There are brothers and sisters to all. I have no wife; it is the men without wives that must go to fight." On these two simple house-holds the news from Gettysburg fell with crushing weight.

"Karl Reutner, killed;" only three words, and there were long columns of names with the same bitter word following them. But into few houses was carried greater sorrow than into these. Wil-helm Reutner and Karl were twins. From their ba-byhood they had never been separated, had never disagreed. Together they had come to the new world to seek their fortunes; together they had slowly built up the business which their father had followed in Berlin; they lived together; and Wilhelm's babies knew no difference in love and care between their uncle Karl and their father. The sister was much younger; Wilhelm and Karl had laid by their first earnings to bring her out to join them, and for some years they had all lived in one family in such peace and happiness as are not often seen among laboring people of American birth. No thought of discontent, no dream of ambition for a higher position, entered their heads. Home love, comfort, industry, and honesty — these were the watchwords of their lives, the key-notes of all their actions. When Wilhelm and Annette were married, there was no change in this atmosphere of content and industry, except an immeasurable increase of happiness as child after child came, bringing the ineffable sunshine of babyhood into the two households.

Just before the sad news of Karl's death, a new and very great element of enjoyment had been introduced into Wilhelm's family. Margaret Warren had come to live in his house.

Margaret Warren was the daughter of a Congregationalist minister. Her life had been passed in small country villages in the Western States. She had known privations, hardships, discomforts of all sorts; her father was a gentleman and a scholar, and wretchedly out of place in the pioneer western life; he did not understand the people; the people misinterpreted him; his heart was full of love **for**

their souls, and a burning desire to bring them to
Christ ; but he wounded their self love, and they
offended his instincts, at every step ; the consequence was, that he found himself at a middle age
with an invalid wife and six children, a disappointed,
unsuccessful man.   Margaret was the eldest daughter, and for the first fourteen years of her life,
her father's constant companion.   The only un-
alloyed pleasure he had was in the careful training of her mind.   Margaret Warren was, at sixteen,
a rare girl ; she was far better fitted than most boys
are, to enter college.   But all this learning did not
in the least unfit her for practical duties.   She was
her mother's stay as well as her father's delight ;
she understood housekeeping as well as she did
Greek, and found as true a pleasure in contriving
how to make a garment out of slender material, as
in demonstrating a problem in Euclid.   Until her
seventeenth year she had been unflaggingly brave,
hopeful, content, in this hard life.   But as she saw
the years slowly making all the burdens heavier ;
her mother growing feebler, the family growing
larger, she began to ask herself what the end would
be ; and she found no answer to the question.   A
vague feeling, that she herself ought to find some
way of making her mother and her five little
brothers and sisters more comfortable, haunted her
thoughts by night and day.   She saw the secret of
her father's failure more clearly than the most
discontented of his parishioners ever saw it.   She

knew things could never be any better. "Oh, why did papa ever undertake to preach," she said to herself, over and over; her affectionate reverence for him made her feel guilty in the thought. Yet it pressed upon her more and more heavily.

"Each place we go to is a little poorer than the one before it," she repeated, "and yet, each year we need a little more money instead of less; and mamma is growing weaker and more tired every day. If I could only get a good school I could earn as much money as papa does by preaching. I know I could teach well; and then I could learn too." Unconsciously to herself, the desire for a wider knowledge and experience of life entered largely into Margaret's desire to be a teacher. She had uncommon executive ability, and, without knowing it, was beginning to be cramped by her limited sphere.

Through the help of a clergyman in Chicago, an old class-mate of Mr. Warren's, Margaret realized her dream. It was a bitter day for the little household in the parsonage when she left them. With tears streaming down their cheeks the children clung to her, and her mother was pale and speechless with grief; but Margaret bravely kept back all traces of her own sorrow, and went away with a smiling face. The next day she wrote to her mother : —

"Dear, precious, tired Mamma; it would break my heart to think of you working away without me

to help you, and when I recall your face on the
door-step yesterday, if I were not borne up by an
instinct that I shall very soon help you much more
than I could at home. Only think, I can already
send you seventy-five dollars every quarter — half
as much as papa's salary ; and I know I shall very
soon save a great deal more."

Margaret was right. Such a teacher as she had
only to be known to be recognized. Her text-book
training had been singularly thorough and accurate, but this was the least of her qualifications as
a teacher. In the first place she loved children
with all her heart ; in the second place, she loved
nature and truth with the passion of a devotee.
That life could be dull to a human being was a
mystery to her ; every new discovery in art or
science was a stimulus and delight to her ; the simplest every day fact had significance and beauty to
her ; her own existence was rich, full, harmonious,
and out of her abundance she gave unconsciously
far more than she dreamed to every being that
came in contact with her. There was not a pupil
in her school who was not more or less electrified
by her enthusiasm and love. The standard of
scholarship was rapidly raised ; but this was a less
test of her power than the elevation and stimulus
given to the whole moral tone of the school in
which she taught. Teachers as well as pupils
were litted to a higher plane by intercourse with
her.

At the end of two years Margaret was the principal of the highest school in the city, at a salary nearly twice as large as her father's. But her ambition was not yet satisfied. She longed to be at the head of a school of her own, where she should be untrammeled in all respects, and free to carry out her own theories. This was her one air-castle, and, with a view to this, she planned all her life. Three hours every day she spent in hard study or reading. Only the best of constitutions could have borne such a strain ; but Margaret had come, on her mother's side, of an indomitable New England stock. It was in carrying out this scheme of educating herself more perfectly that Margaret had come to live in Wilhelm Reutner's house. Wilhelm's two little daughters had been in her first school. They were singularly gentle and well-bred children, and held themselves always a little aloof from their companions. One day Margaret discovered accidentally that they spoke both German and French fluently. "How is this, little ones," she said ; who taught you so many languages ?

"Oh, papa always speaks to us in German, and mamma in French," said they.

"And Uncle Karl, too," added the youngest, with a sad face. "Uncle Karl that has gone to the war."

That afternoon Margaret walked home with the children from school. As they drew near a block of small two-story wooden houses, Margaret's eye was attracted by two balconies full of flowers. " Oh, how lovely ! " she exclaimed.

" That 's our house. Those are Uncle Karl's flowers," cried both the children in a breath; " we take all the care of them now he has gone. He said we might."

The front of the little house was like a terraced garden. Margaret had never seen anything like it. Every window-sill had its box of flowers, and above the door was a balcony full to overflowing of geraniums, nasturtiums, fuchsias, and white flox. Margaret stood for so long a time looking at them that the children grew impatient, and pulled her with gentle force into the house.

Annette came forward with a shy, sweet courtesy to meet the unexpected guest.

" We talk your name very much, Mademoiselle," she said ; " to see you will be to the father a happiness." Then Wilhelm thanked her with warm fervor for her goodness to the children, and before he had finished speaking, the children, who had disappeared upon entering the house, came running back with their hands full of scarlet, yellow, and white blossoms, and showered them upon Margaret's lap.

" But my children, my children ! " remonstrated their mother.

" Uncle Karl said we might pick always some 'or a pretty lady," cried they ; " and is not the teacher pretty? Did we not tell you she looked like the Madonna?"

"It was not the first time that Margaret's face had been compared to that of the Sistine Madonna; always, however, with a qualification, for that calm and placid Madonna had far less joy in her face than was in Margaret Warren's bright countenance.

"Yes, the children say rightly, young lady. They have done well to bring you the flowers, as our far away Karl would have done," said Wilhelm, gravely, still standing before Margaret.

Margaret felt as if she were in a dream. She had come expecting to find two plain, honest working people, to whom she could without difficulty say that she would like to come and board in their family for the sake of learning to speak German and French. Instead, she felt as if she had been received by a prince and princess in disguise: so subtle a power have noble thoughts, simplicity of heart, and love of beauty to invest men and women with a dignity greater than splendor can give.

Margaret made stammering words of her request. It was received with great surprise, but with the same dignified simplicity of demeanor and speech.

"We have never thought that a stranger could come under our roof, and pay for the food," said Annette, with a shade of pride in her voice; and t might be that our living would displease you."

"The teacher is not as a stranger, when Annettechen and Mariska so love her," said Wilhelm, who was on Margaret's side from the beginning. "But do you remember, young lady, that you have never known such ways as are our ways? It would be a great shame to my heart if you were not at ease in my house; and we cannot change."

With every word that Wilhelm and Annette spoke, Margaret grew more and more anxious to carry her point.

"It is you who do not know," she said, "how very simply and plainly I have always lived at home, and it is so that I would wish to live even if I had much money. My father is a poor minister; my mother has never, in all her life, had so pretty a home as this."

And Margaret sighed, as she looked around at the picturesque little sitting-room; its white porcelain stove was now converted into a sort of altar, holding two high candlesticks, made out of the polished horns of antelopes — a crimson candle in one, and a yellow one in the other, and between the two a square stone jar of dark, blue and gray Flemish ware, filled with white amaranths. Low oaken chests, simply but quaintly carved, stood on each side the stove, and a row of tiles, maroon colored and white, with pictures of storks, and herons, and edelweiss flowers, and pine trees on them, was above each chest. The

furniture was all of oak, old and dark. It had
belonged to Annette's mother, in Lorraine. The
floor was of yellow pine, bright and shining, and
gay braided rugs, with borders of tufted worsted
balls, covered the greater part of it. Flowers
filled every window, and on the walls were prints
of Albert Durer, of Teniers, of Holbein, of Raphael — cheap prints, but rendering the masters'
works truthfully. In one corner stood a large
violoncello, and in another, above a shelf filled
with music, hung a violin case wreathed with ever-
greens. This was Karl's. In the other two corners were odd oaken cabinets with glass doors,
and a figure of St. Nicholas on the top. On the
shelves were wax and glass and wooden toys.
These were the Christmas gifts of many years.
The whole room was like a bit of the quiet German Tyrol set in the centre of the bustling and
breathless American city; but Margaret did not
know this. She only felt a bewildered sense of
repose and delight and wonder, mixed with a
yearning recognition of the beautiful life which
must be lived in this simple home.

When Annette heard that Margaret's father was
a poor pastor, her face lighted up. "My mother
also was the daughter of a pastor," she said; and
is it then that the good pastors are poor in this
country also?" Annette had thus far known only
rich and prosperous ones in the rich and prosperous city.

Wilhelm, also, felt that a barrier was removed between him and the "teacher" when he heard that she had lived as a daughter lives, in the home of a poor country pastor. He no longer feared that she could not be content in his house; and his heart had been strangely warm towards Margaret from the first moment.

"There is Karl's room, which would be sunny and warm, if it were not too small," he said inquiringly, turning to Annette.

"And the big closet with a window — would it not be that the teacher could use when she would study? said Annette, who remembered the little room in which her grandfather had kept his few books, and sat when he was writing, and must not be interrupted.

Margaret's face flushed with pleasure. The matter was evidently settled. It was already beginning to be a matter of hospitality in these kindly hearts, and the only question was how they could make her happiest and most comfortable. The children danced with joy, and taking Margaret's hands in theirs, they drew her towards the stairway, saying:

"Come, see Uncle Karl's room; it is the nicest in the house."

It was, indeed, a lovely room, with its one window looking out on the great blue lake.

"It is too small," said Annette, as she stood with Margaret on the threshold; "but there is also this closet," and she threw open a door into a second still smaller room, also with one window to the east.

"Oh !" exclaimed Margaret. " Can you spare them both ? That will be perfect. My good friends, I cannot thank you enough."

Wilhelm looked at Margaret with a steadfast, half-dreamy gaze. The German nature is a strangely magnetic one, under all its phlegmatic and prosaic exterior.

" I have a belief that it is I and my house who are laid under debt by you, teacher," he said, with singular earnestness.

So it was settled that Margaret should come to live with the Reutners, and should have Karl's room till he returned from the war.

She wished to come at once, but Wilhelm insisted on a week's interval. Annette looked puzzled ; she knew of no reason for the delay ; but Wilhelm was firm, and Margaret did not press the matter.

Seven days later, when Margaret went home again, with Annettechen and Mariska, — this time really going home, — she hardly knew the little rooms. Wilhelm had painted the walls of a soft gray ; he had taken away the closet door, made the door-way into an arch, and hung it with curtains of plain gray cloth, of the same shade as the walls. A narrow strip of plain crimson paper bordered the rooms ; a set of plain book shelves on the wall were edged with the same crimson paper. A small table, with a crimson cloth, and a comfortable arm-chair, also of crimson, stood in the room which had been called the closet. Under each window he had put a larger balcony shelf, and filled it with gay flowers, such as were on the shelves below.

Margaret's eyes filled with tears. She turned, and saw Wilhelm and Annette standing behind her, their faces glowing with welcome and hope that she would be pleased.

"Do not try to say that you like it, teacher," said Wilhelm; "we see in your eyes that you are more glad than we had hoped we could make you." And with a delicacy which touched Margaret even more deeply than she had been touched by the adorning of her rooms, he drew Annette away, and left her alone.

One month from this day, Wilhelm, Annette, and Margaret were sitting alone in the little sitting-room. The children had gone to bed. It was a sultry evening. Annette had put out the large lamp, and Wilhelm was reading the newspaper by the light of a candle in one of the Tyrolean candlesticks. Suddenly he groaned aloud, dropped the candlestick, and fell back in his chair. The candle was extinguished, and they were left in darkness. Helplessly the two women groped for another light, Wilhelm's heavy breathing terrifying them more and more every moment, and poor Annette crying : —

"Wilhelm, oh, my Wilhelm! He is dead! He 's dead!"

Wilhelm Reutner was a strong and robust man.

It was the first time in his life that he had ever lost his consciousness. But the fatal words, "Karl Reutner — killed," had flashed upon his eyes with an indescribable shock of surprise and anguish. He had not known that Karl's regiment was at Gettysburg. He was reading the accounts of the battle with no especial interest, and it was by accident that he had glanced at the lists of killed and wounded. When he came to himself he gasped out, "Karl, Karl!" and then fainted again.

"Oh! our Karl is killed!" cried Annette; "it will kill my Wilhelm, too;" and she fell on her knees, clasping her husband's head to her bosom, and calling: "But, Wilhelm, thou hast the little ones, and thou hast me. Oh, do not die, darling!"

He soon revived, but could not speak. He turned most piteous looks first at Annette, then at Margaret.

"Yes, Mr. Reutner," said Margaret, who had taken up the paper, and saw the name, "we know it, too. It is your dear brother's name. But you must remember that these lists are often wrong. A great many people have been reported killed who have been only taken prisoners. I do not believe your brother is dead."

Wilhelm groaned. Hope could find no place in his heart. "Oh why did I not compel him to stay at home?" he said. "What is this cursed country to us that we should die for it?"

"Oh! yes," sobbed Annette, "we all knelt to

Karl! Wilhelm had tears like the rain on his face, to beseech that he would let us pay that another man should go; but he said that the man with no wife should go to the fight, and he was angry at the last, even with Wilhelm.

"I think your brother was very right," said Margaret quietly, taking Wilhelm's hand in hers; "if he were my own brother, even if he had been killed, I should still rejoice that he had been noble enough to give his life for the right."

"For the Fatherland, yes," said Wilhelm; "but not for this land we need not to love. It is not anything to us, except that we must live. We are Germans; we are not of your blood;" and Wilhelm looked almost fiercely at Margaret.

"All men are of one blood, when the fight is that all men may be free, my friend," said Margaret, still more quietly, with a voice trembling with sympathy, and yet firm with enthusiasm. "Whatever land it had been which first began the fight for freedom to all, I would send my brothers to die under its banners. I would go myself! But I do not believe your Karl is dead. I cannot tell why I have so strong a feeling that he is still alive, but I have no doubt of it — none!"

Margaret's hopefulness was not shared by Wilhelm. He refused to listen to any of her suggestions. Weeks later a letter came from Karl's friend, Gustave Boehmer, who was in the same company, and was lying in the trench, next to Karl,

when he was shot. Wilhelm read the letter aloud,
without a tear or a sob, and said, turning to Margaret, "You see the brother's knowledge was more
sure than the stranger's. I knew in that first second
that my Karl was gone."

A black ribbon was twined in the evergreen
wreath on Karl's violin, a wreath of white immor-
telles put around Karl's picture on the wall, and
the little, grief-stricken household went on with its
daily life, brave and resigned. But Wilhelm Reutner's face was altered from that day ; night after
night the little children gazed wistfully into his
eyes, missing the joyous look from his smile and
the merry ring from his voice. Night after night
poor Annette had cried as she had cried on the
night when the sad news came, " Liebling, thou
hast the little ones and thou hast me : do not die
for the love of Karl." And Wilhelm answered,
" Be patient, I had not thought it could be so hard.
The good God will make it easier, in time. It
must be that the twin bond is strong after death
as it is before birth. I feel my Karl all the while
more near than when he was alive."

On the wall of Karl's room, now Margaret's,
there hung an oval picture of the beautiful Königsee Lake in Bavaria. On the margin of the print
was drawn, in rough crayon, a girl's head. It was
a spirited drawing, and the head had great beauty.
Around the picture was a wreath of edelweiss.
Annette had told Margaret that this head was the

portrait of a young girl in Ischl whom Karl had loved when they were little more than children. She had died just before Karl and Wilhelm had set out for America, and this rough and unfinished sketch, drawn by Karl one day, half in sport, when they were sailing on the Königsee, was the only memento he had of her. The edelweiss flowers Karl had gathered on the very glacier of the Watzman, the day before he bade good-by to his home.

Ever since Margaret had occupied the room, she had found a special fascination in this picture ; but now she was conscious of a new magnetism in it. Every morning the first rays of the rising sun slanted across this picture, bringing out into full relief each line of the girl's head, and still more, every fine, velvety fibre of the snowy petals of the edelweiss. The picture hung at the foot of the bed, and sometimes when Margaret first opened her eyes and saw this golden light on the lake and the girl's face and the edelweiss wreath, she fancied that there were rhythmic sounds in the light ; that she heard voices fainter than faintest whispers, and yet clear and distinct as flute notes in the air, speaking words she did not understand. She grew almost afraid of the picture ; it seemed a link between her and the unseen world. Yet she never believed that the link was with Karl. It was with the unknown maiden of Ischl ; the immortal Love Blossoms seemed to bind it, to symbolize it, and in the tremulous sunlight to utter it. Margaret

was not superstitious, and she had not a touch of
sentimentalism in her nature ; but it was out of
her power to shake off the influence of this picture.
"Königsee" floated through her brain, even in
school hours, like the refrain of a song ; when she
looked off into the sky, the clouds took shapes
like the shape of the sides of the Königsee, and
whenever she gazed on the blue lake, she found
her fancy walling it in with mountains, like those
which walled Königsee. By night she dreamed of
sailing in shadowy boats, with the shadowy maiden,
on Königse ; and she waked from these dreams
only to find the sunbeams on her wall lighting up
the shadowy maiden's head, and making golden
bars across the water of Königsee. The young
maiden of Ischl had loved Karl Reutner very
much ; she loved him still ; else, whence came this
thrilling personality in the mute picture record
of her and of the sunny day when she and her
lover had sailed on Königsee ! Had Karl gone to
her ? Had her love drawn and lifted him up,
past the stars, and over the golden wall of Heaven ?
Were they together now ?

Constantly Margaret asked herself these questions, and constantly one answer came. " No !
Karl is alive." Ah, well must the shadowy maiden
of Ischl have loved Karl ! Well does she love him
still. Else, how does she always and ever, through
the mute picture record of that summer day on
Königsee, say to Margaret, " Karl is not dead !
Karl will come home ? "

Six months had passed. Karl's name was oft-
ner spoken now in his home. Wilhelm could bear
the sound. The faithful little children still called
their geraniums and fuchsias and roses "Uncle
Karl's flowers," and laid the fairest buds and blossoms by the "teacher's" plate at breakfast. Margaret was as thoroughly at home in the family as
she could have been in her own father's house,
and yet there was a shade of reverential deference
in Wilhelm's and Annette's manner towards her,
and in their regard for her. They loved her as a
sister, but it was as they would love a sister who
had become a princess. To their simple and un-
learned souls her acquirements seemed greater
than they really were, and a certain unconscious
reticence of nature which Margaret had, in spite of
all her overflowing enthusiasm and frankness, surrounded her with a barrier of personal dignity
which every one felt, and which no one ventured to
disregard.

On New Year's night Margaret returned home
late from a party. As she drew near the house
she saw to her surprise a bright light burning in
the sitting-room. Fearing that some one was ill,
she opened the door of the room quickly ; a strange
sight met her eyes. Wilhelm was on his knees,
his face uplifted, and tears streaming down his
cheeks. Annette stood opposite him, with her
hands clasped, looking at him with an expression

of unspeakable rapture. Neither of them spoke as Margaret approached.

"Oh, what is it? What has happened?" exclaimed Margaret, too terrified by their strange attitudes to see that their expression was one of great joy, and not of grief.

Wilhelm stretched one hand towards the table, and his lips moved, but no sound came from them. Annette turned to the table, took up a letter, and gave it to Margaret, saying, "Karl! Karl! He is alive. He comes home."

Margaret sank into a chair. Strong as her instinct had been that Karl was not dead, the certainty came to her with almost as great a shock of surprise as it had come to his brother and sister.

The letter was from Karl's friend, the young lady in the Philadelphia Hospital. It was long and full, giving an account of all that Karl had suffered in the months in Libby Prison, of his almost miraculous preservation at City Point, and of his present convalescence. At the close she said : —

"The surgeon says that if Karl has no drawbacks he will be well enough to come home in a month. He most earnestly advises that you do not come here. Karl is absolutely comfortable, and wants for nothing ; the excitement of talking would do him great harm. He himself begs that you will not come. I will see him every day, and write to you every week."

At the bottom of the sheet Karl had written : —
" Beloveds, do not come to me. I will the
sooner come to you. God be praised.

" KARL. "

Grief has no tears like joy. A stranger would
have supposed for the next few days that the whole
household was in sorrow. Everybody's face was
red with weeping. Nobody could speak in a steady
voice. Wilhelm sat silent, by the hour, looking
into the fire, and wiping his eyes.

" Oh, Miss Margaret," he said ; " Oh teacher,
taught of some angel, why did I not believe you ?
Why is it that you, who have not known our Karl,
should be the one to be told, and not I ? "

Margaret was on the point of telling him that
the maiden of Ischl had told her because she found
her sleeping in Karl's room. But a vague shame
sealed her lips. She need not have hesitated. It
would not have seemed a strange or an incredible
thing to Wilhelm Reutner.

The next letters were not so cheering. The excitement of hearing, even by letter, from his friends,
had caused a slight relapse of Karl's fever, and the
physician now thought that it might be six weeks
before he could safely travel. It was a hard thing
for Wilhelm to sit quietly at home and wait for so
many days. Only Margaret's influence withheld
him from going to Philadelphia at once.

" I need not to see him," he said ; " I could go each
day to the door and ask if he is better. No hurt

could be to him in that; it would not be so hard for me as is this to stay here; and the doctors do not always know the right; no one can do for my Karl so as I can do. "

" But, Mr. Reutner," urged Margaret, " you do not dream how much harder it would be for you to bear not seeing him, there; it is almost more than you can bear here, three days' journey from him; if he were in the next room, nobody could keep you out; and then if he were to have another fever from the excitement of seeing you, you would never forgive yourself; and it might kill him. He must be very weak."

This last fear restrained Wilhelm. " Yes, if it were to hurt him. That would not be love!" he said over and over to himself, and tried to keep his heart and hands busy in making preparations for Karl's comfort after his return; but the days seemed longer and longer to him, and his face again grew worn and haggard, almost as much as it had in the first few weeks after the news of Karl's death.

One night he sprang up from the tea-table, say-ing, " Annette, come to the theatre! I cannot sit in this room, thinking how it will be when Karl is again in his corner with the violin. I wish we could live in another house till he is here. It will never be done, these two months!"

After they had gone, Margaret drew her chair in front of the fire, and fell into a long reverie, a

strange thing for her to do. She reviewed her
whole life ; first as the eldest daughter in the poor
minister's household ; then as the unknown teacher
in the great city ; now the successfull instructress,
highly esteemed, sought after by people of culture
conscious of influence and power, having in a great
measure realized her early dreams. But the early
dreams had been succeeded by later ones no less
vivid, no less alluring. Margaret Warren had in
her nature a vein of intense ambition. It was not
a vulgar craving for power as power ; it was rather
that a consciousness of power craved room, craved
action. Her studies, her reading, had opened to
her new worlds, and made life seem to her more
and more a vista upon which she had as yet barely
entered.

Her æsthetic sense was fast developing into a
passion which must have food ; beauty in little
things, beauty in great things, beauty perpetually
she was learning to demand. A verse of Keats
could so stimulate her, so lift her into delight, that
she would find jarring and offense in things which
her practical good sense told her were as true, as
harmonious in their way as the color and rhythm
of Keats's peerless lines. She recalled herself
constantly ; she reproached herself constantly ; she
said sternly to herself many a time, " Dignity and
truth are the same in all ages. This Wilhelm
here is great ; and Annette, and the children, they
are representative. Socrates knew no more than

they live, each year, each hour, in their simplicity. If I dwelt in a court, the king could be, after all, only a man. All knowledge is open to me. I have but to take it. What do I want?" But that she did want Margaret knew very well. She wanted the delights of the companionship of the very wisest and highest men, the delight of the sight and sound and sense of utmost beauty, and still more, the delight of feeling in herself the wisdom, the beauty, the elevation. It was partly a noble, and partly an ignoble craving ; partly selfish and partly pure ; but stirred and kindled and fed by such lofty enthusiasms and purposes, that Margaret must be called a noble woman even in her discontent.

She was roused from her reverie by sounds of strange voices in the hall. As she laid her hand on the door to open it, it was thrown violently open, and she had barely time to spring back, when she found herself clasped in the arms of a tall man, and kissed on cheeks, forehead, eyes, lips, neck.

She was so stunned, so bewildered, she could not speak ; also, strong arms held her so tightly that she had no breath, and the first words came from the servant, who ran into the room, calling vociferously, " Howly Vargin, but it 's not the misthress, at all, at all, that yee 's kissin'. It 's the tacher, sir — och, Miss Margaret, it 's the mistress he is a takin' ye for."

That was a moment not to be forgotten. In the

dim fire-light, Karl and Margaret having disentangled themselves, stood for a second looking blankly in each other's faces: Karl, the picture of inexpressible chagrin and confusion; Margaret, scarlet with excitement. But her strong sense of the ludicrous soon conquered every other feeling, and, with laughing eyes, she said, " Never mind, Mr. Karl, I will give them all to Annette as soon as she comes home, and I am very glad to see you back, indeed I am," she added, stretching out both her hands to him; " we did not look for you for weeks yet. "

As she took his hands in hers she felt that they were cold as ice, and saw that his face was turning white. His strength of a moment before was only the passing strength of a great excitement. He had set out against the advice of his physicians and nurses, had journeyed day and night, and now the false strength given by the desire to be at home was fast ebbing away.

" Oh, pray lie down, Mr. Reutner, you look very ill," exclaimed Margaret; and she led him like a little child, to the lounge. Like a little child he lay down upon it, and looked up in her face, while with the servant's help, she took off his heavy wrappings. Then he shut his eyes, and murmured, "The four leaf of clover."

Margaret was terrified. She thought he was delirious; she dared not be left alone with him, and yet she felt that she ought to send for a physician.

3

She bathed his forehead; she chafed his hands; she looked helplessly into the servant's face, saying, "Oh Mary, what shall we do?"   At the sound of her voice Karl opened his eyes, and said, feebly, "Do not have fear. I will rest. That is all, and if there is wine, it will make me strong." Then he looked long into Margaret's face with a strange, unseeing gaze, and murmured again, as he shut his eyes : —

"The four leaf of clover. It have come true."

When Wilhelm and Annette returned, they found Karl asleep on the sofa, and Margaret siting close by his side, her face pale and full of distress. It had been a terrible hour for her. As soon as she saw Wilhelm and Annette, she burst into tears, exclaiming, "Oh, thank God, you have come ; he is not quite in his senses, and I have not known what to do ! "

Hardly daring to breathe, lest they should waken the sleeper, the three sat motionless for an hour.

At Karl's first movement, Wilhelm threw himself on his knees, and clasped him to his heart ; no word was spoken ; but the two men sobbed like women. While they were in each other's arms Margaret stole softly away.

When Karl looked up he said, "The four leaf of clover, where has she gone?" Wilhelm did not understand the first words, but replied simply to the last, "She has gone to her room. It is the good teacher, Miss Margaret; she lives with us. You will love her as we all do."

Karl smiled.

The next morning, when Margaret came into the sitting-room, Karl, still lying on the lounge, fixed his blue eyes steadily on her face, and said abruptly, "It was then that I so frightened you, to make your cheeks so white, last night. To-day they are red, like red lilies and white lilies in one field," and the blue eyes dwelt on the face till the red lilies had driven all the white lilies away.

Margaret passed her hand impatiently across her cheek. "Oh, I always have color," she said. It did not please her that Wilhelm Reutner's brother should have looked at her in that manner. In a second more, her kindliness of heart triumphed over the slight unworthiness of resentment, and going nearer him, she added, "I was indeed very much frightened about you last night. You seemed very ill, and I was all alone with Mary. I hope you are better ; you look better."

Karl's eyes had fallen to the ground. As clearly as if it had been written in letters on Margaret's brow, he had read her first thought, and had been pained.

"Yes, I am better ; I am well. It is the home which could cure me," he said, in a tone whose grave simplicity was like Wilhelm's, and had in it an inexpressible charm.

In a moment more, he said, earnestly, "Have you ever found one four leaf of clover ? " and, taking out his pocket-book, he turned its leaves over slowly, searching for something.

"Oh dear," thought Margaret, "he is certainly crazy. That was what he was talking about last night. Poor fellow!"

"Oh, yes, Mr. Reutner," she replied. "Four-leaved clovers are very common. I have often found whole handfuls of them."

"I thought you had. And have you ever one dream at night that you find the hands full of them, and give them to some one?"

Margaret looked puzzled, and was about to reply, when Wilhelm and the children entered the room. Karl laid a little folded paper, which he had held in his hand, back into the pocket-book, and opened his arms to the children, who sprang into them, and covered him with kisses until he was forced to cry out for mercy.

All day long Margaret was haunted by the words, and the voice in which they were spoken, "Have you ever found one four leaf of clover?" "What could he have meant?" she thought. "He does not seem in the least like a crazy man. I wonder what he had in that paper;" and more than once, the scholars received irrelevant answers to their questions, because their beautiful teacher's thoughts were full of this perplexing memory.

That night the mystery was cleared up. After the children had gone to bed, Karl told the story of the four-leaved clover, and took from his pocket-book the little relic leaf. Wilhelm took it in his hands, and looked at it with stern eyes.

"But why dost thou keep it, my Karl? Ach, it has cost thee dear!"

Karl reached his hand out hastily, as if to rescue the leaf.

" But it have bring me home," he said. " I will keep it so long as I live," and as he laid it back in the pocket-book, he smiled with the smile of one who recalls a bliss known only to himself.

It was indeed the " home which could cure." Karl grew better hour by hour. The wound healed, and, although the physicians said that the lungs must always be weak, Karl was in two months a strong man.

Margaret did not grow wonted to his presence in the family. It disturbed her, she hardly knew how, or why, and she chided herself often for the unreasonable feeling. Since that first morning, when with his blue eyes blazing with admiration, he had compared her cheeks to red lilies, he had never by word or glance betrayed any feeling other than the respectful affection with which his brother and sister treated her. His eyes met hers with the same clear, steady response that Wilhelm's always did, and he listened to her words with a simple reverence like that the children showed her. Often when she was speaking, he sat with his head slightly bowed, his eyes fixed on the ground ; and an expression of rapt attention ; it was as a man might 'isten to the words of a priestess. Sometimes when he looked earnestly at her, there was, for a second, a beseeching and remorseful look, as of one who implored forgiveness; but the look was gone so quickly that Margaret never fathomed its meaning, and no one else saw it.

Margaret often wished that Karl had not come home; and yet, she never said this to herself without being in the same instant conscious that in numberless, and in some hardly definable ways, her comfort had been much increased since his return. Karl had seen more of the world than Wilhelm and Annette, and had, moreover, a curious faculty of divining Margaret's preferences and tastes.

"The teacher would like this, or that," he had said to Annette, again and again; and Annette had replied, "How dost thou know? Has the teacher said it to thee? She was pleased before." But when Karl had carried his point, Annette always found that there came in a few days, a strong expression of grateful pleasure from Margaret.

And so the spring and the summer wore away, and the winter came back, and the long months had brought no apparent change in Wilhelm Reutner's house. But deep down in one heart under that roof, were working forces mightier, subtler than any which had ripened the spring into the summer, and the summer into the garnered harvest of autumn. Karl Reutner loved Margaret Warren. His love was so entirely without any hope of return, that it partook of the nature of the passion of a spiritual devotee, and was lifted to a plane of almost superhuman unselfishness. To say that he never thought of Margaret as a man thinks of a woman who might be his wife, would not be true. Margaret was a very beautiful woman; and Karl Reutner was a man in whose veins ran blood both strong and pure; he could not hear the rustle of Margaret's gown without a faster beat to his pulse. Yet, when he thought of Margaret's possible wifehood, it was never of her wifehood to him. He could not forbear thinking what wifehood, what motherhood would be to her; he could not forbear thinking what it would be to a man, if Margaret were to put her arms around him; he could not forbear thinking how Margaret would look with her child at her breast. But it was as a man might think, kneeling before the holiest of Raphael's Madonnas. His sole desire in life was that Margaret should have happiness. Each smallest trifle in which he could add to that happiness, was a joy unspeakable; that she seemed content, even glad in the quiet home life which he shared, was a blessing so great, that even one day of it could almost be food for a lifetime, it seemed to him. The thought that it could not always be thus, he resolutely put away. But from the thought of asking Margaret to be his, — Karl Reutner's, — wife, his very soul would have recoiled as it would from a blasphemy.

And yet the day came when Margaret found herself obliged to say to him that she could not love him.

It was a strange chance which brought it about.

Karl's love of flowers was a passion such as only Germans know.   How, in addition to all the hours he devoted to his business, he found hours enough to make flowers grow in every window-seat, nook and ledge in and outside of the house was a marvel.   But he did, and the little house was known far and wide for its blossoms.   Margaret's sitting-room was a conservatory; as soon as a plant showed signs of decay it was removed, and replaced by a vigorous one.   Bloom succeeded bloom ; in season and out of season she was never without flowers of red and of white.

One Saturday in February, a year from the day Karl had come home, Margaret was sitting alone in her room.   It had snowed, and the day had been dreary ; at sunset the sky cleared, and a beautiful rosy glow spread over the lake.   Margaret sat watching it, and wondering, as all lonely people have hours of wondering, why, since the world is so thronged with its millions, there need ever be one lonely man or woman.   Some one knocked at the door so gently that she thought it was one of the children, and answered without looking around. The door opened, but no one spoke.   Margaret turned her head ; there stood Karl, holding in his hands an oblong box of daisies in full blossom.   He had been for weeks coaxing and crowding the little things until there was a thicket of the dainty nodding disks, pink, white, red, and the green leaves also crowding thick and bright. The box was surrounded by a fine lattice work, painted white, which came up like a paling, two inches above the top of the box, so that one could fancy it a mound in an English garden fenced in with white.

"It is for you, Miss Margaret. Where shall I set it," said Karl.

"Oh, Mr. Reutner, you are too kind," exclaimed Margaret, her face crimson with pleasure. "It is the loveliest thing I ever saw," and she bent her face down close to the daisies, still held in Karl's hands.

Margaret had never been so near to Karl before. The rosy lake and sky, and snowy clouds made of the window-panes behind her a background such as Raphael never painted. Her beaming face and thrilling presence lifted Karl to heights of exaltation, and, placing the daisy-box on the floor at her feet, he said, "They are but daisies, beautiful Miss Margaret; that was the fitting flower, for it is like my love for you. It is low on the ground, but it would bloom for you always, and you will not forbid that they should live always in your room?" And for the second time Margaret saw the blue eyes kindle as they kindled when he had told her her cheeks were like red lilies.

Margaret grew more crimson still. No words came to her lips.

It seemed as ruthless to hurt this man's love as 'o trample on a daisy. Yet Karl Reutner must be

made to understand that there could be no thought
of love between him and her. Even in that glori-
fied moment, when he stood before her, tall, strong,
upright, fair as an old Saxon viking with his golden
beard and blue eyes, and pure, she well knew, as
Adam in Eden, Margaret Warren remembered that
Karl Reutner was beneath her in what the world
calls station. There was a shade of something not
wholly kind in the very kindness and gentleness
with which she said:

"But, Mr. Reutner, I cannot let you give me the
daisies to mean that. I am so sorry, so grieved to
pain you, but I must be true."

Margaret's eyes filled with tears as she saw the
look of distress on Karl's face. He stooped to
pick up the box without saying a word. Margaret's heart could not bear this.

"But, Mr. Reutner, you need not take the daisies away. I would love to have them in my room,
now that you understand me. You were so good
to make them grow like this for me. They will be
beautiful all winter," and Margaret laid her hand
gently and caressingly on the edge of the box.

"Oh, Miss Margaret, I thank you," said Karl,
in a very low voice. "You need not to fear that
the daisies should say words to you, if you are
willing that they live at your feet. They have but
eyes; they will not speak. You will let them
stay?"

"Oh, yes, indeed I will," replied Margaret, trying to speak in a natural voice, as if it were an every-day gift, and making room for them on a little stand by the window. Then, while Karl was arranging the box and the saucer, she went on talking with a forced rapidity and earnestness of manner.

Karl listened as one who only partly heard the words. When she stopped he said in his old, grave, calm tone, lifting his eyes to hers steadily as usual: "Thank you, Miss Margaret," and left the room.

Margaret burst into tears. She was very unhappy and utterly perplexed.

"Whoever heard of a man's thanking a woman like that, and going away looking so content and glad when she had just told him she could not marry him!" said Margaret to herself, "and what is to become of me now? I cannot live in the house with him any longer; it will not be kind; I must go away. Oh, I wish he had never come home," and Margaret threw herself on the bed and cried herself to sleep.

When Annette knocked at the door to ask why she did not come down to tea, Margaret roused herself from her heavy sleep, and looked into Annette's face with a bewildered expression of distress. She could not remember at first what had happened. In a second it all flashed into her mind, and burying her face in the pillow she groaned aloud. Annette was frightened. She had never

seen the " teacher " lose self-control.   She thought
she must be very ill.

"Oh, Miss Margaret, what have you ?   It is a
fever " — for Margaret's face was of a scarlet color.
"Karl must bring the doctor," exclaimed Annette.

"No, no, Mrs. Reutner," cried Margaret.   " I
beg you will not say a word to any one.   I am not
ill.   I have slept too heavily.   I will not come
down-stairs to-night, but I shall be well to-morrow."

It was the first time that Margaret's chair at the
table had been vacant.   Annette's explanation of
her absence did not lessen the sense of gloom
which every one felt.

Margaret ill !   It was incredible.

" She have never looked so beautiful as I saw
her not three hours ago," said Karl incredulously.

Something in his tone fell strangely on Wilhelm's ear.   He turned a keen, quick look upon
his brother's face ; but Karl met it with one open
as day, in which nothing could be read except un-
feigned anxiety and wonder.

When Annette went to Margaret's room later in
the evening, Margaret's face was pale, and all
traces of feverish excitement had passed away.
She had had two hours of hard struggle with her
self ; but she had resolved that she must seek another home, and, having come to this resolution,
she wished to lose no time in carrying it out.

"Sit down, dear Mrs. Reutner," she said, " I
must have a little talk with you."

Annette looked uneasy. She had never seen Margaret look as she looked now. She knew that bad news was coming.

"My dear, good, kind friend, I must go away from you," said Margaret, and her voice trembled.

Annette gazed speechlessly into Margaret's face.

"Oh, Miss Margaret, what is it? Is it that you must go home?"

Margaret shook her head. "No, Mrs. Reutner, I have no expectation of leaving Chicago; but I must find another home. It is not best for me to live in your house any longer."

Great tears rolled down Annette's face, and she sobbed: "Oh, Miss Margaret, is it nothing we can do to make all better for you. It will break the father's heart and the little ones'. Will you not tell us? We have much more money now; we can buy all for you, if you will only show us how it is to be;" and Annette cried heartily.

Margaret was distressed. It seemed disloyal to Karl to give her reason; cruel to Annette and Wilhelm to withhold it. She remained silent for some time. Annette sobbed again a few broken words; "Miss Margaret, you do not know what it is to the house that you are in it. Karl said, only yesterday, that you were the good angel to each one in the house. Tell us, Miss Margaret. Is it that you must have larger rooms? Wilhelm will build all you want, — one, two, more."

The mention of Karl's name gave Margaret more strength to proceed.

"I will tell you, my kind friend," she said, "the real truth. It is for your brother that I must go away. He loves me; he told me so this afternoon; and it is not delicate or kind after that for me to live in the same house with him. I shall never be so happy anywhere else. Nobody will make me so comfortable, and I am very, very sorry to go away; but I must," and Margaret, in her turn, was very near crying.

Annette had dried her tears, sprung to her feet, and now stood gazing at Margaret with such stupe- faction in her face that Margaret could scarcely keep from smiling in spite of her distress.

"Karl — tell you he love you — to be his wife?" gasped Annette. "Oh, Miss Margaret, it has been a mistake. Karl has never told you that; Karl could not."

Margaret colored.

"I am not likely to be mistaken, Mrs. Reutner," she said, a little coldly. "I regret it more than I can say. But it is so, and I must go away."

Annette seemed like one in a dream. She was in haste to be gone. She replied at random to all Margaret said, and at last sobbed afresh : —

"Oh, Miss Margaret, I must go now. To-mor- row I will hear you again. I think not that the good God sent you to our house to take you away like this ; " and Annette was gone.

Wilhelm and Karl were seated in the dining- room, smoking. Annette, with streaming eyes entered the room, and hurrying breathlessly to Karl, exclaimed : —

" How daredst thou to ask the teacher to be thy wife ? It was thou that hast made her ill, and she will go away from our house because of thee, and — " Annette stopped for lack of breath, and because the two men had both sprung to their feet, and were gesticulating violently, — Karl with an angry voice.

" God in Heaven ! What dost thou take me for, Annette ? Dost thou not know I would as soon ask one of the angels in Paradise to be wife to me ? Who has told thee this tale ? "

And Wilhelm, " Annette, art thou mad, or dost thou think Karl is a madman ? "

Annette looked tremblingly from one to the other. She herself had felt like this when Margaret had first told her. In a hesitating voice she began : —

" But Miss Margaret has said that thou — "

Before she could finish her sentence, Karl's face, — white as the face of a dead man, — was bent close to hers, and Karl's voice, strange, husky, was saying, in slow, gasping syllables : —

" The teacher — said — I — asked — her — to — be — wife ? "

Annette nodded, too terrified to speak.

Karl strode to the door, and opened it. Annette ran to hold him back, but Wilhelm restrained her. In that short moment Wilhelm had understood all.

"He must speak to her," he said ; "let him go. It must be told to her. She has mistaken ; it was not that Karl asked her to marry him. But he has let her to know that he has worship for her. And she need not be angry for my Karl's love, if he ask nothing," added Wilhelm, proudly ; but his head sank on his breast, and he said, in a low tone to himself : "Oh, my poor Karl ; my poor Karl!"

Margaret knew Karl's step. As she heard it rapidly drawing near her door, her heart beat and her cheeks flushed. What had Annette said ? What new distress and embarrassment were coming to her now ? Almost she resolved not to admit him. But Karl forestalled that intention. Knocking lightly on the door, he spoke at the same instant : —

"Miss Margaret, for God's sake, I ask to come and speak to you one minute, — only one minute ; it must be."

The anguish in his voice moved Margaret strangely. She opened the door.

Karl entered almost staggering, and with his hands clasped : —

"Oh, mine God," he exclaimed, "give it to me what I shall say! Miss Margaret, beautiful Miss Margaret, angel of God, I did only ask that the 'ove and the daisies should lie together under your feet. I could die here before you in one second, if vou do not believe that never, no never, in all this world, I could have asked you what you have said to Annette. You are to me as if I saw you in Heaven; you are angel of God in my brother's house. If you go away because I have said such love as this, then will I, too, go, and never shall my Wilhelm see my face again, so help me, my God!"

Before Karl had spoken three words, Margaret divined all. Shame, resentment, perplexity, and unspeakable distress mingled of all three, were in her face. She could not speak. This man, then, had never dreamed of asking her to be his wife. True, he acknowledged the utmost devotion for her, and more than implied that the reason he could not ask her to marry him was that he revered her as an angel of God; but the mortifying fact remained that she had not only rejected a man who had not asked her to take him as a husband, but she had told the matter, and compelled him to come and undeceive her. It was a bitter thing. Margaret could not speak; she could not look up.

Karl went on, more calmly: "Beautiful Miss Margaret, it will come that you forgive me when you have thought. And you would have seen that it was only the love like the daisy, at the feet, if you had come down-stairs before you had spoken, you would have seen that you need not to go away. It is not kind to the daisy that there be no more sun."

Margaret could not speak. Karl walked slowly

4

to the door. As he opened it, Margaret sprang towards him, and holding out her hand, said : —

"Forgive me, Mr. Reutner. That is the only word I can say."

Karl took her hand in his, looked at it with no more trace of earthly passion in his eyes than if it were the hand of a shrined saint, lifted it to his forehead, bowed, and was gone.

Now was Margaret's distress complete. Turn which way she would, she saw only perplexity and mortification. Mingled with it all was a new, strange feeling in regard to Karl, which she could not define to herself. He had never looked so manly as when he stood before her, saying, "So help me, my God !" It was the only moment in which he had ever, in her presence, seemed stronger than she. Usually his great love bound him as with withes, and laid him helpless at her feet.

A low hum of voices came to Margaret's ears from the room below. Karl and Wilhelm were talking earnestly. Only too vividly Margaret's fancy pictured what they were saying. She walked the floor ; she wrung her hands ; she was too wretched to shed a tear. Deep down to its very depths her proud heart was humiliated. It was a kind heart, too, spite of its pride ; a loving and a grateful heart ; and it was sorely wounded to have brought such sorrow to friends.

An hour passed ; all grew quiet down-stairs. Margaret still walked the floor. Suddenly she neard soft steps outside her door; a low knock, and Annette's voice said, entreatingly: "Dear Miss Margaret, may Wilhelm come and speak to you?"

Margaret threw the door open instantly. She was so wretched, so perplexed, that she was glad of any help from any source. She had already thought of Wilhelm, and wished that his clear-eyed and tender wisdom could in some way be brought to bear on this distressing problem.

"Miss Margaret," said Wilhelm, very quietly, "it is not much that I can say. A grief has come to us all; but that cannot now be changed: that is as if it were past; and if you will only stay in our house it can become as if it had not been. It is no shame to you that my brother have seen that you are more beautiful and good than any other woman. It is so that any man must see, Miss Margaret. I, also, who am the father in the house, I have said to Annette all this year that you are one good angel. And I could kneel to pray you to stay. I know my Karl. It is not with him as you think. It is only a joy to him that you stay, as it is to me and to Annette. And he will keep the vow he have vowed. If you go he will go away for ever. Give to us our brother, oh, Miss Margaret," and tears stood in Wilhelm's eyes.

"Mr. Reutner," said Margaret, very earnestly, "do you truly believe that it will do your brother no harm, I mean, cause him no pain to live with me as before?"

Wilhelm fixed his eyes on the floor in silence for some seconds.   Then he said : —

" Miss Margaret, that you are content, are glad, is joy to Karl and to us.   So long as you find to be content, glad in our house, it is great joy.   When you are more glad in your own house that will be greatest joy to Karl, to us.   There will come the year when Karl will have wife and house as I. He has the great father heart which must have the children to love.   You will do his life no harm.   To have seen that you are God's angel shall be only light to him, not cloud.   I know my Karl.   Oh, Miss Margaret, will you not for one month try if it cannot be ? "

So Margaret promised to stay.   The first meeting with Karl was what she most dreaded ; but it was over almost before she knew that it was near, and Karl's beautiful simplicity of nature made it easier than could have been foreseen.

He was standing alone in the window of the drawing-room when she went to breakfast the next morning.   He had just broken a beautiful tea-rose from its stem, and was about to lay it on her plate. As she crossed the threshold he went towards her, holding it out, and saying : —

" You are like a new guest in our house to-day. Oh, Miss Margaret, let the rose tell to you how we all thank God that you have come."

The tone, the look, were calmly, gravely, affectionate as ever.   The old life was taken up again, the stormy break in it put away forever. Margaret's heart leaped with a sudden rapture in the consciousness that she still had the same quiet, peaceful, dear home as before.

Again the spring and the summer wore away, and the winter came, and no change was visible in Wilhelm Reutner's household. No change visible ! But — ah ! beneath its surface had again been at work far deeper forces than those which ripen spring into summer, and summer into the garnered harvest of autumn.

Margaret loved Karl ! What subtle triumphs love knows how to win for his own ! Karl Reutner's heart had no more hope in it now than it had a year before; no less now than then, it would have seemed to him like blasphemy to ask Margaret Warren to be his wife : yet there were days when Margaret could not see daisies without tears, so bitterly did her heart ache to recall the hour in which she had rejected the love which they had once symbolized to her.

It was hard to tell how this love had come. Its growth had been as slow, as uninterrupted, as immutable, as unsuspected as the silent growth of crystals deep hidden in chambers of stone. It was long before Margaret had dreamed of it, and very long before she had admitted it to herself. She wrestled with it bravely ; it was against her will ; she did not choose to love Karl Reutner. She was no less proud a woman this year than last.

She had no less dreams and purposes for the future, and to be the wife of Karl Reutner was not among them. Nevertheless it had come to pass that his presence meant happiness to her, and his absence meant a vague sense of discomfort and loss. Vainly she asked herself why. Reason was silent. The great interest of her life had been, — still was, — in books, in study, in progress in the broadest sense. Karl Reutner had not studied, had not read ; he cared more for the laughing eyes of a happy child than for all the discoveries of a century. To him flowers were events ; a blue sky, and a bright sun, and smiles at home were life.

The new world of which he had glimpses through Margaret's conversation, — the world of history, the world of art, the world of science, — seemed to him very great, very glorious. He kindled at mention of noble deeds, at descriptions of stirring scenes ; but it was partly because Margaret found the scenes and events thrilling, and he always returned to his flowers and his music with a sense of rest.

Sometimes when playing one of Mozart's early sonatas, so divine in its simplicity and sweetness and strength, he would say, " Ah, Miss Margaret, it is only the simple tones which can speak the truest. Listen to this ; " and while Margaret listened, it would seem to her that the world and its kingdoms had all floated away in space.

" To be very good, and to make that all are

happy, Miss Margaret, is that not enough?" he said one day. He had grown nearer her, and dared to speak as he could not have spoken a year ago. "Is not that enough? Why must the little men think they can understand all? This world is not for that. It is that we are made pure in this. There comes another world for the rest. That is my creed, Miss Margaret."

But Karl did not add the rest of his creed, which was, that Margaret had the light of both worlds in her soul.

Often Margaret felt abashed before the spiritu-- ality of this man's nature ; often she thought, while she looked at him, that he had indeed entered the kingdom of God by becoming "as a little child." Then again, the worldly, the ambitious side of her nature gained the ascendency, and she said, " This is a merely material life he leads after all ; day's work after day's work, and a peasant's song at the end! What have I in common with him?" Oh, very stoutly the carnal heart of Margaret Warren wrestled with the angel which was seeking a home in it. But the angel was the stronger. More and more clearly shone the celestial light ; more and more clearly Margaret saw the celestial face.

It was a year and a day since Karl came home. Margaret had looked forward to the anniversary day with mingled dread and hope. The pretty daisy-box had long ago been taken away from her room ; the daisies had bloomed their day out, and died, and other flowers had taken their place. Margaret wondered if Karl would give her another such token. Except for the deep yearning desire in her heart that he should so do, she would have known that nothing was less likely than that he should do anything on that day to remind her of its being an anniversary. The day passed without even an allusion from any one to the past. In all hearts there was too sore a memory of the last year. Margaret felt this keenly. "Alien that I am in this house," she thought, "I make it impossible for them to keep the festivals of their love. Two years since Karl came home — only two years; and it seems to me that it is a life-time."

It was near sunset. A rosy glow was suffusing the lake, and Margaret sat again at her window watching it. Again came a low knock at her door, and again she answered without turning her head, and Karl entered.

"Miss Margaret," he said, "may I come and talk with you? It is that I wish that we all go to another house to live. This is not as it should be; it is small. I have talked much with Wilhelm, and I can pay all the money, but he will not. He is wrong; and will not you, Miss Margaret, help me to make that he sees the truth? For the little ones, when they are large, it will be that they must know more people; this place is not right. And you too, Miss Margaret, it is always grief to me that your ⁻ooms are so small. You should have large rooms, and many windows for the south sun until night."

Margaret glanced lovingly round the rooms.

"I love these little rooms," she said, impulsively; "I should be very sorry to leave them." As she spoke, a sudden memory of the daisy-box flashed into her mind. Her eyes filled with tears, and she could not hide them.

Karl stretched out both hands with an eager gesture, exclaiming, "But Miss Margaret, Miss Margaret, it shall not be, if it is pain to you. I did not dream that you would be sorry to go. I will no more say."

"It is not that, Mr. Reutner," said Margaret, "not at all. I believe it would be better for all to have a larger house; I did not mean that I would be really unwilling to leave these rooms; I was thinking of something else," and again the tears filled her eyes.

"Oh, Miss Margaret!" cried Karl. He had never seen tears in her eyes before. The sight unmanned him. His "Oh, Miss Margaret!" was a cry from the very depths of his heart.

The hour had come. Who keeps calendar for the flowers that each blossom bides its time, and blooms at its fated second by sun, by moon, by star, or by breeze! Who keeps calendar for hearts?

The hour had come. Margaret looked full into Karl's face, and said in a low voice, "I was thinking of a year ago yesterday, Mr. Reutner; and I was so sorry for having made you unhappy then."

Astonishment and wounded feeling struggled on Karl's features for a second. That Margaret should voluntarily allude to that bitter day seemed heartless indeed. In the next second, something in her face smote on his sight, dazzling, bewildering, terrifying him. The celestial light in her heart shone through her eyes.

Karl gave one piercing look, piercing as if he were seeking to read some farthest star, — then sank slowly on his knees, buried his face in Margaret's lap, and spoke no word. Margaret laid one hand lightly on his head. Tremblingly he took it, lifted his head, still without looking into her face, and laid his cheek down on the firm soft palm.

Karl Reutner could not speak. He did not distinctly know whether he were alive. With her free hand, Margaret stroked his hair as she might that of a tired child. An ineffable peace filled her soul.

At last, Karl said, very slowly, almost stammeringly, without lifting his head, "Miss Margaret, beautiful angel of God, I cannot look in your eyes ; to see them again would make my heart stop to beat. Will you let that I go away from you now, out under the sky ? When I can come back, even if it is a long time, may I come to you ? "

Margaret bent her head and whispered, "yes, Karl."

He stooped still lower, kissed the hem of the gown on whose folds he had been kneeling, and then without one look at Margaret, went slowly out of the room. When he came back, the twilight was nearly over ; stars were beginning to shine in the sky ; Margaret had not moved from her seat ; the door stood still ajar as he had left it ; softly, so softly, that his steps could hardly be heard, he crossed the room, and stood, silent, before her ; then he lifted his hands high above her head, and opening them, let fall a shower of daisies : on her neck, bosom, lap, feet, everywhere, rested the fragrant blossoms.

"Now you will let that they tell you all," he said ; "now you will let that they lie at your feet."

His tone was grave and calm ; his looks were grave and calm : but his eyes shone with such joy, such rapture, that Margaret, in her turn, found it hard to meet them.

An hour later, when Karl and Margaret went into the dining-room, hand in hand, Wilhelm and Annette gazed at them for a moment in speechless wonder. Then Annette ran out of the room sobbing. Wilhelm said aloud : " God be praised ! " Then walking swiftly towards them, he looked first into Margaret's face, then into Karl's, and exclaimed again : " God be praised."

"Wilhelm," said Margaret, "will you, too, forgive me for the day I made sad for you a year ago? Karl has forgiven it."

Wilhelm's answer was a look. Then he fell on Karl's neck, and was not ashamed of the tears that would come. Not often do two men love as did these twin brothers.

It all seemed to Wilhelm and Annette impossible, incredible. Their eyes followed Karl, followed Margaret with an expression which was half joy and half fear. But to Karl and Margaret the new happiness seemed strangely natural, assured. Like a crystal hidden in stone, it had grown, and now that the store had been broken open, and the crystal set free, every ray of the sun that fell on it was multiplied, and the brilliant light seemed only inevitable.

Later in the evening Karl put a ring upon Margaret's finger. It was dark, and she could not see the design.

"Could you promise not to see till the sunlight should come to-morrow?" said Karl. "I would like that the sun should light it up first for your eyes."

Margaret smiled. "Oh, foolish Karl! I will try not to look; but you ask a great deal."

Karl turned the ring round and round on the finger, as Margaret's hand lay in his.

"I have a long time had this ring,—more than one year. It was to be for you if I died, or if you were to be married to——" Karl could not now pronounce the words "another man." He went on: "I thought that then you would wear it and not be angry. I not once thought I could put it on for you with my own hand;" and Karl lifted both Margaret's hands, covered them with kisses, laid them against his cheek, on his forehead, on his heart.

It was strange to see this lover, in these few hours, already so free from fear. His child-like simplicity of nature was the secret of it. Knowing Margaret to be his own, he joyed in her as he joyed in sunlight. He took the delights of seeing and touching her, as freely as he would bask under the blue sky. He could no more feel restraint from one than from the other.

"Karl, if you really do not want me to see the ring, you must roll a tiny bit of paper round it," said Margaret. "It feels very large."

"Yes, it is large. It could not be small to tell what it tells," replied Karl, rolling a fine tissue paper carefully over and under it, and twisting it firmly. "Mine own, mine own," he said, kissing the hand and the ring, "when the to-morrow sun shines from the lake to your bed, lift your hand in the light and look."

When the "to-morrow sun" first shone on Margaret's bed, Margaret was asleep. When she waked, the room was flooded with yellow light. Dimly at first, like memories of dreams, came the recollections of her new happiness; then clearer and clearer in triumphant joy. She raised her left hand in the great yellow sunbeams, which seemed to make a golden pathway from the very sky to her bed. Slowly she unwound the rosy tissue paper from her ring. A low cry of astonishment broke from her lips. She had never seen anything so beautiful. On a broad gold band was curled a tiny thread-like stem, bearing a four-leaved clover of dark green enamel. The edge of each leaf was set thick with diamonds, and the lines down the centre were marked by diamonds, so small, as to be little more than shining points. Margaret's second thought was one of dismay. "Oh, the wicked Karl! To spend so much money! It would almost furnish our little house. What shall I do with such a ring as this?"

But surprises were in store for Margaret. When she gently reproached Karl for having spent so much money on the ring, his face flushed, and he hesitated a moment before replying. Then he said, with inexpressible sweetness, taking both her hands in his, "My Margaret, I have much money. I was glad before, for Wilhelm, and the little ones. But now that I can make all beautiful for you, I so much thank God. It was a chance that I have it. I know not how to find it, as your people do. It was the land."

Karl Reutner was indeed a rich man. Lands which he had bought a few years before, for, as he said, "such little of money," were now a fortune in themselves. And it was in consequence of this increase of his wealth that he had so earnestly besought his brother Wilhelm to let him provide a new home for the family.

"But now, my Margaret, it shall be for you," he said. "I hope that there shall be enough that you have all things you have ever had dream of."

Margaret sighed. Almost she regretted this wealth. It was not thus she had pictured her life with Karl. But her love of beauty, of culture, of art, was too strong for her to be long reluctant that the fullness of life should come to her.

"Oh Karl! Karl!" she said, "I cannot believe that I am to have you, and all else in life besides. Dear one, I do not deserve it."

Karl was lying at her feet, his head resting on her knees, as he had bowed it when he first knew that she loved him; only that now he dared to gaze steadily into her eyes. He did not reply for some moments, then he said : —

"The good God knows, my Margaret. Perhaps there will come sorrow for you, if it needs for his Heaven that you be more of angel than you are. But for my love, that is only like the daisies. It is enough that it can make a beautiful ground where you walk."

Since these things which I have written, many years have gone by, and have not yet brought sorrow to Margaret. The windows of her beautiful home look out on the blue lake ; and into the nursery where her golden-haired children sleep, the morning sun sends its first beams, as it used to send them into her tiny room, in Wilhelm Reutner's house.

On the wall of Margaret's own room hangs the picture of Königsee, and the head of the shadowy maiden of Ischl still wreathed with edelweiss blossoms.

" I love her, my Karl. She told me that thou
wert not dead. She is glad of thy joy each hour,"
Margaret often says.

On the right hand of the portrait of Königsee,
framed in velvet and ivory, and also wreathed by
edelweiss blossoms, hangs an oval of soft gray surface, on which is a tiny and faded and crumpled
clover, " the four leaf of clover ; " — " which saved
my papa's life," little Karl says, pointing to it with
his chubby finger, " my papa says so." When little Karl is older he will understand better. This
too is wreathed with edelweiss blossoms, fresher
and whiter than the others. Margaret also has
sailed with Karl on the Königsee, and she gathered
these edelweiss flowers on the edge of the Watzman
glacier.

Above these hangs a quaint old bit of heraldry.
It is the coat of arms of the Whitson family, and
belonged to Margaret's grandmother, who was a
Whitson, and well-to-do, years ago in England. It
is an odd thing, and to some minds much more
than an odd thing, that this old coat of arms should
be an oak tree in a clover field, and that there
should be a tale how once when a sorely pressed
king of England was escaping from his pursuers
he came to a field of purple clover, with an oak
tree in its centre ; and that a churl Whitson, to
whom the field belonged, and who chanced to be
mowing it that day, helped the king up into the
oak tree, and lied bravely to the pursuers, saying

that no man had passed that way; so the king, grateful for his life, gave lands to the churl, and the right to a crest bearing the oak and the clover.

This, I say, is an odd thing, and to some people more than an odd thing. To Karl Reutner, for instance, who is so impressed by it, that he has had garlands of oak and clover leaves carved on the cradle in which all his babies sleep; garlands of oak and clover leaves carved over the doors and windows of his wife's room; garlands of oak and clover leaves wrought on silver and on glass to hold choice fruits and wines; and wrought of gold and gems in many a dainty device for his wife to wear. And those who look closely at these garlands find that there is not one without a four-leaved clover.

5

FARMER BASSETT'S ROMANCE.

IT began at a camp-meeting; and the odd thing was that John Bassett should have been at a camp-meeting at all. He had no more respect for such means of grace than Epictetus or any other stoical pagan would have had. He had no antagonism toward the Methodists; nor, for that matter, toward any of the five so-called religious sects which had places of worship in his native town, Deerway. If the whole truth could have been known, it would have been seen that he classed them all together, and favored them alike with his heartiest but most good-natured contempt. Luckily he was a silent and reticent man, and his townsmen never suspected in what low esteem he held their sectarian bonds, — their spiritual ecstasies and depressions. They only thought that he was "queer," and some of the more zealous Christians among them feared he might be an infidel, or at best a pantheist, though as to what that latter manner of man might be, there were very vague ideas in Deerway. The truth was, that John Bassett was a pagan, — a New England pagan. There are a few of these in every New England county. They are the offspring of the Westminster Catechism. Apply enough of the Westminster Catechism to a meditative, clear-witted, logical, phlegmatic boy, in his youth ; let him spend most of his days out on sunny hill-sides, thinking it over in silence, and asking nobody any questions, and the chances are that, when he is twenty-one, he will quit going to church, and be a high-minded pagan. He will have absorbed much that is grand and ennobling ; but he will have thrown away, in his slow-growing hatred of the cruel husk, part of the sweet kernel also, and will be a defrauded and robbed man all his days, for lack of true comprehension of the Gospel of Christ, which is loving, and of Christ's Father, who is love.

It is evident that a camp-meeting was the last place one would expect to see John Bassett in. If pools had been the fashion in Deerway, one might have made a fortune betting against the chance of John Bassett's hearing Bishop Worrell's sermon on the last day of the Middleburg camp-meeting. But he did hear it, every word of it.

He had been that day to Northborough, ten miles above Middleburg, to look at a pair of prize oxen he had heard of, and had a mind to buy. If those oxen had not been sold the day before, John Bassett would have bought them, and this story would

never have been written ; for if he had had the
oxen to drive home, he would not have got down
to Middleburg till late at night, and the camp-meeting would have been over. As it was, he got to
Middleburg Crossing at three o'clock in the afternoon ; and there he had to stop, for Jerry, his
horse, had cast a shoe, and John Bassett would no
more have driven Jerry ten miles with one foot un-
shod than he would have walked it barefoot himself ; no, nor half as quick, for Tom and Jerry, the
two beautiful bay horses that he had broken as
colts, and trained into the best ten-year-old team in
all Wenshire County, were the pride and the love
of John Bassett's heart.

So, there is another little "if" which might have
made a big difference to John Bassett, and all the
difference between this story's being written and
not. If Jerry had not cast his shoe, his master
would never have heard Bishop Worrell's sermon.

There are only three houses at Middleburg
Crossing ; the town itself is four miles farther
south. One of these houses is a sort of inn, and
the master, Hiram Peet, is well known to be the
best blacksmith for many a mile round. Here
John stopped and fastened his horse at the door of
the forge, which was black and still.

"Gone to that confounded camp-meeting !" he
exclaimed, as he stood by the anvil and tapped it
impatiently with his whip. "Hang it all. I wonder, if I could find him, whether he 'd come out
and shoe Jerry."

Every blind in the house was shut. The hens walked about with an expression which showed that the family was away from home, and the cat looked out uneasy and suspicious from a high loft over the corn-house.

John walked a few steps down the road and looked at the two other houses. Shut up also; not a trace of life about them. The two Thatcher brothers, who married sisters, lived in these houses. "Well, I don't know what the Thatcher folks have got to do over at camp-meeting," thought John. "They're all Baptists. They don't train in that crowd."

He had thought that he might while away the time by talking with Mrs. Susan Thatcher, who was a woman he had once almost thought he would like to marry. John was much vexed. He walked up and down the road and switched off the tops of golden rod and purple asters in a way that was really shameful. He was at his wit's ends : ten miles from home ; Jerry waiting to be shod ; not a human being to be found. But John Bassett's impatiences never lasted long. He was too good a pagan to fret and fume. He took Jerry out of his harness, led him into the barn, and gave him so delightful a rubbing down that the creature arched his shining neck and looked around at his master's hands, and would have purred if he could, he felt so comfortable. John patted him and talked to him as if he were a child.

"There, there, old fellow," he said, "eat your oats. You shall have four fine new shoes presently; and then we won't get caught this way again very soon."

Jerry whinnied back and did his best to be entertaining; but where was there ever a mortal man who did not weary of wordless affection? John began to be sadly bored. He looked over at the camp-meeting hill, where thin columns of smoke were curling up above the tops of the trees. The Middleburg camp-ground is one of the oldest in New England; it has been used as such for twenty years, and there are some eighty cottages in the "circle." People go there in June, and live in their cottages for two months or more before the camp-meeting week begins. John had often thought he would like to see what kind of a life it was that the Methodist people led on their religious picnics, as the worldly were in the habit of calling them. He began to consider within himself whether this were not a capital chance for doing it without any loss of self-respect on his part. He would go over and see if he could find Hiram Peet. This was not going to camp-meeting. Oh, no!

The camp-meeting grove was not more than a quarter of a mile from the forge. At John Bassett's goodly stride, this distance was quickly walked; and almost before he fairly realized what he had made up his mind to do, John found himself in the throng of people pouring through the outer gate. He and his ways were well known in all this region, — everybody stared to see him coming to camp-meeting.

"Hollo, John! Ez this you?" exclaimed one.

"What's up?" said another.

"Glad to see you in the right way at last, John," called out a gray-haired elder of the Methodist church in Deerway.

John did not like this. At first he made no reply, except a good-natured laugh; but presently, to a townsman who shouted out, across many heads, —

"Why, John Bassett, what on airth's brought you here, I'd like to know," he answered in an equally loud tone, —

"Not any of the tomfoolery that's brought you, I can tell you that. I'm looking after Hi Peet to shoe my horse, back here at the Crossing."

"Oh, Hi? Well, he's in there, in the seats, along o' his folks. But you won't get him to come out till after the sermon. The bishop's jest beginnin' now."

John walked on in silence. The scene was beginning to take a vivid hold on his imagination. From his earliest boyhood he had had a passionate love of the woods. There was not a wood within five miles of his father's house which he did not know as thoroughly as if he had been an Indian or a trapper. The young trees had grown with his growth and strengthened with his strength; he

often pushed his way through some thick wood,
recollecting, step by step, along the path, how
twenty years ago these stalwart trees had been sap-
lings he could bend. No smallest leaf or fern was
unknown to his eye ; no flower, no berry ; yet he
had names for few. To see a great maple and ash
and hickory grove swarming full of human beings,
was at first as strange a sight to John Bassett as it
would have been to a devout Roman Catholic to
come suddenly upon his private chapel and find it
crowded with strangers. John felt a mingled irri-
tation and fascination in the sight. This noble
army of trees seemed to lend something of their
own sacred dignity to the motley multitude they
were sheltering. There were three thousand people
that day on the Middleburg camp-ground. As far
as one could see, the vistas between the trees were
filled by horses, wagons, carriages of all descriptions. These were outside what is called the " circle," a large space of many acres, fenced in, and to
be entered only by gates ; within this circle were
the cottages, all picturesquely disposed among the
tiees ; winding and irregular paths had been trod-
den from one to another, and there was almost the
semblance of a street in some places. But still the
trees were left undisturbed ; the street or the path
turned reverentially to the right or the left, as the
tree might require. Hardly a tree had been cut
down. In the centre of the grove a large space
had been filled in with rough wooden benches in

an amphitheatre-like half circle. Even here stood
the trees, thick and undisturbed, making of the
circle of seats a many-pillared temple, canopied
with green and roofed with blue. Fronting this
had been built an elevated platform for the elders
and the preaching — and on this, at the moment
John entered the circle, had just risen a corpulent,
round-faced, sonorous-voiced man, Bishop Worrell,
who was to preach that afternoon's sermon. John
stopped, leaned against a young hickory tree, and
looked carefully up and down the rows of seats in
search of Hiram Peet. At last he saw him sitting
between his wife and his wife's mother, in the very
middle of the circle, and only five seats back from
the platform.

"I suppose it would be as much as Hi's life was
worth to get up and come out from there before all
these people," thought John. "I might as well
give it up."

Then he fell to laughing so immoderately at Hi's
expression of face, that he had to turn suddenly
away, lest he should shock the sensibilities of the
grave and decorous congregation. As he turned,
he suddenly caught a glimpse of the profile of a
girl who sat in the same seat with Hiram Peet, but
at the farther end of it. The sight of this profile
arrested John Bassett's steps as suddenly as a
strong hand laid on his shoulder could have done.
He stood still, with his eyes fixed on the face. He
did not say to himself, "How beautiful!" he did

not even think whether the face were beautiful or
not — it simply arrested him, that was all. Presently the girl changed her position so that he could
no longer see her face, and with a pang like terror,
he saw it suddenly vanish from his gaze, and become lost and merged in the great mass of bonnets
and hats and faces. He tried to keep his eyes
resolutely on the spot where it had disappeared,
as one tries to keep his eyes fastened on the spot
where something has gone down at sea ; but like
the sea, the mass of faces seemed dancing and
shifting under his look. At last he was rewarded.
The girl turned her head again, so that for one
brief moment he saw her profile, and also noted,
with the eagerness of a detective, that she wore a
black hat, with one single upright feather of bright
scarlet in it.

Slowly, and with a bewildered wonder at himself
all the time, John skirted the great semicircle of
seats, pushed his way through and past knot after
knot of men and women, and drew nearer and
nearer the seat where the girl sat. As one after
another saw him, noted his absorbed and grave
look, exclamations and conjectures were whispered
on all sides. There were many of the Deerway
Methodists on the ground.

John Bassett stood no chance of being unobserved. Many a soul warmed with hope for his
salvation on seeing him in this unwonted place.
One good old Methodist woman who had nursed

his mother through several illnesses, and who had
come to love John very much, as all persons did
who knew him intimately, plucked her neighbor
suddenly by the sleeve, and exclaimed : —

"My goodness, Sarah Beman, if there ain't John
— John Bassett, don't you know? Let's git right
down on our knees here 'n' pray for his soul!
Mebbe the Lord 'll give him religion right now!"
and the two women actually sank on the ground,
and were rocking back and forth on their knees,
wrestling in prayer on John's behalf, as he passed
by them. Perhaps there was never a moment in
his life in which he was more in need of prayers.

When he reached a point opposite the seat in
which sat the girl with the black hat and scarlet
feather, he turned, and slowly looked in her face.
She did not see him. She was listening in rapt attention to the bishop's sermon. Yet it was not the
attention of a credulous or an ecstatic devotee.
Her face wore now the look of one who was striving to penetrate a mystery; to fathom a secret;
there was an expression of something like disapprobation on her features. All this John Bassett
saw at his first glance. At his second, he perceived that the girl was no country girl; he felt,
rather than perceived, that her whole attire, bearing, and atmosphere were of the city : she was a
stranger. The two elderly women who sat with
her were richly clad, and their whole manner be-
okened listless weariness. Up to this moment,

John Bassett could not have told, if he had been asked, whether this girl were fair or not; but now in the more assured composure of his new stand-point of observation, he began to study her features. They were of delicate mold, indicating sensibility rather than strength. Her hair was of so pale a yellow that only its great thickness saved it from looking dead. It was turned back from her low forehead in rippling waves which were too thick to lie flat. Her eyes were of a clear, bright dark blue, and in them shone a sort of restrained energy which gave to her face the strength which the delicate features would otherwise have lacked. It was not a beautiful face. It was very far from a pretty face. But it was a face to arrest one at first sight. As it had arrested John Bassett, it had arrested many a human being, man and woman, before.

But it always came to pass that each human being thus arrested by Fanny Lane's face, very soon forgot all about her face, in a vivid conscious-ness of her personality. Her individual magnetism was something not to be described, not to be de-fined. It was to some persons as powerfully re-pellant as it was to others attracting. There were men and women who had been heard to say that they simply could not stay in the same room with Fanny Lane, so disagreeable to them was her very presence, and there were men and women for whom simply her presence could transform the most cheerless room into a palace of joy; and for whom her love, if they were once sure of possessing it, seemed enough to brighten a whole life-time.

Bishop Worrell's sermon was one hour long. Until the very last word had been spoken, John Bassett stood without once unfolding his arms or once removing his eyes from Fanny Lane's face ; but he stood in such a position that while he looked steadily at her, he seemed to those about him to be looking in the preacher's face, and the intent and grave expression of his countenance gave rise to great hopes in the hearts of many who saw him. After the benediction had been pronounced, there was a general movement in the audience, and all except those who were interested in the special services which were about to follow, withdrew. More than half of the seats were left empty. A little knot of some half a dozen persons had gathered around Fanny Lane, and were all talking eagerly.

"City boarders from some hotel hereabouts," thought John. " I don't suppose I shall ever set eyes on that girl again ; and I 'm sure I don't know why I want to." But he lingered, and waited, and furtively watched to see what the next movements of her party would be.

It was evident that an animated discussion was going on. Fanny Lane said little, but each time she spoke, she shook her head with great decision, smiling as she did so with a smile which was to John Bassett's mind a very perplexing smile ; there

was so much radiance about it, and yet such an expression of immovable will ; it seemed as much out
of the ordinary course of human smiles as a cold
sunbeam would out of the ordinary course of nature.   At last the party divided, and the two old
ladies, wearing very dissatisfied faces, walked slowly
away with the majority, leaving Fanny Lane and
one other young woman alone in the seats.   As
the discomfited elderly people passed the tier
where John still stood, leaning with his arms
folded, watching in feigned carelessness the whole
scene, one said to the other : —

"It's perfectly absurd, Maria, the way you spoil
that girl."

A look of fretful impatience passed over Maria's
face as she replied : —

"It's all very fine to talk about spoiling, Jane.
You know as well as I do, that if Fanny makes up
her mind to do a thing, she's going to do it, come
what will ; and as for my saying 'must' or
'mus'n't' to her, I know better than to try that.
She's just like her father."

"Well, I reckon she's your own child," answered
Jane, "and my child should mind me. I know
that much," and the party passed on.

John Bassett smiled. He liked the picture of
the fair girl triumphing always. He felt already
that it was her right. Before the smile had died
off his face, the old ladies came hurrying back,
they had noticed his grave, honest, clear-eyed face

as they passed, and they had turned back to ask
him one of those anxiously helpless questions
which the average woman is perpetually asking.

"Can you tell us where Mr. Goodenow's wagon
is?" they said.

It happened that John could. It had chanced
that as he walked up the hill, he had observed
young Luke Goodenow sitting in his big farm-
wagon playing cards on the back seat with a
stranger, whose whole appearance had seemed so
suspicious (to John) that he had said to himself as
he passed by, "I wonder if Luke Goodenow 'd
ever be such a fool 's to play for money;" and "I
wonder if that's the reason he fastened his team
down in that hollow," was his second thought.

"Yes," said John. "I can. I will show you,"
and he led the way, thinking, as he walked.

"So these folks are the Goodenows' boarders.
Now I can find out all about them."

Luke little understood John Bassett's affable
kindness in helping him put in his horses, and being so very careful in examining the harnesses, before they set off. John was listening with strained
ears to what one of the elderly women was saying
to Luke.

"Miss Lane and Miss Wheelwright are not coming now. They wish to stay till the end of the
meeting. They have friends there from the hotel
who will take care of them, and you are to drive
back after them at nine o'clock to-night."

"Well, I swanny," was Luke's reply. "I donno what I'm goin' to do for hosses."

The city lady looked calmly in his face with the city lady's usual incredulity of anything being impossible in the country town where she is spending her summer, and said : —

"Oh, it won't hurt these horses to come back."

Luke did not deign to argue this point, but answered reflectively : —

"Mebbe I can git Smith's. Hisn warn't out when we come off, an' if I don't go for the girls, they can come home in the hotel coach ; that warn't full."

"Oh, no ; I should much prefer that you should go for them," said the bland lady. "You can surely get horses somewhere."

"There ain't any 'somewhere' in our town mum," replied Luke, sententiously. "If yer don't know jest where a thing is, 't ain't anywheres. But I'll see that Miss Fanny's got home somehow or another."

If Fanny Lane had heard Luke's reply, the unconscious and inimitable philosophy of its first clause would have given her a keen delight ; but it was all thrown away on Aunt Jane, or if not thrown away entirely, passed for nothing more than the unintentional impudence of a farmer's lad. So that her orders were obeyed, as she would have called it, she was content and unobservant ; and, luckily for her complacent peace of mind, wholly unaware how far from the thoughts of her landlord and his sons was any comprehension of the idea of obedience as she understood it.

When John Bassett returned to his post of observation by the young hickory-tree, he found the seat on which his attention had been so long concentrated occupied by two elderly women from Deerway, — his own next door neighbors. With a smothered ejaculation of contempt at his own folly, he made a hasty retreat, not however before both the women had seen him, and had beckoned to him with eager gestures to come and sit by their side. He shook his head and walked rapidly away in the opposite direction, as if he were about to leave the grounds ; each moment, however, his keen eyes were roving to the right and to the left in search of a scarlet feather. Scarlet feathers there were in plenty, and knots of scarlet ribbon, as he found to his cost, after he had been for half an hour lured vainly about, first in one direction then in another, by them. His scarlet feather was nowhere to be found. To look for one person, among three thousand people roaming about in a grove of several acres, is like searching for a needle in a hay-stack ; and so John said to himself at last, and vowed he would look no longer. He had been asking all the time for "Hi Peet," and had several times narrowly escaped finding him. The truth was he did not now so much want to find "Hi Peet," but he liked to give himself the

6

shelter of that ostensible errand, and so he kept
on asking. At last some one said in reply to his
stereotyped question, " Why Hi? — Hi 's up in the
Franklin tent at a big prayer-meetin' they 've got
goin' on there. You might 's well give up all idee
of gettin' hold of Hi Peet to-night. You 'll have
to wait till morning. Hi 'll keep you over night
fust rate; though I suppose they won't break up
here till midnight."

This was precisely what John Bassett had in
his own mind determined to do, but he replied with
a diplomacy worthy of a deeper game : —

" Well, I call that pretty hard, to have to wait all
night to get a horse shod, don't you ? "

The man laughed, and answered : —

" Well, yes, I do.   But you see, it 's just your
luck that makes it happen so.   They don't have
camp-meetin' but once a year ; and they don't have
but one last night to each camp-meetin': an' you
could n't ha' ketched Hi away from hum one o' the
other three hundred an' sixty-four nights ; so you
see it 's nothin' but your luck."

This curiously illogical logical speech made John
laugh heartily, and a half shamed consciousness of
the scarlet feather in his thoughts made him also
flush a little as he replied : —

" Well, I don't believe in anything's being luck."
Just as he spoke these words, he heard a voice behind him, a voice of a quality such as he had never
before heard.   He did not turn his head.   He list-

ened, and it was an odd thing that as he listened, he said to himself, —

"If that is n't her voice, I 'm mistaken."

The voice said : —

"Can I sit for a few moments in one of these chairs, till my friends return ? "

The voice was so near that John walked away a few steps, before he turned to see who had spoken. He walked on and on for a rod or two, so sure was he that when he turned he should see the face of which he had been in search. He was not mistaken. There she sat, — the strange, vivid, yellow-haired, blue-eyed stranger, — alone in a chair on a raised platform; the platform was full of camp chairs of all sorts which had been brought there by an enterprising Middleburg tradesman, to sell to the camp-meeting pilgrims. The tradesman had gone away for the afternoon and left the business in the charge of his wife, a brisk, bustling, dapper little body with a voice like a jew's-harp, and eyes whose sharp shrewdness was saved from being disagreeable only by their kindly twinkle, and lines of good-natured wrinkles at their outer corners. She was holding forth to two friends volubly and loudly on the subject of her grievances in the matter of the chairs.

"Folks seems to think we 've brought 'em over here just for them to set in," said she. " I 've tried every way I could think of ; we turned 'em bottom side up some days, but the chairs don't show so

well that way, an' it don't make much difference :
they turn 'em right over an' flop down, and there
they sit 's long 's they please, 'n' when I say,
'These chairs is for sale,' they say, 'Oh, I don't
want to buy, I only want to rest a while,' 'n' I do
declare I'm so mad sometimes I tell Eben he'd
better take the chairs home before they're all worn
out. There's some on 'em now that looks just
like second-hand. I fixed some folks yesterday,
though," and she gave a hearty peal of unrestrained laughter at the thought : "they come along,
a whole party — three on 'em, a man and two
women, 'n' down they sot without so much 's a
word ; 'n' I steps forward 'n' sez I, 'We charge for
these chairs bein' sot in, a cent a minnit !' You'd
better believe they jumped up 's quick 's if the
chairs had been red hot, and one o' the wimmin
she said, 'Well, I never !' 'n' sez I, 'Well I never,
nuther,' 'n' I laughed an' I laughed till I thought I
should ha' died to see 'em goin' off 's mad 's if the
chairs had been theirn 'n' not mine."

John watched Fanny Lane's face during the whole
of this long speech, which she could not have failed
to hear. He had come slowly nearer and nearer
until he stood within a few feet of her chair, but so
much behind her that she could not see his face unless she turned her head. Various shades of amusement and sympathy flitted over her expressive face
as she listened to good Mrs. Cross's troubles ; but
she was evidently now absorbed in watching the

faces of all who passed by. She scanned each one intently, closely, as if she were looking for a face she knew; her face wore the same expression of mingled perplexity and disapprobation which it had worn during the sermon. The longer John looked at her, the surer he felt that he understood the mental processes through which she was going.

"She's fighting this thing out for herself, just as I did ten years ago," he thought. "She can't swallow it all down, and yet it bothers her to let it go. She'll come out all right, though, — no fear about a woman with such eyes in her head as those."

It was half an hour before Miss Lane's friends returned. They came up laughing and chattering, and gathering around her, exclaimed : —

"Oh, Fanny! it was too bad to leave you so long. We got off farther in the woods than we meant to. Have you been awfully bored, dear, waiting?"

"Bored!" exclaimed Fanny Lane. "I was never farther from it in my life. This is one of the most interesting sights I ever saw. I can't in the least make it out."

"Make it out! What do you mean, Miss Lane?" cried young Herbert Wheelwright. "Does it strike you as a conundrum? I think it is a confounded bore myself, except for having you girls to take care of."

"Be quiet, Herbert," interrupted his sister ;

"don't be so rude to Fanny ; you don't understand her."

Herbert shrugged his shoulders and walked to the side of another young girl in the party who was not likely to oppress him with any psychological perplexities. As the group moved on, Fanny Lane turned back, and holding out a piece of silver to the proprietress of the chairs, said in the same low vibrant voice which had so stirred John Bassett's nerves at his first hearing of it, —

"You must let me pay you for the use of your chair. You were quite right in saying that it ought to be paid for."

The woman stretched out her hand to take the money, but her husband, who had returned and stood by her side, pushed down her hand impatiently, and exclaimed : —

"No, no, Miss. We 'd be happy to have you set here 's long 's you like. You ain't the kind we meant."

Fanny smiled, but still held out the money.

" I 'm very heavy," she said roguishly, " and should hurt the chair quite as much as anybody. Please take the money and buy something for your pretty little boy," and she pointed to a bright-eyed chubby fellow, some four or five years old, who was clinging to his mother's skirts, half in and half out of the folds, after the manner of shy country children. Thus conciliated on the side of his paternal affection, the man took the money, saying

with a clumsy but well-meant attempt at respectfulness : —

"Much obliged to you, Miss, much obliged to
you, I'm sure, if it's a present to Sammy. Thank
the lady, Sammy."

But Sammy only burrowed the deeper in his
mother's skirts, and evinced no gratitude whatever;
as, indeed, why should he, since the chances were
so small that he could have any hand in the spending of that half dollar!

As Miss Lane and her friends walked away,
John Bassett turned suddenly in the opposite direction, and plunged into the woods. He was conscious
of a sudden unwillingness to see this girl put off
the face she wore when she was thinking, and
alone, and put on the face she wore when she was
talking. Already he had perceived that she was
like a chameleon in her change of expression;
and of the expressions he had thus far seen, the
only one which did not jar and perplex him was the
one she wore when she was silent and undisturbed
by antagonistic or interrupting magnetisms. He
roamed on till he reached the outer edge of the
wood, where all was as still and peaceful as if it
were a wilderness. Here he threw himself on the
ground, and surrendered himself to his reveries.
He was not much given to analyzing his own emotions; he had always been too healthy and too
busy, and, moreover, had had very few emotions.
He was affectionate and loyal in the relations in

which he had found himself placed ; but beyond
one or two strong friendships for men who had been
his playmates at school, he had not added to his
list of affections since he was a little boy. He had
never been in love, though he had often thought
very sensibly about being married, and had done
his share of taking the Deerway girls on sleigh-
rides, and home from singing-schools in the winter ;
but he did it partly as one of the duties of a good
citizen of the town, and partly from a quiet sort of
good-fellowship, which would have walked or ridden almost as contentedly with a young man as
with a young woman, if so the customs of young
people had decreed. He was not without his preferences among the Deerway young women, but he
had also his preferences among the Deerway young
men ; and he could have given as clear and satis-
factory reasons for them in the one case as in the
other, unless, perhaps, in the case of a little girl
named Molly Wilder, whose mother was a widow,
and took summer boarders in Deerway. They were
very poor, and had lived on one of the Bassett
farms ever since John could remember ; and one of
the earliest things he recollected was hearing his
father say to his mother, —

"Well, Sam Wilder 'll never earn his salt in this
world, but I sha'n't turn him out o' that farm 's
long 's Molly lives. She 's no kind of a woman to
be left without a house over her head."

At last Sam Wilder died of a disease so linger

ing and vacillating in its nature, that one of his neighbors was heard to say one day : —

" It don't seem 's if Sam Wilder could even die like other folks. He 's just a shilly-shallyin' along with that, 's he has with everything else he 's ever undertook."

The day after the funeral poor Mrs. Wilder sent for her landlord, and told him the simple truth, that she had not a cent of money in the world, and no property except the little stock which they had put in the farm.

" Never you mind," said John Bassett's father ; " you shall stay on this farm 's long 's you like. I 'll take the hay off the meadow land, and we 'll call that the rent. If you can manage to make a living for you and the girl somehow, you 're welcome to the house and the rest of the farm."

Ezekiel Bassett could well afford this, for the " Bassett farms," as they were called, were many and large, and comprised the greater portion of the best lands in Wenshire County. Nevertheless, it was a very generous thing for Ezekiel Bassett to do ; and from that day the Wilders seemed to be a sort of outlying colony of the Bassett house. All the odds and ends of clothes and of food, which the Bassetts could spare and the Wilders could use, found their way to the little gray house down in the meadows ; by the time John Bassett was ten years old, it seemed to him as natural to take blue-berries to Mrs. Wilder as to his mother ; he knew no distinction in the rights of the houses. And when little Molly was old enough to go to school, John led her in summer and drew her on his sled in winter, as if she had been his sister. Nothing else — nothing less would have seemed possible. When he was twenty and Molly was fifteen, occasions were less frequent for him to take care of her, for she was hard at work all day at her home, and he was hard at work all day at his, but he never lost the sense of responsibility for her ; and if nobody else took her to the quilting, or the sleigh-ride, or the singing-school, he did. If he found that some one else was intending to ask her, he was content; so that Molly had the good time, he was satisfied. She never became a burden to him, for no girl in all Deerway had a sweeter face or more winning ways, or more admirers among the young farmers of the region. But all that John Bassett had ever yet thought about Molly, as in distinction from the other young girls he knew was, that somehow he always had a better time when he took her than when he took anybody else. He thought it was because he was so used to her. What Molly thought is neither here nor there in this story as yet.

Every summer Mrs. Wilder's little house was filled with summer boarders ; and a hard time she and Molly had of it from June till October. Not the least hard part of it to Molly was that for all these months John hardly came near her. John

disliked the very sight of a "summer boarder."
He disliked their clothes, their ways, their general
bearing. He disliked the annual invasion of the
quiet of the town; the assumption which so many
of them showed only too plainly, that they felt that
the Deerway farms and farmers were created
chiefly for the purpose of making summer comfortable to city people who must leave home. So John
never crossed the threshold of Mrs. Wilder's house,
if he could help it, while there was a single, summer boarder left; and this had been the source of
many a half quarrel between him and Molly, who,
gentle as she was, could not help resenting and
misinterpreting his absence.

And here was John Bassett, at the Middleburg
camp-meeting, absolutely spending a whole afternoon and evening in watching a "summer boarder,"
following her about, looking at her face and studying it, as he never studied a woman's face before!

" All for the want of a horse-shoe nail."

John's reverie did not last long. It passed by
quick and easy stages into a sound sleep. When
he waked it was almost dark. He sprang to his
feet in bewildered wonder, but soon recalled the
whole situation of his affairs. Sentiment and excitement had yielded in him, by this time, to fatigue
and heat and hunger; and it must be acknowledged
that as he walked briskly back toward the centre
of the grove, his thoughts of himself and his behavior were not complimentary. He was as nearly

surly as it was in his nature to be ; and by a curious sort of moral metonymy all his impatience centred on the thought of Hi Peet. So when he found himself face to face with Hi, in one of the restaurant tents, he spoke to him with a gruff displeasure, which was, to say the least of it, uncalled for, and made Hi laugh heartily.

"Why, man alive," he said, "you did n't suppose I was bound to stay to hum year in and year out, on the chance of a man's wantin' his horse shod, did you ? 'Tain't more 'n once a week or so that I git a job o' shoein', anyhow. 'T was jest your luck, you see, a-comin' to-day."

"Well, you're the second man that's said that very thing to me," replied John, "so I suppose it must be true." And as he was by this time much rested, and no longer hungry, agreeable reminiscences of the scarlet feather floated at once into his mind, and arrested on his very lips the last clause of his reply, which was about to be as before, "But you see I don't believe in any such thing as luck."

The people were already crowding into the seats in front of the platform. The elders and the preachers sat with their hands over their eyes, engaged in silent prayer. This was the last night of the camp-meeting, and most earnestly did they long for some especial signs and tokens of the Lord's presence before they should separate.

Again John walked slowly around the circle, scan-

ning each seat attentively in search of Fanny Lane.
This time he was more successful; in a very few
moments he found her. She and her friends were
sitting where Hi Peet had been in the afternoon,
only five seats back from the pulpit, and near the
central aisle. Fanny herself sat in the outside
seat, with her face turned away from the platform,
and her eyes bent earnestly down the long vistas
of twinkling lights between the trees. It was a
beautiful and impressive spectacle. Lanterns were
hung upon many of the trees, and their light
brought out the foliage above them in a marvelous
gold and black tracery; in every direction long
shadowy aisles seemed to stretch away, with alter-
nating intervals of gloom and radiance; and over-
head was a clear, dark sky blazing with stars. No
wonder that in such a scene as this hearts are
newly wrought upon by memories and appeals.

The sermon was not a long one. At its close,
the usual invitation was given to all those who
wished the prayers of the congregation to come
forward into the seats reserved for them. Many
went forward. Then rose the sweet wild hymn, —

> "Come to Jesus! Come to Jesus!
> Come to Jesus just now."

The tender plaintive cadences seemed to float up
among the trees, and to be prolonged there, in the
upper air, as if the echoes were entangled in the
leaves; then came prayers, — earnest, wrestling

prayers by men who believed with their whole souls that for many of the men and women sitting there, that night would be the only chance of salvation. Nothing in this life can be more solemn than such a moment to those who hold the Methodist belief. Tears flowed down the cheeks of strong men. Women sobbed hysterically ; here and there could be seen a mother pleading with a child, a wife with a husband. The elders walked up and down in the aisles, urging and encouraging the timid and the hesitating ; every few moments the presiding elder on the platform would strike up a new strain of song, — tender, plaintive, and subduing beyond all power of words. With each stanza there came forward more and more, till the seats were nearly full.

" Bless the Lord, here is another soul that 's going to be saved," the ministers would cry, as each person came forward. Heartfelt " Amens " and "Glorys" rose from the whole congregation. The cool evening wind rustled at intervals through the trees ; and it needed no faith in the Methodist creed, no excitement of spiritual ecstasy, to make one thrill all through with the consciousness that the leaves rustled as if invisible hosts were passing by. Whatever be one's religious belief, however he may disapprove of all his class of abnormal influences, he cannot witness such a scene unmoved, unless he be of a hard and scoffing nature. John Bassett was astonished. He was too sincere and earnest himself, not to recognize earnestness and sincerity wherever he saw them. He had regarded the Methodist methods as akin to the methods of mountebanks and jugglers. He felt to-night, in every nerve of his being, that he had been wrong. He was affected in spite of himself — so powerfully that more than once he felt tears spring in his eyes.

He hardly dared look at Fanny Lane, so intense was her expression; her cheeks were flushed, her lips were parted; she bent forward unconsciously and looked up into the face of each person who passed her to take a seat among those who were "anxious." Whenever the singing broke forth, her lips trembled, and she fixed her eyes on the ground. John had taken his seat just opposite her — only the narrow, grassy aisle separated them. He could have reached her with his hand; and he felt again and again an impulse to do so, when he saw her excitement increasing.

At last she rose slowly, and turning toward her friends, said in a low voice, which John heard distinctly : —

"Don't say anything; I am going down into that seat to sit with those people."

And before her mortified and alarmed companions could utter a remonstrance, Fanny Lane had glided quietly three steps forward, and had seated herself by the side of an old woman, who was bent over nearly double with her face buried in her nands, sobbing.

John Bassett felt a strange, irrational rage at this sight, then a still stranger and more irrational desire to go and sit by her side. He gazed at her with a sort of terror, wondering what she would do next. He had not long to wonder. One of the elders approached her, and began to put to her the usual questions. She waved him gently aside, and said in a low, clear voice : —

"Thank you, I am not in the least unhappy. I did not come down here for that. I thought I should like to have all these people praying for me : — that is all."

Solemn as was the scene, and profoundly as John was feeling at that moment, he had to pass his hand quickly over his face to hide a smile, at the sudden and utter bewilderment of the discomfited elder. There was evident, at first, a quick, angry suspicion, that this finely clad city lady had taken her seat there out of pure irreverence ; but one look into the steadfast blue eyes slew that suspicion ; and with a grave "May the Lord bless your soul, my sister," the elder passed on.

When it was evident that no more persons would come forward to be prayed for, the whole congregation kneeled down, and the prayers began. Prayer after prayer — some quaint, simple, and touching ; some incongruous and distasteful ; but all earnest and impassioned. Fanny Lane sat still as a statue, her fair head unbowed, her eyes fixed steadily on each one who prayed. So strange, so foreign, so inexplicable a sight was never before seen on a camp-ground. More than one good Methodist man had his attention diverted and his devotion jeoparded by that startling face. And as for the good Methodist women, there was but one opinion among them of poor Fanny's conduct.

" Never see anything so brazen in my life."

" I wonder that Elder Swift did n't put her out."

" Should n't wonder ef he thought she was crazy, an' there might be a row that ud break up the meeting," were some of the indignant whispers at Fanny's expense.

Before the prayers ended, John stole softly away. He was uncomfortable. He had a vague instinct of flight from the place, — of flight from this girl whose atmosphere affected him so strangely. He found it no longer agreeable. His feeling toward her was fast becoming something like fear. Midway down the aisle, he stopped, turned, took one more look at her, and met her eyes, steadily, unmistakably fixed upon him. With a sense of something still more like fear in his heart, he turned abruptly and walked on.

When Hi and Hi's folks reached home, considerably past midnight, they found, to their great surprise, John Bassett fast asleep on the kitchen settee.

Hi shook him awake by degrees, exclaiming : —

" Why, John, how in airth 'd ye get in ? "

" Through the buttery window," laughed John.

"I stood it over at your camp-meeting as long as I could, and then I came out. If I'd have dreamed that you'd left a window open in all your house you wouldn't have caught me over there at all, I can tell you."

It was arranged that Hi should shoe Jerry as soon as it was light in the morning. And John would be off for Deerway by six o'clock, for there was mowing to be done that day which could not be put off. Then John went to bed, and as he settled himself to sleep, he said : —

"Well, that's the end of that."

But the end was not yet.

Two weeks later, as John was driving Tom and Jerry leisurely along the road past the Goodenows' farm-house, just at sunset one night, he heard his name called loudly from the piazza, and saw Luke Goodenow running down the pathway toward him. John felt, rather than saw, that the piazza was filled with people. He never passed the house without having a secret conscious wonder whether the blue-eyed, yellow-haired girl would be in sight ; but he had never seen her since the night of the camp-meeting. Now he felt sure that she was on the piazza, for the whole family had gathered there, to look at the sunset, which was one rippling wave of fiery gold from the western horizon nearly to the zenith. John did not turn his head, but reined up his horses and sat waiting for Luke.

With true New England circumlocution Luke opened his communication thus : —

"Ain't very busy now, John, are you ? "

Taken unawares, John said, frankly : —

"No; did the last of my haying yesterday. Why ? "

"Well, father 'n' I was a wonderin' if you would n't do a job o' drivin' for us. Ef yer would, 't 'ud be an awful help to us. We 're jest about drove out o' our senses. You see we hain't got hosses enough for all our folks; yer can't calkillate on boarders no how ; one year there won't nobody want to ride at all, 'n' yer hosses 'll eat their heads off ; an the next year, ye 'll cut down on hosses, and then everybody 'll want to drive from mornin' till night, and not make a mite of allowance for you nuther. Now, Kate, she 's gone lame ; a feller here raced her up meetin'us hill last week, and pretty nigh killed her — I 'd like to break his darned neck for him ; an' that breaks up our best team ; and you see there 's some o' our folks we 'd agreed to take regular every afternoon, and they 're just upsot about it, an' I 'm afraid they 'll go off if they can't have their rides, — it 's about all they do. I wish such folks 'd bring up their own hosses. Now could n't you jest take 'em for us? they won't be here more 'n a month. They 'll pay ye first rate, they 're rich, they don't care what they pay for any-thing."

John laughed out.

"Why, Luke," he exclaimed, "I'd do 'most any·
thing to oblige you, but I can't really turn hack-
driver.   I'm sorry."

Luke's face fell.

"I don't suppose ye'd let anybody else drive
Tom and Jerry, would you? Father'd always go
himself if ye'd let us have 'em," he said in desper-
ation, for this was really Luke's last hope.

"You'd better believe I wouldn't," said John
Bassett, a little proudly.   "I'm real sorry for ye,
Luke.   Well, summer boarders are nothing but a
pest anyhow."

"Well, some on 'em is, an' some on 'em isn't,"
replied the sententious Luke.   "There's folks in
our house I'd jest as lieves disappoint as not, and
a little lieveser; but I do hate to disappoint Miss
Fanny an' her ma, the worst kind."

"Oh, it's women folks, is it?" said dishonest
John Bassett, with a bound at his guilty heart; "if
it's only women folks, I might take 'em, perhaps;
but I'll be hanged if I'll drive any o' these city
fellows round."

Luke jumped eagerly at this suggestion.

"No, indeed," he said; "there ain't no man in
the party; jest the two old women and Miss Fanny,
an' they're jest the nicest folks we've ever had in
our house, I tell you.   Miss Fanny, she's a smart
one.   The old aunt, she's some stuck-up, but she's
no account, anyhow.   It's Miss Fanny's ma that
pays all the bills.   You jest come right up here

and make your bargain with 'em now," urged Luke, anxious to strike while the iron was hot.

"Bargain!" shouted John Bassett, with a look of indignation which nearly paralyzed Luke. "I'm not going to make any bargain. You can tell 'em that a friend of yours is going to do it for you. I don't want any of their money."

"But John," began Luke, "Father won't take it."

"Settle it among you as you like," cried John; "I sha'n't take any money. Let me know when you want me to come," and he gave Tom so sharp a stroke with the whip that Tom reared and plunged forward at a pace that whirled the wagon out of sight in the twinkling of an eye.

"Well, I swanny!" ejaculated Luke as he walked up the hill, "John Bassett is a queer one. I wonder how we'll fix it!"

"I swanny" does such universal duty as an oath throughout New England that the expression merits some attention as a philological curiosity. No one can sojourn among rural New Englanders for any length of time without being driven to speculate as to the origin of the phrase. Could it have come down through ages of gradual elimination from some highly respectable Pagan formula, such as, "I will swear by any of the gods," for instance? This seems a not wholly incredible supposition, and lifts the seeming vulgarism at once to the level of a "condensed classic."

No perplexing considerations of the question of

pay hindered the elder Goodenow from grasping gratefully at John Bassett's help in the matter of driving.

"They can pay us all the same," he said to Luke; "an' ef John Bassett 's such a fool 's not to take the money, he can go without it, that 's all. I sha' n't sue him to make him take it, I reckon."

And so it came to pass that on the next day, at three o'clock in the afternoon, John Bassett sat in his big strong wagon with Tom and Jerry shining like satin, and prancing in their harness before the Goodenow's gate, waiting to take three " summer boarders " to drive. He felt uncomfortable. He was sorry he had said he would do it, but he would not withdraw now; neither was he sure that he wanted to withdraw. In fact, just at present, John Bassett was not sure of anything. Minute after minute passed. Tom and Jerry pranced more and more.

"Look here, Luke," said John; "if this 's the way your folks keep horses standing, they can't drive with me. I 'll take a turn and come back, — it fidgets Tom so to stand," — and he drove down the road at a rapid rate.

"What does the man mean?" exclaimed Aunt Jane, who had just appeared at the door, and was leisurely wrapping herself up. Fanny Lane also ooked impatiently after the swift-going horses, and exclaimed, " How very queer! "

Luke hastened to explain.

"Ye see, Miss Fanny," he said, "John Bassett's horses aint like ourn. They wont stand a minute."

"What, are n't these horses quiet?" screamed Aunt Jane. "I sha' n't go a step. Maria, this man's brought skittish horses; we'll have our necks broken, and these country people never do know anything about driving."

Luke could not bear this.

"Well, mum," he said, "if you say that after you 've driven with John Bassett, I 'll eat my head. There aint no circus man can do any more with horses than John can. His horse plays hide-and-seek with him in the yard, just like a boy, — you 'd oughter see it."

Fanny Lane listened with delight.

"Oh, how charming!" she said, with one of her bewildering smiles bent full on Luke. "What good luck it was, Luke, that you found such a nice driver for us, and such nice horses! How did it happen that he was not engaged?"

The truth was very near escaping from Luke's lips in spite of himself; he was so tickled at the idea of John's being "engaged" as a "driver;" but he prudently choked both his laughter and the truth together and answered diplomatically: —

"Oh, he would n't drive for everybody, John would n't," — which was certainly true, though it served Luke's purpose as well as a lie.

When Luke, with some confusion and mixing up of genders and pronouns, had succeeded in in-

troducing John Bassett to the three women whom
he was to take charge of for the afternoon, Fanny
Lane looked full in John Bassett's face and
said, —

"I have seen you before, Mr. Bassett — I saw
you at the camp-meeting. You went out in the
middle of the last prayer, and I thought it was
so very wrong of you."

John was dumbfounded. All the old bewilderment of senses and emotions which he had felt at
his first sight of this girl, rushed back upon him
now, — also something of the old terror. How
could he be sure that she had not seen him during
the whole time he had spent in watching her? How
could he be sure that she had not read his thoughts
and feelings in his face? How could he be sure
that she was not at this very moment reading
clearly all his discomforts and perplexity? Heartily, John wished himself and his horses safely back
on the Bassett farm.

But all that Miss Lane saw of this mental per-
turbation was a slight hesitancy and slowness of
speech, which she set down to the natural shyness
of a rural man — unaccustomed to be at ease with
city women ; and she found something very quaint
and amusing in John's concise reply : —

"I do not think any one heard me go out. No
one looked up that I saw."

As Miss Lane's eyes were probably the only eyes
'n that whole congregation which were not de-

voutly closed at the moment when John stole away
so noiselessly on the grass, John had the best of
this little opening passage at arms, — how much
the best he did not dream, and would have been
astonished if he had known that his companion
was saying to herself at that moment: "How
clever of him! Of course I should never have
known that he had gone out if I had not been
gazing about at everything," and Fanny Lane
looked with a new interest at John Bassett's face.
It was a face that a sensitive and timid woman
might fear; but one that a high-spirited and independent woman might welcome with a quick and
hearty sense of comradeship and trust. Very calm,
very strong, very straightforward was the expression of the face in repose; the eyes were dark
blue-gray; the eyebrows and lashes jet black; his
smooth-shaved chin was too long and too heavily
molded, and his lips were thin rather than full,
though the outline of his mouth when closed was
rarely fine, and when he smiled it was beautiful.
Yet, the face was on the whole a stern one, and
oftener repelled than won advances from strangers;
it compelled confidence, but did not invite familiar-
ity. The more Miss Lane looked at her escort, the
more she took satisfaction in his appearance.

"Really," she thought, "this is a godsend; such
horses as these, and a man who is not in the least
stupid if he is a farmer! We shall have a lovely
time on our drives."

And she settled herself back in the broad front seat with a content and pleasurable anticipation which radiated from every feature, and made itself felt like sunshine.

"Is n't this lovely, mamma?" she exclaimed. "What a lucky thing that old Kate went lame! These horses are a thousand times better that Mr. Goodenow's. In fact," she added, "that 's no way to speak of them; they would be superb horses anywhere; they 're not to be spoken of as the same sort of animal as Mr. Goodenow's."

"No," said John quietly.

The tone of the monosyllable meant so much that Fanny Lane exclaimed —

"You love your horses very much, Mr. Bassett, do you not?"

"They are my only brothers," replied John, "I have taken care of them since the day they were born."

"Oh, how perfectly delightful!" cried Fanny. "That 's the very thing I have always thought I should like to do, — have a colt for my own in the very beginning, when I could play with it as I would with a kitten."

"Yes, that 's the only way to have the real comfort of a horse," said John. "They are more intelligent than dogs, and much more loving, if they ever had a chance to show it. You ought to see Tom play hide-and-seek with me; he will hunt the whole place over and never give up till he finds

me ; and he knows just as quick in the morning
if there 's a little difference in my tone of speaking
to him ; if I don't happen to feel quite first-rate
myself, he 'll poke his nose into my hand, and
whinny uneasily, till I speak in a chirker voice to
him. I don't really need any reins to guide them.
See here," and John suddenly said in a low tone —
"Whoa, Tom! Whoa, Jerry!" The horses were
trotting at a rapid rate down a little hill. So suddenly that they fell almost on their haunches, the
beautifully trained animals came to a full stop, and
stood still with their necks arched, their heads
down, snorting a little in impatience. The sudden
stop had given a severe jar to the wagon, and un-
fortunately had jolted Aunt Jane forward from her
seat.

"There! I told you so, Maria! Let me get out!
let me get out! We 'll have our necks broken.
Young man, let me get out this minute ; do you
hear?" screamed the terrified old woman.

"Oh, Aunt Jane," cried Fanny, who could barely
speak for laughing, "don't be absurd. There is
nothing the matter. Mr. Bassett stopped the horses
himself to show me how quick they would mind
his voice. It 's all right."

"I did not realize that it would give the wagon
quite such a jar, ma'am ;" said John, gravely, though
he corners of his mouth quivered. "I am very
sorry it frightened you so."

Aunt Jane was not very easily appeased.

"Don't do it again. Don't do it again. I v((y nearly went out into the middle of the road, — a most dangerous trick for horses to have. I always am afraid of country horses," she said.

Any alarm in Aunt Jane's mind always broke out in a jerky, monosyllabic, incoherent, but quick-running chatter, like nothing under heaven except the cackle of a frightened hen. Nobody could help laughing at the sounds she produced ; let the danger be ever so extreme, it would be impossible not to be amused at them. Fanny broke into an unrestrained peal of laughter in which John could not help joining, — a fact which completed Aunt Jane's discomfort, and reduced her to a state of ill-humor and absolute silence for the rest of the drive.

Mrs. Lane enjoyed and loved fine horses as much as her daughter did, and it was with a really cordial and unaffected tone, quite unlike her usual languid manner, that, when they reached home, she thanked John Bassett for the pleasure they had enjoyed.

"Yes, indeed, Mr. Bassett," echoed Fanny. " It is the very nicest thing we have had in Deerway. Now, you wont let anything keep you from coming every afternoon, will you ? We shall depend upon it ; I want to explore every inch of the whole region within fifteen miles round. It is the loveliest country I have ever found in New England. Remember, now, two o'clock exactly ! We wont keep you waiting to-morrow. Good afternoon ! " and she ran up the pathway like a fleet deer.

"Did n't touch his hat. Don't even know enough to touch his hat. What boors these country people are ! " grumbled Aunt Jane, as she laboriously toiled up the piazza steps, lifting her fat ankles slowly, and swinging alternately to right and left, as a duck does when it waddles up-hill.

"Well, why should he touch his hat, Aunt Jane?" exclaimed Fanny aggressively. "He is n't a coachman, and he has never been taught that gentlemen ought to lift their hats to ladies, — nobody does in Deerway. If he had been born in the city he would have known better. It is n't his fault."

Aunt Jane was half way up-stairs, and wheezing audibly, but she stopped, whirled with difficulty on the narrow stair, and exclaimed : —

"It 's my opinion, Fanny Lane, that you 've got some notion in your head of flirting with that strapping fellow, and I 'm just going to put your mother on her guard.'

Fanny flushed. "Oh, how could mamma ever have had such a coarse sister ? " she thought, but she answered merrily.

" I 'm not afraid. Mamma knows much better than to believe anything you tell her about me."

And then Fanny Lane sat herself down in a corner of the piazza, and looked off into the vast golden twilight in the west, and said to herself deliberately : —

"It's a very odd thing that I like that man's face so. I have never yet seen a face I like so much. He's as strong as a lion, and as true. What'll he ever do for a wife here in Deerway, I wonder."

The story of the next six weeks of John Bassett's life is as well told in one page as in hundreds ; yet its vivid details of delight would need no spinning out, no exaggeration to fill the hundreds of pages ; and as for color, it had the palette of the New England autumn, and the light of love, from which to paint its pictures.

It was an unusually beautiful autumn; the forests were like altar fronts in old cathedrals ; they glittered with colors which gems could not outshine. Heavy September rains filled the brooks to overflowing, and left the air cooled for the October sunlight. Deerway lies on one of the highest plateaus in New England ; this plateau is in places broken into myriads of conical and interlapping hills. These hills are thickly wooded with maple, ash, hickory, oak, chestnut, pine, cedar, hemlock, larch : not a tree of all New England's wealth of trees is lacking.

For miles and miles in all directions the roads run through forests and by the sides of brooks and streams. Then when you come out on the inter vals and opens between these hills and forests, there are magnificent vistas of view to distant horizons where rise the peaks and ranges of New England's highest mountains.

Over these roads, under these trees, across these lifted plains, drove John Bassett and Fanny Lane, side by side, every afternoon for six weeks. The two elderly ladies behind, wrapped in their cloaks and shawls, and often half asleep, little dreamed of the drama whose prelude was so quietly and fatefully arranging and arraying its forces on the front seat.

Fanny Lane was a genuine and passionate lover of the country. As soon as she entered it, the artificiality, the paltry ambitions, the false standards of her city life, fell away from her like dead husks. She was another woman. Had her whole life been passed thus face to face with the nature she was born to love, she had been indeed another and a nobler person. As it was, all that her few months' interval of each year of summer and out-door life did for her was to give her a marvelous added physical health, a suberabundance of vitality, which country life can never give to any one who does not love it with his whole soul. There seemed sometimes almost a mockery in the carrying back to the senseless dissipations and excitements of a gay city winter the zest and capacity to endure and to enjoy, born of woods and fields and sunrises and sunsets. But this was what Fanny Lane did

year after year. It was like living two lives on
two different planets ; no one who knew her only
in one would recognize her in the other, — would
believe the other possible to her. How should John
Bassett dream that this girl, who knew every tree,
every wayside weed by name, who climbed rocks
with exultant joy like a chamois, who came home
from her drives, day after day, with her arms loaded
with ground pine and clematis, with big boughs of
bright leaves, with lichens and mosses, would be
transformed one month later, in her city home, to
a nonchalant, conventional woman of society, entirely absorbed in a routine of visits and balls ?

Fanny Lane was also an artist by nature. No
spot of color in the woods, no distant shading
of tint in the horizons, no picturesque grouping
of work-people in the fields, no smallest beauty of
their rude homesteads, escaped her eye ; she noted
every one ; and she spoke of each one with the
overflowing tone of delight which belongs to the joy
of the true artist nature. How should John Bassett dream that all these things which she seemed
so to love and delight in, she loved and delighted
in as a spectacle, as if they were painted on a
canvas ! and that she would use the same tones
and show the same joy, a few weeks later, over
rare jewels and beautiful raiment, over an exquisite
equipage or a fine-flavored wine ! How should
John Bassett dream, when she jumped lightly from
the high wagon-seat to the ground, at one bound

without touching his hand, and cried, "Oh, what a lovely drive we have had; I never had such a good time in my life, Mr. Bassett," that her happiness was as purely a sensuous one as if she had been a faun, and that she had said the same thing thousands of times before? Her faculty of enjoyment was simply a superb gift; it was the health and mirthfulness of a young animal added to the keen susceptibility and passionless passion of the artist nature : the overflow of all this, the effervescence of these two qualities, gave a sparkling enchantment to her life and behavior, which was contagious and irresistible to all persons who did not pause to analyze or question it. John Bassett neither questioned nor analyzed it. In the intervals of his absence from her, he simply recalled her. When he was with her, he simply felt and heard her.

And so the six swift weeks sped on, and the day came at last when John Bassett had to say good-by to Fanny Lane at the little Deerway railway station, to which he had driven them early one crisp October morning. In the hurry of checking luggage and bestowing Aunt Jane and her canary bird and her many parcels in the train, there was little chance for farewell words; but just at the last moment, Mrs. Lane said very cordially, for she had come to have an honest liking for the grave and manly young farmer : —

"Whenever you come to town, Mr. Bassett, be

8

sure and come and see us;" and she shook hands with him warmly.

" Oh, yes, Mr. Bassett, you must come," cried Fanny; " I shall be so glad to see you. I shall miss Tom and Jerry horribly. Our horses are not half so nice, and our stupid park will be so dull after the Deerway woods. Oh, dear me! I wish I could stay here all winter. Good-by! Now, be sure and come and see us if you are in town," and the cars whirled away, bearing Fanny Lane out of John Bassett's sight.

He jumped into his wagon as if he were in great haste, and drove away at a furious rate. As soon as he was out of sight, he said to Tom and Jerry: " Walk, boys," flinging the reins loose on their necks, and never once roused from his reverie of thought and emotion till the whole six miles had passed, and the horses turned of their own accord into the farm-house gate. Then he started, and exclaimed : —

" Bless me! I meant to have stopped at Molly's, but it is too late now."

Little Molly had been looking out for John all the morning. It so chanced that their last boarders had gone to the station that morning, and Molly had seen John drive by with the Lane party, and had perceived, much to her joy, that they were also going to the train.

" Oh, I 'm so glad!" said Molly. " It 's all done with for this year. Now we can have peace and comfort again."

How many times John had come laughing within a few hours after the last boarders had taken leave, and exclaimed as he opened the door : —

"Thank heaven, the last summer boarder's out of the way!"

So Molly felt very sure he would stop now on his way back from the station; and surprised enough she was, to be sure, when she saw him drive past the house, — Tom and Jerry walking as lazily as if they were in the pasture, and John sitting with his hands on his knees and his eyes fixed on the dasher.

"Why, what a brown study John's in!" exclaimed Molly. "I wonder what he's thinking about."

And this was all she thought, for Molly was a sweet, gentle, unsuspicious little girl; and besides, did not she know John Bassett through and through — almost as well as if they had been rocked in the same cradle? If anybody had suggested to Molly that John might be in love with one of the "summer boarders," she would have laughed merrily; she knew better than anybody else how he hated the very sight of all those city people; and she had often thought in the past few weeks how good it was of John to take those three women to drive every day, — "just to help the Goodenows."

Poor little Molly! It was some weeks after Fanny Lane's departure before the thought of asking her to be his wife took actual shape of purpose in John Bassett's mind. He was almost benumbed,

he missed her so ; and he spent whole days driving
vaguely round and round in the roads where he had
driven with her ; he knew well enough what all this
misery meant, but while it was at its first height, he
could not even grasp at any ray of comfort or hope.
He loved this woman with the whole intensity of
his reticent and long-restrained nature, though his
common sense told him (when he let it lift up its
voice at all) that it would be folly for him to think
of her as his wife, — folly on all accounts : her
utter unfitness for a farmer's wife ; the utter im-
probability of her loving him. "Pshaw," he said
to himself, a hundred times a day. "John Bassett,
you are a fool ! " Nevertheless, day by day, and
night by night, a cruel hope whispered to him. He
recalled every word Fanny had said of her glad
delight in the Deerway life.

"I 'm sure," he thought, "no human being could
be happier than she was here. She belongs to the
country. She 's country all over. There is n't any
of the city lady about her. Not a bit.

"She said she wished she could stay here all
winter. She need n't ever lift her hand to do a
stroke of work. I could keep two or three girls for
her, just as well as not ; " and good John Bassett
thought over, with true manly pride, how he could
give to his lady-love all which, in his simplicity of
heart, he could conceive of even a city lady's re·
quiring.

"I 'd build her any sort of a house she wanted,

if she did n't want to live here with mother. Or I 'd take her anywhere in the world she wanted to go. There 's money enough ; " and so the treacherous hope allied itself to the blinded love, and both together lured John Bassett on until one day in midwinter he rang the door-bell of the grand house in which Fanny Lane lived " in town." He had not come with any assured hope ; not at all ; toward the last, his strong, good sense had come to look on the step more as a·desperate remedy for a desperate hurt, than as a probable healing of the wound by the gentle and blessed healing of happiness. He said to himself, grimly : " It 's the only way I 'll every get free from it. I 've got to know the truth once for all ; and I 'm not ashamed to ask her."

Mrs. Lane's black servant man had never seen at Mrs. Lane's door a person of precisely John Bassett's bearing. His first impression was, that he was some sort of tradesman, and he was on the point of giving him a seat in the hall, when John's quick and decisive tone — " Will you please say to Miss Lane that Mr. Bassett, from Deerway, wishes to see her," caused him to change his tactics, and usher this unclassed gentleman into the drawing-room.

On the very threshold of this room, John got his first blow. People who have been accustomed all their lives to laces and velvets, and paintings and statues in their rooms, can form no conception of the bewildering impression which such splendors produce on the mind of simply reared persons, seeing them for the first time. John's only experience of splendor, or what he thought splendor, had been in theatres, where he had, a few times in his life, seen plays put on the stage with considerable magnificence of appointment. He would not have conceived that even in kings' palaces could there be rooms so adorned as was this room in Fanny Lane's home. The only thing which he saw, which did not give him a sense of dazzling bewilderment, was the conservatory which opened from the farther end of the room. With a vague instinct of seeking refuge, he walked toward it ; but even here all seemed unreal ; the plants were, to him, as new as the soft carpets and the floating draperies of cobweb lace ; not a familiar leaf or flower ; only a great exuberant bower of strange colors and strange shapes, and an overpowering spicy scent which seemed, to his fresh and uncloyed nerves, almost sickening. Involuntarily he looked about him for a window ; he wanted fresh air and a sight of the blue sky. Draperies and veils shut out one and hid the other ; he felt as if he were in an enchanted prison, and it seemed to him a measurelessly long time before the black servant returned, and holding out to him some newspapers said, with a much increased respectfulness of demeanor : —

"Miss Fanny says, sir, that she is very glad, indeed, to see you, but she will have to keep you

waiting awhile, for she is just dressing for a dinner. She sent down the morning papers, thinking
you might like to look them over."

Mechanically, John took the papers and sat down
in the simplest chair he could find, and as near to
the wonderful window draperies as he dared to go.
Mechanically, he fastened his eyes on the printed
words; but he did not read one. He was wondering what would be the next scene in this play.
Fanny Lane's face, as he had seen it the last summer, in a simple white chip shade hat tied loosely
under her chin, with a branch of wild roses floating
down on her shoulder, seemed dancing in the air
before him. Would she look as she looked then?
He had sat thus, wondering and dreaming for a
long half hour, when a soft, silken rustle fell on his
ear, and a swift, light step, and the voice he knew
so well said, in the door-way : —

"Oh, Mr. Bassett, I 'm so glad to see you; and
you must forgive me for keeping you waiting so
long, but you see I am going to a stupid dinner at
six o'clock, and I was just dressing for it. But
now I am all ready, and have nothing to do but
sit and hear all about Deerway, and dear old Tom
and Jerry. I 'm ever so glad to see you; have you
been well?" and the vision held out its hands,
which looked like Fanny Lane's hands, and recalled
John Bassett a little to his senses.

This was what Fanny Lane had done : —

When the servant brought to her Mr. Bassett's

name and message, she sprang to her feet, and ex·
claimed, " Why, the good soul ! I 'm so glad to see
him. Tell Mr. Bassett I 'll be down in a moment,"
but before the man had left the room, she exclaimed : " Wait, William." Then turning to her
mother she said : —

" I believe I 'd better dress before I go down, for
it 's four o'clock now and he 'll be just as likely to
stay two hours as one, and I never could hurt his
feelings by telling him I had an engagement."

" Yes, dear, I think so too," assented Mrs. Lane,
though she did not in the least think so, having a
very distinct impression of the incongruity between
Fanny's evening toilet and her Deerway visitor.
Then Fanny went to her room, saying in her heart
as she went : —

" It may be all a ridiculous fancy of mine, but it
wont do any harm ; and if the poor fellow has
really come down here with any such idea in his
head, nothing would cure him of it so soon as to
see me in evening dress. I know John Bassett well
enough for that."

Fanny Lane had never forgotten ; she had often
wished she could forget, — the look on John's face
just as the train moved out of the Deerway station,
the day she had bade him good-by. It smote her
with a pang, — not of remorse, for she was not conscious of having by look, word, or deed done anything to invite or to awaken his love, — but of bitter and bootless regret. She liked and esteemed

John Bassett heartily; more than that, she recognized in him the elements of a true manliness of the sort that she most admired; and she had more than once gone so far in her secret thoughts as to admit to herself that not one of the men with whom she had thus far been brought into contact could compare in point of fine native grain and honesty clear through to the core with this uncultured and unmannered farmer. Through all Fanny Lane's worldliness and ambition and conventionality, she had kept unsullied her womanly instinct of reverence for, and tenderness to, all real love. To break, or to hurt a heart wantonly was as impossible to her as it would be to John Bassett himself. Very sorely she suffered during the half hour that she spent in arranging herself to go down to meet this man whom she feared she had wounded; and it was a serious and pensive face that looked back at her from the long pier-glass, as she surveyed herself at last, and noting every point of the perfection of her attire, thought sadly, —

"I am sure if he has thought of such a thing, he will see now he has made a great mistake."

Kind, wise Fanny Lane! When John first looked up, he literally did not know her. The dazzling white neck and white arms were all he saw at first, and at sight of those he felt an honest and quick displeasure. To his unenlightened and uncultured sense, they were unseemly. He knew, he had read, that this was the way of the

world ; and he had often seen actress women thus
bared to the eyes of men; but even in the theatre
he had disliked it : he was so simple-hearted, so
pure-minded, — this man of the fields, — and now,
nearer, within the close and unrestrained reach of
his eyes, he disliked it more.   Yet it was not this,
powerfully as this affected him, which slew on the
instant the purpose with which he had sought
Fanny Lane.   For this he could have had patience
and comprehension, seeing that all the influences
and circumstances of her life made it inevitable.
The thing which slew the purpose, almost the desire, within his heart, was the thing which Fanny
Lane had divined beforehand would slay it, and
had purposely plotted should slay it ; it was the
whole atmosphere of luxury, artificial elegance in
her dress.   She had chosen the showiest and cost-
liest of her gowns : a heavy wine-colored silk, with
a sweeping train trimmed profusely with white lace ;
white chrysanthemums, so daintily and truly made
that it was hard to believe them artificial, looped
the folds of the silk, and were scattered in the lace ;
white chrysanthemums, made of pearls with yellow
topazes for their centres, shone in her hair, on her
neck and on her arms.   She was superbly beautiful
in this toilet, and she knew it ; but she knew or
believed that it was a kind of beauty which would
bring healing and not harm to the heart of John
Bassett.   It did.   It did its work so quickly that to
her dying day, Fanny Lane never felt sure — and

it was many years before she ceased to wonder —
whether the healing had been needed or not.

"Very well, thank you, Miss Lane," said John
Bassett, with an untroubled and warm-hearted smile,
in reply to her first inquiry. "I am always well.
Have you been well? and your mother and aunt?
You asked me to come and see you, if I came to
town, and so as I was here to-day, I called. Are
you well?"

"I'm very glad you did," said Fanny; and with
an uneasy instinct which she never felt in a ball-
room, she drew close up to her throat the fleecy
shawl she had thrown over her shoulders as she
came down-stairs. Without knowing what she felt,
she had felt the avoidance in John Bassett's eyes.
"Yes, I am very well."

"You do not look as well as you did in Deerway," said the honest man, looking at her more
closely now that he could; "you are not out-of-
doors enough, are you?"

"Oh, yes, but it's a different out-of-doors," said
Fanny. "It's only one degree better than in-
doors; but it's all we can have till summer comes,
and we can get back to Deerway."

"Will you be in Deerway next summer again?"
asked John.

"Oh, no, Mr. Bassett, nor for two or three summers; we are going to Europe in May, to stay three
years!" exclaimed Fanny, with great animation.
"I'm so delighted. It has been the dream of my

life. But, Mr. Bassett, do tell me about Tom and Jerry; and how the pine woods look now the snow has come. I wish I could see Deerway in the winter."

Then John told her about Tom and Jerry, and about the pine-trees, with great avalanches of snow on their lower branches, and about the sledding, and sugaring-time, which would soon come; and before he knew it, it was already dark and time to go. As he rose, Fanny exclaimed : —

"Oh, let me give you some flowers, Mr. Bassett; come into the green-house."

Very ruthlessly, Fanny Lane cut the rare flowers, not even sparing the tremulous and spiritual orchids, of which she had a few. Putting the fragrant and beautiful mass of bloom into a basket which stood on the table, she said, with a sudden impulse : —

"Give some of these to that pretty little Miss Wilder I saw in Deerway, the one that sings in the choir. She lives near you, does n't she ?"

"Oh, yes ;" said John, "she is just like my sister; she is very fond of flowers."

"She has one of the very sweetest faces I ever saw," said Fanny, earnestly; "I never have forgotten it."

John looked a little astonished. He did not know that Molly's face was sweet; but he knew that *she* was.

"Molly 's a very sweet, good girl," he said

warmly; and oddly enough, those were the last words, except good-byes, which passed between John Bassett and Fanny Lane.

After Fanny went up into her mother's room, she stood for some minutes at the window watching John's tall, broad-shouldered figure, as he walked away. Then she sighed and sat down.

"What's the matter now?" said Aunt Jane.

"Nothing," said Fanny, "only I was thinking that country people are a great deal happier than we are."

"Pshaw!" said Mrs. Lane, languidly, "I wonder what Mr. Bassett thought of your gown. I don't suppose he ever saw a really handsome silk gown before."

"He didn't appear to think anything about it at all," said Fanny, half petulantly. Could it have been that, side by side with her good, true purpose of saving John Bassett from speaking words he might wish unsaid, she had had a petty desire that he should, at least, confess her more beautiful in her silks and jewels?

"What could you expect?" sneered Aunt Jane. "I don't suppose he'd know a pearl marguerite with a topaz middle, from one of the ox-eye daisies on his farm!"

"Yes, he would," retorted Fanny, "and like the ox-eye daisy a great deal better; and that's where he is happier than we are."

John Bassett went back to Deerway. The purpose, nay, even the desire to ask Fanny Lane to be his wife was slain, as we have said, in an instant by the sight and the sense of the Fanny Lane whom he had never seen, never known, till he saw and knew her in her city splendors. But there remained still the memory, the consciousness of the other Fanny Lane whom he had seen and had known during all those long, sweet, bewildering summer hours. This memory and this consciousness were not so easily slain. They died hard, and John was, for many months, a man bereft. If there had been in the Deerway grave-yard a mound under which he had laid away the dead body of a woman he had loved, his sense of loss would not have been much greater. The winter was a long and cold and sunless one. If it had been summer, John's loneliness would have been far less ; nature would have helped to cure him through every pore, and every nerve ; but the New England winter is a bitter season in which to be shut up alone with a grief ; it takes a serene and ever-abiding joy to reconcile one to its imprisoning cold. The months seemed very long to John. They seemed very long to Molly Wilder also. The instinct of love is like the subtle added sense by which the blind know the presence or the approach of a person they can neither see, nor hear, nor touch. What had happened to John, Molly did not know, could not imagine ; but that something had changed him, she felt so keenly, that she could hardly keep back tears when he spoke to her. Sometimes she fancied that he must have discovered that he had some deadly disease of which he knew he would sooner or later die; but he said that he was well; and he looked well. Sometimes, she fancied that she had in some unwitting way displeased him; and a hundred times a day, the gentle girl said, " I will ask John what I have done;" but a shy consciousness which did not clothe itself in words made it impossible for her to ask the question.

Molly was unhappier than John. Meantime, he came and went all winter in the old fashion, so far as times and seasons counted, and never dreamed that he was seeming unlike himself; never noticed, either, that Molly was pale, and was growing thin, until one day in April, when all the young people were out on a sunny hill-side looking after arbutus blossoms, he came suddenly upon Molly sitting alone on a mossy log, with a few violets lying loosely dropped in her lap, her hands crossed above them, her eyes fixed on the far horizon, and an expression of patient suffering on her countenance. He ran toward her.

" Why, Molly, what is the matter? Have you hurt yourself?" he exclaimed.

She flushed red, and replied : —

"Nothing. I am only tired."

But John saw that there had been tears in her eyes, and with a sudden lightning flash of con-sciousness, his heart pricked him.

"Dear little Molly!" he thought. "I do believe I 've been cross to her all winter. I 've been thinking about something else all the time, and she has n't anybody else but me.

From that hour, John's manner toward Molly changed, and the color began to come back to Molly's cheeks. Nothing could be further from love-making than his treatment of her; and yet she was comparatively happy, for the old atmosphere of brotherly fondness and care had returned, and gradually, the old, good cheer came too.

Molly did not dream that anything more would follow; if ever the thought had striven to enter her pure, maiden heart, that it would be a joy to be John's wife, she would have blushed with shame at herself, as if the thought were a sin; but it must have been hard for Molly to keep the thought away all through these days, when John was deliberately permitting himself to wonder whether, after all, little Molly were the woman who would bring him true peace and content. He was very honest with himself. He knew he did not love Molly as he had loved Fanny Lane; but he also knew clearly that his love for Fanny Lane was a mistake, — was a glamour of the senses, — and he was fast coming to feel, by Molly's side, a serene sort of happiness which he believed was a better and truer thing than the other. There was not a trace of coxcombry in John Bassett's nature. He did not once feel sure that Molly could love him as a husband , but he said to himself : " If I feel that I can make her happy, I believe she is the woman I ought to marry. I 've loved her ever since I can remember anything, and that ought to be the best sort of love."

And as the summer grew fair this feeling grew strong, and John and Molly grew happier and happier, until one October day when everything except grapes had ripened, this too ripened and fell, and Molly gathered it. When John said to her : —

" Molly, do you think you could love me well enough to have me for your husband ? " she looked up into his face and said only : —

"Oh, John, do you think I should make you happy ? " And in that instant something in the look on Molly's face, and in the tone of Molly's voice, smote the inmost citadel of John's heart which had never before opened, and never would have opened to any other or different touch.

There is an evil fashion of speech and of theory, that a man's love for a woman lasts better, is stronger, if he be never wholly assured of hers for him. This is a base and shallow theory ; an outrage on true manliness ; it has grown out of the pitiful lack of true manliness in some men ; out of the pitiful abundance of selfish counterfeit loves and loving. Nothing under heaven can so touch, so hold, so make eternally sure, the tenderness, the loyalty, the passion of a manly man, as the consciousness in every hour, in every act of life, that

9

the woman he has chosen for his wife lives for him, and in him, utterly and absorbingly.

Before snow fell, John and Molly were married. Molly went up from the house on the meadow to the house on the hill to live, and that seemed to be almost the only change, except in the gladness of her heart and John's, and that was a change no-body knew much about except themselves. A little change there was also in Molly's clothes, though not the usual metamorphosis which brides undergo. She was as quiet in her tastes as a Quaker, and the only adornment which she wore when she first went to church as John's wife, was a wreath of small white chrysanthemums in her hat. They were singularly becoming to her fair and rosy face. It cannot be denied that when John first saw them, he started a little, and remembered some he had seen a year before, made of pearls and topazes. But he thought these much prettier than those ; and as Fanny Lane had said, " an ox-eye daisy on the farm " prettier than either.

We may not dare in this world to wonder why the sad people live and the happy people die. At times one is so overwhelmed by the terrifying con-sciousness of this cruel habit of fate, that one hardly dares rejoice at his fullest, for fear of being slain and removed from his joy.

John Bassett and his dear and beloved wife, " little Molly," lived together only one short year. Then with his own hands he laid her and their

baby daughter, who had never breathed, in one
grave under the apple-trees in the south orchard,
where he could see the mound from his chamber
window. Now was John Bassett, indeed, bereft.
The blow told on him heavily. It changed him
month by month by a slow benumbing process into
a man sadly unlike what he had been before. He
had lived, as we said, like a noble pagan. He
suffered as the noble pagans used to suffer, with a
grim stoicism, an unwilling and resentful surrender
to powers he was too feeble to oppose.

Before little Molly was taken ill, she had had a
presentiment that she would die, and she had set
all her house in the most careful order to leave
behind her. Her few little personal ornaments,
her two or three bits of lace, and her two silk
gowns, — only two, and of the simplest fashion, —
she had laid away with bags of lavender in one of
the deep drawers in an old-fashioned chest which
stood in their chamber. Her common clothes she
had packed in a box, and had said to John one
day : —

" If I don't get well, dear, just give that box to
mother ; all the things will be of use to her ; but
the things in the drawer I 'd like to have kept for
the baby. I don't believe God will take us both
away from you ; and I am sure it will be a girl, —
a daughter would comfort you more than a son,
would n't it, dear ? "

And so it came to pass that after Molly was buried, there was hardly a trace left of her in the old Bassett house except her little work-basket, which stood on the stand by her bed, and held a little baby's sack of flannel, on which she had been working that last day. This basket John would not allow to be moved. It hurt him like a new sight of Molly's dead face whenever he looked at it, and yet he could not bear to have it taken away. He would often turn over the spools, the worn and discolored bit of bees-wax, the thimble, the scissors ; he would take up the little sack, and look at it almost with thoughts of hatred. If the baby had lived, he would have come to love her in spite of her having cost her mother's life ; but now he felt that Molly had gone childless out of the world, he was left childless in it ; this miserable, frustrated, useless life, that was never a life at all, had separated him from Molly, — it was bitter. One day he felt in one of the silk pockets of the basket a rustling of paper ; clumsily, and with difficulty, he thrust his big fingers deep down into the little receptacle, and drew out a crumpled bit of newspaper. It had been folded and refolded so many times that the creases were worn almost through. He opened it and read the following lines : —

"THE WIFE'S REVERIE."

O HEART of mine, is our estate, —
Our sweet estate of joy, — assured ?
It came so slow, it came so late,
Bought by such bitter pains endured ;
Dare we forget those sorrows sore,
And think that they will come no more ?

With tearful eyes I scan my face,
And doubt how he can find it fair ;
Wistful, I watch each charm and grace
I see that other women wear ;
Of all the secrets of love's lore,
I know but one to love him more !

I see each day, he grows more wise,
His life is broader far than mine ;
I must be lacking in his eyes,
In many things where others shine.
O Heart ! can we this loss restore
To him, by simply loving more ?

I often see upon his brow,
A look half tender and half stern ;
His thoughts are far away, I know ;
To fathom them, I vainly yearn ;
But nought is ours which went before ;
O Heart ! we can but love him more !

I sometimes think that he had loved
An older, deeper love, apart
From this which later, feebler, moved
His soul to mine.   O Heart ! O Heart !
What can we do ?   This hurteth sore.
Nothing, my Heart, but love him more !

Tears filled John's eyes : " Oh, what could have made Molly keep that ? " he said to himself. " Dear little girl ! I never really loved anybody in this whole world, but her, and I never will."

The lines haunted him for days. He put the paper into the upper drawer where he kept his col- lars and neckties. He did not like to leave it in the basket, lest, some day, it might be read by some one else. Every morning, when he was dressing, he took it out and read it again, and it always brought the tears to his eyes. After awhile, he read it less often ; and after another while, it was gradually pushed farther and farther back in the drawer till, it being out of sight he forgot it ; and at last, some day, it might have been a year, it might have been two or three, — nobody will ever know, — the little worn wisp of paper over which sweet Molly Bassett had, in spite of all her quiet happiness, shed some tears, slipped through a wide crack at the back of the drawer, and fell down into the drawer beneath, — the drawer which held Molly's clothes, fragrant with the undying lavender. Here the verses lay for years, forgotten, and un- disturbed, — forgotten, — for John Bassett had become a grave, silent, steady-working, contented farmer ; — undisturbed, — for the key of the drawer lay where Molly had laid it, in the till of the chest, and John never saw it without thinking of her, and wondering uneasily what would be done with those garments when he should die. The verses he had forgotten all about. But it was not because he had forgotten Molly that he had forgotten the verses; neither was it because he had forgotten Molly, that when he was, in the Deerway vernacular, "just turned forty," he one day rode over to Middleburg Crossing and asked the widow Thatcher to marry him. He was lonely; he was uncomfortable; he had borne with the eye-service, the short-comings, the ill-nature of hired women in his house as long as he could; and just as the Deerway people had fairly settled down into a belief that "nothing under heaven would induce John Bassett to marry again," that "there was a man who was really true, from first to last, to his first love," they were electrified one fine morning, by finding posted up on the brick meeting-house walls, on the ominous black-board containing the announcement of intended marriages, the names of John Bassett and Mrs. Susan Thatcher.

Mrs. Susan Thatcher was the most notable housekeeper in Wenshire County. She was something of a farmer, too, and had "done very well for a woman," everybody said, with 'Siah's farm since his death. She made the best butter and cheese in the region; dried more apples, and pickled more pickles, — sweet, sour, and "mixed," — than any two other women. Her bread always took the premium at the County Fair; and as for her "drawn-in rugs," they were the wonder and the admiration of everybody. She was a spinner,

too, and stoutly discountenanced the growing dis-
favor into which that ancient and picturesque art
was fast falling. "You can always spin at the odd
times when you would n't do anything else," she
said, and by chests full of home-made linens and
woolens, she made good her words. With all this
notable industry and skill, she was also warm-
hearted and cheery; had a pleasant word for
everybody, and was a master hand at "bees" of
all sorts, especially at "quiltings."

She was generous, too, and gave away her
turkeys at Thanksgiving, and her chickens in July,
with a cordial liberality not common in the country.
She was generous, moreover, with what costs more
than food or money, sympathy and help; she was
confided in and leaned on by everybody; and even
if her words sometimes seemed a little brusque or
hard, it always turned out that, in their sense and
substance, they were right, for Susan Thatcher was
the incarnation of common sense.

As soon as Deerway recovered from its first
shock of surprise at the announcement of John
Bassett's intended marriage, the town was unan-
imous in its approval.

"The very best thing he could have done,"
they said; I wonder nobody 's thought of it before."

" He could n't have found a woman in all the
country who 'd have gone right on to that farm, an
worked everything 's Susan Thatcher will."

This was quite as clear to John Bassett as it was
to any of his neighbors ; and it was with a great
sense of assured satisfaction and calm content-
ment that he took his second wife home and installed her in his house. He felt for her a great
esteem and an honest liking, and the sort of calm
affectionate regard, which was all he had to offer
her in the way of love, was all that Mrs. Susan
Thatcher would have known what to do with.
More would have embarrassed and annoyed her ;
for she was, as we have said, the incarnation of
common sense.

When in the course of her setting to rights all
things in the house, she came upon the locked
drawer in John's bureau, she said to herself : —

"Here's some of Molly Wilder's things, I expect. I guess I'd better let 'em alone. If he
wants me to have 'em, he'll say so when he gets
ready ; " and she asked no question about the
drawer.

The little work-basket, with all its contents, now
so yellowed and dusty with age, — for it was eight
years since Molly died, — John had burned the
night before he married Susan.

"I don't believe little Molly would like to have
Susan have that," he thought, "and I don't think
I want her to neither," he added, with a deep sigh
and a yearning recollection of Molly's sweet face,
as he watched the crisp straw crackle and the fine
fiery lines of the threads quiver and turn from red

to gray. Then he recollected the locked drawer,
and said to himself : —

"Some day I 'll give Susan the key to that
drawer. I suppose the things might as well be
used first as last."

When John gave his wife the key, and told her
what the drawer held, she said in her clear, resolute, kindly tone : —

"Well, just as you like, John. Of course, I
have n't any feeling one way or another about it ;
but there 's so many folks in need of clothes, it
seems a pity to let anything be lying by idle."

As soon as John had gone out to his work, Susan
went up-stairs to open the drawer. It must be con-
fessed she had her own curiosity to look into it,
especially as John had said to her, a little huskily :

"I have n't ever opened the drawer. It 's just
as Molly put the things in before she was sick."

"Poor little thing ! " thought Susan, as she
turned the key and slowly drew out the drawer ;
"it was real hard for her, but I can't say I 'm
sorry exactly," and Susan's eyes took on a softer
light. She had found out that she loved John
Bassett better than she had ever loved Josiah
Thatcher. She shook out the folds of the two
silk gowns, — one black and one of a pale gray.

"I don't know as there 's any reason why I
should n't use this black," she thought, rolling a
bit of it between her thumb and finger, and mentally estimating that it must have cost at least ten-
and-sixpence a yard.

"Black silk 's black silk, whoever 's worn it ; nobody could tell one from another, and I might have the gray one dyed for a petticoat ; no, I 'll give that to Molly's cousin, Sarah Beman ; she never has anything pretty, poor soul ! John 'u'd never see it on her, or he would n't know it if he did ; she 'd make it up with red, most likely."

And so good Susan Bassett went on through the simple wardrobe, apportioning it in her own mind as seemed best, and quietly saying to herself at last : —

"I guess I 'd better not say anything to John about it ; he 'll know I 've disposed of 'em some-how, and I reckon he 'd rather not know where they went. It 's only natural he should have some feeling about the things ; 'taint so very long yet."

As she took out the last article from the drawer, she saw far back in the right-hand corner a small folded paper. She took it out, opened it, and see-ing that it was poetry, was just about to throw it on the floor (Susan never read poetry) ; but suddenly recollecting the circumstances under which this drawer had been closed, she felt a curiosity to see what the verses were which had been put away so carefully with Molly's best clothes.

If "The Wife 's Reverie" had been written in Sanscrit, it would have been but little more re-moved from Susan's comprehension. She read it slowly with a look of increasing contempt on her face.

"Pshaw!" she exclaimed, as she finished the last line. "If that is n't just like Molly Wilder ; she always was a silly little thing," and Susan crumpled up the paper, and tossed it on the bed. Then she put back the clothes, locked the drawer, and put the key in her pocket. The morning was slipping away fast, and she was in a hurry to be about her work. She had been cutting out some unbleached cotton shirts for John the day before, and as she left the room, she noticed a few of the yellow threads and bits of cloth on the floor ; she stopped and picked them up ; then she took "The Wife's Reverie" from the bed, and rolling it and the rags together in a tight ball, hurried down-stairs to oversee the churning. At the foot of the stairs, behind the door which opened into the kitchen, hung a big rag-bag made of bed-tick. It was so full that the mouth bulged open.

"Dear me," thought Susan, "I do wish that peddler 'd come round. The bag 's running over full ;" and as she impatiently crammed in her little ball of ravelings and paper, and her eye fell again on a line of "The Wife 's Reverie," she said to herself complacently : —

"It 's the queerest thing, when a man marries again, how sure he is to pick out such a different kind of a woman from his first wife. I suppose they find out what they really do want."

MY TOURMALINE.

I HAD arrived, late one November afternoon, at a wretched little tavern in a small village in Maine. I was very unhappy. It was of no consequence to me that I was young; it was of no consequence to me that I had superb health. I was very unhappy. How compassionately middle age smiles, looking back upon the miseries of its healthy youth! How gladly to-day would I be sent away in disgrace from college, to rusticate for six months in a country parson's house, if I could feel the warm, strong blood bound in my veins, as it bounded that night when I jumped from the top of the stage to the ground under the ugly, creaking sign of that village tavern.

It was a dismal afternoon. A warm rain was slowly filtering down through the elm-trees with which the street was too thickly shaded. The ground was sprinkled with golden-yellow leaves, and little pools of muddy water filled every footprint on the grass-grown sidewalk. A few inert and dispirited men lounged on the tavern steps with that look of fossilized idleness which is peculiar to rural New England. In other countries, idlers look as if they were idling because they liked it ; or perhaps because illness or lack of employment had forced them to idle ; but the New England idler, on the steps of his native tavern, or by the stove of his native "store," looks as if he had been there since the prehistoric ages, and had no more volition or interest in his situation than a pterodactyl five hundred feet under ground.

Spite of the rain, I had persisted in riding on the outside of the stage. I took a perverse pleasure in being wet through, and chilled to the marrow. I remember I even thought that I hoped I should take cold and have a rheumatic fever, so that the President might see what had come of sending a fellow down into Maine to spend a winter. Jim Ordway, my chum, had been rusticated with me. His offense was simply calling the President an "inhuman old fool" to his face, on hearing of my sentence of rustication. Jim was a warm-hearted fellow. I have always wondered I did not love him better. He was snug and warm inside the coach, and had been exasperating me all day by breaking out into snatches of the old college songs. For the last hour he had been quiet, and when I sprang down from the top of the coach, and called loudly to him, "Come, jump out, old fellow ! Here we are, and an infernal hole it is to be sure, " I was half paralyzed with astonishment at hearing him reply in a whisper, " Be quiet, Will ! She 's asleep." Slowly and carefully he came down the coach steps, holding in his arms a limp and shapeless bundle, from which hung down two thin, little gray legs, with feet much too big for them, and made bigger still by clumsy shoes.

"Good heavens, Jim," I exclaimed, " what is it ? where did you pick her up ? " I added, for I saw tangled yellow curls straggling over his arm from the folds of the old plaid shawl in which the poor little thing was rolled.

" Hush, hush ! Look after him, will you ? " he said, nodding his head toward a man who sat in the corner of the coach, and made no motion to get out. The driver took hold of him roughly and shook him. He swayed helplessly to and fro, but did not speak nor open his eyes ; horrible fumes of rum came from his wide-open mouth. He was drunk and asleep. We carried him into the house as if he had been a log, and laid him on a buffalo-robe on the floor in the corner of the office. The loungers turned their slow dull eyes on him. One said : —

" Drunk, ain't he ? " with a slight emphasis of surprise on the verb.

" Wall, yes, I sh'd say he wus," replied a second, the least talkative of the group, also conveying his sense of the unusualness of the incident by emphasizing the final verb of his sentence ; and then the group returned to their vacant contemplations.

No such indifference was shown in the parlor, where Jim had carried the little girl, and, leaving her on the grim hair-cloth sofa, had summoned the landlady to care for her.

"The poor little creatur ! Now, I never ! Ain't she jes' skin an' bone," ejaculated the kind-hearted woman, as she bustled about, with pillows and shawls ; "and, good gracious ! I do declare, ef her feet ain't jest as stun cold as ef she wus dead," she cried out, beginning to rub them so energetically that the poor little waif shrank and screamed, even in her sleep, and presently opened her eyes — the most beautiful and most terrified eyes I ever saw, hazel brown, large, deep-set, with depths of appeal in their lightest glance.

"Where is my father ?" she said, beginning to cry.

"Don't cry, dear. Your father is asleep in the other room. I 'll take care of you," said Jim, trying in his awkward boy fashion to stroke her head.

She looked up at him gratefully. "Oh, you 're the kind gentleman that picked me up in the stage," and she shut her eyes contentedly and was asleep again in a moment.

It seemed that she and her father had taken the stage some ten miles back. I had been too absorbed in my own dismal reflections to notice them. The man was almost unconscious from the effects of liquor when he got into the stage, and had placed the child so carelessly on the seat, that at the first motion of the wheels she had fallen to the floor. Jim had picked her up, and held her in his lap the rest of the way. It was pathetic to see how he had already adopted her as his special charge. He was an impulsive and chivalrous boy, with any amount of unmanageable sentimentalism in him.

"I say, Will," he exclaimed, as soon as the land-lady had left the room, "I say! That man out yonder will kill this child some day. He is a brute. She trembles if he looks at her. I wonder if we could n't keep her — hide her away somehow. He 'd never know where he lost her. He did n't know he lifted her into the stage. I 'd just like to adopt her for my sister. I 've got plenty of money for two, you know, and it would be jolly having the little thing down here this winter."

"Oh, bother!" said I. "It 's lucky you 've got a guardian, Jim Ordway, I know that much. You can't adopt any girls for five years to come; that 's one comfort. Come along; let 's see if there 's anything to eat in this hole. She 'll sleep well enough without your watching her."

But Jim would not stir. He sat watching the tiny, sleeping face, with an abstracted look, unusual to him. He did not even resent my cavalier treatment of his project. He was too much in earnest about it.

"No, no; I sha'n't leave her here alone," he
10

said, in reply to my reiterated entreaties to him to come to the dining-room. " If she wakes up and finds herself alone, she will be frightened. And you can see, by her face, that she has cried herself almost sick already."

It was true. There were deep circles, swollen and dark, around the eyes, and a drawn look about the mouth, pitiful to see on such a little face. She could not have been more than eleven years old, but the grief was written in lines such as might have been written on the face of a woman.

On my way to the dining-room I passed through the office, and looked at the drunken man, still in his heavy sleep, lying where we had laid him on the floor, like the brute he was. It was indeed a bad face — bad originally, and made more hideous still by the unmistakable record of a long life of vile passions. I shuddered to think of that child's pleading hazel eyes lifted up in terror to this evil countenance, and I no longer wondered at Jim's sudden and chivalrous desire to rescue the little one by almost any means. But her rescue was already planned and nearer at hand than we could have dreamed. Only a few moments after I had taken my seat at the supper-table, I heard excited voices in the office, the quick trampling of feet, and then a pistol-shot. I sprang up, and reached the door just in time to see the drunken man's body fall heavily on the floor, while the blood spouted from a bullet-hole in his throat, and the men who had been grappling with him staggered back on all sides with terror-stricken faces. In a second, however, they gathered round him again, and lifting him up, tried to stay the blood. It was too late; he was dying; a few inarticulate gasps, a dim look of consciousness and fear in the blood-shot eyes, and he was gone.

Loud and confused talk filled the room; men crowded in from the outside; pale and agitated, in the doorway, stood Jim, his eyes fixed on the dead man's face. "Will," he whispered, as I pressed closer to him, "I feel just like a murderer. Do you know that just before that pistol went off, I was saying to myself that I wished the man were dead, and I believed it would be a good deed to shoot him! Oh God, it is awful!" and Jim shuddered almost hysterically. In the excitement, everybody, even Jim, forgot the little girl. Presently, I felt my coat pulled by a timid touch. I turned. There, to my horror, stood the child. Her brown eyes were lifted with their ineffable appeal, not to my face, but to Jim, who stood just beyond me, and many inches taller; she had touched me only as the sole means of reaching him.

"Kind gentleman," she began. Before I could speak, Jim leaped past me, caught her in his arms, folded her on his breast as if she had been a baby, and carried her back into the parlor. She was beginning to cry with vague terror. Jim was too overwrought himself to soothe her.

"Where is my father," she said.   " Has he left me ? "

Jim looked at me hopelessly.

" Why," said I, " does he often leave you ? "

" Yes, sir, sometimes," she said, in a matter-of-fact tone, which was pitiful in its unconscious revelation of the truth.

" What do you do when he leaves you, dear ? " said Jim, tenderly as a woman.

" A boy that lived in the room under our room took care of me the last time.   He was very good, but he was away all day," replied the waif.

" Well, I 'm the boy that 'll take care of you, this time," said Jim ; " if he leaves you here, I 'll take first-rate care of you."

A queer little wintry smile stole over the pinched face.

" But you 're not a boy. You 're a big gentleman — the kindest gentleman I ever saw," she added in a lower tone, and nestled her head on Jim's neck.   " I like you."

Jim looked at me proudly, but with tears in his eyes.

" Did n't I tell you you never saw anything like it ? " he said ; then, turning to the child, he looked very earnestly in her face, saying, —

" If you think I 'm a kind gentleman, and will take good care of you, will you mind me ? "

"Yes, sir, I will," she replied, with the whole strength of her childish little voice thrown on the " will."

"Very well. My friend and I want to go into the other room for a few minutes. I want you to promise to lie still on this sofa and not stir till I come back. Will you?"

"Yes, sir, I will," again with all her strength on the "will."

Jim stooped over and kissed her forehead.

"You know, I shall come back in a few minutes," he said.

"Yes, sir, I do;" and she looked up at Jim with an expression of trust which was as much too old for the little face as were the lines about the mouth. Both were born of past suffering. As we went towards the door, the brown eyes followed us wistfully, but she did not speak.

As soon as we had closed the door, Jim took both my hands in his and exclaimed: —

"Now, Will, don't you see, I've got to take her! It's a clear Providence from beginning to end; and if you don't help me through with it, I'll cut loose from you, and college may go to the devil. I've got five hundred dollars here with me, and that to these country folks is a fortune; they'll be glad enough to have me take her off their hands."

"But, Jim," I interrupted, "you talk like a crazy man. You don't know that she is on their hands, as you call it. There may be twenty relations here to the funeral before to-morrow, for all you know. The man may have lived in the very next town."

"No, no, I know all about them," said Jim. "I

mean," he added shamefacedly, " I know they
did n't live anywhere near here. They 're English.
You might have known it by the sweet tones of her
poor little feeble voice. They have only just come
from the ship ; she told me so ; and her mother is
dead ; she told me that too."

We were interrupted by the appearance of the
landlord, who came hurrying out of the office, his
face red with excitement, which was part horror
and part a pleasurable sense of importance in having his house the scene of the most startling event
which had happened in the village for a half century.

" Oh ! " he said, " I was jest a lookin' for you ;
we thought mebbe ye knowed suthin' about the
miserable critter, as ye come in the stage with him."

" All I know," said Jim, " I know from the little
girl. The man was nearly dead drunk when they
got into the stage. They are English, and have
only just come to this country. She has no brothers and sisters, and her mother is dead. He was a
cruel, inhuman brute, and it is a mercy he is dead.
And I am going to take the little girl. I am an
orphan myself, but I have friends who will care for
her."

The landlord's light-blue eyes opened wider and
wider at each word of Jim's last sentences. A boy,
eighteen, who proposed to adopt a little girl of
eleven, had never before crossed Caleb Bunker's
path.

" Ye don't say so ! Be ye — be ye rich, in yer — yer — own right ? " he stammered, curiosity and surprise centring together on the one-sided view which the average New England mind would naturally take of this phenomenal philanthropy. " I expect ye be, though, and uncommonly free-handed, too, or else ye would n't think o' plaguin' yerself with a child, at your time o' life," and the inquisitive eyes scanned Jim's tall but boyish figure from head to foot.

"You 're a professor, I reckon," he added in a half earnest, half satirical tone.

Jim looked utterly bewildered. He had never heard the phrase, " a professor," except at college, and was about to disclaim the honor in language most inexpediently emphatic, when I interposed.

" No; neither my friend nor I have yet made a profession of religion, Mr. Bunker. We have come to study with Parson Allen this winter, and " — I had a vague intention of closing my sentence with a diplomatic intimation that we hoped to be spiritually as well as intellectually benefited by Parson Allen's teachings ; but Mr. Bunker interrupted me in tones most unflatteringly changed.

" So, ho ! You 're them two young college chaps, be ye ? We 've heerd considerable about ye ; the parson was over a lookin' for ye, last night."

" Yes, Mr. Bunker," interposed Jim with great dignity, which, although it simply amused me, was not without its effect on Mr. Bunker : " we are the young college chaps ; and if we had behaved wisely at college, we should n't be here to-day, as you evidently know. But we are going to study hard with the parson, and go back all right in the spring. And about this little girl, I am entirely in earnest, in wishing to take care of her. Parson Allen will advise me as to the best way of doing it. In the meantime, perhaps your wife will be so kind as to get some clothes for her ; the poor little thing is very ragged. Will this be enough, do you think, to get what she needs at present ? " and Jim quietly put a hundred dollar bill in Mr. Bunker's hands. Its effect was ludicrous. Not very often had Caleb Bunker even handled a hundred dollar bill, and the idea of such a sum being spent at once on the clothing of a child stunned him. He fingered the bill helplessly for a second or two, saying "Wall — wall, reelly — naow — Mr. — I beg yer pardon, sir, — don'no 's I heered yer name yit."

" Ordway," interrupted Jim. " My name is Ordway."

" Wall, Mr. Ordway, reelly — reelly — I 'll speak to Mis' Bunker ; " and the bewildered Caleb disappeared, totally forgetting in his astonishment at Jim's munificence, that the dead man still lay uncared for on the office floor.

" Will," said Jim, " you go in there, and tell those men I 've taken the child. I don't want them coming near her. And if there 's any trouble about burying that brute, I 'll just pay for it. I ex-

pect, by the way the man glared at that bill, they 're
an awfully poor lot up here. No, no, I can 't go
in," he exclaimed, as I tried to persuade him to go
with me. " I don't want to see that infernal face
again. I won't forget it now as long as I live. I
am thankful I did n't kick him out of the coach.
I came near doing it a hundred times. You just
manage it all for me, that 's a dear fellow. I 'm
going back to the child."

The story of the hundred dollar bill had evidently reached the bar-room before I did. As I
entered, the hum of excited conversation was succeeded by a sudden and awkward silence, and I was
greeted with a respectfulness whose secret cause I
very well knew. The dead body had been carried
to an upper room, and the arrangements for the in-
quest were under discussion. There was no dis-
agreement among the witnesses of the death. The
landlord had ordered the hostler and the stable
boy to carry the drunken man to a room. On being lifted, he had roused from his sleep, and with a
frightful volley of oaths had demanded to be let
alone. As they persevered in the attempt to lift
him he had drawn the revolver from his pocket,
aimed it at random, and tried to fire. In the scuf-
fle, it fell from his hand, went off, and the bullet
had passed through his neck, making a ghastly
wound, and killing him almost instantly.

It was a horrible night. Not until near dawn
did silence settle down on the excited house :

neither Jim nor I shut our eyes. Jim talked incessantly. His very heart seemed on fire; all the lonely, pent up, denied brotherhood in his great warm nature had burst forth into full life at the nestling touch of this poor little outcast child. He was so lifted by the intense sentiment to a plane of earnestness and purpose, that he seemed to me like a stranger and grown man, instead of like my two years' chum and a boy some months my junior. I felt a certain awe of him, and of the strange, new scenes, which had so transformed him. Mixed with it all, was a half defined terror lest he might not be quite in his senses. To my thoroughly prosaic nature, there was something so utterly inconceivable in this sudden passion of protecting tenderness towards a beggar child, this instantaneous resolve to adopt her into the closest relation but one in the world, that no theory but that of a sudden insanity could quite explain it. Jim had one of those finely organized natures, from whose magnetic sensitiveness nothing can be concealed. He recognized my thought.

"Will," he said, "I don't wonder you think I'm crazy. But you need n't. I was never cooler-headed in my life; and as for my heart, every bit of this love has been there ever since I was a little shaver. I never tell you fellows half I think. I never have. I know you'd only chaff me, and I dare say you'd be half right, too, for there's no doubt I've got an awful big streak of woman in me.

But a fellow can't help the way he's made ; and I
tell you, Will, I cried myself to sleep many a night,
when I was along about ten or twelve, because I
did n't have a sister like most of the other boys.
And since I have been a man [dear Jim, seventeen
years and six months old] I have had the feeling
just as strong as I had it then ; only I 've had to
keep it under. Of course, I know I 'll have a wife
some day. And that 's another thing, Will, I
never can see how the fellows can talk about that
as they do. I could n't any more talk about my
wife lightly and laughingly now, while I don't
know who she 'll be, than I could do it after I
had her. I can't explain it, but that 's the way I
feel. But it 'll be years and years before I have
a wife, and do you know, Will — I suppose this
is another streak of woman in me — when I think
of a wife, I never think so much of some one who
is going to be all feeble and clinging, dependent
on me, as I do of somebody who will be great
and strong and serene, and will let me take care of
her only because she loves me so much, and not a
bit because she needs to be taken care of. But a
sister is different. I 'd just like to have a sister
that could n't do without me. And, by Jove, if ever
a man had the thing he wanted put right straight
into his hand, I should think I had. Don't you ? "

"Yes, I should think you had, you dear old
muff," I said. "But what in thunder are you
going to do with the child ? You can't carry her
back to college with us."

" I know that; but I can have her at school there, and see her every day; and we can keep her with us here, this winter, and she 'll get to loving me first-rate before spring."

" Well, as for that, the little beggar loves you enough already, — that 's easy to see. It 's a case of love at first sight, on both sides," I said, carelessly. Jim flushed.

" Look here, Will," he said, very soberly, " you must n't speak that way. We 'll quarrel as sure as fate, old boy, if you do it ; you must remember that from this day, Ally is just the same as if she were my own sister, blood-born. And is n't it strange, too, that Alice was my mother's name ? That 's only one more of the strange things about it all. Supposing, for instance, we 'd gone the other road, as we came so near doing, we should n't have got here till day after to-morrow, and she 'd have been in their infernal poor-house by that time, I dare say ; is n't this what you might call Fate with a vengeance ? I don't wonder the old Pagans believed in it as they did. I believe I 'm half Pagan myself."

" Now, Jim," I interrupted, " don't go off into the classic ages. If you are really going to be such a ——"

" Say fool, and be done with it, Will ; I don't mind," he laughed.

" Well ; if you 're really going to be such a fool us to adopt ' Ally,' and really want to keep her

with us at Parson Allen's this winter, the sooner we
drive over and see the old gentleman and break the
news to him, the better. Oh, Jim ! " — and I roared
at the bare thought of how queer a look the thing
had on the face of it — " what will become of us
if the parson has a keen sense of humor ! Two
college boys rusticated for serious misconduct, ar-
riving at the door of his house with a young miss
in their charge. I never thought of this before.
It 's enough to kill one ! "

Jim laughed, too. He could not help it. But
he looked very uneasy.

" It is awkward," he said ; " there 's no doubt
about that ! I 'd rather face the President again
than this old parson, but I 've got a conviction that
this thing is going to be all of a piece right straight
through, and that the parson 'll be on my side."

" The parson's wife is more important, I reckon,"
said I. " It 'll all turn on how she takes it."

" Well, I think she 's all right," Jim replied.
" Old Curtis, my guardian, knows her. He says
she 's an angel ; he knew her before she was married, and something in the dear old man's face,
when he spoke of her, made me wonder if it was n't
for her sake he 'd lived an old bachelor all his life.
She was a Quaker, he said, and they have n't ever
had any children. You know that it was Curtis
who asked the President to send us here, don't
you ? "

I had not known this ; it gave me a great sense

of relief, for, "Old Ben Curtis," as he was always called, was a man whose instincts were of the finest order. A tenderer, purer, gentler, more chivalrous soul never lived. His lonely life had been for forty years a pain and a mystery to all who loved him. Was it possible that two careless college boys were to come upon the secret of it, in this little village in the heart of Maine?

When we went down-stairs, Alice was fast asleep. She began already to look younger and prettier; the dark circles under her eyes were disappearing, and the pitiful look of anxiety had gone from the forehead. Mrs. Bunker stood watching her.

"She's as pooty a little gal as ye often see," she said, turning to Jim, with an evident and assured recognition of his paternal proprietorship. "I'll be bound ye won't never regret a-taken' on her, sir. I suppose ye'll send her right to yer folks?" she added, endeavoring to put the question carelessly, but succeeding poorly in veiling the thought which was uppermost in her mind.

"No, Mrs. Bunker," said Jim, "I shall not send her away if I can induce Parson Allen to keep her for the winter. I want her here very much."

Mrs. Bunker's countenance fell. Plainly she had had hopes that the child might be left in her own hands. But the native loyalty and goodness of her heart triumphed speedily, and she said, in a hearty one, —

"Lor' me! I never once thought of that! But

I reckon it would be jest what Mis' Allen would like. She's dreadful fond o' children. She an' the parson hain't never had any o' their own."

Jim glanced at me triumphantly.

"Yes," the good soul went on ; " I do reely think there's a kind o' Providence in the hull thing from fust to last. I've often heerd Mis' Allen say that she an' the Parson hed thought of adoptin' a little gal, but they never quite see their way to do it. You see, his salary's dreadful small.' 'Tain't much we kin raise in money down here, and there's a sight o' men folks moved out o' town 'n the last few years. So I reckon Mis' Allen's given up all idea on't long ago. Did ye ever see her? She's jest the handsomest old lady ye ever sot eyes on. There ain't a gal in the meetin'us, not one, that's got such cheeks as Mis' Allen, an' she's goin' on sixty. She's a Quaker, for all she's married the parson, an' they do say there's somethin' in the Quaker religion that's wonderful purifyin' to the complexion. I don'no how 't is. But there ain't no such cheeks as Mis' Allen's in our meetin'us, old or young ; I'll say that much, whether it's the religion makes 'em, or not."

Fairly launched on the subject of Mrs. Allen, good Mrs. Bunker would have talked until noon, apparently, if Jim had not interrupted her to say that we must go at once to report our arrival to Parson Allen, and to see what arrangements we ¢ould make for Alice there.

" Remember, Mrs. Bunker," he said, with great earnestness, "if Ally wakes, she is not to leave this room, and I do not wish her to see any one except yourself; she must not be told that her father is dead by any one but me. I hope very much that she will sleep till we return. I think she will, for she is very much exhausted." Jim's magnetism of nature always stood him instead of authority, and was far more sure of obtaining his ends than any possible authority could be. He simply mesmerized people's wills so that they desired and chose to do the things he wished done. It was perfectly plain already that so far as Ally was concerned, Mrs. Bunker and her whole household were at Jim's command.

As we drew near the parsonage, our hearts sank. Our errand grew more and more formidable in our eyes. Jim's face took on a look more serious than I had ever seen it wear, and he said little. I felt impatient and irritable.

"Oh, bother the thing!" I exclaimed, as I opened the gate; "I don't see how we 're going to have the face to ask them to take the child. If it were only a boy, it would be different."

Jim turned a slow look of unutterable surprise on me.

"Why, I don't see what difference that would make. I guess girls are not so much trouble. And I should n't have taken her if she 'd been a boy. It was a sister I wanted. I 've got you for brother, you know."

I felt guilty at heart.

"You dear old boy," I exclaimed, "go ahead ; I won't go back on you."

We walked slowly up to the door, between two old - fashioned, narrow flower-beds. They were brown and rusty now, but in spring must have been gay, for there were great mats of the moss pink, thickets of phlox, and bushes of flowering almond. Now, the only blossoms left were the old-fashioned " Ladies' Delights," which were still plentiful, and seemed to have been allowed to run at will from one end of the beds to the other. The house was a large two-story house, square, white, with nine windows on the front ; on one side of the door stood a scrawny lilac-tree ; on the other, a high bush of southern-wood. As Jim lifted the big black knocker, he said, under his breath : "Well, there 's room enough, anyhow. Look at the windows ! I wonder what the parson lives in such a big house for, if it is n't on purpose to take us all in."

"Perhaps he don't have the whole of it," said I.

At that instant, before the knocker fell, the door was opened, and there stood " Mis' Allen." I had broken a bit of the southern-wood, and was crumpling the sweet-bitter leaves in my fingers as the door opened. To this day I can never smell southern-wood without recalling the picture of Mistress Dorothy Allen as she stood in that door-way.

"No such cheeks," indeed ! Well might **Mrs.**

11

Bunker have said it. They were of such pink as lines the innermost curves of the conch shell; and the rest of the face was white and soft. Her eyes were as bright-brown as little Alice's, but were serene and grave. Very thin white hair was put smoothly back under a transparent lace cap, which was tied under the chin by a narrow white ribbon. Her dress was of a pale gray, and fell straightly to her feet. Folds of the finest plain white lace were crossed on her bosom, and fastened by two tiny gold-headed pins, joined together by an inch or two of fine thread-like gold chain — the only thing bordering upon ornament which she ever wore.

"How does thee do? And thee?" she said, holding out motherly hands first to Jim, and then to me. "Come in. We were just about to have family prayers, and waited, because I had seen you at the gate. It is a good hour to have come home;" and she smiled upon us so warmly that we could not remember to speak, but followed her into the house, bewildered by our welcome.

Parson Allen sat at a window; the bright autumn sun streamed in across the open Bible which lay on his knees. Nearly in the centre of the room stood a tall oleander-tree, in full bloom. The sunlight poured through and through its pink blossoms, and seemed to fill the room with a rosy glow.

"I am glad to see you, my sons," said Parson Allen. "I take it as a sign from the Lord, that you should have reached my house just at this

hour; we always begin our days with prayer."
There was not a trace of anything sanctimonious
or pharisaical in his manner. It was as simple and
hearty and loving as if he were speaking of his
affection for an earthly friend, and his habit of
morning greeting to him. As he waved his hand
to us to be seated, and said, "After prayers, we
will tell you how glad we are to see you, wife and
I," by some sudden, undefined association, the
words, "Christ, our elder brother," floated into my
mind. I glanced at Jim. His eyes were misty.
The religious element was much more fully developed in his nature than in mine, and he was much
more profoundly impressed than I, by the spiritual
atmosphere of the scene. He afterwards said to
me, that he could think of nothing while the parson was speaking, except that this must be the
way angels welcomed new-comers into Heaven, if
they happened to arrive while the singing was going on. We sat down together in one of the deep
window-seats; more than once, at some Bible verse
read in a peculiarly impressive manner, Jim's hand
stole over to mine, and his eyes dropped to the
floor. But what was our astonishment when, after
the Psalm, came these words from the "Enchirid-
ion" of Epictetus : —

"There are things which are within our power,
and there are things which are beyond our power.
Within our power are opinion, aim, desire, aversion,
and, in one word, whatever affairs are our own.

Beyond our power are body, property, reputation, office, and, in one word, whatever are not properly our own affairs.

" Now the things within our power are by nature free, unrestricted, unhindered ; but those beyond our power are weak, dependent, restricted, alien. Remember, then, that if you attribute freedom to things by nature dependent, and take what belongs to others for your own, you will be hindered, you will lament, you will be disturbed, you will find fault both with gods and men. But if you take for your own only that which is your own, and view what belongs to others just as it really is, then no one will ever compel you, no one will restrict you ; you will find fault with no one, you will accuse no one, you will do nothing against your will ; no one will hurt you, you will not have an enemy, nor will you suffer any harm."

Jim and I had been wild boys. We had come down to this far away village in disgrace, with something of bitterness and resentment entering into all our resolutions of good behavior. But in our first hours in the parsonage, the bitterness, the doubt, the resentment, melted away, and there was sown in our souls a seed of reverence, of belief, of purpose, whose whole harvest has never been gar-nered, neither indeed can be, since in Eternity is neither seed-time nor harvest.

In less than half an hour after prayers were ended, Jim and I had told to our newly found friends the whole story of little Alice, and of our desire to bring her to live with us at the parsonage for the winter. Mrs. Allen's eyes glistened at the thought.

"Husband," she said, slowly, "I feel myself much drawn toward this little girl. Does thee not think it is a clear call that this young man's heart is so set upon bringing her to live under our roof?"

"Dorothy, thee knows that it shall be as thee likes," said Parson Allen, his eyes resting as lovers' eyes rest, on the smooth cheeks, whose beautiful pink was deeping a little in her eager interest; "but we must consider whether James's guardian will think we have done wisely in permitting him to undertake the charge of a child. My mind misgives me that most people would not approve of his taking this burden upon him."

"Benjamin Curtis is not of the world's people at heart," said Mistress Dorothy, gently. "He cannot have changed in that, I am persuaded, though it is thirty-five years since I saw him. If, as James says, he has these thousands of dollars each year to spend, Benjamin Curtis will joy to see him spending it on another rather than himself."

"That he will," burst in Jim. "He's the most generous old boy in the world. Why, he goes looking like a beggar himself half the time, he gives away so much of his own money; and he's never so pleased with me as when I go and tell him that I've just given away my whole quarter's allowance, and am dead broke."

Mistress Allen's eyes were fixed dreamily on the oleander-tree, but her mouth was tremulous with intent interest.

" Did thee say that thy guardian was frequently impoverished himself, by reason of his gifts to the poor ? " she asked. " That is like the boy I knew forty years ago."

"Why, no, I can't exactly say he's impoverished, because he's got heaps of money, you know," replied Jim ; " but he's so full of other people's troubles and needs that he don't remember his own, and he goes pretty seedy half the time, bless his old heart ! He's the biggest brick of a guardian a fellow ever had. I know just as well, Mrs. Allen, that he'll be only too glad to have me adopt Ally for my sister, and take care of her all the rest of my life, as if I'd asked him ; and it will only take four days to hear from him ; I sent a letter this morning. You'll very soon see that it is all right."

" In the mean time, the little girl would be better off with us than in that wretched place where she is now," said Mrs. Allen. " Mrs. Bunker is a kindly woman, but there are sights and sounds there which the child should know nothing of. Thee had better bring her over this afternoon, that is," she added, turning to me, " if thy friend will share thy room for a few days, and give up to the child the one we had prepared for him. We have not had need for many rooms, and have had no money to spend on anything but needs ; so most of our chambers are still unfurnished ; " and a shade of what would have been mortification thirty-five years before, but was now only sweet resignation to a cross, passed over the beautiful old face.

The dreaded errand was over ; the difficulties had all vanished, as Jim's prophetic sense had assured him they would ; and we parted from Parson Allen and his wife, as we might have parted from our father and mother, eager to come back to our home at the earliest possible moment.

It was a mile from the parsonage to the hotel ; Jim drove furiously, and hardly spoke during the whole distance.

" I 'll never forgive myself for staying so long, if Ally 's waked up and cried," he said. " We might have done it all in one half the time. Will, did you ever, in all your life, see such a heavenly old face ? It 's enough to make a saint of a fellow just to look at her ! I sha' n't ever call her ' Mrs. Allen ! ' I 've got to call her ' mother,' or ' aunt,' or something. Guardy was right, she 's an angel," he exclaimed, as he jumped out of the buggy, and throwing the reins to me, bounded into the house.

Ally was still asleep ; Mrs. Bunker said she had roused once, and asked for " the kind gentleman," and on being told that he had left word that she must not stir from bed; had asked pitifully : " Does he keep little girls in bed all day, every day ? " and had then fallen asleep again almost immediately.

"I don't wonder, sir, that Mr. Ordway's so taken with her," said Mrs. Bunker to me, as we stood together in the front door. "She's jest the winnin'est child I ever laid eyes on; she's jest like a lamb, yit there ain't nothin' stoopid about her. But, ain't it strange, she never so much's asked for her pa? I was all over a tremble for fear she would. I reckon it's a mercy the Lord's taken her out o' his hands."

I did not see Jim or Ally for some hours. I went several times to the door, but I heard Jim's voice talking in a low and earnest tone, and I knew he was telling the child of her father's death and of his intention of adopting her as his sister, and it was better that they should be alone. At last Jim called me in. He was sitting at the head of the bed, and Ally's head was on his shoulder. I never forgot the picture. Ally had been crying bitterly, but her face had a look of perfect peace on it. Jim had been crying also, but his eyes shone with joy and eager purpose.

"Ally," he said, as I entered, "this is Will. He is just the same as my brother; so he is just the same as your brother, you know."

"Yes, sir," said Ally, looking at me with a grave and searching expression. "Shall I kiss you?"

"Yes, indeed, you dear little thing," I exclaimed; and as I stooped over, she put one tiny thin arm around my neck, — the other was around Jim's, — drew my head down to her face, and kissed me once, twice, three times, with the sweetest kisses lips ever gave. I thought so then ; I think so still. From that moment my fealty to Alice was as strong as Jim's. Wondrous little maid-child! Alone, unknown, beggared, outcast, she had won to her service and forever two strong and faithful hearts with all the loyalty of manhood springing in them.

Two days later, Jim and Alice and I were all so peacefully settled down in our new home that it seemed as if we had been living there for weeks. Never did household so easily, so swiftly adjust itself to new bonds, new conditions. The secret laws of human relations are wonderfully like those of chemistry. An instant of time is enough for blending, where the affinity is true ; an eternity is not enough, if the affinity do not exist. Oh, the years and strength, and vital force which we waste in the vain endeavor to make antagonistic currents flow smoothly together! When Mrs. Allen first looked into Ally's face, tears sprang to her eyes, and she exclaimed involuntarily: "Dear child, dear child ; does thee think thee could call me mother?" Ally flung both her arms round the old lady's neck, and said, in a tone so earnest that it made her simple answer more emphatic than volumes of asseveration could have been : —

"Yes, ma'am ; I'd like to very much, if you will be my brother Jim's mother, too."

"Oh, Mrs. Allen, please let me!" said Jim, in a tone as simple and earnest as Ally's.

"And me, too ! I can't be the only orphan in the house," exclaimed I.

The sweet old face flushed, and she turned smilingly to her husband, saying : —

"A quiver full — is it not, husband ?"

"He setteth the solitary in families," replied Parson Allen, solemnly and tenderly. "God bless you all, my children." And he drew Ally to his arms very fondly.

It was thought best that Ally should know nothing of the circumstances of her father's death, nor of his funeral. It was enough for her trusting little soul to be told that he had died. There was no bond of love between them. He had represented to her only terror and suffering, since her babyhood. The strongest proof of this was the fact that she never mentioned his name ; of her mother she had no recollection ; her life had been almost incredibly sad ; it was hard to conceive how a child could have lived to be eleven years old, and have had so few associations stamped on her mind, either with places or people. Her memories seemed to be chiefly of hunger and loneliness, and terror of her father ; of room after room in which she had been left alone, day after day, and sometimes night after night, for weeks and months ; and of long journeys which were one shade less dreadful than the solitary confinement had been, because, as she said quietly : "Everybody spoke to me, and I liked that."

It was a marvel how, in this hard life, had grown
the grace and instincts which made Ally so lovable.
She had had no books, no toys ; she had known no
other child ; she had spent whole years of days, simply watching the sun and the sky, as a little savage
might in the forest ; but in place of the savage's
sense of freedom, she had had the constant pain of
constraint and fear.   There was a certain fine fiber
in her nature, which had saved her from being benumbed and dulled by these ; had transmuted the
suffering into a patience all the more beautiful that
it was so unconscious.   It was certain that this fine
organization must have come from her mother.   If
only we could have known, — if only we could
have found a clew to her history !   But Ally had no
recollections of her ; and the few papers found in
her father's possession threw no light on his past or
his plans for the future.   What could have brought
him to this remote spot, no one could divine ; and
where their luggage had been left, Ally did not
know.

"It's just as if she had been dropped out of the
skies to me," said Jim, one day, as we were talking
it all over ; "and that is just where I used to look
up, and think I saw little girl angels flying, when I
was a little fellow, and used to cry for a sister.   I
remember once, when I was only eight years old,
I spoke right out loud, in church, at prayer-time
and asked my mother, 'Oh, mamma, is n't there the
'east chance of my ever having a little sister ? '   And

afterward, when she talked with me about it, she
cried so, that I never said another word about a
sister to her till she died.   But I remember I said
to her then : ' I know I 'll have a sister some day !
I know I will !   You see if I don't !   How can you
be so sure God never will give me one ? '   And now,
you see, I have got one."

Yes !   It was indeed as if Ally had been dropped
out of the skies into Jim's hands.   We were her
only friends in the country, — so far as we knew, in
the world, — and all that she could tell us of herself
was that she was eleven years old, and that her
name was Alice Fisher.

She was a marvelous child.   Mrs. Bunker's
homely words told the exact truth of her ; they
came to my mind constantly in the course of our
first days at the parsonage.   " She 's jest like a
lamb, and yit there ain't nothin' stoopid about her."
She obeyed, with an instant and pathetic docility,
the slightest suggestion from any one of us ; she
rarely made a movement of her own accord.
Wherever we placed her, whatever we gave her to
do, there she stayed ; with that thing she continued
to occupy herself until some one proposed a change.

This was the result of the long patience she had
learned in her sad years of solitude and confinement.   But her eager brown eyes watched with in-
tensest interest everything that happened within
her sight, and no word that was spoken escaped her
attention.   At family prayers, while the Bible was

being read, her face was a study. She had known
but dimly of God and of Christ, and she had never
in her life said a prayer until she had knelt by her
new mother's side on the first evening of our arrival.

The next morning, immediately after prayers, we
were all startled by this question from her : —

"Why don't you go into the room where God is ?
Is it that one ? " pointing to the closed door on the
opposite side of the hall.

The little, ignorant child had felt to her heart's
core the same atmosphere which had so impressed
us when we first heard Parson Allen pray. She felt,
as we knew, that he was speaking to some one very
near. Every fiber of motherhood in Mrs. Allen's
heart twined around this sensitive, loving, helpless
little creature.

" She seems to me like a babe," she said ; " like
a babe found in the wilderness. I hope we may be
guided to nurture her aright, for I believe she is a
child of very rare gifts. She has not known the
name of Christ, but she has lived his life, and I
have a conviction that she is one of his chosen
ones."

No danger but that Ally would be nurtured aright
in the house of which Dorothy Allen's sweet soul
was the central warmth, and the man she loved
was the light and strength. I have seen many
households, households of wealth and culture,
households of simple and upright living, but I have

never seen one which so filled my ideal of a home as this plain and poor little parsonage. The secret of it all lay in the fact that its life was idealized; idealized, first, by Dorothy Allen's lovingness and her fine sense of beauty and grace; secondly, by her husband's fine sense of moral truth, and his devotion to thought and study. Parson Allen was a rare scholar. Only his great modesty prevented his being known as one of the finest Greek scholars in the country; but all his learning did not in the least detract from the "simplicity of Christ," with which he was filled. I shall never, in any world, hear a grander outburst of praise from lips of saint or angel than these words seemed to me, pronounced as he often used to pronounce them at the end of his morning prayer: "For the sake of our Lord Jesus Christ, the blessed and only Potentate, the King of kings, and Lord of lords; who only hath immortality, dwelling in the light which no man can approach unto; whom no man hath seen nor can see; to whom be honor and power everlasting. Amen."

His enthusiasm for study, his recognition and love of high thoughts, were no less hearty than his enthusiasm for Christ and his love of souls. There were no limitations to his religion. Life, from Adam until now, was to him all one great, beautiful revelation of God. He was a devoted disciple of Christ; he believed with all his heart in the Christian dispensation; but he walked also with Socrates and Plato, and was broad enough to feel that he did Christ's words no dishonor when he read side by side with them at our morning prayers, the bravest and most religious words of men who, dying before Christ was born, yet saw and preached and lived the truths for whose sake Christ died. Ah, never did two boys sit at the feet of a wiser, stronger, sweeter teacher than Parson Allen. Our winter with him was worth more to us than all our after years in college. The lessons which we recited to him from text-books were the smallest part of the education he gave us. The Plato that I read to him I have forgotten. The Plato that he read to us is part of my life.

No less rare than his power of compelling us unconsciously to assimilate intellectual truths was his wife's power of giving us spiritual tests, and arousing in us a need of the highest living. We did not know, as the noiseless and gentle days slipped by, how much beauty they bore. We did not know in what their charm lay ; but when we went into the presence of those who lived on a lower plane, for smaller ends, and with a less love of beauty, less depth of insight and feeling, we recognized the change in the atmosphere, as one does who comes suddenly from pure, outside air, into the confined and impure air of a house. I might write pages in the endeavor to explain this fact ; to analyze the fine flavor which Dorothy Allen knew how to give, **or,** rather, could not help giving, to life ; but my

words would be vain. It was not that she was
always gentle, low-voiced, dainty, and full of repose ;
it was not that she knew how to produce iu her
simple household, and with small means, the effect
of almost luxury of living, in all matters of food
and service, and personal comfort ; it was not that
she had, spite of her Quaker training, a passion for
color ; and from December round to December,
never permitted her home to be one day without
the brightness of blossoming flowers ; it was not
that her warm, active nature was thoroughly alive
to all the events, all the interests of the day, and
that she had ever some new thing to speak of with
eager interest, and found the days far too short for
inquiring into all the matters which she desired to
search out. It was no one of these ; it was not all
of these. I have seen women of whom all these
things were true, but they did not create a home as
did this woman. Neither was it the great lovingness of her nature, marvelous as that was : God
makes many women who are all love and lovingness. It was — so far as language can state it — it
was because in all these traits, into every one of
the acts springing from them, there entered a deep
significance, a symbolic meaning, a spiritual vitality,
born of her intensity of temperament and purity
of nature. The smallest thing had its soul, as well
as its body ; and the soul radiated through and
through the body until transfiguration became an
ever-present reality. For thirty-three years she had

every morning laid by her husband's plate, before
breakfast, a bunch of flowers — or at least, a green
leaf, if no flowers were to be found. When Jim first
saw her do this, he came to me, and said, "Will,
that's the way the Lord meant a woman and a
man should love each other. That geranium-flower
she put down by his plate this morning was n't simply a geranium-flower — either to her or to him.
Oh, if I were a poet, I 'd just write what I saw in
her eyes. They said, 'All the summers of the
world, all the sun, all the light, all the color, have
gone to make up these blossoms ; since the beginning of time, the moment has been journeying on
at which it should bloom, in the spot where my
hand could gather it for thee ; my vow is no less
than its ! Love it for to-day, my love ! reverence it,
and to-morrow another blossom will bloom either
here or in eternity, also for thee ! ' "

"Oh, Jim," I said, "You ought to have been
a woman. I don't believe the dear old mother
thought any such thing. She knows that Dominie
loves flowers ; that 's all ! "

"All !" exclaimed Jim, "I tell you the flower 's
nothing ! It might be a pebble ; it might be a
crown of diamonds and pearls. It 's the soul of
love, and the symbol of life, when she lays it down
there of a morning. It 's just so when she hands
him a newspaper, for that matter. I 've seen him
look up at her as if she had just that minute given
him herself for the first time, dear old lovers, that

12

they are. And if you watch, you 'll see that he has
that flower about him all day somewhere; if it is n't
in his fingers, it 's lying on his desk, or in his but-
ton-hole. I 've seen him read a whole forenoon
with it in his hand. I wonder if anything like it
will ever happen to you or me, in this world, Will ?"

"May be to you, Jim ; not to me. I 'm too prosaic. I should n't understand it. I don't half
know what you mean now, " replied I. But, in
spite of my words, I did know dimly, and wondered, as Jim had wondered, if it were ever to be
mine.

"I don't know, old fellow," said Jim. " I 've a
notion that the Dominie was something such a fellow as you are ; he is n't a bit like her, anyhow.
That 's the reason he worships her so. Now, I am
like her. I know just how she feels about fifty
things a day, when you are only listening to what
she says, and trying to make it out that way, just as
you do with me, you dear, old, honest, sturdy,
strong, slow fellow, worth a thousand of me, any
day. But if I were a woman, and you loved me,
you 'd understand me just as the Dominie under-
stands mother."

In this warmth of love and care, little Alice
bloomed out like the geraniums in the deep window-seats. At the end of two weeks no one would
have known the child, except by the hazel-brown
eyes. Suffering and feebleness had not disguised
or dimmed the beauty of those ; neither could joy

and health add to it. They were simply and forever perfectly beautiful. One looked from them to
the shining, yellow curls, and then back from the
yellow curls to the brown eyes, in almost incredulity
of the wonderful combination. Each day we feared
to see the golden hue change on the sunny head ;
but it never changed, never !

It soon became our habit to take Ally with us on
all our rambles. She was as nimble and as tireless
as a squirrel, and so full of joy in all things she
saw that she was a perpetual delight to us. She
ran between us, holding a hand of each ; she ran
before us, her golden curls reaching far back on
the wind ; she lagged behind, hiding mischievously
behind a tree or rock, and laughing loud like an
infant to hear us call her. Sometimes we clasped
our hands together and carried her proudly aloft
higher than our heads, and holding on clingingly to
each neck. When we put her down, she always
kissed Jim, saying : "Thank you, brother Jim,"
and then, turning to me : "Thank you, too, Mr.
Will ; would you like to have me kiss you ? "

One day I said to her, as we were sitting under a
tree : "Ally, you always kiss Jim without asking
him. How do you know he likes it ? Why don't
you kiss me without asking me ? "

"Why, he is my brother," she said instantly ;
"he wants me to kiss him always," and she sprang
up with a wonderfully agile spring which he had
taught her, and lit on his shoulder, where she sat

perched like a bird, kissing him over and over.
Then she said, more gravely : " Brother Jim did n't
say you were my brother. He said you were just
the same as my brother.   There is n't any same as
brother about kisses."

Oh, marvelous maid-child of eleven ! Jim
laughed, but I had a strange sense of pain in the
child's words, and I waited sorely for days and days,
for her to kiss me, spontaneously and freely as she
kissed Jim.

The Indian summer lingered late and long. The
maples turned scarlet and gold, the ash-trees to
purple and yellow, till the forests outvied the sun-
rise and sunset. Little Alice had never seen this
sight. It gave her delight so great that it bordered
on pain. Day after day she filled the house with
the bright boughs. Not a corner, hardly a chair,
but had the glittering leaves lying in it; it was as
if they floated down among us through the roof ;
and Ally was never seen without them in her hand,
or placed fantastically around her belt or in her
hair. It grieved her very heart that they must
die.

"Oh, why do they not stay on all the winter,
brother Jim ? " she said. " Why can they not be
this color all summer ?   I suppose God likes green
best ? Is there any other world where He lets the
trees be red and yellow all the time ? "

One afternoon, we were returning very late from
a ramble in the woods, now nearly leafless. Ally

had made a long wreath of crimson oak-leaves, and we had thrown it round and round her shoulders and neck, till it looked like a mantle of red, with long ends trailing down behind. Her golden curls fluttered like sunbeams across it, and as she ran lightly before us, and, lifting up one end of the crimson wreath in her hand, looked archly through it over her shoulder, laughing and crying out, " Now, I am an oak-tree running away from you," Jim drew a long, sighing breath and whispered to me : " Oh, Will, does she look like a mortal child ? I think she is an angel and will fly away presently."

At that instant she stumbled over a projecting root of a tree and fell heavily to the ground without a cry. She was several rods in advance of us ; before we reached her she had fainted.

We were almost paralyzed with terror ; we were two miles from home, and on the top of a rough and rocky ledge, the face of which was so thickly grown with scrub oaks that we had found great difficulty in forcing our way through. " Oh, Will, how are we to get her home ? " gasped Jim, as he lifted her up. The poor little white face, with its yellow curls, fell limp and lifeless on his shoulder, and the torn oak wreaths tangled themselves around his arms. She looked as if she were dead ; but in a few moments she opened her eyes, and said : " I am not hurt brother Jim, not a bit. Where is the pretty green stone ? "

"Oh, Ally dear, are you sure you 're not hurt?" exclaimed Jim; "never mind about the stone; was it that made you fall?"

"But I must mind about the stone," said Ally. "You have n't got any such stone among all yours; it was as pretty almost as the leaves; it 's right down here, under the old root that tripped me up. I wanted to get it for you, brother Jim," — and she tried to slip away from his arms to look for it.

"Stay still, Ally, stay still. I 'll find it," said I. "What sort of stone was it?"

"Oh, beautiful," said Ally; "it shone, and it was shaped like my prisms! Oh, do find it, Mr. Will."

I searched in vain; the old tree had been partially uprooted, and its scrawny underground branches exposed to light, had twirled themselves into strange shapes. Stones and earth had piled up around them, and a big mullein was growing on the very top of the root; coarse white pebbles and sharp bits of granite were lying all about, but no such stone as Ally described could I see.

"Dear little Ally, you must have fancied it; as you fell, things looked different to you; there is n't any such stone here."

Ally rarely contradicted, or urged any point; but her child's heart was too firmly set on the pretty stone to abandon it without a further effort.

"But, Mr. Will, I saw it before I fell. It was that tripped me up. I mean, I went to stoop over and pick it up, and I caught my foot." This was

logic irresistible. I searched again, but with no
better result. All this time, Jim had been anxiously
studying Ally's face, and paying little attention to
the search for the stone.

"Ally," said he suddenly, "where does it hurt
you? Something hurts you, I know by your face."

"My foot, just a little bit, brother Jim, but not if
I don't move it," replied Alice.

"This one?" said Jim, touching it very gently.

Ally moaned in spite of herself.

"Yes, that one, brother Jim ; please don't touch
it. It will be well pretty soon."

Ally had sprained her ankle. That was evident.
The slightest movement or the slightest touch was
more than she could bear. It was very near sunset, and fast growing cold. To carry the child
down that rocky ledge, and through the scrub oak,
without giving her greater torture than she could
bear, seemed impossible. But it must be done.

Jim rose up very slowly, with her in his arms,
saying, "Now try, dear little Ally, to bear the
pain."

"Yes, brother Jim, I will ; it " — but the sentence ended in a groan. Ally was very much hurt.
At last, I arranged a sling from Jim's right shoulder
in which both her legs could rest, and in this position she bore the motion better. As we moved
slowly away from the tree, the gentle brown eyes
looked back wistfully; in spite of the pain she
could not forget the stone. Suddenly she cried out
joyfully : —

"Oh, there it is, Mr. Will. Mr. Will, there is the stone!" and she pointed to a crevice in the tree-roots, higher up than I had looked.

There it was; and a most beautiful stone indeed; Neither Jim nor I had ever seen one like it. It was a crystal nearly two inches long, of a brilliant green color, shading through paler and paler tints to a clear white, and then from white to a deep rose red. For a second we almost forgot Ally in our wonder at the gem. There was nothing like it in the cabinet of our college; we had never read of any such stone.

"Oh, let me carry it, Mr. Will," pleaded Ally. "I won't drop it, and it will help me bear my foot better;" and the sensitive child fixed her eyes with passionate delight on the crystal.

Presently she said, feebly, "Take the stone, Mr. Will. I can't hold it. It pricks."

As I took it from her, a sharp shock of pain ran up my arm. What was this weird bit of crystallized red and green on which we had stumbled? Had we, unawares, linked ourselves to unseen dangers, hidden spells? I was ashamed of the vague sense of terror with which I walked on through the twilight recalling the whole scene: the little flying maiden, with her fantastic red wreaths and golden curls, the strange stone, the mystic bond between her and it, the sharp and inexplicable pain which had shot through my frame on taking it from her hand.

Ally's sprain proved a serious hurt ; it was almost a fracture. In two hours after we reached
home, the slender ankle was firmly bound with
splinters, and the patient little face looking up
from pillows on which the Doctor had said she
must probably lie for some weeks. As he was leav-
the room she said : —

"Oh, please, Mr. Will, show my pretty stone to
the Doctor."

Dr. Miller reached out his hand eagerly for the
crystal as soon as he saw its shape and color.

"Why, bless my soul, what's that," he exclaimed.
"You found that up on Black Ledge ? Somebody
must have dropped it. It's an emerald. No, it
is n't, either. Look at this red in it."

The Doctor was thoroughly excited. He turned
the stone over and over, held it up to the lamp-
light, all the while muttering to himself, "Most extraordinary ! Never saw or heard of such a stone
as this before;" "looks like magic ;" "and, by
Jove, I believe it is," he said, dropping the stone
suddenly on the floor, and rubbing his fingers
violently. "It's given me an electric shock."

"It made my hand prick," said Ally. "I could
n't hold it either."

The Doctor and I stooped at once to pick it
up, and our hands touched it simultaneously. Instantly the same sharp thrill of heat flamed up my
arm as before. I drew back, and again I glanced
uneasily at Ally, and felt that there was something

supernatural in the bond between her and the stone. The Doctor sprang to his feet, thrust both his hands in his pockets, and stood looking down at the crystal. Then he put the lamp on the floor. The carpet was of a pale gray. The gem shone out vividly upon it, and green and rose-colored rays gleamed and flickered through it as we moved the lamp from side to side. Very quietly Mrs. Allen bent down, and, after looking at it earnestly for a second or two, lifted it and laid it on the silver snuffer tray on the stand. On the polished silver it looked still more beautiful. Ally clapped her hands with delight.

"It is evidently some jewel which has been lost," said Mrs. Allen. "We ought to seek for the owner. Does thee not think it may be of great value?" she asked, turned to Dr. Miller.

"I don't know anything about it, Mrs. Allen," replied the Doctor. "I am inclined to think there's some kind of witchcraft about the thing, anyhow."

"But thee does not believe in any kind of witchcraft about anything," said Mrs. Allen, with a placid twinkle in her eyes. "Thee knows that very well. Can thee not judge if it is a carven gem, or if it is in a state of nature? I think I have read of various stones having a certain electrical power."

"Oh, it is not cut," said the Doctor. "It's a natural crystal. It's the color that poses me. I have never read of such a stone."

"Please let me take it a minute," said Ally.

I laid it in her hand. She stroked it softly with the other hand, then raised it to her cheek.

"It gets brighter every minute Ally holds it," exclaimed Jim.

Indeed it did. As we watched the motions of it in the child's hands, it seemed almost as if a distinct light came from it, and played upon her features. Suddenly she dropped it, with a little cry.

"It pricked again, brother Jim. Is it alive? Does it hate to have us handle it?"

We gathered around the bed. There lay the gem, silent, shining, rosy red and emerald green, on the white sheet, between Ally's two little outstretched hands, which she held to right and left of it, as if afraid it might escape her. Her cheeks were scarlet and her eyes dilated with excitement. She watched it as if expecting it to move. I think it would have astonished none of us if it had. We watched it for some time in silence. Then Mrs. Allen laid it again on the silver tray, and placed the tray on a high shelf, saying, quietly, "I do not feel any of these singular sensations myself in touching the stone. It is a most beautiful jewel. We must seek for the owner to-morrow, and now this child must go to sleep."

Late into the night we sat around the fire talking about the magic stone and making the wildest conjectures about its nature, its history. Dr. Miller was as excited as Jim and I, and the Dominie seemed carried out of himself by the sight of it. "It brings more to my mind the thought of the crystal gates of the heavenly city," he said, "than anything I have ever seen. Who knows but it may be one of the gems mentioned in Revelations whose names are not now well known.

Dr. Miller smiled, half reverently, half pityingly.

The village called Dr. Miller an atheist, because of the blunt speech in which he set his contempt for creeds which they held sacred. But so much the more, by all the scorn which he felt for the pict- ure of God as framed in the phrases of men, did he love the picture of God as framed in a rock, or a mountain, or a daisy.

"I've a notion, parson, that God makes jewels for more practical purposes than for gates to his heaven," he said. "If we've got a mine up on Black Ledge of such gems as this, it's a fortune for some of us. I own a big piece of the ledge to the south myself, and I'm going up the first thing in the morning with these boys, to see if there are any more stones like this one."

Dominie smiled, also half reverently, half pity- ingly. The two men loved each other.

At dawn Jim and I sprang up. Jim went to the window. In a tone of utter despair he ejacu- lated : —

"Will ! "

The ground was white with snow — deep, solid, level snow. It must have snowed furiously all night. Winter had come in utter earnest. Side by side we stood and looked out on the scene. The air was thick with snow-flakes. We could not see ten rods from the house.

"Plague take this climate," said I. "When it once comes down this way there's no let up to it till spring; I know all about it. I spent a winter in Vermont once, and from the first of December till the middle of March we never saw an inch of bare ground. I just hate it. Now, we can't look after those stones for three months."

"I don't believe there are any more of them, Will," said Jim, speaking slowly and in an earnest tone. "I believe there was just that one left there for Ally, by angels, for all I know. Did you see how that light flickered on her face when she stroked her cheek with the stone? And if there were any such stones would n't Dr. Miller know? Should n't we have seen some in the cabinet?"

"Oh, pshaw! you dear old Jim," I said. "I agree with Dr. Miller that God don't make stones on earth for gates to heaven, nor for angels to give to earthly children — not even to Ally!" I added, with a sudden conscience-stricken memory of the picture of her the night before, with the tangled crimson oak wreaths and the yellow curls and the flying feet, and how I myself had shuddered in the twilight to recall the thrill of hot pain which shot through my nerves when she first handed me the stone.

"I dare say we'll all get some money out of that old ledge yet. New minerals are all the time being discovered."

"Money!" said Jim, contemptuously. "I believe if a feather should drop off an angel's wing you'd pick it up and wonder what it would sell for."

"Yes, I would," said I, very composedly; "not wearing angels' wings myself, and having no kind of use for that kind of feather! I'd sell it as a curiosity and buy a pair of cassimere trousers; and so would you, old fellow, if you hadn't any more money than I have."

"Oh, forgive me, Will, dear Will, I didn't mean to be rough on you!" exclaimed Jim, with his whole face grieved at his own thoughtlessness. "But you know I do hate money-making, and money-talking, and money-worshiping. If I hadn't had money to begin with, I'd never have made a cent more than just enough to get bread with."

"I don't believe you'd have made that, old boy," laughed I. "You would have sat on the sunny side of the almshouse, perfectly rapt in content, watching angels in the clouds, and treasuring up their feathers if they happened to drop any! And then you couldn't have adopted Ally."

"No," said Jim, thoughtfully. "After she came, I think I'd have carried the angels' feathers to market, and made as sharp a bargain for them as you yourself, Will."

I was right. It was the winter which had set in. All that day, and all the next day, it snowed without stopping. The village seemed slowly, steadily sinking in a silvery morass ; bush after bush, stone-wall after stone-wall, fence after fence, landmark after landmark, disappeared, until the vas ttracts of open country lay as unbroken as an Arctic Ocean, and the very chimney-tops of the town looked like the heads of hopelessly overwhelmed travelers. On the morning of the second day, Dr. Miller came in, trampling, puffing, and shaking off snow from shoulders, pockets, beard, everywhere ; he shed the powdery avalanches as a pine-tree sheds them when it is rocked by a sudden wind.

"Ha, boys," he exclaimed; "no hunting for precious stones on Black Ledge this year! We're snowed up for three months at least. How'll you youngsters like that? And how's the ankle, Pussy," he said, in a softer tone, turning to Ally with such a smile as seldom came on his rugged face. A little bed had been brought into the sitting-room and set across the south window. In this Ally lay, under a marvelous coverlet which the parishioners had presented to Mrs. Allen at the last Donation Party. It was called the "Rising Sun" pattern, the villagers never having heard of the word Aurora. But there was something pathetic in the embryonic conception which these hard-working New England women had stitched into their bed-quilt of flaming Turkey red and white. A scarlet sun in

the centre shot myriad spokes of red to the outer
edge ; and minor suns with smaller spokes were
set at regular intervals around it.   When Ally first
saw this, she was so captivated by its splendors,
that Mrs. Allen's motherly heart could not resist
giving it to her ; so Ally had, as she said, "twenty-
five suns to keep her warm at night."   The child's
passion for color was intense.   It was the forerun-
ner of the exquisite artistic sense and worship of
beauty in all things which marked her later devel-
opment.   She lay now, idly following with her tiny
forefinger, scarlet ray after scarlet ray on the coverlet.   The south window held two high abutilon-
trees in full flower.   Their striped orange bells and
broad green leaves nodded above her like a fairy
canopy; and at the foot of the bed stood the
glossy, dark-leaved oleander-tree, with a few pink
blossoms left on the upper boughs.   The sun
streamed in at the four windows, and the reflected
light from the snow world outside was almost too
dazzling.   Close by Ally's side sat Mrs. Allen, her
pale gray gown, soft white hair, and filmy lace,
making a delicious tone of relief for the sunlit reds
and yellows.

Dr. Miller put his hands behind him and stood
before the fire for some moments, silently drinking
in the picture.   Then he turned suddenly to us,
and said in a gruff tone : —

"Boys, how d'ye like it, here ?"   Jim laughed
outright.

"Just about as well as you'd like it yourself, Doctor."

Jim had been watching the Doctor closely. The Doctor chuckled, and clapped him on the shoulder.

"Pretty good for you, boy. Bring out that stone of yours. Let's look at it by daylight. The confounded thing kept me awake last night. I can't imagine what it is."

Ally raised herself slowly on one elbow, and, fumbling under her pillow, brought out from a miscellaneous store of treasures a tiny blue silk bag. In this was the crystal.

"Mother said I could have it to sleep with," she said; "but in the night I heard it crawling in the bag, so I moved it from under my head. It's alive. I guess it'll get to know me."

Again I felt a strange shudder at the child's words, and at the eager look with which her eyes followed the gem as she gave it into the Doctor's hands. Again we experienced the same singular sensation, like shocks from an electric battery, in passing it from hand to hand. Again we fancied that the colors deepened while Ally held it, and that a peculiar iridescent light flashed from it when it was held near her face. It was very evident that she grew more and more excited while the stone was in motion in the room. Her cheeks grew red and the pupils of her eyes dilated, and she was restless; she did not like to have it out of her possession ; still she could not hold it for many minutes.

"What does make it pinch so?" she said. "Poor little Stonie, is that all the way it can speak? Mother said the wasp pricked me to say 'Let me alone;' but this does not hurt. I like it."

Mrs. Allen looked uneasy. "Does thee think, Doctor, it can harm the child?"

"No," replied the Doctor, in a perplexed tone. "No, I think not. If it is, as it seems to me, simply a natural electricity, it may do good; but it is a strange thing. I'd give a good deal to know what it is."

Broad sunbeams were resting on Ally's bed; the coverlet was soon warm to the touch. Ally laid the crystal carefully on one of the white spaces. "Stonie does not look pretty on the red color," she said. One of the abutilon blossoms had fallen, and she was slowly tearing the bright striped bell into strips and arranging them in fantastic patterns on her breast; the feathery stamens also lay scattered about like a shower of golden threads. Suddenly Ally cried out : —

"Oh, see! The flowers like Stonie; they follow him."

We all ran to her bed, and stood transfixed with astonishment at the sight. Yes, the flowers did follow the stone! As Ally drew it slowly along, the tiny shreds of the abutilon petals and the slender filaments of the stamens followed it. On touching

it they adhered slightly to the surface, as magnetized objects to a magnet. " Is Stonie eating
them ? " said Ally. " Is that what he lives on ? "
This persistent disposition on Ally's part to speak
of the stone as a living and sentient thing, childish
as it was, and as we all the while knew it to be,
heightened our half superstitious sense of mystery in
the thing. For the first time Mrs. Allen's face experienced a shade of the same feeling.

" My mind misgives me," she said, slowly, " that
it would be well for us to return this mysterious
visitor to the place from which he came."

"Oh, no, no, mother dear," cried Ally ; " not out
in the cold snow, my dear Stonie," and she lifted
it to her lips and kissed it. With a little cry, she
dropped it quickly, exclaiming, " He is hot as fire,
I left him in the sun too long ; he pricked me to
say he did not like it," and she picked the stone up
again cautiously, and, with a timid air, half appealing, half resolute, dropped it into the little silk bag,
looking all the time in Mrs. Allen's eyes, and saying, " Please let me keep him, mother ; he is such
a pretty Stonie, and he 'll get to know me."

" Oh, yes, let her keep it," said Dr. Miller, " it 's
only a crystal. We 're foolish to be so stirred up
about a bit of stone, just because we never saw anything like it before. I dare say there are a few
more stones on the earth we don't know. We 're
nothing but ignoramuses,— at least I am,— beg-
ging your pardon, Mistress Allen."

Mrs. Allen smiled. " I know only too well how ignorant I am of all the treasures in this wonderful world," she said. " The word that thee used did not stir any resentment in my heart, I assure thee. But does thee really think it is safe for the child to have for a plaything a stone which has such strange properties as this? And does thee not think it may be a jewel of value lost by some stranger on the hill ? "

Dr. Miller sprang to Ally's bed and bent over it. In that moment, almost before she had put the stone fairly back into the bag, the child had fallen asleep. It seemed an unnatural sleep to have come so suddenly, and yet her breathing was peaceful, her pulse regular, and her cheeks were less flushed than before.

" It's the electricity ; it must be," said the Doctor, more to himself than to us. " No," he continued, " I do not see any danger in the thing. The electrical properties of the stone must be slight, and the child will soon weary of it as of any other toy. But the first thing we'll do, boys, when the snow breaks up, 'll be to go to Black Ledge, and hunt up the rest, if there are any more. There s something worth looking into. I 'm confident of that, but I must not spend my time this way ? " And the Doctor was off almost without a good-by.

The Doctor's prediction that Ally would soon weary of the stone was not fulfilled. Six long weeks the patient little creature lay on her bed, in the south window, under the abutilon canopy, and the mysterious crystal was her inseparable plaything. When she was not holding it up and turning it over and over in the light, she kept it in sight, laying it always on the white spaces in the coverlet, and as far as possible from the scarlet; and I observed that when she was lying still, apparently in a reverie, her eyes were usually fastened upon the stone. We grew familiar with its strange electric and magnetic phenomena, and even amused ourselves by passing it rapidly from hand to hand after it had been heated by friction and by the sunlight.

As our superstitious uneasiness about it wore away, our interest in it diminished, and sometimes for weeks we did not think of it, except when Ally called our attention to its beauty or its mysterious powers. She still persisted in speaking of it as if it were alive, and caressing and loving it as if it could reciprocate all her affection.

"Stonie knows me now," she would often say. "He does not know any of the rest of you ; you don't love him. He hardly ever pricks me now ; he only purrs on my fingers."

It was an odd thing that Mrs. Allen never felt this sensation. Her nerves were so strong that the powerful influence, whatever it might be, produced no disturbance on the equipoise of her system. Jim was more sensitive to it than any one except Ally herself. He knew instantly on approaching

Ally if she had been playing with the stone. He could tell with his eyes shut, by touching her hands, in which hand the stone lay ; and he never entirely lost the first feeling of fear and repulsion with which we regarded the gem. He said again and again to me : —

"Will, I'm ashamed of the feeling, but I do hate to have Ally keep that stone. I can't shake off a sort of presentiment that evil will some day come to her through it. I do wish it could be lost, but it is never away from her one second. At night she hides it under her pillow, and by day she carries it in her pocket. I do believe there is a spell about the thing."

"Well, it isn't a spell that does the child harm, anyhow," I always replied to him, "for certainly never in this world did a child grow strong and tall and beautiful faster than she is growing. You have it so firmly fixed in your head that she isn't a mortal child, like other children, that you can't see anything connected with her as it really is."

I was not conscious of the feeling, but a deep-rooted jealousy of Jim was already growing up in my heart, and distorting my thoughts of both him and Ally. Gentle and loving as she always was to every human being, there was a certain spontaneous, exuberant overflow of affection toward Jim, which made her manner to every one else seem cold by contrast. I was not sure, but it seemed to me that even dear Mrs. Allen felt this. I sometimes saw her eyes rest upon the two when they were frolicking together, with an expression of pain. The day came when I understood what that pain had meant.

Long before spring we had ceased to talk about going to Black Ledge to look for the magic stones, but Ally never forgot it. One bright day in April, when the drops falling from the eaves had melted a little circle around the roots of the lilac-tree, and brought to light a few tiny pale green shoots of grass, Ally turned from the window, and said to me : —

"Mr. Will, see, there is the ground again! Pretty soon the snow will be gone, and we can look for Stonie's friends. Poor Stonie! he would have been very lonely all winter if it had n't been for me. We 'll take him up with us, and he will show us the way."

" But, Ally, how can a stone show people the way ? That's a silly speech, little girl," said I.

" No, Mr. Will," she answered gravely. " It is n't silly, because it is true. Stonie won't show you, because he don't know you ; but he will show me. He tells me a great many things when we are all alone together, don't you, Stonie ? " And she took the little blue silk bag from her pocket and laid it against her cheek. As she did so her eyes dilated and her cheeks flushed, and again the uncomfortable sense of something supernatural in the stone, and in the bond between Ally and it, swept over me. " Who knows but Jim is right, after all ! I wonder if we should love Ally any less if she did n't have that stone?" I said to myself, as I pondered her words and looks.

The thaw was rapid and general. Not for years had such a body of snow disappeared so quickly. The river rose alarmingly ; even little pools became dangerous. A large part of the village was under water. One feeble old man was actually drowned at the foot of his own garden, and for a few hours there was great cause for alarm ; but the waters fell as fast as they had risen ; a high wind rose and blew steadily for three days, and at the end of a week the whole country lay bare and dry, with a tender green tint everywhere struggling through the brown.

Dr. Miller had not forgotten the trip to Black Ledge. While the freshet was at its height he ran in one morning to say, " Boys, if this lasts we can go to Black Ledge by Saturday. The snow 'll be all gone."

" And me, too?" said Ally. " Will you take me?"

" No, indeed, Pussy," said the Doctor. " It will be too wet and muddy."

" But you can't find Stonie's friends without me," said Ally. " I know you can't. Don't you know, Mr. Will, you could n't see Stonie, look all you could, and there he was right in plain sight all the time. Don't you remember?"

True, so it was. Again a vague distrust and fear

flashed through my mind. It had seemed to me at the time inexplicable that, searching so carefully and long, I had not seen the stone. Ally continued : " It won't be of any use for you to go unless you take Stonie, at any rate. Perhaps he will tell you the way if I ask him to."

Dr. Miller looked at Ally with a surprised face.

" What nonsense is this you 're talking, Pussy ? " he said.

" That 's just what Mr. Will said," replied Ally, archly, and yet with a strange earnestness in her tone. " Nobody believes that Stonie knows me and tells me things, but he does. Some day you 'll all believe it."

" Pshaw — what a notional little woman it is, to be sure," laughed the Doctor, patting her on the head, as he hurried out.

" Never mind. You 'll see," said Ally quietly, putting back into her pocket the blue silk bag which she had been fingering dreamily while she talked.

Saturday was clear and bright. We set out early. Ally made no request to be taken with us, but watched all our movements with intense interest. I observed that she had the blue silk bag in her hand and raised it often to her cheek. She bade us good-by very quietly, but, as we cleared the gate, we heard her call, " Doctor, brother Jim, wait a minute," and she came flying down the walk, with the blue silk bag in her hand. " Here, Doctor," she said "you must take Stonie. You can't find the way without him. He has told me where his friends are; and I have asked him to tell you. There are n't any more of them on the old tree-root. You need n't look there. Most of them are down deep, and you 'll have to dig; but there are some up on the very tip-top of the rocks. I know just how they look there. Stonie showed me."

The Doctor laughed and dropped the little bag in his pocket, saying, " I 'll take good care of your Stonie," and Ally ran back, kissing her hands to us all.

" She 's a most fanciful child," he said, as we walked on; " that imagination of hers will give her trouble some of these days; though she 's got a splendid physique to offset it."

" Are you sure it is all her imagination about this stone, sir? " asked Jim, hesitatingly.

Dr. Miller stopped, turned, and looked Jim squarely in the face. " God bless my soul, boy, what else do you suppose it is? You 're as bad as the child, upon my word. They don't teach a belief in witchcraft at your college, do they? I 'll be bound Will here don't believe any such nonsense," turning to me.

I felt my face grow red, and my answer was as hesitating as Jim's question.

" No, sir; I don't believe it exactly, but it is very odd how Ally — "

" Ha! ha!" chuckled the Doctor. " It is n't at

all odd how Ally — But you two are beginning rather young to see through a woman's eyes. Let it alone, boys, let it alone, only torment comes of it ; " and the Doctor fell into a reverie, such as we had often seen him in before, and which we knew better than to interrupt.

It was a wet and ugly climb up Black Ledge that morning. In the hollows of the rocks and under the giant oaks there still lay patches of slippery snow and ice ; but the air was soft and balmy, and one blue hepatica welcomed us. It was growing almost under the trunk of the fallen tree in whose root Ally had found the stone.

" Ally said it was n't of any use to look here," said Jim, unthinkingly.

Dr. Miller looked at him almost severely.

"Youngster," says he, " are n't you a little ashamed of yourself ? "

" Yes, sir, a good deal," replied Jim, frankly enough to disarm the most contemptuous critic. "A good deal. But I can't help it. I do believe, if we find the stones at all, we shall find them where Ally said they were."

" And I suppose you believe, too, that this stone here " — tapping his waistcoat pocket, — " told her where its 'friends,' as she calls them, were ? " said the Doctor, with kind, twinkling, compassionate eyes. " Poor boy — if Ally, at ten, does this to your senses, what 'll she do to you six years hence ? "

"Love me, I hope," said Jim, "as well as she does now. She's all I've got in the world, Dr. Miller, and please don't laugh at me any more. You wouldn't if you knew how I love that child, would he, Will?"

"No," said I, pretending to laugh. "It's no laughing matter, Doctor."

But the words, "She's all I have got in this world," echoed strangely in my ears. Dear, generous Jim; how little our boys' hearts could have dreamed in that hour of the barrier into which those few words were destined to be built!

We searched long around the roots of the old tree. I think Dr. Miller was determined to falsify Ally's prediction by finding the stones there.

"That one stone couldn't have been all alone," he said. "There's no such thing in nature; there must be more where that came from."

"But, Dr. Miller," said I, "that one was in a crevice of the roots; it probably came from deep down in the earth," and I showed him, as nearly as I could recollect, where the stone had lain. He examined the earth on the roots very carefully, and we looked for the cavity from which the tree had come, but there was no trace of it. Probably many years had elapsed since the storm which uprooted the old oak. "It might have grown a long way farther up the hill for all we can tell," said the Doctor, scratching his head and looking puzzled.

At this instant we heard loud shouts from Jim

He had spent very few minutes looking in the vicinity of the old tree, but had climbed rapidly up the ledge, and had been out of sight for some time.

"Oh, Will! Will! Doctor! Doctor! Hurry!" he cried, in tones so shrill and earnest, that I feared he was in trouble.

" He 's found them, I do believe," exclaimed the Doctor, and .we ran breathlessly up the steep and slippery rocks.

On the very top of the ledge knelt Jim, — his hands clasped.

"Oh, look, look!" he exclaimed. "Was not Ally right ? "

We stood still in amazement. Glistening, sparkling in the sun, there lay dozens of crystals as if they had been just thrown down by some careless hand.

" I have n't touched one," said Jim ; "I did n't dare to."

Dr. Miller did not speak for some moments. Then he cried out : —

" By Jove, I 'd like to know whether we' re in Maine or in Brazil ! It looks as if we 'd been living at the foot of an emerald mine all our days, and might have gone on living so if it had n't been for that blessed child. However, somebody nad to find it out sooner or later. Pitch in, boys , pitch in, we 'll get all we can this trip. The whole town 'll be up here to-morrow, for I take it we

have n't got any right to keep it to ourselves.
Nobody 's ever thought of owning Black Ledge.
I guess my line comes up higher 'n anybody 's ;
but I 'm a good way down yonder ; this is the
town's property up here."

Eagerly, silently, with an undercurrent of consciousness that we were coming very close to some
strange secret of nature, we gathered up the crystals. There were many of great beauty, but none
so fine as the first-found one, Ally's " Stonie."
Many of them were broken ; some looked as if
they had crumbled slowly into fragments ; but all
were transparent, brilliant, and of colors of ineffable beauty, — dark green, light green, pink,
yellow, blue, rose-red and white.

It seemed utterly incredible that such treasures
could long have been lying exposed on this hill-top.

" I don't suppose there are many villages where
it could have happened," said Dr. Miller, " but
there is n't a man or woman in this town that
would ever think of walking a rod for pleasure, except me, and I 'm too busy always to get so far
from home 's this. I suppose I 've looked up at
this Black Ledge a hundred times and resolved to
come up here at sunset some night, but I never
have. I guess I 'm glad I did n't. It 's worth a
good deal more to come on it this way, with you
boys along, and that Ally down below waiting."

" Oh, what will she say ? What will she say ? "
exclaimed I.

"She won't be surprised," said Jim. "She's known it all winter. She told me a long time ago that there were ever so many up here; that Stonie said so. And she says: 'You know that the most of them are down deep;' that we'd only find a few on the top."

"So she did; so she did," said the Doctor, unconscious of the amount of confidence in Ally betrayed by his reply. "It's odd how the child knew; but that's the way it must be. These crystals have been formed deep down among these rock. I don't know what has laid them bare. It takes ages for rocks to decompose, but this looks like it. We'll dig down just at the base of these biggest rocks. This soil has washed down round them."

In our first wonder and delight at the crystals, we had scarcely observed the rocks; but in looking more closely, we found that they, too, were of rare beauty. There were great masses of a rose-red stone, magnificent rocks of quartz, and shining surfaces of mica. On the cold gray of the granite ledge these glittering colors stood out in sharp relief, and produced an effect of design in spite of all the chaotic confusion.

"I believe the gods began a temple here once," said Jim, "and left their jewels behind them."

"Quit Maine for want of worshipers," chuckled the Doctor, as he tugged away at his digging. Suddenly he threw down his spade, fell on his knees, and began fumbling in the loose earth with his fingers.

More crystals! We looked on in speechless astonishment. The cavity into which his spade had broken was some two feet deep. The bottom was filled with sand, and loose in this sand, as if they had been packed in it for safe keeping, lay many crystals of the finest colors we had yet seen. Their shapes were not perfect, and many of them were cracked or fissured as if they had been at some time exposed to the grinding of other stones upon them, but the colors were superb. Carefully we sifted the cavity to the very bottom, not leaving a single fragment of the gems in it. By this time the sun was well down in the western sky.

"We really must go home, boys," said the Doctor; "they will be anxious about us, and I am hungry; and you ought to be, though you are not," he added, scanning our excited faces with a professional eye.

Hungry! — we had no more thought of hunger than we should have in Aladdin's palace. Our eyes were so feasted that the whole body seemed fed. It was simply impossible to carry down the ledge all the crystals and crystal-bearing fragments of rock we had collected. We hid some of the least beautiful specimens under the old tree-root, and we were then so heavily burdened that the walk home was a serious toil. Ally was at the window watching for us. At the first sight of our overloaded arms she clapped her hands and bounded to open the door.

"Oh, I'm so glad, so glad!" she exclaimed, jumping up and down, and springing first to one, then to another. "I thought Stonie would help you."

"You foolish Pussy," exclaimed Dr. Miller, "we've got a hundred stones just like him."

"No," said Ally, gravely, "you have not got any just like him. There is not one among them all just like him."

"By Jove, she's right," muttered the Doctor, as we slowly set down our loads; "there isn't one just like hers."

"I told you so. I said she knew all about them," whispered Jim, under his breath.

We spent the whole evening in sorting and arranging the stones; they seemed more and more beautiful the more we studied them. There were no two alike; very few of them were perfect in shape, but they were all of superb colors. There was not one, however, which was so large, so regularly shaped and beautifully tinted as Ally's Stonie. As we held up crystal after crystal, exclaiming, "This is a perfect one!" "Oh, this is the most beautiful of all!" Ally would place hers by the side of it, and without saying one word, look an arch interrogation. When the last crystal was laid in its place, she said, quietly : —

14

"Stonie is king. These are his people. But there are many more in the hill."

"How does thee know, dear?" asked Mrs. Allen. "Can thee tell me how it is?"

"Stonie tells me, mother," replied Ally.

"But how does he tell thee?" said Mrs. Allen, humoring the child's fancy by speaking of the stone as she herself did. "He does not speak in words. He makes no sound."

Ally looked perplexed. "No," she said, slowly, "I know that. But he likes me. He makes me see."

This was all the explanation she could ever give of the way in which she received impressions by means of the magnetic stone—"He makes me see." The next morning we inclosed a few of the smaller crystals in a letter and sent them to the Professor of Geology in our college, giving him a full account of the crystals, and of the locality where we had found them.

How anxiously we awaited his reply. Our brains teemed with the wildest hopes and projects; even Dr. Miller built air-castles, in which rubies and emeralds made walls and floors. The whole village was in a ferment of excitement. Black Ledge swarmed thick with eager crystal hunters. Many beautiful specimens were found, but no more of the perfectly formed crystals like ours. At last the letter came. Jim and I ran with it to Dr. Miller's office, and we read it together. It was long and full.

Our crystals were not emeralds, not rubies. They were tourmalines. The mineral was a rare one. Early in the eighteenth century, some experiments had been made before the French Academy, showing the wonderful electric properties of the stone, and for a few years considerable interest had been taken in the subject. But, owing to the scarcity of the gems, the investigations had not been continued, and even at the present day the stone was almost unknown, except to professional mineralogists.

Commercially, the gem had no fixed value. A superb group of them, which had been presented to the British Ambassador to the Burmese Empire, in 1795, and was now in the British Museum, had been valued at one thousand pounds sterling. The deep red variety, when clear and flawless, would command the price of rubies. It had been surmised that the famous ruby in one of the diadems of the Russian crown jewels was a species of tourmaline. The Professor concluded his kind letter by heartily congratulating us on our discovery, and thanking us, in the name of the college, for the specimens we had sent. He also offered to put us in communication with some amateur collectors in Europe, if we wished to dispose of the remaining crystals. As these were the only ones which had been discovered in America, he believed that they would be largely sought after.

"Well, they're not real jewels after all, then," said the Doctor, drawing a long sigh. "I did hope they'd turn out to be a fortune for somebody. But I don't care to dabble with the amateur collectors the Professor talks about. I've had one such man on my farm already after bird tracks. I never made anything out of him. You can have all my share, boys; but I think you'd better send some of the very handsomest specimens to the college, don't you? Those little fellows we put in the letter weren't anything. If the British Museum has got one five-thousand dollar specimen, 't aint anyways likely they want another. It's easy enough, though, to 'value' a thing at five thousand dollars, when a grand Mogul of the Burmese Empire's given it to you for nothing. I can set one of these big quartz rocks with the green crystals in it up on my mantel-piece and 'value' it at five thousand dollars, too, any day."

We were crestfallen and disappointed; but the romance remained, though the hopes of pecuniary gain had departed. There was something in the very word tourmalines, Jim said, which went far to reconcile him to their not being rubies, and we felt somehow linked to the past century, to the French Academy, and to the Russian Empire, — we boys in the heart of Maine who could amuse our-selves of an evening with handfuls of gems such as savants had vainly desired to possess and Empresses had worn.

When we read the letter aloud at home, Mrs. Allen looked at her husband with so significant an expression, and he returned it with one so full of earnest meaning, that I exclaimed: —

"Dear Dominie, dear Mrs. Allen, what is it?"

Mrs. Allen did not speak. The Dominie glanced at her before replying. Then he said: —

"My son, our hearts were much troubled at the new thoughts which these jewels had brought into the life of our household. We do not desire money for ourselves; we fear it for those we love. We must grieve that your hopes are cast down, but we cannot help being glad that the chief mission of the wonderful stones is, after all, nothing more than to give us all one farther glimpse into the wonders of God's house in which we dwell."

Jim sprang from his seat, went to the Dominie, took his hand reverently in both of his, and pressed it without speaking. The Dominie's words had gone to the very bottom of his heart.

"God bless you, my son," said the Dominie. "When your hair is as white as mine you will think as I think."

"I do now, sir," said Jim, in a low voice, "and I believe I should think the same if I had not been rich."

"Much you can tell about that, old fellow," said I. "Wait till you 've had to go without half the things you wanted for years and years. You 're just like a blind man talking about colors."

"The Dominie and mother have had to go with-out most things they wanted," said Jim, impul-sively.

The two aged lovers again exchanged glances. This time it was Mrs. Allen who spoke.

"Nay, not so. We have not gone without the things we have not had. But that is something thee cannot understand yet," and the placid, tender eyes turned to Ally involuntarily.

Ally had listened with absorbed interest to the reading of the letter and to the conversation which followed. Her face showed that not one of the ideas escaped her comprehension. The mental growth of this child in the last six months had been simply wonderful. In technical and text-book knowledge she was still far behind most children of her age, and must, of course, continue to be so for a long time. The lost years of her sad, un-trained childhood could not easily be made up. But, on the other hand, every moment of her life now contained true education; and her suscepti-bility to influence was so exquisite that each new germ of thought sprang up quickly, bearing its hundred fold. Except for the innate gayety of her temperament, and for her fine English physique, she would have been in danger of becoming an in-troverted and too thoughtful child. But the mirth-ful heart and the abounding animal life saved her.

As Mrs. Allen finished speaking, Ally came slowly to the table, drawing the blue silk bag from her pocket.

"I would like to send Stonie to the gentleman who wrote that letter. Stonie is king, and ought to go," she said.

"Can you spare Stonie?" asked Jim, tenderly. "You will miss him very much, little one."

"I can have another all for my own, can't I?" said Ally, anxiously.

"Why, yes, pet, a dozen, if you want them," replied Jim; "but they won't be like Stonie. There isn't one just like him."

"I know that," said Ally. "There isn't one in all the hill just like him. But he is king; he ought to go, and he wants to go, too. He has told me so."

With a tender, lingering touch she laid the beloved crystal down on the paper where we had already placed some of the specimens to be sent to the Professor. It was, indeed, king of them all. Both ends of the crystal were perfectly formed. It was transparent and flawless throughout. Two thirds of its length were vivid green; the other third rose-pink. At the green summit was a layer of solid opaque white, looking like a cap, though only a line wide. In no other specimen did we see any trace of such a formation of white.

"That is Stonie's snow crown," said Ally, laying her finger on the white end of the crystal. "You see none of the rest have crowns."

She found it hard to make a choice. She tested every stone by laying it against her cheek.

"I want one with a voice like Stonie," she said.

We were so accustomed now to this strange manner of speaking of the stone that we treated it
merely as a child's fancy for thinking a toy alive.
But there was much more in it than we knew. At
last she made her selection, — two of the longest and
slenderest crystals, of precisely the same length,
one solid green, the other green and red.

"Are these too nice for me to have?" she asked
timidly. "They are the best of all you have."

"You generous pussy," exclaimed Dr. Miller,
"as if you had n't given us the very gem of the
whole."

"Oh, Stonie was n't really mine! — only to keep
for a little while," said Ally. "He was king."

The next day Dr. Miller was to set out on a long
journey to the West, and he proposed to deliver
our precious package of tourmalines, with his own
hands, to the Professor.

I 'd like to tell him, too, about you boys," he
said, roguishly. "If I report all your misconduct
faithfully, he 'll get your sentence extended another
six months."

"Oh, if he only would!" we both exclaimed.
"We do hate to go away."

The time was very near — only four weeks more.
We could not bear to hear any one mention the
days of the month. They sounded in our ears like
the notes of a clock striking hour after hour of a
happy day. Oh, the marvel of this thing which we

call time ! — which is, and which is not ; a moment
of which can seem like an eternity of pain ! an eternity of which can seem too short for a moment of
joy ?

Some weeks after Dr. Miller's departure I observed, one morning at breakfast, that Ally was
unusually grave.

" What is it Ally ? What are you thinking about ? "
said I.

" Stonie," she replied, in a sad voice.

" Do you want him back ? I was afraid you
would, " said Jim

" Oh, no, brother Jim. It is n't that ; " and the
child's lip trembled.

" What is it, then ? Do tell me, dear," exclaimed Jim, his face full of trouble, as it always
was at sight of an instant's unhappiness on Ally's.

" I can't," said Ally ; " I don't know. It's
Stonie. When will Dr. Miller come home ? "

" Why, not for three weeks yet, Ally," replied
Jim ; " but he has n't got Stonie now. Stonie's
safe in a great big box on high legs, with a glass
cover to it, by this time." And he tried to divert
her mind by telling her about the college cabinets.
She listened absently, and at last shaking her head,
and saying, " Stonie is n't there," she slipped from
Jim's lap and walked slowly away.

That night there came a letter to Jim in a hand
writing he did not know. He glanced at the signature, and exclaimed : —

" Oh, the good Doctor ! He's written to tell us about the tourmalines ! "

As he read the letter his face lengthened. I did not interrupt him with any question, but I said to myself : —

" The tourmalines are lost, and Ally knew it this morning. I wish we 'd never heard of the things, anyhow. They 're bewitched. "

Presently he threw the letter to me, saying, " Read that, Will. I don't care about the con- founded stones, but I 'd rather run a gauntlet of wild Indians than tell Ally. Hang the thing! I wish we 'd never seen Black Ledge."

Dr. Miller's letter was highly characteristic : —

" DEAR BOYS : I may as well out with it. Your — my — Ally's — all the tourmalines are lost. I don't know but the Dominie was right, after all. Maybe they are used for gates in heaven, and angelic archi- tects lay violent hands on them whenever they find them. The worst of it is, that I can't swear that it is n't my fault. The beastly stage driver that we rode with day before yesterday upset his stage just before dark, and nearly broke all our necks. There was a woman with a little boy in it, and the child's leg was broken, and I was up all night with them ; and I 'll be hanged if I ever thought once of the package of tourmalines till late the next day. I had it in my inside pocket, and felt of it about once m an hour or so up to that time. I spent most of yesterday ransacking the bushes and sand where we tipped over, and questioning everybody, but it 's no use ; the thing 's gone, and I 'll have to push on to-morrow. I hate to leave this woman with her boy worse than I ever hated to do anything. The child can't be stirred for three months, and they 're as poor as the dogs. You can tell Ally about this lit-tle boy and his broken leg, and that 'll divert her from Stonie. Don't blame me any more than you can help, boys ; I 'm cut up enough about it, any-how. I expect you thought I was old enough to be trusted. DAVID MILLER.

" P. S. I 'm ashamed of myself for thinking such a thing, but I can't get it out of my head that Caleb Bunker has got the tourmalines. He sat next me in the stage, and he has been like a man possessed about them from the very first ; but, of course, I can't ever say à word to him, and I 've no business to you. He was terribly officious in helping me look after them yesterday morning, and all of a sudden he disappeared. If he got them I shall find it out some day, for he 's such a fool. D. M. "

To our great relief Ally took the news of the loss of " Stonie " very quietly. She was prepared for it.

" I knew something had happened," she said, " but it is no matter. Stonie will be king, you know, wherever he is. I dare say he did not want to be shut up in that box you told me about."

When we were alone Mrs. Allen said quietly to Jim :—

" I am very glad thee was discreet enough not to read before the child the Doctor's suspicions of Mr. Bunker. She has gratitude to him and Mrs. Bunker, and I would be sorry to have it disturbed. I fear that the Doctor is right. There was all the essence of dishonesty in the manner in which he spent thy hundred dollars for Ally."

Our sorrow at the loss of the tourmalines was soon swallowed up in our grief at the near prospect of going back to college. To leave Ally and Mrs. Allen and the Dominie was harder to me than it had ever been to leave my own home ; and, as for Jim, poor boy, it was the first home he had ever known.

" If I were n't ashamed, Will," he said, " I 'd quit college and turn my back on the world and settle down here with Dominie."

" What to do, Jim ? " said I. " Study and hunt, and teach Ally till she 's old enough for me to take her to Europe, replied he with kindling face. " I believe I 'd know more at the end of six years that way than I will now. College is an infernal humbug, Will, and you know it as well as I do. Have n't we learnt more in these six months with Dominie than in all the rest of our lives put together ? Anyhow, I 'm thankful Ally's got such a home. Blessed little angel, how could I ever have thought of her being marched up and down the streets in those processions of boarding-school girls, and learning to flirt with the students. It makes me feel like knocking these country fellows down now whenever I see them looking at her, and I don't know what I 'd do with her at college."

" Break a dozen fellow's heads every term, I expect, old boy, — what with the ones that made love to her, and the ones that chaffed you about her," laughed I.

" Chaffed me about Ally!" exclaimed Jim. " What do you mean, Will ? Who ever heard of a man being chaffed about his sister ? "

" Nobody," said I satirically ; " but Ally happens not to be your sister."

" Will, it 's just the same as if my father and mother had adopted her instead of me ; exactly the same. She is my sister, I tell you," said Jim emphatically.

" There is n't any same as brother about kisses, " came into my head, but I forebore to quote the words. My heart was already sorer than I knew how to explain, by reason of this little maiden's exclusive love for her brother Jim.

The dreaded day came swiftly, as only dreaded days can ; it was a sunny May morning. To go away by stage from a home one sorrows to leave is infinitely harder than to go in any other way. There is such a mockery of good cheer, of a pleasure drive, in the prancing of the horses eager to be off. There is such a refinement of cruelty in the composure of the driver, waiting whip in hand for

you to decide for yourself when the last words have
been said, the last kiss taken. There is such a
prolongation of the pain of last looks, as at turn after turn of the winding road you discover that you
can still see the dear forms on the doorstep, or
the gleam of the home through the trees. The authoritative "All aboard" of the conductor, and the
pitiless shriek of the steam-engine at the railway
station, are mercies for those who find it hard to
part. All this I thought as we rode away from the
beloved parsonage, looking back and back again
between the pink apple-tree tops to the group of
loved ones in the door-way. The parting had been
singularly brief and quiet. Mrs. Allen's placid
brown eyes were full of tears, but her last words
were simply, to both Jim and me: "Thee will
write, thee will write often;" and the Dominie's
voice shook a little as he said, "God keep you, my
boys. Remember that this is your home always."

Ally spoke no word; she kissed first me, then
Jim, with a swift kiss quite unlike her usual clinging, loving kisses, and then turned her head away
and hid it in the lilac boughs. The clusters of
purple flowers bent down and rested on her golden
hair as if to soothe her. All I could see of her face
was the patient, sweet mouth, which was firmer
shut than usual.

And so we went back into the world again: the
city, the college, the men, the women, all seemed
unspeakably strange, and the strangeness did not

wear off. For weeks our feeling was not so much one of homesickness as of bewilderment. No foreigners in a strange land ever found the atmosphere of their lives newer, more inharmonious. The very speech jarred on our ears. For six months we had heard but three voices, and those singularly low, sweet, rich.

"Oh, Will, is this the same language they used to speak at the Dominie's?" exclaimed Jim, in the middle of our first breakfast at our boarding-house; "I can't stand it! It is like jews-harps. It never sounded like this before."

"How have you ever made out to live through the winter in that outlandish place, Mr. Ordway?" at this instant called our spinster landlady in shrill tones from her high seat at the head of the table; "I assure you we have all sympathized with you deeply."

Jim's look of surprise was almost an angry stare.

"I was never so happy in my life, madam," he retorted, "and I assure you this place is the outlandish one and not that!"

Significant looks were exchanged among the boys at this outbreak. "Oh, Jim, be quiet," I whispered; "the boys will chaff you to death if you make such speeches."

"Yes, I'm a fool, Will," he answered, under his breath, and then, resuming his more courteous tone, he endeavored to soothe the ancient maiden's resentment and disarm suspicion by a graphic ac-

count of the beauty of the winter in northern
Maine, and of the rare characters we had found in
Parson Allen and his wife.

But the mischief was done. College boys do not
easily lose sight of the clew to a possible joke, and
the secret of Jim Ordway's attachment to Maine
was the staple of current banter for months. I
was not there long to help poor Jim bear and
baffle it. In the third week of the term I was
called home by the sudden death of my father.
His business was left in disastrous confusion, and
the only chance of saving the property seemed to
lie in my giving up my college education and going
into the counting-house. It was a severe test for a
boy eighteen years old, but I never regretted that
it devolved upon me. I was better suited for a
business life than for any other, and the four years
of college would not have been sufficient help to me
in it to have compensated for the delay. Here,
therefore, the currents of life divided me from Jim.
After four years — three at school and one at college — in which we had lived like brothers, we
were now thrown widely apart.

The separation was much harder to Jim than to
me. As I said in the beginning of my story, I have
always wondered why I did not love him better.
His idealistic, dreamy, poetic, impulsive nature had
great fascination for me, but with the fascination
was mingled a certain impatience, almost scorn, of
his lack of practicality, and an element of pity

which is fatal to the strongest love between man and man. It was only in a woman's nature that I could wholly love the combination of qualities which made Jim the sweet-souled fellow he was, and made him dearer to almost everybody than he could ever be to me, whom he loved with his whole heart. Yet I feel a sharp sense of disloyalty, in writing these words, in acknowledging even to myself this fatal flaw in my regard for him. He was so pure, so unselfish, so true; he lived habitually on so much higher a plane of thought than I did, that I always felt in his presence that the flaw was in me, rather than in him, that my love could not grow warmer. His gentle, affectionate sweetness, his enthusiastic sympathy, moved me greatly. But the instant he was gone from my sight my consciousness of the lack in his nature returned in undiminished vividness, and I knew that I must forever receive far more affection than I could give, in my relations with him.

The story of the next three years is summed up in a few words. Jim was faithfully working away in the college routine, which he more than half despised, but would not let himself abandon. I was working alone and unhelped, as men work in a shipwreck, striving to save the remains of my father's little property. It was a terrible strain, and has told on my whole life. I used up in those years physical capital which could never be replaced, but I gained a business knowledge and

15

capacity which no less severe training could have given me. In saving my father's hundreds I learned to make my own thousands, and I am content. Jim wrote very often. I wrote seldom. This was partly because of my temperament, partly because I was so overworked. Through him I heard from the dear home in Maine, and through him sent to them my warm recollections; but after the letters at the time of my father's death I left off writing directly to him. This, again, was partly because of my temperament, partly because I was so overworked; but partly, also, because I had an instinctive consciousness that the thought of Ally must not become an element in my daily life. Strange that in the boy's heart the man's instinct should have been so strong; should have so recognized in the little unformed child the mature woman; should have had so prophetic a sense of all which lay hid far, far in the future! When the news of my misfortune reached the parsonage, Mrs. Allen and the Dominie each wrote me a loving and sympathizing letter. Mrs. Allen said: —

" Thee knows that we ourselves set little store by money, nevertheless we can sorrow with those who lose it. If it is best for thee to have riches, it is very easy for the Lord to lay them in thy hands."

Enclosed in the letter was a small bit of paper, on which Ally had printed in large and angular etters: —

"DEAR MR. WILL, — I am very sorry for you to have to go away from brother Jim.

"I would kiss you if you were here.

"ALLY."

I have this precious bit of paper now; the letters are faded, and the paper is worn thin and ragged; it is many years old. Jim's letters were full of Ally, especially during his vacations, which were always spent at the parsonage. Sometimes he was grieved at my seeming lack of sympathy about the child. He once wrote : —

"I don't know if I bore you about Ally. You never ask a question about her, and sometimes I think you have forgotten our life in the old parsonage, you say so little of them all. But it don't seem like you, Will, to leave off loving anybody that loves you, and they all do love you just as well to-day as the day we rode off together on the stage. If you don't care about them as you used to, and would rather not hear so much about them, do tell me, so I need n't write it any more."

Leave off loving! No, it was not like me. In my reply to this letter I said : —

"I hope you will never think, because I do not speak of or to people, that I have ceased to love them. I do not love you, or Dominie, or Mrs. Allen, or Ally any less than I did three years ago. You will never learn, I suppose, that words are not with me natural expressions of feeling."

Jim was relieved, but not satisfied.

"I cannot doubt the truth of all you say, dear Will," he replied, "but I wish it had a different sound to it, somehow."

Ah, the "sound to it!" How many a heart like my faithful Jim's, has half broken for the lack of a certain "sound" to words which were spoken in all loyalty and affection, and really meant all which the aching, listening heart craved, but could not learn to understand in any other language than its own!

This letter was just before Jim's graduation. I had promised to be present at the Commencement. The Dominie and Mrs. Allen and Ally were all to be there, and perhaps Jim's dearly beloved old guardian. Jim's heart was over-full with delight and anticipation. His letters made even me, prosaic, calm-blooded man that I was, feel like laughing and crying together.

"Oh, you dear old Will!" he wrote; "will you just think of what currents are coming together next week? Guardy hasn't seen Mrs. Allen for thirty or forty years, and I know he used to love her — I know it by lots of things; and you haven't seen Ally for almost four years. I shan't tell you a word about her, only just you be prepared to lose your breath, that's all. I will tell you one thing, though. She's almost as tall as I am, Will! What do you think of that for a girl of fourteen? Oh, I'm proud of her! And you, old fellow, have you got such a beard I shan't know you? Oh, but I'm

afraid I shall cry! Hang it all! I wish there
was n't such a streak of woman in me."

Ally, almost as tall as Jim! I could not form
any such fancy of her.

She lived in my mind, always in one picture ; a
little bounding child, with a wreath of scarlet oak-
leaves over her shoulders, and golden curls shining
in the wind; and whenever I recalled this picture,
I recalled as vividly the sharp thrill of electric heat
which shot up my arm as I took from her tiny hand
the red and green crystal. My life during these
three years at home had been so secluded, so dull,
so hard, that the memory of the winter at the parsonage was in no danger of being effaced by new
impressions. On the contrary, it but brightened
day by day. The traveler cannot forget the oasis
while he is still in the desert. My mother and sisters were good women. I loved them dutifully, but
they gave me no joy; they invested life with no
grace, no exhilaration, no stimulus ; they were, like
me, affectionate, realistic, faithful, plodding; except that I had known Mrs. Allen, had breathed
the atmosphere of her house, I should have ac-
cepted them as types of the highest sort of women
— so true, loyal, upright, steadfast were they; but,
I had learned the gospel of a new dispensation ; I
had been led up to heights whose air had expanded
my spiritual nature as the air of great altitudes ex-
pands the lungs. All the more that I compre-
hended my own incapacity to create or even fully

understand the atmosphere of an idealized life, I
felt that I needed it, and knew that I longed for it.
Hour by hour, in these long three years, while Jim
had suspected me of forgetting the dear ones at
the parsonage, I had yearned for them with a yearning born of such need and loss as Jim could never
have felt, and never have borne. I hesitated long
whether I should go to the Commencement. The
promise had been of such long standing it seemed
an obligation; and well I knew that Jim's loving
heart would be wounded to the quick, if I failed.
My inmost instinct warned me against going, told
me that after a week in such companionship it
would be only the harder to return to the associations and the burdens of my inevitable life : on the
other hand, it seemed a selfish thing to deprive my
friends of a pleasure solely to save myself a pain.
" Supposing life is made a little harder," I said to
myself, bitterly, "what then ! I can bear it." Oh,
how worthless a faculty is imagination when we use
it to gauge an untried burden ! As well ask the
eagle's vision to measure the load that a beast of
burden may draw !

I went to the Commencement. An accident to a
train delayed me many hours, and I did not arrive
until nearly noon of the Commencement day. The
exercises had begun some two hours before. The
church was filled to overflowing. To enter by the
doors was simply impossible. A step-ladder had
been set at an open window on the left hand of the

pulpit, and by this the guests who were to have seats on the platform had climbed up. From this window I could see the whole house. I had not stood there many minutes before I caught Jim's eye. He was in the second row of pews, in front of the platform, looking no more like a senior than he did the day we were rusticated for our freshman frolic. Dear, child-hearted man. Not a line of beard on his cheek; not a trace of wordliness in his face ; every line, every feature, full of spirituality, enthusiasm, simplicity.

When he caught my eye his whole face flushed, and he involuntarily half rose from his seat; then recollecting himself, he sank back with a comic look of despair, and began to make signals to me which I could not in the least comprehend. In my absorbed attention to these signals, I did not observe that I was obstructing the entrance to the platform, and that some one was waiting to pass me. Suddenly, I heard a low voice saying, "Will you have the kindness, sir, to let my father pass?" and the old electric shock flashed up my arm like fire. Without turning my head I knew that it was Ally who had spoken, and that she had the Tourmaline in her possession. I sprang back. She lifted her beautiful brown eyes to me as calmly as to a stranger, thanked me, and stretched out her hand to Dominie, saying : "Come down here, father, we have kept a seat for you."

Dominie also looked in my face as in the face of

a stranger, and bowed courteously as he passed. Then for the first time I realized what the years had done to my face. But how then should Jim have known me so instantly? A sudden sense of aggrieved pain stole over me. I said to myself: "They would have known me if they had not forgotten my face." As Dominie took his seat, I heard him say to Ally : —

"He has not come. It is very strange. I am afraid there is some accident."

I knew then that he had been to the station to meet me. The temptation was very strong to make myself known, but the temptation to study Ally's face for a few hours unobserved was still stronger.

To say that she was the most beautiful human creature I had ever seen seems to desecrate her. Comparison between Ally and other women was impossible. Moment by moment as I looked at her I grew incredulous of my eyes. Was that a girl fourteen years old? Was that the outcast child fostered in a lonely New England village by the village pastor's wife? It was a woman of such superb stature that one half inch more of height would have made her look masculine. It was a woman of such self-poise of manner and bearing — such elegance of dress — that out of America one would have thought her of some royal house. If she had had no beauty, the elegance and the grace of her bearing would have produced the effect of it; but what words can describe the charm produced by the combination of these with beauty which more than fulfilled the promise of her childhood? There were the same soft yet brilliant brown eyes, the same exquisite complexion, the same golden-yellow curls. The curls were no longer falling on her neck, but no looping could wholly confine them. I could have sworn that one which drooped and fluttered on her right shoulder was the very one I had so often threatened to cut off. The expression of her face was singularly like that of Jim's. I had sometimes noticed this at the parsonage, but now the resemblance had deepened. There was the same simplicity, spirituality, enthusiasm. There was, however, in spite of the enthusiasm, an expression of placid repose, which Jim's face had not. In this her face was like Mrs. Allen's, and no one seeing them sitting there side by side could have failed to suppose them mother and daughter. Mrs. Allen's face had grown wrinkled and thinner, and yet so tender and holy was its beauty that it did not suffer by contrast with the fresh young bloom at its side.

Ally's dress was black, of a fine transparent material. A wide, floating scarf of the same, quaintly embroided in tiny poppies of scarlet and gold, was thrown over her shoulders. Her bonnet was of the finest black lace, its only ornament two scarlet poppies and one golden bud. It was a toilette an Indian princess might have worn if she had also been a poet.

"Jim must have sent to Paris for that for her," said I to myself. "Lucky fellow that he is with his money!" I was wrong. It was a toilette that Ally had devised, and her own hands had wrought the poppies in scarlet and gold.

The President rolled out his sonorous Latin sentences; my old classmates came and went on the stage; disquisitions, discussions, orations, were all alike to me. I heard the words as one hears words in a dream. I was fully conscious of but one sense, and that was the sense of Ally's personality. It was not the fascination of her beauty; it was, as it always remained, the vivid sense of her as of an expansion of my consciousness of myself. This is the nearest analysis which words can give of the bond which held me to Ally. As I stood with my eyes dreamily fixed on the scarlet and gold poppies of her scarf, I recalled the wealth of scarlet oak-leaves which she had worn on that autumn morning, and I knew that the two hours were linked together by a bond as enduring as eternity. While I was thinking of the strange coincidence in material color of these two most vivid pictures in my brain, I was suddenly conscious of another sharp, electric thrill; not running as before, up my arm, but seeming to come from the floor beneath my feet. It was very sharp, — so sharp that I involuntarily leaned against the wall to steady myself for a second and shut my eyes. When I opened them I saw that Ally's head was turned; she seemed to be eagerly looking for some one, yet the expression was not wholly one of expectancy; it was of a vague anxiety. Her eyes moved slowly from face to face in the seats behind her. As they came nearer and nearer to me my heart beat violently. Was she about to know me at last? Had the tourmaline bond revealed me to her? Her eyes met mine. I had resolved that no change in my face should assist the recognition, but I felt the blood mount to my temples, and I could no more have withdrawn my eyes from hers than I could have lifted the old church in my arms. For a second her eyes fell under mine, then she lifted them again with the old appealing look which I remembered so well, her cheeks flushed, and a reproachful expression gathered around her mouth. If she had said : " I know it is you; how can you be so cruel, pretending not to know me? " it could not have been plainer. I smiled, and in one second there broke all over her face a light of rosy color and laughing gladness, and turning to Mrs. Allen and the Dominie, she spoke one eager word, pointing to me. In a moment more the dear old Dominie had my hands in his, and, too regardless of the place, we were talking breathlessly. It was well for us that an intermission in the exercises arrived at that moment. Once the barriers of my incognito were broken down, words could not come fast enough.

"I am very glad to see thee once more," were all the words of welcome Mrs. Allen spoke, but the eyes said more. And Ally, beautiful Ally, how shall I describe the myriad ways in which the child heart spoke through the woman's eyes and voice! The three years' interval seemed obliterated in her consciousness ; it was again "Brother Jim" and "Mr. Will," and the glad, merry, loving old life seemed to be going on, as fresh and untrammeled as ever, there on the platform of the old meeting-house, and under the eyes of hundreds of people.

"I knew you were here some time ago, Mr. Will," said Ally.

"How, Ally?" said I. She colored, but did not reply. "You have spoken to me once this morning, and did not know me," I continued. "That made it hard for me to be sure you knew me just now."

"Oh, no, Mr. Will," she said, earnestly. "That is not possible. I knew your face the instant I saw it. I had been looking slowly into all the faces near me to find you. I had been looking for an hour. I knew when you came in, I think."

It was probable, then, that when I had believed her eyes were lifted to my face, they were really fastened on Dominie, who was close behind me, and she did not see me at all. As I sat near her, the folds of her dress touching my feet; again the sharp electric thrill flashed from the floor to my brain. I bent over her and whispered,

"Ally, do you carry Stonie in your pocket?"

"Oh, no, not Stonie. He was lost, you know.

But I have Stonie's two friends here;" and she threw back her scarf and pointed to the two tourmalines hanging at her belt. They were fastened together by a twisted silver wire in shape of a cross, and swung by a long loop of the wire from her belt clasp.

"I keep them always with me," she went on. "I am just as much a baby as ever about them. Do you recollect?"

"Yes," I said.

"Well, it is just so now. Mamma thinks I shall outgrow it, but I do not believe I shall grow any more. Do you, Mr. Will?" she said with delicious archness. "And if I do, I believe the crystals will keep on telling me things as long as I live. If I put my hands on them I feel their power, and I can see things while I am touching them — things which are happening away from me. But mamma does not like to have me talk about it to any one. So I never do."

"Oh, dear me!" exclaimed Jim, "Tourmalines again! I'll cut them off your belt some day, Ally. They bewitch you and make you too bewitching, and she is bewitching enough without them. Isn't she, Will?" turning to me.

I could not answer. Something in his tone jarred upon me indescribably. Was this the Jim who had said to me once that he could not understand how boys spoke lightly of the wives they would one day have? Was it he who was speaking

in this jesting way of the witchery of the girl whom
he was to marry? Ally laughed, and her laugh
jarred upon me still more.

" No use, brother Jim," she said. " I should go
to Black Ledge and get others. Besides, Stonie is
coming back to me some day, and he is king."

Ally's child-like unconsciousness of self prevented
her seeing what we all saw, that the eyes of the
whole assembly were upon her. Her beauty, her
remarkable stature, her indescribable charm of
voice and smile, awaked the attention of every one
and held it spell-bound.

" Ally, my child," at last said Mrs. Allen, " thee
must not forget that thee is not at home. There
are many strangers here observing us."

Ally was as high-spirited as she was beautiful.
The old lamb-like docility had gone with the days
of suffering which had created it.

" Why should they observe us? How dare they
be so rude?" she said, with her eyes flashing and
turning suddenly toward the front of the platform,
unconsciously taking in the whole house in her
swift glance of resentment, and looking more superb than ever.

" By Jove, Will," exclaimed Jim, in a whisper,
" look at the galleries! We 'll have the whole college at her feet to-morrow!" and his face flushed
with pride.

" Oh, Jim," said I, " do let us get her away. I
can't endure to see them stare at her so."

"Why, you queer old Will," said Jim, "what do you mean! You ought to be just as proud as I. She's just as much your sister as mine."

"She is n't either your sister or mine, old fellow," said I, "and it's no place for a girl like her — up on this platform for a mob of men to look at. I'm going to take her farther back;" and I easily persuaded them all to move into a more retired seat, where we could talk more quietly.

The memory of the next two weeks is to me like the memory of a dream — a dream of a lifetime passed in some fairy land, through whose scenes floated one peerless being, robed in such robes as mortals do not wear. There were evening parties, and there were drives, and there were breakfasts and dinners, and there were days in cars, and days on mountain tops. After the exercises of the Commencement were over, we went to the White Mountains for a week, and then home to the parsonage. It is certain that I moved and spoke through it all like a calm and rational man, for no one wondered or demurred at anything I did; and the atmosphere of all our hours together was one of affectionate and unbroken hilarity; but the best proof of the overwrought state in which I was really living is the fact that when all was over, and I sat down at home to recall the incidents of the journey, I had literally not one single memory of any of the scenes through which I had passed. I had only a series of pictures of Ally, sometimes with a floating background of clouds, and sky, and silence ; sometimes with an equally misty one of the heads and faces and voices of people ; but all this, merely as background, frame-work for the one vivid, gleaming picture of Ally in her marvelous attire. Never before was woman so clothed. Her passionate, artistic sense, spent and wrought itself in the fashioning of every garment she wore. She would not allow Jim to send her any gowns except of plain colors, and made in absolute simplicity of style. Then she herself, with silks and flosses of the most exquisite hues, wrought upon each gown its chosen ornament. Embroidery was to her as inevitable an expression as verse to a poet. It was like no other embroidery ever seen, except in some of the rarest Japanese tapestries. How into the heart of this lonely little girl, in Maine, entered the conception of thus repeating and rendering nature, by simple stitches of silk, is one of the secrets of divine births which no common law explains. No one taught her. No one could learn from her. She copied a grass, a flower, a bird, with her needle, rapidly, as another artist might with a pencil. The stitches were strokes of color. That was all. They were long and massive, or they were light and fine, as need was ; looked at closely they were meaningless, and seemed chaotic ; but at the right distance the picture was perfect, — perfect because copied from nature, with that ineffable blending of accuracy and nspiration which marks the true artist.

One of the gowns she wore was a blue silk, — blue of that pale yet clear tint which summer skies take on at noon of the hottest days. On this were wrought pond lilies, cool, white, fragrant, golden-centred — just a lap full, no more — with a few trailing stems and green glistening pads, reaching to the hem, and falling back to right and left, — one big knot at the throat, and a cluster of buds and coiling stems on the wrist of each sleeve ; that was all ; but a queen might have been proud to wear the gown. Another was of soft white crape ; upon this she had wrought green and amber and silver white grasses, in a trailing wreath, yet hardly defined enough to be a wreath, across the shoulders, to the belt, from the belt carelessly across the front, to the hem, and then around the hem, which lay heavily on the ground. These gowns she had wrought especially to wear for "brother Jim," to do honor to his Commencement Day.

"Did they not take a great deal of time, Ally ? " said I. In my ignorance of the great difference between her type of work and ordinary embroidery, I had been sorry and surprised to see such evidences of love of mere ornamentation. I could not understand how Mrs. Allen had permitted it.

Ally laughed a little merry laugh.

"Not half so much time as to hem ruffles, Mr. Will," she said. "I did it at odd minutes."

"Can thee not show him how it is done, Ally,

dear ? " said Mrs. Allen, very quietly, with a twinkle in her eye.

Ally took the Dominie's white silk handkerchief
roguishly from his lap, saying : "I want it to give
Mr. Will an embroidery lesson on, papa." Then,
sitting down on a low cushion at my feet, she
looked up in my face, and as she threaded a large
needle with crimson floss, asked : —

"Now, what flower will you have, Mr. Will ? "

" A rose, Ally," I said, " if that is not too much
trouble."

"Oh no," she said.   "That is very easy."

In and out, in and out flew the needle — making
long loops at every stitch, as a crayon might make
long curves ; and in less than ten minutes a perfect,
many-leaved crimson rose had blossomed on the
silk.

" Now I will show you how easy it is to unmake
a rose," she said, smiling, half sadly ; "the petals
can go almost as quickly as they do in the wind."
After a few quick, short snaps of the scissors rosy
ends of the floss fluttered to the floor ; she pulled
out the rest, and held up the handkerchief spotless
white again.   "That rose has had its day," she
said, and fixed her eyes dreamily on the crimson
threads on the floor.   "It was n't a rose after all ;
is any rose a rose, Mr. Will ? "

Dimly I understood her, but my dull sense groped
vainly after the words which should carry my meaning.

"Yes, I know," she went on; "you are one of the people that believe that a rose is a rose. It is so many drachms of so many sorts of chemicals, and that's the end of it. But brother Jim and I — we don't think so. A rose is a great deal more than a rose; and the rose you see is a great deal less than the rose; and there's a conundrum for you," she laughed, tossing back the golden curls as if shaking off the sober thought.

"Brother Jim and I." The words sank into my heart. Yes, they two thought alike; they saw into the secrets of the rose. What was I, practical, realistic clodhopper that I was, to dare even to worship this glowing woman, whose soul could so illumine, possess, and interpret nature and life? And another sentence came to my memory at this moment — a sentence which Jim had spoken three years before. "She is all I have got in the world."

"May God do so to me and more also," I said to myself mentally, "if even in my heart I permit myself to long for my brother's wife — "

"Yes, Ally," I said aloud. "I can believe that a rose is a great deal more than a rose; but the rose I see is more than all roses, and there's a conundrum for you, my sister."

She looked at me for a second with an expression I could not fathom. I had never before called her sister.

"I am not your sister. I am brother Jim's sister," she said half petulantly. "You must n't think I love you as well as I do brother Jim, Mr. Will."

"No danger of that Ally," I said, laughing. "You told me a long time ago that there 'was n't any same as brother.' If you 'll love me half as well as you do brother Jim I 'll be satisfied."

"I remember the day I told you that," replied Ally. "It is very true," and she left the room.

I do not like even now to recall the memory of the first few weeks after I returned home from that fortnight's dream. The world believes that the keenest suffering and deepest joy are known by the idealistic and imaginative temperament. There seems a manifest absurdity in the attempt to compare the emotions of opposite temperaments. How can either measure the other, and shall one man know both? I dissent, however, from the world's verdict on this point. I believe that the idealist enjoys more but suffers less than the realist. The realist accepts his pain as he accepts other things in life, for what it is — actual present hopeless, irremediable. Face to face with the fact of it, he sits down and sees no escape. In the idealist, hope is always large and strong, and a certain joy in the great significant, solemn, undercurrent of life is never absent from him, even when the waters seem going over his head. I am quite sure that no possible future could have looked to either Jim or Ally so like a pall as my future life did to me during these days. Nothing but a strong physique, a certain quality of dogged pride, saved me from succumbing to the sense that life had nothing worth living for. How I cursed my folly in having exposed myself to the suffering! "The child I should have forgotten; the woman I never, never can forget," I groaned to myself daily. I destroyed Ally's picture. I destroyed every note I had of hers except the little bit of paper on which were written in the big childish letters: "If you were here I would kiss you." That I could not destroy. When I bade her good-by she gave me one of the tourmalines from her cross, and this I laughingly promised to wear always as a charm.

"Have a care, Will. There's more in those stones than you think," said Jim.

Indeed there was. I was distinctly conscious many times of an electric effect produced on my nerves by the stone. I unconsciously acquired the habit of holding it in my hand while I was reading, or whenever I sank into a reverie. Sometimes for days it would not give me any sensation whatever. Then suddenly, — whether from my own physical condition or from the state of the atmosphere, or from some subtle bond between it and its magnetized fellow hanging at Ally's belt, I cannot say, — it would give me sharp shock after shock, would seem, as Ally had said when she was a child, to "purr" in my hand, and would make me "see things" as it used to make her see them. Often, at such times, I would see the interior of the parsonage as vividly as if I were there. I would sink into a sort of clairvoyant trance, out of which I would rouse only by a strong effort of my will, and find myself cold, my hands and feet numb and pricking, and partially paralyzed for a few moments. I firmly believe that many times in these trances I saw as clairvoyants see things which were happening hundreds of miles away. There were many coincidences which I cannot relate here which established this point fully to my own mind, though they might not do so to others.

The hard and dreary days grew into weeks, months, years. Jim was studying at a theological seminary. His tender heart had drawn him strongly to seek some way of helping souls, and he had resolved to become a preacher. The parsonage life was going on placid, beautiful as ever. The Dominie and his wife were slowly nearing harbor, with the radiant light of a glowing sunset illumining their faces. Ally was the central delight and support of their lives. Jim's letters kept me fully informed of all which happened to them as well as to himself. His letters were fuller and fuller of Ally. I could not tell him that such letters gave me pain, neither was I wholly sure that they did me harm. They heightened my consciousness of the indissoluble bond between him and his adopted sister. Ally's genius was fast developing in many ways. Her passion for study was as great as her passionate love of beauty. As no summer could satiate ner heart with sunshine and flowers, so no knowledge could satiate her soul. When she was not drinking in nature or reproducing it in the wonderful tapestry-like embroidery, she was absorbed in study.

"Only think, Will!" Jim wrote in one of his letters. "Dominie has begun to teach Ally Hebrew. She begged so hard that he could not refuse her, and Ally says she likes it better than Greek; it is so much grander. Dominie says he has never had a pupil who learns languages as Ally does. She has intuitions about them just as she does about other things, and she never forgets."

Again he wrote: "Ally's flowers grow more and more wonderful. I only wish you could see the panels she has made for the corner cupboards in the sitting-room! You'd never know the old room. It is a perfect picture-gallery. I brought one of her pieces up to town last week, and the artists all say it is one of the most beautiful things ever seen in America, and entirely unique in its way. One of the fellows made me so angry. 'Why,' said he, 'this young lady could make thousands of dollars if she would put these things in the market. They would command any price for draperies of rooms or panels in doors.' Fancy Ally! I said very coldly that 'luckily this young lady was in no need of earning money,' and the man had the impudence to say that it was not 'luckily' at all; that art would be advanced if such works were known. I wanted to say to him that art was advanced whenever one true and beautiful thing was done, whether it ever came into what he called his market or not, — whether it were ever seen by any other eyes than the artist's or not. I 've a notion that art is only one form of truth, and that laws of growth of truth are as sure and steadfast as the laws of growth of a crystal. I reckon the tourmalines in Black Ledge never stop growing one second from the day they began, whether we are to find them to-day, or our children's grandchildren are to find them a hundred years hence. But I did 'nt argue with the fellow. He paints great pictures of Western territories, a county or two at a time, warranted to fit the largest dining-rooms, and gets thirty thousand dollars apiece for them. What 's the use of telling him that my darling's pansies and fox-gloves on a bit of white crape set in an old mahogany door in a Maine parsonage are dearer to the heart of the God of Art, and really a higher water mark in the Art Record, than all his acres of canvas ? "

It was not only that Jim's letters grew fuller and fuller of Ally. They grew fuller and fuller of expressions of fondness for her, of delight in her. While these maddened me, they also slowly awoke in my heart a feeling akin to scorn of Jim's love.

" He speaks of her as his darling to a third person," I said to myself. I could as soon hold up one of her golden curls to passers-by in the street and say, " Look at this for a color, my masters ! "

I was bitterly unjust to Jim in these days. Forgive me, my brother, forgive me.

It was near the end of the third year that I took from the post-office one day a letter addressed in Jim's handwriting. As I put it in my pocket I touched the tourmaline swinging from my chain, and felt a sharp electric thrill. I took the stone in my hand and fancied that it was warm. The electric pricking was stronger than I had felt it for months. "The letter is full of Ally, I suppose," I said to myself, and I went to my own room to read it. I fully expected that the letter was to tell me of their approaching marriage.

Like a man stunned, blinded, I groped my way through these opening sentences : —

"DEAR WILL, — I have something to tell you which will surprise you very much. I have made up my mind to go out to India as a missionary. This is no new idea. I have been thinking of it for months, but I thought it best, and kindest too, to say nothing of the plan until my resolution was fully taken. I have had for a long time a growing and unconquerable instinct that this was my proper work and my proper field for work. Of course you know me well enough to know that I have no intention of going out as the delegate, employee, or representative of any sect or any organization. I shall go independently, and after I get there I shall work as I see fit, just as I might in any city or town here. My fortune will enable me to do this, thank Heaven,

and to give material as well as spiritual help to the
people over whom my heart so strongly yearns.
The good missionaries in India will, no doubt, call
me a Buddhist, and include me in their labors. But
perhaps I can love them into liking me enough to
let me alone."

Here I threw the letter down. I could read no
more. I buried my face in my hands. "Oh, my
God!" I said, "to take that glorious girl to India,
to kill her, body and soul!"

Whenever I had dared to picture to myself Ally's
future as a wife, it had always been as the centre of
a perfect home, surrounded by all that her rich nature craved and could use of beauty, of culture, of
luxury. I had fancied the whole world itself laid
under tribute for her growth, her joy, as I myself
would have laid it had I won her love. Only too
well I knew the uselessness of attempting to influence Jim when one of his sentiments had suddenly
become a conviction and crystallized into a purpose.

"It is no use," I grieved. "He has taken India
just as he took Ally — into his very heart of hearts.
No earthly power could have moved him or can
now."

I picked the letter up and read on.

"I have made all my arrangements to go in a
month. Good-byes are hard, even when one has
so few to say as I have. The sooner they are over
the better. I have but one anxiety in going. Of

course you know what that is. It has been so great
that it has many times brought me to the verge of
abandoning my purpose. It is the leaving Ally,
my dear, sweet, darling sister. But she has a father
and a mother, and may I not say, dear Will, a
brother? I have settled on her unreservedly half
of my fortune, and dear old Guardy is to take care
of it for her as he always had for me."

Mechanically I folded the letter. Mechanically,
but with breathless rapidity, I moved about my
room, making all my arrangements for going to Jim
by the next train, which would start in a few minutes. I had but one distinct consciousness in my
brain ; it whirled back and forth, and back and
forth, in the one question : If Jim could leave Ally
like this, had he loved her as I thought? I must
know.

A day and a night and a day I rode with that
question, in a million shapes, mocking, comforting,
racking my soul. When I stood face to face with
Jim, in answer to his alarmed and eager "Why,
Will, Will, what has brought you? Are you in
trouble?" all I could do was to gasp out slowly,
syllable by syllable, the same question, —

"Jim, if you love Ally, how can you leave her
so ? "

My face more than the words told him the whole
story.

"Oh, my Will, my Will ! " he said, putting his
hands on my shoulders, and standing so closely

breast to breast with me that his breath was warm on my cheek. " I never once thought of Ally as a wife, never! God be praised that you love her. Oh, my grand old boy, how did you ever torture yourself so for nothing ? " he burst out, impatiently, throwing one arm around my neck in our old boyish fashion.

I had not slept, I had scarcely eaten, for seventy hours. I staggered and reeled, and Jim caught me in his arms. I felt that I looked up in his face helplessly, as a woman might. For one brief moment in our lives, he was the stronger man. He gave me wine, and tried to persuade me to rest. To all his persuasions I had but one answer, —

" I must go to Ally. There is no rest for me till I know."

It was a marvelous thing how strong a hope had sprung into instantaneous life in my heart. I had no shadow of reason to believe that Ally loved me. Yet I believed it.

" I will come back to you, Jim ; I will come back at once," I said, " but you must let me go. It is of no use to try to stop me."

He proposed to go with me. I was too overwrought to consider the cruelty of my words, and I exclaimed : —

" Not for worlds ! "

It seemed to me at that moment that to have seen Ally meet us, and throw her arms around her " brother Jim," before I knew that he was to her a brother as she was to him a sister, would have made of me a Cain.

Jim's nature was too thoroughly sweet for resentment !

"You are right, my dear fellow," he answered, "I should only be in the way."

Again I rode a day and a night and a day in the ceaseless din of the cars, with one question whirling back and forth and back and forth in my restless brain. The spring was just opening. All through New England's lovely meadows the appletrees were rosy pink and white. The sweet bridal colors flashed past my eyes, mile after mile, in significant beauty ; my life, too, had had a long winter ; I felt the thrill of its coming spring.

It was near sunset when I reached the town now so dear, which had looked so dismal and wretched to me when I first saw it six years before. I walked slowly toward the parsonage. For the first time since I left Jim's rooms, a misgiving forced itself upon me, whether I had done wisely in coming unannounced, and I dreaded the first moment of meeting. I need not have done so. It was true and right I should lose no second's time in hasting to Ally ; and the right always arranges itself. A few rods from the parsonage was a clump of tall firs. I paused behind these and gazed earnestly at the house. "Oh," I thought, "if Ally would only come out !" Involuntarily I laid my hand on the tourmaline, and recalled Ally's childish fancies

about her "Stonie." The crystal was highly elec·
tric at that moment, and I felt a sharp shock. At
that second the door of the house opened, and
Ally — my Ally — stood on the threshold.

She wore a white gown, and had a dark purple
scarf thrown over her shoulders. She looked up
and down the road as if expecting some one, —
then sat down on the door-step and leaned her
head against the wall, as she had done the morning
Jim and I had ridden away on the stage six years
ago. The clusters of purple lilac blossoms seemed
now, as they did then, to caress her golden curls —
curls as golden to-day as then. I was hidden from
her sight by the firs. I watched her for some mo·
ments. She sat motionless ; I could see that she
held in her fingers something swinging from her
belt. "Why does not the tourmaline tell her I am
here ?" I thought, and I laid my hand on my own
crystal, as I walked toward the house.

She rose slowly, looked earnestly toward me, and
then came with hesitating steps down the walk.
The almond flowers shook down a cloud of rosy
petals at the floating touch of her gown. I reached
the gate first, folded my arms on its upper bar, and
waited. She came toward me with her lips parted
in a smile such as I never saw on her face before
— such as I shall never see again, unless God takes
her first to heaven, to wait my coming there. No
trace of surprise — no shade of strangeness was on
her countenance.

" I thought you were coming to-night, Mr. Will,"
she said, as simply as she would have said it six
years before.

"Oh, Ally, how could you know!" I exclaimed.

"The same old way," she replied, smiling, but
still with a certain solemnity in the smile, and touching the tourmaline which swung at her belt. " I half
saw you, Mr. Will. I am all alone in the house.
Mother and father have gone to the prayer-meeting.
But I can be glad enough for three till they come
home."

" Can you be glad enough for the fourth, Ally ? "
said I.

She looked at me perplexedly.

"Oh, Ally — Ally," I exclaimed in a tone which
needed no syllables further to convey its meaning.

She did not tremble nor flush — she gazed steadily into my eyes, as if reading my inmost soul. Her
look was not one of gladness — it was of unutterable solemnity. We had reached the doorstep.
The lilac trees waved above our heads, and the
strong, sweet odor of the blossoms seemed to wrap
us as in a fragrant cloud. Still her bright, fearless,
loving, child-like, woman-full eyes gazed steadily
into mine, and she did not speak. I could not.

I put in her hand the little worn bit of paper
which had lain on my heart for five years. She unfolded it and read her own childish words : —

" If you were here I would kiss you, Mr. Will."

A faint rosy color mounted to her temples — to

her golden hair ; the look of solemn, earnest seek-ing deepened on her face, but into it there came a tenderness, an ineffable love, and, lifting her face to mine, she repeated in a low whisper the dear old childish words : —

" Shall I kiss you, Mr. Will ? " —

An hour later the bent figures of the beloved Dominie and his wife came slowly up the path un-der the firs. Arm in arm, with an unconscious and touching revelation of tenderness in their clinging hold on each other, they paused under the trees and looked up at the stars.

" Let us go and meet them, Ally," I said.

Hand in hand we walked swiftly toward them. When they first saw us they stopped in surprise for a second, then hurried on with ejaculations of joy and wonder. Mrs. Allen's clear-visioned eyes saw all in the first moment of our meeting.

" Oh, my children ! " she exclaimed, and even in the twilight I saw tears of gladness in her eyes. " Husband, husband," she continued, " they love each other."

Dear Dominie's slower sense but dimly compre-hended her meaning. As he looked into our faces it grew clear to him, and, lifting up both his hands, he blessed us. Then Ally left me and clung to her father's arm, and we walked slowly homeward. Mrs. Allen and I lingered at the door.

" I used to hope for this," she said, " in the first months of our knowing thee. Thee has the tem perament which our child requires. My great fear for her has been that she would love some man of an organization similar to her own. It is the danger of women of her temperament and mine, but I have learned that the great need of such a temperament is a trustful sense of rest, of calm tenderness, and the tendency to restrain rather than to stimulate the nervous life. Thee will do my child good as well as make her happy, just as my beloved husband has done for me."

" God bless you, mother, for saying this ! " I exclaimed. " Do you not really think there is danger of my being a clog to Ally? I feel so utterly unable even to comprehend her sometimes. I only know that I worship her."

" Undoubtedly thee will be a clog, as thee terms it, on a part of her nature, but it is a part which needs to be held down," replied the sweet, low, wise voice. " Thy tenderness will perpetually calm her unrest, thy practical wisdom will direct her swift fancy, and it will not be long before thee will smile to think that thee ever said thee could not comprehend her; and she will create in every hour of thy existence a new life of which thee has never so much as dreamed."

When I entered the sitting-room I started back, exclaiming : " Good heavens ! what room is this ? " Jim had told me often of the transformations that Ally's art had wrought in the room, but I was unprepared for it. I gazed from wall to wall in bewilderment. Ally stood by delightedly, saying : —

"Is it nice? Do you like it? We do, but nobody else who knows has seen it except brother Jim, and he thinks it is lovely because I did it, and if it were hideous he would think so all the same. The village people, some of them, say it is 'heathenish,' and when I told them that I was glad of it; that the people they called heathens knew a great deal more than we did, they looked at me as if they thought I was crazy."

"I wish thee had more patience with such ignorance, my daughter," said Mrs. Allen, quickly. "Thee could teach them what true beauty is, if thee would."

Ally shook her head impatiently.

"It would n't be of any use, mother dear. Nobody was ever taught what beauty is by being told. It 's just like my telling you it is warm by the thermometer when you are shivering. You don't mind a bit about my telling you it is over seventy degrees."

The Dominie laughed heartily at this sally. The one sole discomfort in the parsonage winter life was dear Mrs. Allen's need of a higher temperature than the Dominie's and Ally's more robust blood could endure.

"Nobody learns beauty," Ally went on. "You feel it in one second, if you ever can. If this room is beautiful, there will now and then come into it people who will see what it is, and they will be the better for it. It only hurts and hardens the others to tell them they ought to like it. And, as for explaining why a thing is beautiful, you can't. There is n't any why."

The room was indeed beautiful. Across three of the corners had been fitted book-shelves with doors of mahogany. The wood had been brought to the town by an old sea captain. He had brought it from Brazil, and it had lain a quarter of a century, waiting for him to grow rich enough to build a house. Before that time came he died, and the mahogany boards went to auction, with old sea chests and other rubbish. Dusty and unplaned as they were, the rich, dark wine-colored planks caught Ally's eye, and she had bought them herself, to the Dominie's great amusement. The doors were finished in long, narrow panels with a single molding. In the centre of each was framed one of Ally's flower-pieces ; in one, purple pansies on white ground ; in another, pale, shadowy white foxglove blossoms, in a cream-colored jar on a dark claret ground ; and in the third, amber and green and dark-red grasses on a light-blue ground. In the fourth corner stood the abutilon-trees, now grown to the ceiling, and branching wide like lilac bushes. A mantel-shelf and several brackets had been cut simply of the same mahogany, and along their front edges were set, like tiles, bands of the same flower embroidery, or of fantastic patterns like mosaics.

Cornices of the same were at the windows. The cornices were all of one pattern — mingled woodbine sprays of deep crimson on light blue. These were the most beautiful things in the room.

"That's the way our woodbine branches look in November, blowing between your eyes and the blue sky," said Ally, eagerly, as I was studying them and wondering how the combination could be so daring and seem so simple. The effect of all this dark mahogany was heightened by a pale uniform gray tint on the walls and in the carpet. There was no bright color on the floor except in the rug before the fire. The rug was of heavy gray felt. In one corner were two palm-trees, with gorgeous blue and red parrots swinging from their branches, the palm-trees copied truly from a photograph of a palm, and not looking in the least like the tall, flattened feather dusters which are the conventional rendering of the theoretical palm-tree. A mahogany easel stood in front of the abutilon-tree, and on this was a superb photograph of the Venus of Milo. The pure white statue gleamed out among the rich dark colorings about it. The furniture was covered with crimson and blue chintz, and the curtains were of a creamy white, of some curious filigreed Indian material, which had come from the treasures of the same old sea captain who had unwittingly brought all the way from the Brazil forests the settings for Ally's pictures.

"I hope the old man sees his mahogany now,'

said Ally, dreamily, " and I think he does. I often feel conscious of him, and in very hot days the wood purrs sometimes a little as my crystals do. They are of kin."

"Oh, Ally, what a room! what a room!" I ex· claimed. It was all I could say. The vivid, intense personality of the room overpowered me. It seemed strange that they could all be living a quiet every-day life in such surroundings.

"I'd love just to make a whole house like it," said Ally, sighing. The bareness of the parsonage was a grief to her; her artistic sense demanded harmony throughout.

" You shall, my Ally," I whispered, and forgetting that we were not alone, I folded her in my arms.

There is but a brief story left to tell of Ally's life and mine. I mean that the story which I shall tell is brief. When happiness begins, history stops. There is, however, in "Stonie's" life one more incident which belongs rightfully to the readers of this story. Ally and I were married before that year's apple blossoms had all fallen. There was no reason why we should wait; and Jim had made his one last request of us, that we would go with him to Europe on his way to India. Very earnestly he begged the Dominie and Mrs. Allen to go with us; but the old lovers refused.

" We are too old," they said. " The cities of this world do not draw us as they did. We expect very soon to see a fairer one."

They were right! God rest their souls! They died within one week of each other, in less than a year from the day of Ally's marriage.

Mrs. Allen died first. The Dominie died apparently of the same disease, but we who knew, knew that he died of her death.

Our first Christmas day was spent in Vienna. We lodged there with a queer old Professor whom Jim had met on a trip in the Austrian Tyrol. He was not poor, but spent all his money in making botanical and geological collections, to the displeasure of his wife, who had at last resolved to take lodgers as an offset for her husband's scientific extravagances.

" He will us ruin, mine Franz," she said, shrugging her shoulders. " He will, to sell the clothes off his back for one small stone ; and it is not that one can eat and drink from stones ! " But for all that Frau Scherkle was very fond of her Professor, and told us always when he was asked to dine at great houses, " because that he so much do know, they do not care for his so shabby coat."

As we were sitting at dinner on Christmas day, Professor Franz burst into the room unannounced, in a state of great excitement.

"Come, come all," he exclaimed. " Come this minute to the Museum. There are stones from your country, like the stones the beautiful madame wears at her belt. They are unpacking the casket now. Come, come ! The dinner is no matter."

Ally turned pale. I observed that she clasped her tourmaline cross in her right hand as she rose from the table.

"Let us go at once," she said, and in a few moments we were in the street, hurrying to keep up with the little Professor, who ran before us. "It is Stonie, Will," said Ally, in a low tone to me. "You need not laugh, I know it is."

Prof. Scherkle had admittance to all parts of the Museum. He led us to a large basement room, where we found workmen busily engaged in unpacking boxes of minerals. Those which had already been taken out were arranged upon a table in the centre of the room.

Ally walked swiftly to the table and pointed directly to a small red box.

There, in a cotton-lined compartment, alone by itself, transparent, flawless, rose red and vivid green, lay "Stonie!" We, who had known the stone so well, could never mistake it. There were other tourmalines in the box; all of them looked like ours; but of none of them could we be sure, except Stonie. It was the only one which had both terminations complete. It was the only one which had the layer of solid white, the "crown."

"King still," was all that Ally said. She was moved to her heart's depths.

We were all deeply stirred at this mysterious incident. All that we could learn from the persons in charge was, that these minerals had been bought

by the Austrian Government in Holland. They
had belonged to the antiquary Van der Null; and
this box of tourmalines was labeled simply "from
America."

"Could any of the stones be bought?" we asked.

"Nothing was less likely," we were told. "The
Imperial Museum did not trade."

"Oh, Will, I can't leave Stonie," pleaded Ally.

"You shall have him, love, if I can buy him and
have money enough left to take care of you with,"
whispered I.

What I paid to the illustrious Government of
Austria to buy back our own tourmaline I would
rather not tell. However, the sum, though large
for me, was small to them, and I know very well
the stone was not bought so much by money as by
Ally's eyes, and by the sweet voice and looks with
which she told the whole story to the Baron Roe-
derer, who introduced me to his cousin, the di-
rector of the Museum.

Stonie is very safe now; he is locked up every
night in a tiny jewel-box, which is also of tourmaline, and has a bit of history of its own. It is
an exquisite thing, made of thin layers of amber
and yellow tourmaline, fastened at the corners by
curious gold clamps, with serpents' heads. Jim
sent it to Ally on the anniversary of our wedding
day. In the letter accompanying it he wrote: —

"I send you a magic box to keep Stonie in. It
also is tourmaline. You see I can't escape the

mineral any more than you. Ceylon is full of them. This box was made by my most devoted lover and convert, Phaya Si Zai. He sat on the veranda of my cottage every day last week, tinkering away on it. That is the way the native jewelers do here. They bring their little furnaces and tools, squat on your veranda, and make your jewelry under your eye. Phaya will not take a cent for making this box, though it has cost him six days' work. The chasing, you will see, is very finely done. He has seen your picture hanging in my room, and when I showed him the stones and asked him if a box could be made of them for the pretty lady with gold hair, he said, eagerly: 'Yes, yes. Me make, me make.' When he brought it to me just now he said: 'Lady of gold hair — this — Phaya kiss the hands — stones make lady see Phaya; see good brother.' So you see even the Ceylonese know the spell of the tourmaline."

Our little girl seems to have the same love for and relation with the stones that her mother had. She will play with them for hours, as Ally did when she lay in her little bed, under the abutilon-tree, in the parsonage parlor. The child's name is Alice; but I have fallen into the way of calling her " Tourmie," and strangers stare when they ask what that means, and I reply: " Short for Tourmaline."

JOE HALE'S RED STOCKINGS

It was a hot day in August, and it was hotter in the linen room of the Menthaven Hospital than it was anywhere else on the New England shore. At least so thought Netty Larned, as she sank back in her chair, — if one can sink back in a wooden chair, — and exclaimed : —

"Thank heaven, the last of those stockings is darned."

Sarah Lincoln and her cousin, Netty Larned, in a fit of mingled patriotism and romance, had undertaken the charge of the linen room in the Menthaven Hospital for the summer. Their cousin, Clara Winthrop, was superintending the diet kitchen, and Rebecca Jones and Mrs. Kate Seeley, and several more of Menthaven's "first ladies," were nursing in the wards. It was in the second year of our war ; just at the time when the fever of enthusiastic work for the soldiers and the cause was at its greatest and most unreasonable height among the women of the North. Not to be sacrificing one's

self in some way on the shrine of the country's
need seemed to prove one to be next door to a
traitor — in fact worse. It seems ungracious, even
at this distance of time, to call in question either
the motives or the results of this great outburst on
the part of the women ; but no one who was familiar, in even a small degree, with the practical
results in many of our hospitals of the average
headlong enthusiasm of the average woman, will
deny that in very many instances it could have
been advantageously dispensed with.

The meek and satirical gratitude of the soldier
who, being inquired of by one of these restless
benevolences, if she should comb his hair for him,
replied : "Thank you, ma'am, you can if you want
to ; there's nineteen ladies has done it already to-
day," pointed a moral which was too generally
overlooked.

Some dim suspicions as to the common sense of
their work had more than once crossed the minds
of both Sarah Lincoln and Netty Larned. They
were clear-headed, energetic women, without a
trace of sentimentalism about them. It had appeared to them in the outset that there was a grand
field of work in the Menthaven Hospital, and that
it was clearly the duty of the Menthaven women to
take hold of it. Being, as I say, clear-headed, they
had too distinct a consciousness of their incapacity
as nurses, to undertake ward work ; in fact, when
they came to discuss seriously what they could do,

the charge of the linen room was the only thing they were not afraid to undertake.

"I can keep things in order, and mend, and make out lists, and give out clothes," said Netty; "and that's about all I can do and be sure of doing it well."

"I think so too," said Sarah, "and we'll take it together, and then we can change with each other and have a day's rest now and then; we shall not be very busy, and one or the other of us can go about in the wards and write letters for the men, or help the nurses. But I would n't take any responsibility about them for anything."

"Nor I either," said Netty.

But when they saw Clara Winthrop, who had never in her life cooked anything more nutritious than sponge-cake, and who was used, in her father's house, to having four servants at her command, gravely assuming the entire control of the diet kitchen; and flighty Mrs. Kate Seely, who could not even be trusted with her own baby when it had croup, installed as head nurse in one of the largest wards, Sarah and Netty looked at each other, and said, in the expressive New England vernacular, —

"Did you ever!"

And when they saw, day by day, the sentry opposite their linen room door, simply overborne and disregarded by numbers of most respectable women of their own acquaintance filing in, with baskets of all sorts of edibles, proper and improper, which they proposed to distribute indiscriminately among the patients, they looked at each other again and again, and said : —

"Would you have believed women were such geese ? "

"Did you tell those women that Doctor Hale's strict orders were that no one should be admitted to the wards without a pass from him ? " exclaimed Sarah one day, indignantly, to the sentry.

"Indeed ma'am, and I did," he replied, "but it did n't stop her. She said she knew Doctor Hale very well, and he would let her go in."

"But they must not go in," persisted Sarah. "It is against orders."

"What am I to do ma'am ? " said the sentry.

"Put your bayonet straight across the door, and hold it there, John," said Sarah.

"Ah, ma'am, an' I could n't to a woman. If it was a man I could ; but I could n't to a woman. Besides, she 'd jump over."

The next time, however, John tried it. Sarah heard a parley and flew to her door to reënforce John by the moral support of her countenance.

What to her horror did she see ? Her own aunt, Mrs. Winthrop, red with rage, and Clara behind her, both abusing the poor sentry in no measured terms, and threatening to report him for insolence.

"I am in charge of the diet kitchen," said Clara, "and my mother can go where she pleases in this hospital."

John lowered his bayonet, and the two angry women walked past him, darting withering glances at his discomfited face.

"It's no use, Netty," said Sarah after this. "It's no use. I do believe that ninety-nine women out of a hundred are absolutely destitute of logic. If you were to talk to Clara till the millennium, you could never make her see that her being in charge of the diet kitchen gives her no right to break Doctor Hale's rules."

As week after week went by, and Sarah and Netty set in the two hard wooden chairs in the linen room, mending, mending, mending, eight hours a day, there began, as I said, to cross their minds a dim distrust of the common sense of their proceedings.

"How much do you suppose I have saved the United States Government by mending that stocking?" said Netty, one day, holding up on her little round fist a stocking whose foot was one solid mass of darns.

Sarah laughed. "Oh, Netty," she said, "what did you mend that for? It wasn't worth it."

"I know that as well as you do," retorted Netty. "But we have barely enough to go round, and to-morrow's Saturday. I did hope that box from Provincetown would have had some stockings in it, but there was only one pair. Look at them!" and Netty held up a pair of socks knit of fine scarlet worsted on very fine needles. They were really beautiful socks, barring the color, which was a fiery yellow scarlet, but one remove from orange.

"Goodness!" exclaimed Sarah. "What lunatic ever knit those stockings? I don't believe a man in this hospital would put them on; do you?"

"No," said Netty. "It would n't be any use to offer them to them. I 'll put them at the bottom of the pile." As she slipped them under, she felt something in the toe of one. "Why, there is something in the toe," she said, and turned the stocking wrong side out. A small bit of pink paper, folded many times, fell to the floor. Netty picked it up and unfolded it. It was a half sheet of pink note paper, with a little stamped Cupid at top. In the middle of the sheet was written in a cramped but neat hand —

> "Miss Matilda Bennet,
>> "Provincetown,
>>> "Mass."

Netty exclaimed as she read this: "Why, how queer! Some girl 's put her name in here. What do you suppose she did that for?" and she read it aloud —

> "Miss Matilda Bennet,
>> "Provincetown,
>>> "Mass."

'What could she have done it for?" I wonder if she knit the stockings?"

"Perhaps she has a brother or lover in the war, and does n't know where he may be, and thought the stockings might happen to hit him," said Sarah, reaching out her hand for the paper, and looking at it curiously. "Is n't it odd? Who knows, now, but the man she meant that for may be in this very hospital!"

"I guess not," said Netty. "There is n't a single Massachusetts man here. They 're mostly from New York, and Maine, and Connecticut, so far as I have found out. I suppose I 'd better put it back," she said, folding the paper up, and holding the stocking open.

"Yes, indeed," said Sarah. "Put it back, by all means. Who knows what 'll come of it. It 's something like a letter in a bottle at sea!"

"What!" exclaimed Netty, in unutterable amazement; "like a bottle at sea! What 's the matter with you? What do you mean?"

Sarah colored: hidden very deep in her heart she had a vein of romance which did not show on the surface of her shrewd, active nature, and which never took form in words.

"Why, I mean," she replied, "that it is trusting a thing to just as blind chance to stick it in a stocking and send it to the Sanitary Commission to be allotted to any hospital between Maine and Mississippi, as it is to cork it in a bottle and toss it out in the Atlantic Ocean. Of course that girl put that name in that stocking to reach somebody, and I just hope it will reach him. I don't suppose it ever will, though, and yet, I imagine stranger things have happened."

" Perhaps she put it in just for fun," said Netty, as she pushed the little roll of paper tight down again into the stocking from which she had taken it. " I think that 's quite as likely. "

"Why, I don't see any fun in it," said Sarah.

" Nor I either," replied Netty; " but then things may seem funny in Provincetown which would n't anywhere else. It 's a real New England name, ' Matilda Bennet. ' I wonder how she looks. An old maid, I guess. I don't know why I think so."

" Well, if she did it for fun, as you say, it 's more likely to be a young girl," said Sarah. " A girl too young to think whether it were proper or not."

Early every Saturday morning clean clothes were given out in the hospital. All the convalescent men who were able came for their own ; and the ward nurses came for what they needed for the men who were in bed. It was always an interesting day to Netty and Sarah. They liked to survey the faces of the men, and to watch their behavior as they received the clothes. It was pathetic to see the importance which the little incident assumed in the lives of some of them, the child-like pleasure they would show in an especially nice garment, the difficulty they would find in selecting a pocket-handkerchief. The stockings were Netty's especial department; and she had endless amusement on the subject of sizes.

"Never yet did I hand a man a pair of stockings," she said, " that he did n't look at them, turn them
18

over, and hand them back to me, and say he'd like a pair either a little longer or a little shorter. It's too droll."

On this particular Saturday morning, Netty was much afraid the stockings would not hold out to go round. One or two pairs had come out of the wash so hopelessly ragged that even her patience had not been equal to the trials of mending them; and the washerwomen were still in arrears with part of the wash, so that the piles on the stocking shelf looked ominously low. By noon there were not a dozen pairs left.

"I'm going to begin to offer the scarlet ones, now," said Netty. "It's a shame not to use them, they're so nice. Perhaps I can put them off on somebody who is color-blind."

No man so color-blind as not to be startled at that flaming red! Man after man refused them. Netty held them out, saying with her most winning smile, "Here is a very nice pair of stockings; perhaps you like red;" but man after man replied, some timidly, some brusquely, that they'd rather have any other color. At last came a man who wanted two pairs, — one for himself, one for the man who slept in the next bed to him, and was asleep now; and the nurse thought he'd most likely not wake up before night, for he'd been taking laudanum for the toothache.

"Here's my chance," thought Netty, and laid the red stockings on the pile of clean clothes to be carried to the unconscious victim of the toothache

"I suppose he'll like these red stockings as well as any," said she, quietly. "They are very nice."

The man looked askance at them.

"Powerful bright, aint they? I should n't like 'em myself; but perhaps he won't mind;" and he walked away with them.

"What'll you wager they don't come back?" said Sarah.

"Nothing," said Netty. "I expect them."

The afternoon wore on, and the red stockings did not come back. The last man from the last ward had come, taken his Sunday ration of clean clothes, and gone, and not a single pair of stockings was left on the shelf.

"Was n't it lucky I put those red stockings off on that poor toothache fellow in his sleep?" laughed Netty. "I should have come one pair short if I had n't." The words had not more than left her lips when a shadow darkened the linen room. She looked up; there in the door-way stood the man who had taken the red stockings; he held them in his hand, and fidgeted with them uneasily as he said : —

"Sorry to trouble ye, marm, but Wilson's waked up, and he won't have these stockings no how; and I had to bring 'em back, if it would n't trouble ye too much to change 'em for something else; anything 'll do, he said, that aint red."

Netty pointed to the empty shelf; "I'm very sorry," she said; "but you can see, that is my stocking shelf; I have n't a pair left."

With a crestfallen face the man laid the stockings down and turned to go.

"Don't you think he would rather have those
than none?" asked Netty.

"No, marm," replied the man. "He said he'd
rather go barefoot than wear 'em. He can make
the ones he's got do."

"I will give him a clean pair as soon as some
more come in from the wash," said Netty. "You
tell him he won't have to wait till next Saturday;
by Tuesday we shall have more;" and she put the
rejected stockings back on the empty shelf. Sarah
was shaking with suppressed laughter.

"Poor Miss Matilda Bennet," said she, as soon
as the man had gone away. "Her red stockings
will never reach their destination, I fear. Who
knows? Perhaps the very man they were for has
already refused them. You'd better mention the
card in the toe to the next man you offer them to.
You might hit the right person."

"No," said Netty, "I shall not offer them any
more. I'll give them to a poor man I know in
town, who will not be so particular. They are
really beautiful socks. Any gentleman might wear
them."

The linen room was darkened again; another
tall figure stood in the door-way. It was Joe Hale,
the tallest, handsomest, best-natured man in the hospital, — favorite alike with surgeons, nurses, and
men; so brave while he lay ill with a terrible wound

in his shoulder ; so brave when the arm had to come off ; so jolly — which was the best bravery of all — now that it had been off and buried for many a week, and he was only waiting for his discharge papers to come from Washington before starting for home.

He stood in the door-way, twirling his cap nervously in his right hand ; luckily for Joe, it was the left arm which had gone.

Netty looked up.

" What can I do for you, Mr. Hale ? " she said.

" Have you got a pair of red stockings here? " he said, and a gleam of respectfully restrained mirth twinkled in his bright blue eyes.

Netty laughed outright.

" To be sure I have," she said, and took them from the shelf. " Here they are. I can't find anybody who will wear them."

" I 'll take them," said Joe, holding out his right hand, cap and all. " I gave mine to Wilson ; he is sort o' sick and fussy, and he was so mad with Craig for bringing them to him, it seemed to quite upset him — that and the laudanum together ; so I gave him mine. I had n't put them on ; and if you have n't any use for the red ones, I 'll take them, and obliged to ye. Craig said they were the last you 'd got left."

" So they are," replied Netty, laying them on the cap in Joe's hand. " I 'm very glad you don't dislike red. It 's a beautiful pair of stockings."

"Would you be so very good, ma'am, as to just put them in my pocket here?" said Joe, awkwardly. "I can't manage it very well."

Netty put them in the pocket, and with a military salute, Joe lifted his cap to his head and walked away.

"How thoughtless of me," said Netty, "to have laid them on the poor fellow's cap in his hand! He could n't put his cap on without their falling on the ground. Was n't it nice of him to give his to Wilson? I don't believe he likes the red any better than the other men did."

"It's just like Joe Hale," said Sarah.

"The ward-master in his ward told me the other day, he had n't the least idea what he'd do when Joe went away. He said he was equal to any two nurses in the ward. I've a notion, though, that he has a great fancy for the color red, for I've seen him a dozen times with a bit of red geranium or red salvia in his cap; he always picks out the red ones when Mrs. Winthrop brings her flowers."

Joe Hale was a methodical fellow. When he was preparing to go to bed, he laid all his clean clothes on the chair at the head of his bed to be ready in the morning. On the top of the pile he laid the red stockings.

"Hullo! Fire away, Joe!" called out one man. And another : —

"Warm yer toes, Joe, won't they?"

And another : —

"What possessed a woman to knit stockings o' such a color's that, do you suppose? Why, the turkey-cocks 'll chase ye, Joe, when ye get them things on."

Joe only laughed good-naturedly.

"Go it, boys," he said. "I can stand it's long's you can. I think the stockings are a real handsome color."

"So they be," said the first speaker. It was the very Wilson who had rejected them with such scorn. "So they be, a splendid color for a rooster's wattles; that's the only thing I ever see sech a color."

Joe took one of the stockings up and began mechanically to turn the heel out; he felt the paper in the toe, drew it out in surprise, looked at it, read the name, and slipped the paper quickly into his pocket. The whole thing had not taken a minute, and nobody had chanced to notice it.

"What in thunder did any girl go and do that for?" thought Joe.

Presently he rose and walked out of the ward.

"Say, Joe, don't leave them red stockings o' yourn out that way; they might be stole," called one of the men.

"All right, boys," he said, "laugh away. It's good for you; cure you quicker'n medicine;" and Joe walked away. He wanted to look again at the queer little pink paper. Underneath the big lan-

tern swung at the door of the surgeon's room, he
stood still and read again the words : —

> " Miss Matilda Bennet,
>> " Provincetown,
>>> " Mass."

He looked attentively at the little stamped Cupid
on the top of the sheet. Joe had no experience in
mythological art, and did not know a Cupid when
he saw one.   A naked baby with a bow and arrow
was as much of a puzzle to him as an unprecedented
fossil to a naturalist.   The word " Provincetown "
also set Joe to thinking. He recollected dimly
how on the map he studied at school the word
Provincetown stretched away from the tip of Massachusetts out into the blue space of the Atlantic
Ocean beyond.   It seemed to fly like a signal at a
prow, and the little dot which represented the
town had been half on, half off, the coast, he remembered.   " Poor thing ! " he thought, " she lives
away down there.   I wonder what sort of a girl she
is, and what she ever stuck her name into these
stockings for.   I might write and thank her for
them."

This last idea Joe dismissed with a scornful
laugh at himself as a " silly booby ; " but he folded
up the little pink paper, and put it away carefully
in his big leather wallet.

Three days later Joe Hale lay flat on his back

delirious with fever. He had been devoted in his
attentions to a poor fellow who was dying in one
of the outside tents from a gangrened wound, and
in some way that subtlest and most dangerous of
poisons had penetrated his veins.   For several
days he lay at the point of death; a general gloom
pervaded the hospital ; the surgeon-in-charge himself spent hours at Joe's bedside ; everybody grieved
at the thought of the brave, cheery fellow's dying.
But Joe's time to die was a long way off yet ; good
blood, and a constitution made strong by an early
out-door life on a farm, triumphed, — to everybody's
surprise and joy. Joe began to get well.   He
was as weak as a new-born infant at first, and sat
propped up in his bed among pillows, fed by spoon-
fuls at a time, looking a strange mixture of giant
and baby.   There was great danger of Joe's being
spoiled now, it became such a fashion to pet him.
All the visitors wanted to see him ; everybody
brought him something, generally something to eat ;
as for quince marmalade and tamarinds, for years
afterward the very name of them made Joe ill, he
had such a surfeit of them now.   Every day, as
soon as his too generous friends had left the ward,
he would summon the boys around his bed and distribute his supplies ; and very sumptuously that
ward fared for a good many weeks.   Foremost and
most devoted among Joe's admirers was Clara Winthrop.   There were petty-minded and gossiping
people about who even declared that Miss Win-

throp really neglected the diet kitchen, she spent so much time over "that Hale." One day, early in Joe's convalescence, Clara went to the linen room and called Sarah.

"Come here," she said. "I want to tell you something. You know that splendid fellow, Joe Hale, that's been so ill. Well, he is n't going to die. He's had his senses perfectly clear for two days now, and Dr. Wilkes says he'll pull through."

"Yes, I know," said Sarah. "I saw him this morning and he knew me perfectly."

"Oh, you saw him, did you?" said Clara, with a little dignified surprise in her manner.

"Oh, yes," said Sarah. "Netty and I have seen him every day."

"Ah!" said Clara, "I didn't know you had been seeing him all along."

Not least among the semi-comic things inwoven with all the tragedy of hospital life, was the queer, sexless sort of jealousy which women unconsciously and perpetually manifested among themselves, in regard to one and another of their pet patients.

Clara continued : —

"Well, I'm perfectly sure that he is engaged to some girl, or in love with her; and I think she ought to be sent for. Thomas, the ward-master, has been telling me about it. Thomas says that all the time Joe was out of his head, he was talking about a Matilda Somebody. He never made out the other name; but Thomas says he'd talk

about her all night, and about red stockings ; was n't
that queer ? Thomas said he had on a pair and
the men laughed at him about them. Now, don't
you think we ought to ask him about the Matilda,
and write to her ? "

Sarah opened her lips to say hastily, " Oh, I
know all about that," but suddenly recollecting
Clara Winthrop's constitutional inability to keep
a secret, she merely said : —

" I don't think he would like to know he had
been talking about his affairs that way. Joe is n 't
like the common soldiers here ; he is a very different sort of man. I should just ask him if there
was any friend or relative he 'd like to have written
to, and if he wants to have her sent for."

" Oh, yes," said Clara. " That would be a great
deal better. I 'll do that," and she hurried off, to
lose no time in following Sarah's advice.

" Why did n't you tell her ? " said Netty.

" Tell Clara Winthrop ! " ejaculated Sarah. " I
should think you 'd known the Winthrops as long
as I have. Why, I wouldn 't tell her anything which
I should have the slightest objection to seeing up
in posters on Main Street."

Netty laughed.

" Oh, that 's too bad," she said. " Clara would n't
tell anything that she thought would do any harm."

" I dare say not," retorted Sarah ; " but she
never thinks beforehand whether a thing will do
harm or not. She is not a bit malicious ; but she

does twice as much harm as if she were; a malicious person plots and plans, and has intervals and occasions of reticence; but Clara, — why, Clara's conversation is like nothing in earth but a waste-pipe from a cistern; as soon as it is full it overflows, no matter where, when, or on whom. Give me a good, malignant, intentional gossip any day, rather than one of these perpetual leaky people. What do you suppose she'll say to Joe now?"

" Oh, just what you told her to," said Netty.

" She is a well-meaning soul, and always ready to take advice."

" After all," said Sarah, "we don't know that Joe never heard of Matilda Bennet, except in that stocking."

" And as for that matter," continued the sensible Netty, "we don't know that it is not some other Matilda he was talking about."

" No," said Sarah, "of course we don't. I never once thought of that."

" Here are the red stockings again," said Netty, taking them out of the basket at her feet. "They don't want mending; that's one comfort. I'll lay them up till Joe gets well; I should n't wonder a bit if he fancied them. It will be a long time, though, poor fellow, before he'll do much walking."

That evening as Sarah and Netty and Clara were walking home from the hospital together, Sarah said : —

" Did you write a letter for Joe Hale to-day?"

"Oh!" exclaimed Clara. "That's just what I was going to tell you. It's the queerest thing about that Matilda ; I don't believe there's any such girl at all. I guess it was nothing but crazy fancies. I asked him this morning if there were not some one he would like to have me write to, — somebody who could come on and stay here with him till he got well ; and do you think, the poor fellow said, 'Miss Winthrop, I have n't a near relative in the world, — nothing nearer than a cousin ; and I don't know any of my cousins ; they all live in Iowa, and I 've never seen one of them.' Then I said, 'Well, have n't you some friend that could come ? or at any rate that you 'd like to have me write to ?' And he said, 'No, I have n't any friend that could come, unless it were a neighbor of mine, Ethan Lovejoy, he might come, but I guess I don't want him. I 'm getting on first rate.' 'Is n't there any woman ?' I said. I just was determined to see if there was n't something in it. And he got as red in the face as if I 'd asked him something improper, and said he, 'Any woman ! Why I told you I had n't any relative in the world. I had one sister, but she died when I was little. I don't remember her ; and the only aunt I have lives in Iowa, I told you.' So I gave up then. Is n't it too bad ; the poor lonely fellow ! I 'm really disappointed. I thought it would be so interesting if that Matilda should come on, and we could see them together. Perhaps there has been something in it, some time or other ; but it 's all broken off now. If it was only craziness it 's very queer he should stick to that one name all the time."

Sarah and Netty exchanged glances, but said nothing ; and the voluble Clara ran on and on, with her loose-jointed talk, till they reached the gate of her father's house. After she had gone in, Netty said to Sarah : —

" I 'm going into that ward to-morrow to write letters for Wilson and Craig. I think I 'll offer to write a letter for Joe, and see what he says to me. I think it 's just possible he did n't want Clara to write. She always thinks that she knows the men better than anybody else; but the truth is, she does n't know them half so well as either you or I. She is n't quiet enough with them."

" Yes, I would if I were you," replied Sarah ; " but you must n't tell Clara if he does let you write. She would be vexed about it."

" No, indeed," said Netty, " I won't tell her."

While Netty was writing the letters for Wilson and Craig, she saw Joe Hale watching her wistfully. When she had finished, she went to his bed and said : —

" Is n't there anybody you 'd like to send a letter to, Mr. Hale ? I have plenty of time to write another."

Joe glanced to the right and the left : the beds near him were empty ; no one was within hearing distance of a low tone. Speaking almost in a whisper, he said : —

"Well, it does feel real lonesome to see all the boys sending off their letters home ; but the fact is, Miss Larned, I have n't got a relation to write to — not one."

"Oh, I am perfectly sure your neighbors would be very glad to hear from you." Netty said, cheerily.

Joe glanced around again, and then speaking still lower, said : —

"No, there ain't one of them that I 'd bother with a letter. But there is a letter I 'd like to send, if you think it 's proper," and with his feeble right hand he managed to take from under his pillow the big leather wallet, and laying it near the edge of the bed, he tried to open it.

"Let me open it for you," said Netty. "Is the letter you want to answer in here ? "

"'Taint exactly a letter," said Joe. "That 's it," he said, pointing to the little bit of pink paper in one of the compartments, as Netty held them open.

"It ain't a letter," he continued. "It 's only a name. It was in one of those red stockings I took to please Wilson. Do you remember ? "

"Oh, yes, I remember all about it."

"I did n't dislike the color," said Joe, "though the boys did make most too much fun of them. Well, this paper was in the toe of one of those stockings, and I suppose it 's the name of the girl that knit them. Should n't you think so ? "

"Yes, I think it must be," said Netty.

"I 've been thinking," said Joe, "that it would n't

be any more than civil, seeing she put her name in
them, just to write and thank her for them. May
be she 'd like to know the name of the man that
wore them. I thought may be it was some little
girl that would be pleased to get a letter from a
soldier."

"Why, certainly, Mr. Hale," replied Netty. " I
think it would be a very nice thing to write and
thank her for them. I dare say it was some little
girl who would be proud enough to have a letter
from a soldier. What did you say the name was ?"

"It 's on the paper," said Joe, languidly. He
was growing tired. "Matilda 's the first name. I 've
forgotten the last, but she lives in Provincetown."

"Miss Matilda Bennet," said Netty, reading it
from the paper.

"Oh, yes," said Joe, "that 's it."

Netty wrote the address on an envelope, and
then, taking a sheet of note paper, looked at Joe,
inquiringly, and said : —

"Well, what shall I say ? "

"Oh, anything you like," was the embarrassing
reply, and Joe closed his eyes with an expression
of perfect content and assurance that all would be
right.

"Why, Mr. Hale," she said, " I 'm afraid I don't
know what to say. What do you want said ? "

"Oh, just thank her — that 's all," murmured
Joe, sleepily. "I guess it 's a little girl. I suppose
a grown-up woman would n't have sent her name

that way, would she ? You might ask her to write to me. Then I 'd have somebody to write to me. It 's the only thing makes me feel lonesome, when the boys all get letters."

" I 'd better write in my own name, I think," she said, "and tell her about you. Shall I do it that way ? "

"There is n't any use in telling her anything about me," said Joe, more energetically than he had spoken for some time ; only just to thank her, — that 's all."

This is what Netty wrote : —

" DEAR MISS BENNET : You will be surprised to receive this letter from an entire stranger. Perhaps you remember putting your name on a piece of paper in a pair of red stockings you sent to the soldiers. Those stockings came to this hospital, and were given to a soldier by the name of Hale — Mr. Joseph Hale, of New York. He is very ill now, — not able to sit up ; and he asked me to write and thank you for the stockings. If you would like to write him a letter, he would be very glad to hear from you. There is no greater pleasure to soldiers in hospital than to get letters from friends. Yours truly,

" HENRIETTA LARNED."

The coming in of the stage, and the distribution of the mail it carried were the great events of each

19

day in Provincetown. When the stage was on time
it got in at six o'clock; but its being on time de-
pended on so many incalculable chances all the
way along that sandy promontory, that nobody in
Provincetown thought of placing any dependence
on getting his letters the same night they came.
Least of all did the Bennets, who lived over on
Light-house Spit; they had kept the light-house for
twenty-five years, — ever since Matilda, or "Tilly,"
as she was universally called, could remember. It
was a strange life that she had led on that lonely
rock, — child, girl, woman, she had known nothing
else. Her father had been a sea-captain. He had
had a leg broken by the falling of a mast one night
in a terrible storm; had been brought into Provincetown harbor with the leg rudely spliced and
lashed to a spar, and had never walked without a
crutch again. The light-house was the next best
thing to a ship, and Captain Bennet was glad to
get it. The worse the storm, the more the old
tower — none too safe at best — rocked, the hap·
pier he grew. His wife used to say : —

"I believe, 'Lisha, you 'll never be contenteo
till we break loose here some night, and go head
foremost out to sea;" and the old man would
reply : —

"Well, Lyddy, I 'd as soon go that way 's any.
I never had any kind o' fancy for rottin' in a grave-
yard. The sea 's always seemed to me whole-
somer ; and if ye could manage it anyhow, I 'd

like to be buried in it ; but I s'pose ye could n't fix
it so very well."

Mrs. Bennet did not in the least share her husband's love of the water. It frightened her, and it
bored her, and she hated the isolation with which
it surrounded her. She paced the narrow sand-
spit which linked the light-house rock to the main-
land like a prisoner. When Tilly was a baby she
carried her in her arms ; as soon as the little thing
could toddle, she led her by the hand back and
forth, back and forth, on the narrow belt, always
gazing across at the town with a hungry yearning
for its streets and people, and with a restless watching for some boat to put out toward the light-
house. The child soon shared her mother's feeling,
and the earliest emotion which Tilly could recollect was an intense consciousness of being impris-
oned. In the summer there were visitors at the
light-house almost every day. All travelers who
visited Provincetown came over to see the beautiful Fresnel light, and the townspeople themselves
frequently sailed across and anchored for fishing
just beyond the spit. These visitors were Mrs.
Bennet's one consolation ; by means of them she
seemed to keep some tangible hold on life and
dry land ; and, moreover, they were the only foundation of her one air-castle. Poor, lonely, circum-
scribed, discontented woman ! she had but one,
yet that one seemed at first as far removed from
the possibility of her attaining it as could the wild-

est dream of the most visionary worldly ambition.
Mrs. Bennet wanted a melodeon for Tilly.   When
she went on Sundays to church in Provincetown
and heard the first line of the psalm-tune played
over and over on the wheezy melodeon, she thought
that if she could only sometimes hear such sounds
as that in the light-house, instead of the endless
boom and thud and swash of the water, life might
become endurable to her.   She had a marvelous
knack at crocheting mats, tidies, and the like ; and
as soon as Tilly's little fingers were strong enough
to hold a needle, they were instructed in the same
art.   In the long winter months a great stock of
these crocheted articles was accumulated to be
sold to the summer visitors.   Braided rugs, also,
Mrs. Bennet made to sell, and bed-quilts of scarlet
and white cottons sewed in intricate patterns.   The
small sums thus saved she hoarded as religiously
as if they were a trust and not her own.   She did
not reveal her purpose to Tilly for years, — not
until the child herself grew impatient of the mystery, and of being told that it was "for something
nice " the quarters and half-dollars were being put
away.   When Tilly knew what they were for she
worked harder than ever ; and at last, one June,
when she was sixteen years old, there came a day
— a proud day for Mrs. Bennet and a joyful one
for Tilly — when a small sloop pushed out from
the Provincetown wharves and made straight for
the light-house, bearing the melodeon, spick-span

new, smelling horribly of varnish, and not much more musical than a jew's-harp; it was yet beautiful beyond words to the two lonely women who had worked so many years to buy it. In Mrs. Bennet's early youth she had made some pretense of being a piano-player, and she thought that she could now recall enough of her old knowledge to give Tilly the elementary instructions; but she was sadly disappointed; the working of the pedals was a hopeless mystery to her, and the action of the keys, so unlike that of piano-keys, threw her all "out," as she said. "I never mistrusted 't was so different from a piano," she cried. "It's worse 'n a sewing-machine."

There was nothing to be done now but to let the child go to Provincetown to be taught. Luckily the purchase of the melodeon had not exhausted the treasury of the crochet money. There was enough left to give Tilly a winter's schooling in Provincetown; and if she spent more time over her melodeon than over her arithmetic, and tried all her teachers by her indifference to books, it was only a filial carrying out of the instructions of her mother, whose last words to her had been : "Now, learn all you can, Tilly. It's the only chance you'll get; but don't let anything hinder your learning to play the melodeon."

How long the lonely winter seemed to Mrs. Bennet, nobody, not even her husband, knew. For days at a time all communication between the

light-house and the town was cut off, and the poor
mother lay awake by night, and walked the floor
by day, praying that all might be well with Tilly.
But when, early in May, Tilly came home one
afternoon, looking as fresh and blooming as a rose,
and sat down at the melodeon and played "The
Soldier's Joy, with Variations," Mrs Bennet was
more than repaid for all she had borne. The six
months had told on Tilly in many ways. She had
smartened up in the matter of clothes ; wore bows
like other girls, and liked a bit of color in her hair ;
had learned to talk in a freer way, and could even
toss her head a little, when a young man spoke to
her. All the little awkward arts of the Provincetown belles Tilly had observed, and in a manner
caught. Yet she was not spoiled. She was glad
to come home : her mother was still more to her
than all the rest of the world ; and when Mrs. Bennet saw this she was content. Captain 'Lisha took
little notice one way or another of either of them.
His heart had always been, and always would be,
on the sea. He tended and scrubbed and loved
the light-house as he used to tend and love his
ship. He always called the light "she," and if a
point of its machinery seemed clogged, worried
and fussed over "her" as another man might over
a woman who was ill. But of the two women
whose days were spent on this rock because of him,
and whose whole lives revolved around him as husband and father, he thought comparatively little.

They were housed, fed, clothed, and busy; what more did they want? They seemed good-humored and contented; and so was Captain 'Lisha.

The melodeon made a change. Captain 'Lisha had a better ear for tunes than either his wife or his daughter. His whistling was worth hearing, and in his youth he had sung a good tenor. When he first heard Tilly's little feeble tunes mingling with the roar of the wind and water, he laughed, and thought it would do very well to amuse the women; but as time went on, and Tilly, who practiced with an untiring faithfulness worthy of a better instrument and a better talent, began to play something finer than "Fisher's Hornpipe" and "Soldier's Joy," the old man came to take pleasure in it. And this drew the three nearer together, so that after the melodeon had been in the house a couple of years the family were really much happier and had more animation in their life.

"Practice psalm-tunes, Tilly; practice psalm-tunes," her mother continually said. "There's no knowing what may happen," — by which Mrs. Bennet meant that out of her first air-castle had sprung up a second, in this wise: who could tell but that some day Tilly might be asked to play the melodeon in church. The Bennets were good Methodists and never missed a Sunday when the weather was fair enough for their sail-boat to get across to town. The melodeon in church was played by the minister's wife; but he would be going away pretty soon, — his two years were nearly up, and why should not Tilly be asked then to take Mrs. Sharp's place ?

Into the placid, monotonous and innocent dreams of these lives in the Provincetown light-house, the first news of the first days of our great war broke like a thunder-bolt ; nobody in all these United States felt the shock, felt the strain, felt the power of the war, as did lonely and inexperienced women in remote places. Every word of news from bat-tles was pondered by them and wept over; long intervals of no news, harder still to. bear, were en-dured in the meek silence which is born in women who live in solitude. Tilly and her mother were not exceptions to this. They were transformed by the excitement of the time. The melodeon was shut, and for a few weeks Tilly did nothing but implore her father to go to town for news ; and on days when he could not go, she watched on the rocks for the sight of somebody who might tell her the latest tidings. At last, one Sunday, when the minister called from the pulpit for all the women of the church to meet in the meeting-house the next day, to sew, to scrape lint, and to roll bandages, Mrs. Bennet could stand inaction no longer.

"I tell you what it is, Tilly," said she. "We'll go home and cook up a lot of things for your father, and then we'll come over here, and just stay an' work till this box is sent off. He can get along without us for a few days. It's the least he can do."

Captain 'Lisha made no objection, and on Tuesday morning he took Mrs. Bennet and Tilly over to the town, and left them there.

Tilly's cheeks were crimson with excitement. She was the swiftest-handed maiden in the meeting-house that week ; and her mother was not behind her. When on Saturday they went home they took with them an enormous bundle of shirts to be made.

"We can't be idle, either of us," said Mrs. Bennet. " Can we, Tilly ? "

"No, indeed," said Tilly. " I wish I had a hundred hands."

All day long they sewed, saving every minute of time possible from their household toils.

At twilight one evening, Tilly said : —

"Oh dear, I wish we'd brought over some yarn too. There's just this time between daylight and dark when we can't do anything, and I might be knitting."

" So we might," said Mrs. Bennet. "We haven't got any yarn, have we ? "

" There's that scarlet worsted," said Tilly. " I don't see why that wouldn't do. There's enough for two pairs I guess ; and we sha'n't ever use it up in the world."

This scarlet worsted was one of good Captain 'Lisha's blunders. He had been commissioned on a certain day, to buy in Provincetown, a few ounces of scarlet worsted. Mrs. Bennet wanted it for making narrow scarlet edges around some of her tidies and mats. Captain 'Lisha had made the mistake of buying pounds instead of ounces, and the shop-keeper had refused to take it back except in exchange for other goods ; whereupon Mrs. Bennet, not wanting any other goods, and wanting the money very much, had lost her temper, and carried the unlucky worsted home with her.

"It 's pretty bright," said Mrs. Bennet, "but I don't suppose the soldiers 'll be very particular about colors ; and we 've got it, that 's a good deal ; 't won't cost anything. I guess you 'd better set up a pair."

So Tilly set up the red stockings ; and after her hard day's sewing was done, she used to take the bright knitting-work and go out and sit on the rocks and knit, till her mother lighted the lamp in the kitchen, and her father lighted the lamp in the tower. Then she would go in and sew again till nine o'clock. While the women sewed, Captain 'Lisha read them the newspaper. Since the war began, Captain 'Lisha sailed to town every day ; rain or shine, blow high or blow low, his newspaper he must have. In the old times he had not cared if he did not get it for a week ; and sometimes when they had accumulated, did not even take the trouble to bring the whole pile home, which was a sore trial to his wife and daughter.

And this was the way the red stockings were knitted, — at short intervals of twilight on the rocks ; sunset hues, and quivering lights on the far ocean, and an honest-souled girl's reveries and sorrows about the war, — all went into them stitch by stitch, by stitch. What put it into Tilly's head to send her name in the stockings there is no knowing. She said : —

"I do wonder what poor fellow 'll get these. I 'd just like to stick my name in; it would seem sort of friendly, would n't it mother ? "

"Why, yes, Tilly, I 'd put it in. Some poor fellow might be real glad to know who was a-thinking of him."

And Tilly put it in. And the big box from Provincetown was sent up to Boston ; and from the rooms of the Sanitary Commission there it was sent on to the Menthaven Hospital.

One darkish night at Provincetown, Captain 'Lisha was just on the point of going home without his mail, the stage was so late. Not being very firm on his legs in a boat he did not like sailing across after dark.

" Hold on, Cap'n ! " sang out Tommy Swift, the postmaster. " Hold on, I 'll give ye your mail in a jiffy; here she comes."

The great, creaking, swinging coach rolled up to the door in a cloud of dust, the mail-bag was thrown from the top of the coach on to the post-office counter by a dexterous fling, and without even stopping, the coach rolled away again.

The Bennets very seldom had letters. They had
a daily paper from Boston; and they had a good
many miscellaneous newspapers sent them by a
minister uncle of Mrs. Bennet's, who was well to do,
and had more newspapers than he knew what to do
with. But a letter was an event; and a letter to
Tilly was still more of one.

Captain 'Lisha turned Netty's neat little letter
over and over again, and puzzled his brains vainly
trying to make out the postmark of which only the
" . . . haven " could be read.

" There's lots of ' havens ' all over the country,"
thought Captain ' Lisha ; "but we don't know anybody in any of 'em. It's a woman's writing ; it
might be some one of the last summer's folks writing for tidies."

" Here's a letter for you, Tilly," said Captain
'Lisha, as he entered the kitchen.

" A letter for me ! " cried Tilly.   " Why, who can
it be from ? "

" I was a wondering myself," said her father.
" I did n't know you wrote to anybody."

" I don't," said Tilly, slowly cutting the envelope
with a case-knife.

Mrs. Bennet dropped the skimmer, with which
she was taking doughnuts out of the boiling fat,
and came and looked over Tilly's shoulder.

" Oh, mother, mother ! The doughnuts will
burn," exclaimed Tilly.   " I 'll read it out loud to
you ; " and she followed her mother back to the

cooking-stove, and standing close by her side while she held the dripping doughnuts over the kettle, and shook them up and down on the skimmer, read aloud Netty's letter.

"Well, I must say that's a very proper kind of a letter," said Captain 'Lisha in a gratified tone. "That fellow's got the right feeling, whoever he is."

"What a pretty name Henrietta Larned is!" she said. "How pretty it looks written! She must be real nice, I'm sure."

"Well, the man's got a nice name, too," said Mrs. Bennet. "I like the sound of his name, — Joseph Hale. That's a good name. A New York man, she says?"

"Yes," said Tilly, slowly. "Perhaps he's dead before this time. She says he was too sick to sit up."

"Ye'll answer it, won't ye, Tilly?" said her father. "'T wouldn't be any more than civil, just to let him know ye got his message."

"I don't know," said Tilly, very slowly. "I hate to write letters. I haven't got anything to say to him. I might write to her."

"But she says write to him," said honest Mrs. Bennet; "she says they're so glad to get letters in the hospital. Poor fellows, I should think they would be. I expect hospitals are horrid places. I'd write to him if I was you, Tilly."

"You write, mother," said Tilly, laughing. "I don't know anything to say."

"Me, child?" said her mother. "I have n't written a letter for ten years; I could n't write; but I think you ought to. He might be a waitin' to hear; sick folks think a heap of little things like that."

"Well, I might just write and say I 'd got the letter," said Tilly. "'T was real pleasant in him to send me the message."

"Yes," said Captain 'Lisha. "That fellow's got right feelings. I tell you that."

Tilly carried the letter into her little bedroom and stuck it into the looking-glass frame, as she had seen cards placed.

The next morning her mother said : —

"Now, Tilly, I 'd answer that letter if I was you. It is n't often we get a chance to hear anything from the rest o' the world. I wish you 'd write. Besides, " she added, " after sending him your name so, it don't seem friendly not to."

"That 's true, mother," said Tilly. "I never thought of that, and I 'd just as lieves write as not, if I could think of anything to say."

That evening after all the work was done, the little kitchen in order, the lamps lighted, — the big one for the great, wandering ships at sea, and the little one for the quiet, humble family at home, — Tilly took out a small papeterie of dark-blue embossed leather, and, opening it with a sigh, said : —

"I 'll try to write that letter now, mother."

"That 's right," said her mother. "I 'd write if I was you."

This papeterie had been Tilly's one Christmas present the winter that she had been at school in town. It was given to her by a young man, who in a languid and shame-faced way had, in the Province-town vernacular "courted" her a little. But he had never found courage to take any more decided steps than to give her this papeterie filled with pink paper and envelopes all stamped with cupids, which so far as their mythological significance was con-cerned, were as much thrown away on Tilly as on Joe Hale. She merely thought them babies with bows and arrows, — quite ridiculous, and not very pretty. But there was no other letter-paper in the house, except the big sheets of ruled paper on which her father sent his official reports to Washing-ton, and Tilly would as soon have thought of writ-ing a book as of writing on paper of such size,

It was very hard work writing that letter. Tilly could not think of anything to say. She spoiled several sheets of paper, and at last the poor little letter stood as follows : —

"Mr. Hale :

Respected sir, "

This last phrase was suggested by Captain 'Lisha, on being consulted by Tilly and her mother as to what was the proper form of beginning such a let-ter. Captain 'Lisha could not think of anything more appropriate and dignified than the form he himself used when he wrote to an officer of the Light-house Board.

"Respected sir," therefore, the letter began, and continued as follows : —

"I am much obliged to you for your message. Please thank the lady that wrote it. I hope you are better now. We had the red worsted in the house ; that was the reason the stockings were that color. I knit them on the rocks. We live in the light-house. My father keeps it. We hope you are well —— "

"You said that once before, Tilly," interrupted her mother, as Tilly read the letter aloud.

Tilly looked distressed.

"Oh, so I did," she said, turning back, "No, not exactly. I said I hoped he was better. Won't it do ? "

"Yes, yes," said Mrs. Bennet, impatiently. She was quite vexed that Tilly's letter did not sound more like the elegant and flowing epistles which people always wrote to each other in the novels and magazine stories with which she was familiar. "I suppose it will do. It don't seem to me much of a letter, though."

"I can't think of anything to say," reiterated Tilly, hopelessly ; but thus adjured and coerced, she added one more sentence.

"It is very pleasant here now; in the winter it is very cold."

Then there came another interval of perplexity and consultation as to the signature. Captain 'Lisha had nothing better to offer than the "obedient servant" which represented his own relation to the officials at Washington. But to this Tilly stoutly objected.

"I ain't going to say I 'm his obedient servant!" she exclaimed defiantly. "I 'll just sign my name, and nothing more."

"You might say 'your friend,' I should think," said her mother, hesitatingly. "I don't think anybody ends off letters with just the name. I never saw one."

"Well, all the letters we ever have are from real friends or relations," said Tilly, firmly. "This is very different. I don't suppose it 's often anybody does write to a person they don't know."

Mrs. Bennet persisted in her argument for a more friendly ending; but on this point Tilly was firm, and the queer, stiff little letter went off, with its incongruous pink cupids hovering, like false colors at a mast-head, above the curt, cool sentences, and the brusque signature, "Matilda Bennet."

After the letter had gone, Mrs. Bennet frequently referred to it. The incident had really stirred her imagination more than it had Tilly's.

"I should n't wonder if that soldier wrote to you

20

himself some day when he's a gettin' better," she said.

"Perhaps he died," said Tilly; "that's just as likely."

"I suppose 't is," replied her mother. "But somehow I don't feel 's if he did. I wish you 'd written him more of a letter, and asked him to write to us. It would be real nice to get letters regular from somebody in the war."

"Why, mother!" exclaimed Tilly, "perhaps we should n't like him a bit if we knew him; we don't know anything about him."

"Well," said Mrs. Bennet, "I don't believe that lady would have written for him if he had n't been a real good fellow. And anyhow, it was real good his thinking to thank you for the stockings."

"Yes. That was real thoughtful of him," said Tilly, candidly.

How would both Mrs. Bennet and Tilly have laughed and wondered could they have seen Joe when he read his Provincetown letter! He had looked forward to its coming with considerable interest. More than once he had said to Netty : —

"Do you think she 'll answer that letter — that little girl, or whoever 't is, in Provincetown?" and Netty always replied : —

"Yes, I rather think she will, before long; I think she will want to hear from you again."

When the letter came at last, Joe was really astonished at himself, for the eagerness with which he tore it open. He read it twice, then folded it up, laughing heartily as he did so, and put it in his wallet in the same compartment with the first bit of pink paper.

"Now, I guess Miss Larned will say I was right," he thought. "If that ain't a little girl's letter, I never read one," and Joe watched impatiently for a chance to show the letter to Netty. It did not come for many days. Netty was busy, and did not go to the wards as usual. At last Joe could not wait any longer, and made bold to carry the letter to the linen room. He was so far recovered now that he walked about, and in a very few days would be well enough to go home. He found Netty alone in the linen room.

"Miss Larned," he said, "I hope you will excuse me if I interrupt you. I 've had a letter in answer to the one you wrote, and I thought, perhaps, you 'd like to see it, so I brought it."

"Indeed I should, very much," said Netty. "I was wondering the other day whether you had heard."

Joe watched Netty's face while she read the letter. The amused expression which stole over her features as she read did not escape him. His own eyes twinkled as he held out his hand to take the letter, and said : —

"You see it 's a little girl, Miss Larned. I 'll set all the more by them stockings for that ; could n't

I take them home with me if I give you the price
of another pair ? I 'd just like to keep them always,
to think of the little thing, sitting out on the rocks,
knitting away on stockings for the soldiers."

Netty was still studying the letter. She was
somewhat familiar with the constrained and reticent forms of rural New England's letter-writing.

" I 'm not sure yet about its being a little girl,
Mr. Hale," she said. "It may be ; but I incline
now to think that it is a grown-up woman, who
hardly ever writes a letter."

"Do you think so ? " said Joe, earnestly. " Well,
if it 's a woman, I 'd like first-rate to see her. I 've
come to have a real feeling, as if I ought to know
her, somehow."

Netty laughed.

"Nothing easier, Mr. Hale. It is not a very
long journey to Provincetown," she said.

"That 's so," said Joe ; "but it 's the last place
a man 's likely ever to go to, especially from New
York State."

" Sarah ! I do believe there 's a kind of romance
growing out of these red stockings, after all," said
Netty, when Sarah came in. " Joe Hale 's been
here, and showed me the drollest letter you ever
saw, from that Matilda Bennet. It begins : ' Respected sir,' and has just such droll, stiff, short
sentences as country people always write. He
thinks it is a little girl ; but I don't believe it. I
did n't want to tell him so ; but I 've a notion it 's

an old maid — a pretty old one, too. Still, some
of the phrases did sound simple enough for a child.
Joe wants to buy the stockings and carry them
home with him. He says he sets a store by them,
because this little thing knit them."

"Give them to him," said Sarah. "They are n't
any use here ; nobody else will wear them."

"I don't know that I 've any right to give them
away, without putting another pair in their place,"
replied Netty. "I think I 'll let him give me a
gray pair for them. He seems to have money of
his own ; I think I 'll let him buy them."

So a few days later, Joe set out for home with
the red stockings tucked snugly in a corner of his
valise, and a good new pair of gray ones in their
place on Netty's stocking shelf.

"Dear old fellow," said Netty to Sarah, after he
had bade them good-by ; "we have never had his
like in this hospital, and I don't believe we ever
shall."

"His like is n't very often found," replied Sarah,
quietly. "I consider Joe Hale a remarkable man.
If he had had education, he would have been a real
force in the world, somewhere ; he is, as it is, by
the sheer weight of his superb physique and overflowing good-heartedness ; but I 'd have liked to
see what breeding and education could have done
for him."

"Hurt the physique, very likely, and cooled the
good-heartedness," replied Netty. "That 's the

way, too often ; but I don't call Joe Hale exactly an uneducated man, Sarah."

" No, not as uneducated as he might be," replied Sarah. " He is just the sort of man, so far as education goes, which America is filling up with fast ; a creature too much informed to be called ignorant, but too ignorant to be called educated in any sense of the word. I am not at all sure that masses of this sort of well-informed ignorance are desirable material for a nation."

" Oh, you traitor to the republic ! " cried Netty.

" Yes," replied Sarah, severely ; " my countrymen prevent my thinking so well of my country as I would like to."

" Walpole said that better," retorted Netty. " Of all things to plagiarize a treason ! "

Joe Hale's home was in Western New York, in the beautiful Genesee Valley. His father had been one of the pioneer settlers in that region, and the log-cabin in which Joe's oldest brothers and sisters had been born was still standing, and did good duty as a wheat barn. The farm was a large and productive one, and the Hales had always taken their position among the well-to-do and influential people of the county. But a strange fatality of death seemed to pursue the family. Joe's father was killed by falling from a beam in his own barn ; and Joe's eldest brother was crushed to death by a favorite bull of his. It was never known whether the animal did it in play or in rage. Joe's eldest

sister had married and gone to Iowa to live ; the
other had died when Joe was a little boy, and Joe
and his mother lived alone on the farm for many
years. Mrs. Hale was a singularly strong, vigorous woman, but she was cut down in a single week
by a sharp attack of pneumonia the very spring
before the war broke out. This left Joe all alone
in the world, and when he found the men in his
town holding back from enlisting, and buying sub-
stitutes, he said, half sadly, half cheerily, " I 'm one
of the men to go, that 's certain. There 's nobody
needs me."

And now after one short year's fighting, he had
.come home a crippled man, to take up the old life
alone. It was not a cheering outlook ; and as he
drew near the homestead, and saw again the grand
stretches of old woods in which he had so often
made his axe ring on the hickory trees, Joe thought
to himself : —

" I don't know what a one-armed man is good
for, anyhow."

The cordiality with which his neighbors welcomed him back, the eager interest with which
they all listened to his accounts of the battles he
had been in, lessened this sense of loneliness for a
short time. But the town was a small, thinly-set-
tled one ; in a few weeks everybody had heard all
Joe had to tell ; nobody said any longer, " Have
you seen poor Joe Hale with his one arm ?" The
novelty had all worn off, the town went its way as

before, and Joe found himself more solitary than ever.

When he went to the war he left the farm in charge of a faithful laborer who had worked on it for years; this man had married, and he and his wife and children now occupied the house in which Joe had lived so long with his mother. The house was large, and there was room enough and to spare for Joe; but it seemed sadly unlike home; yet any other place seemed still more unlike home. Poor Joe did not know what to do.

"You'll have to get married, Joe, now, and settle down," the neighbors said to him continually.

"Married!" Joe would answer, and point to his empty coat-sleeve. "That looks like it, does n't it!" And an almost bitter sense of deprivation took root in his heart.

One night, when he felt especially lonely, he went up stairs to his room early. He sat on the edge of the bed and looked about the room. It had been his mother's room. All the furniture stood as she had left it; and yet an indefinable air of neglect and disorder had crept into the room.

"I can't live this way," thought Joe; "that's certain. But I don't suppose any woman would marry a fellow with only one arm. I'll have to get a housekeeper;" and Joe ran over in his mind the names of all the possible candidates he could think of for that office; not one seemed endurable to him, and, with a sigh, he tried to dismiss the sub-

ject from his mind. As he undressed, his big wallet fell to the floor, and out of it fell Tilly's little
pink letter. He picked it up carelessly, not seeing,
at first, what it was. As he recognized it, he felt a
thrill of pleasure. There seemed one link at least
between himself and some human being.

"I declare I'll write to that child to-morrow," he
thought. "I wonder if she would n't like to come
up here and stay a spell this fall,—she and her
mother,—and get away from those rocks. It would
be a real change for them," thought kind-hearted
Joe. "I guess I'll ask them. I reckon they're
plain people that would n't be put out by the way
things go here."

And somewhat cheered by this thought, Joe fell
asleep. In the morning he wrote his letter and
sent it off. It was not quite so stiffly phrased as
Tilly's, but it was by no means a fair exponent of
Joe's off-hand, merry, and affectionate nature. It
answered the main point, however. It continued
the correspondence, and it carried Joe's good will.

"Well, really!" exclaimed Mrs. Bennet, after
Tilly had read it aloud to her; "well, really, I call
that the handsomest kind of a letter; don't you,
'Lisha? Of course we should n't think of going,
but I think it was uncommon good of him to ask
us; don't you, 'Lisha?"

Tilly said nothing.

"Ye–es," replied Captain 'Lisha, slowly, as if he
were not sure whether he intended to say yes or

no.   "Ye–es, it's a very handsome invitation, certain; nobody can dispute that; but it seems queer
he should want to invite folks he don't know anything about. It's bounden queer, I think. Let me
see the letter." Captain 'Lisha straightened his
spectacles on his nose, and read the letter through
very slowly. Then he folded it and laid it on the
table, and brought down his hand hard on it, and
said again: "It's bounden queer."

Tilly said nothing.

"What's the matter with you?" said her mother,
a little sharply. "What's your notion about it."

Tilly laughed an odd little laugh.

"He's got the idea I'm a little girl," she said.
"I see it just as plain as anything. That's what
makes him write 's he does."

"No such a thing, Tilly," said Mrs. Bennet, in
an excited tone. "What makes you think so?
I'm sure I don't see it."

It was an instinct rather than a specific inter-
pretation of any one sentence which had made
Tilly so sure; she could hardly justify it to her
mother, though it was clear enough to herself; so
she replied, meekly: —

"I don't know."

Mrs. Bennet snatched the letter, and exclaimed:
"I'll read it again! It's the silliest notion I ever
heard of. I don't see what put it into your head,
Matilda Bennet!"

Tilly said nothing. On a second reading of the
letter, Mrs. Bennet was more vehement than ever.

"It's no such thing!" she exclaimed. "Do you think so, 'Lisha? Do you see anything in it?"

"I don't know," answered Captain 'Lisha, slowly as before. "It's bounden queer; it's a handsome invitation, but it's bounden queer;" and that was all that could be got out of Captain 'Lisha.

"Well, I'm goin' to answer this letter myself," said Mrs. Bennet resolutely. "I aint no hand to letter-write; but I'm goin' to write this time myself."

"Oh, mother, will you?" exclaimed Tilly, with great animation. "That's good. I was dreading it so."

"Humph!" said Mrs. Bennet. "When I was your age, I'd ha' jumped at the chance of getting letters from most anybody, ef I'd ha' been cooped up 's you are on a narrow strip o' what's neither land nor water. But you need n't answer Mr. Hale's letter if you don't want to. I can make out to write something that 'll pass muster for a letter, I reckon; and I think the man's real friendly."

"All right, mother," said Tilly. "I'm real glad you're going to write the letter. You might tell him that I was twenty-six years old last August, and see what he says to that when he writes. You'll find I was right. I know he thinks I'm a little girl," and Tilly laughed out a merry and mischievous laugh.

What Mrs. Bennet wrote they never knew; to neither Captain 'Lisha nor Tilly would she read her letter.

"Seems to me this is a mighty thick letter, wife," said Captain 'Lisha when he took it from her hands to carry it to the office. "What have you been sayin'? "

"Oh, not much," replied Mrs. Bennet. "It 's on that thick paper o' yours. I just thanked him for his invitation and told him how much we 'd like to come; but we could n't think on 't — and a few more things."

"The "few more things" were the gist of the letter. After the opening generalities of courtesy, which Mrs. Bennet managed much better than Tilly had in her little note, came the following extra-ordinary paragraph : —

"Tilly, — we always call her Tilly for short, but her name is Matilda, same as she signed your let-ter, — she 's got it into her head that you thought she was a little girl, from her letter. Now, we 've had some words about this. I don't see anything in your letter to make it out of, and if you would n't think it too much trouble, I 'd take it very kindly of you if you 'd write and say what 's the truth about it. 'T ain't often I care which end of a quar-rel I come out of, so long 's I know I 'm right; but there ain't any knowing who is right in this one, unless by what you say; and Tilly and me we 've had a good many words about it, first and last. Tilly 's twenty-six, going on twenty-seven ; birth-day was last August ; so she and me are more like sisters than anything else. She 's a good girl, if I am her mother; and I 'd have liked first-rate to bring her out to your place if we could have fetched it about; but we could n't nohow. It 's a lonesome place here for a girl.

> " Yours with respect,
>> " MARTHA BENNET.

" P. S. If you should ever be traveling in these parts, which I don't suppose is any ways likely, we should be glad to see you in our house; and a room ready for you, and welcome, if you could get along with the water."

When Joe first read Mrs. Bennet's letter, he said "Whew!" then he read the letter over, and said again louder than before, —

"Whew! Did n't I put my foot in it that time. I don't wonder the girl got her mother to write for her! — She must have thought me monstrous impudent to write her to come out here visiting, — a woman — as old as I am, pretty nearly. By jingoes, I don't know what to do now. I 'd like to see what sort of a girl she is, anyhow. I don't care ! — that letter of hers did sound just like a child's letter ! I expect she 's a real innocent kind of a woman, and that 's the kind I like."

At last, out of the honesty of his nature came the solution of the dilemma; he told the exact truth, and it had a gracious and civil sound, even in Joe's unvarnished speech.

" I did wonder if it was n't a little girl," he wrote,
" because she spoke so honest about the red yarn
and about the light-house, and most of the grown-
up women I know ain't quite so honest spoken.
But the lady at the hospital who wrote for me first
— Miss Larned — said she did n't think it was a
little girl ; and of course she could tell better than
I could, being a woman herself."

Then Joe said that he should like to come to
Provincetown, but his business never took him that
way, and then he reiterated his invitation to them
to come to see him.

"Since I made so bold as to ask you the first
time, you 'll forgive my asking you over again.   I
do really wish you could see your way to come," he
said.   It 's very pretty here in the fall, our apples
are just beginning to be ripe, and there ain't any
such apples anywhere ever I 've been as in the
Genesee Valley."

Then Joe added his "best respects " to Mrs.
Bennet's daughter, and closed his letter.

If there had been in the circle of Joe's acquaintance now one even moderately attractive marriage-
able woman, Joe would have drifted into falling in
love with her, as inevitably as an apple falls off its
stem when its days of ripening are numbered ; but
there was not.   Joe's own set of boys and girls
were heads of households now, and for the next
younger set, Joe was too old.   Young girls did not
please him ; partly, perhaps, because he saw, or

fancied, that they shrank a little from his armless
sleeve. By imperceptible degrees, vague thoughts
began to form and float in Joe's mind, akin to
thoughts which floated in Mrs. Bennet's before she
wrote her letter ; not tangible enough to be stated,
or to be matter of distinct consciousness, never
going further in words than "who knows ; " but all
the while drawing Joe slowly, surely toward Provincetown. He had thought that he would take a
journey to Iowa before the winter set in, and see
his aunt and his cousins and his married sister
there ; but gradually he fell into the way of thinking about a journey to the East first. Now, to suppose from all this that Joe had a romantic sentiment toward the unknown Matilda Bennet would
be quite wrong. He had nothing of the kind.
He had merely a vague but growing impulse to go
and see, as he phrased it, "what she was like."
As week after week passed and he received no reply to his letter, this impulse increased. He had
thought Mrs. Bennet would write again ; she seemed
to Joe to wield rather a glib pen ; he had supposed
he should have an active correspondence "with the
old lady," as he always called her in his own mind ;
but no letter came. Mrs. Bennet builded better
than she knew, when she left Joe to himself so
many weeks. His letter had given her great satisfaction. She read it aloud to Tilly and to her
husband, and consoled herself by her partial defeat
'n her argument with Tilly by saying : "Well, he

only says he wondered ; and the lady told him it was n't a child, and he knew she knew best ; that ain't really making up his mind ; I don't call it so by a long shot ; " and there the quarrel rested. Tilly was content, and if the whole truth were known, a little more than content, that " the soldier," as she always called their unknown correspondent, knew now that she was "grown up." Tilly had built no air-castles. She often thought she wished she could see " the soldier," but she had no more expectation of seeing him than of seeing General McClellan. Tilly was, as her mother had said, a good girl. She loved her melodeon ; and she still spent two hours a day at her practicing. She had for several weeks now played in church, and that gave her a new stimulus to practice. For the rest, she helped her mother, she sewed for the soldiers, and still knitted at twilight on the rocks, stockings — of gray yarn, now — to be sent to hospitals.

One night, late in October, when the stage drove up to the Provincetown Hotel, the loungers on the piazza were surprised to see alighting from it a one-armed man, in a heavy army overcoat. His speech was not that of a military man, and his reticence as to his plans and purposes was baffling.

" Been in the war, eh ? " said one, nodding toward the empty sleeve.

" Yes," said Joe, curtly.

" Discharged, I suppose."

"Yes," said Joe. "They don't have much use for men in my fix."

"Got leisure to look round ye, a little, now, then," said the first speaker.

"Yes," said Joe.

They could not make anything out of him, and the street speculated no little before it went to sleep that night, as to what that "army feller" was after. If anybody had said that the "army feller" had come all the way to Provincetown solely to see what "Tilly Bennet was like," the town would have given utterance to one ejaculation of astonishment, and wondered what on earth there was in Tilly Bennet to bring a man all that distance.

But Joe did not think so the next morning, when, having hired a man to take him over to the lighthouse, he landed on the rocks at noon, just as Tilly was hanging out clothes. The clothes-line was fastened to iron stanchions in the light-house itself, and in high cliffs to the back of it; a gale was blowing; in fact, it had been so high that the boatman had demurred at first about taking Joe across, as he was not used to the sea.

"Go ahead," said Joe. "If you can stand it, I can."

But, if the truth were told, Joe was pretty white about the lips, and not very steady on the legs when he stepped ashore.

" A half hour longer 'd have made you sicker 'n death," said the man, eying him.

" That 's so," said Joe, with a desperate qualm. " Dry land for me, thank you."

" How long do ye want to stay ? " said the boat-man.

Joe looked up at the light-house — then at the tossing white-capped waves.

" Always," he said, laughing, " if it 's going to heave like that — not more than an hour, or may be half an hour," he added, seriously ; " it is n't going to blow any worse, is it ? "

" Oh no," said the man, " it 'll quiet down before long," and he prepared to make his boat fast.

Tilly was hard at work trying to fasten her clothes on the line. They never waited for quiet weather before hanging out their clothes at the light-house. It was of no use. Tilly's back was to-ward the wharf where Joe had landed. Her sleeves were rolled up to her shoulders, and her arms shone white in the sun. She had twisted a red silk hand-kerchief of her father's tight round her head; a few straggling curls of dark hair blew out from under this ; her cheeks were scarlet, and her brown eyes flashed in her contest with the wind. Nobody ever called Tilly pretty ; but she had a healthy, honest face, and at this moment she was pretty ; no — not pretty ; picturesque, which is far better than pretty, though Joe did not know that, and in his simplicity only wondered how a woman could look so handsome, blowing about in such a gale.

Tilly saw a stranger walking up to the light-house door; but she did not pause in her work. Strangers came every day. Joe's left side was farthest away from Tilly. She did not see the loose, hanging sleeve; and the blue of the army coat did not attract her notice, so she went on with her clothes without giving a second thought to the man who had disappeared in the big door of the light-house. Somebody to see her father, no doubt, or to see the light.

When Tilly went into the kitchen and saw the stranger sitting by the table talking familiarly with her mother, she was somewhat surprised, but was passing through the room with her big clothes-basket, when her mother, with an air of unconceal-able triumph, said: —

"Tilly, you couldn't guess who this is."

Tilly halted, basket in hand, and turned her scarlet cheeks and bright brown eyes full toward Joe.

"No, — I haven't the least idea," she said, and as she said it she looked so pretty, that Joe, absurd as it might seem, fe'' in love with her on the spot.

The words "I haven't the least idea," had hardly left her lips, when her eyes fell on the empty sleeve; and, although in no letter had it ever been said that Joe had lost an arm, this sight suggested him to her mind.

"Why, it isn't Mr. Hale, is it?" she said, turning still redder.

"It is, though," said Joe, rising and coming toward her, offering her his one hand. "You and your mother would n't come to see me, and so I came to see you."

Tilly's hand having been all the morning in hot soap-suds, was red and swollen and puckered, but it looked beautiful to Joe; so did Tilly's awkward little laugh, as she said, half drawing back her hand : —

"I 've been washing; that 's what makes my hands look so."

There was something in the infantile and superfluous honesty of this remark which reminded Joe instantly of the sentence in Tilly's letter: "We had the red worsted in the house. That is the reason the stockings were that color," and he smiled at the memory. His smile was such a cordial one that Tilly did not misinterpret it, and his spontaneous reply, as he took her hand in his, was worthy of a courtier.

"I often saw my mother's hands look like this, Miss Bennet. She always did a great part of the washing."

Tilly stood still looking ill at ease, and Joe stood still, also looking ill at ease. There seemed to be nothing now to say. Mrs. Bennet cut the Gordian knot, as she had cut one or two already.

"Go along, Tilly," she said. "Get off your washing duds; it 's near dinner time."

Tilly was glad to escape to her own room. Once

safe in refuge she sank into a chair with a most bewildered face and tried to collect her thoughts. She
seemed like one in a dream. "The soldier" had
come. How her heart ached over the thought of
that armless sleeve!

"He never said anything about his arm being
gone," thought Tilly. "It's too bad. How blue
his eyes are! I never saw such blue eyes!" in a
maze of innocent wonder and excitement. Her
thoughts so ran away with her that when her
mother called through the door, "Dinner's ready,
Tilly," poor Tilly was not half dressed, and kept
them waiting ten minutes or more, which drew
down upon her from her father a rebuke that it
hurt her sorely to have "the soldier" hear. But
"the soldier" was too happy to be disturbed by
small things. Since his mother's death Joe had not
seen anything so homelike, so familiar, as this
dinner in Mrs. Bennet's little kitchen. He made
friends with Captain 'Lisha at once; the old man
could not ask questions enough about the war,
and Joe answered them all with a patience which
was perhaps more commendable than his accuracy.
Tilly sat by, listening in eager silence; not a word
escaped her; when her eyes met Joe's she colored
and looked away.

"I don't care if she is twenty-six," thought Joe,
"she is just like a child."

Mrs. Bennet, with hospitable fervor, had insisted
that Joe should not go back to the town, but should

stay with them; "that is," she added, "if you think you can sleep with the water swash, swash, swashing in your ears. 'T was years before I ever could learn to sleep here; and there's times now when I don't sleep for whole nights together."

Joe thought he could sleep in spite of the water, and with the greatest alacrity sent his boatman back to town for his valise.

"After all," said the citizens, on hearing this, "after all he was only some relation of the Bennets."

But when day after day passed, and he did not return, the town began again to speculate as to his purposes. Some fishermen going or coming, had seen him walking on the rocks with Tilly; and very soon a rumor took to itself wings and went up and down the town, that the one-armed soldier was "courting Tilly Bennet."

The seclusion of the light-house had its advantages now, — very little could the Provincetown gossips know of what went on among those distant rocks. Very safe were Joe and Tilly in the nooks which they explored in the long bright afternoons. How strangely changed seemed the lonely spot to Tilly! Each rod of the wave-washed beach was transformed as she paced it with Joe by her side. No word of love-making did Joe say — not because it was not warm and ready in his heart, but he was afraid.

"Of course she can't care anything about me, all

of a sudden so," said sensible Joe, "She haint been a longing and a longing for somebody 's I have."

So at the end of the week he went away, — merely saying to Tilly and Mrs. Bennet as he bade them good-by, that he would write very soon. But Tilly's heart had not been so idle as Joe thought, and she was not surprised one day, a few weeks later, when she read in a letter of Joe's that he did n't know whether she knew it or not, but he had come to the conclusion that she was just about the nicest girl in all the country, and if she thought she could take up with a fellow that had n't but one arm, he was hers to command for the rest of her life.

Tilly had a happy little cry over the letter before she showed it to her mother.

"Do you think you can like him, Tilly?" asked Mrs. Bennet, anxiously.

"Yes," said Tilly, "I do like him; and he 's real good."

And when they told Captain 'Lisha, he said, vehemently, that nothing short of going to sea again could have pleased him so much.

So it was settled that at Christmas Joe should come back for Tilly.

When the engagement became known in town, there was great wonderment about it. How did the acquaintance begin? What brought the New Yorker to Provincetown?

But Tilly and her mother kept their secret to themselves, and not a soul in Provincetown ever heard a word of the red stockings, which was much better for all parties concerned.

The wedding was to be on Christmas day. Two weeks before that day, there swept over Provincetown harbor a storm the like of which had not been seen for half a century. The steeple of the old church fell ; the sea cut new paths for itself here and there among the low sand-dunes, and washed away landmarks older than men could remember ; great ships parted anchor, and were driven helplessly on the rocks, and the light-house swayed and rocked like a mast in the tempest. In the middle of the night the storm burst with a sudden fury. At its first roar Captain 'Lisha sprang up, and said, —

"Martha, this is going to be the devil's own night. I must go up into the light. I can't leave her alone such a storm's this."

From the dwelling-house to the light-house tower was only a short distance ; the rocks were shelving, but a stout iron railing protected the path on one side. Whether Captain 'Lisha failed to grasp this rail and slipped on the icy rocks, or whether he was swept off by the violence of the gale, could only be conjectured, but in the morning he did not come back. As soon as the storm had lulled a little, Mrs. Bennet crept cautiously across the slippery path-way, and climbed the winding stair to the light.

In a short time she returned, with a white, horror-stricken face, and in reply to Tilly's cry of alarm, gasped : —

"Your father's gone ! "

After the first shock of the death was over, Mrs. Bennet saw much to be grateful for in its manner; in her own inimitable way, she dilated on the satisfaction it must have been to Captain 'Lisha.

"It 's just what he was forever a sayin' he 'd like, to be buried in the sea, and especially to be washed overboard ; if I 've heard him say so once, I 've heard him a hundred times, and the Lord's took him at his word, and I don't believe there 's a happier spirit anywhere than 'Lisha's is, wherever 'tis he 's gone to."

In the Provincetown way of thinking, Captain ' Lisha's death was no reason why Tilly's marriage should be deferred, but rather why it should be hastened. It took place, as had been planned, on Christmas day.

The next day when Tilly and her mother bade everybody good-by, and went away with Tilly's manly, tall, kindly-eyed husband, everybody said, "What a Providence ! " and I make no manner of doubt that Joe and Tilly got on quite as well together, and were quite as happy as if they had known each other better and taken more time to consider the question of marrying.

It may not be foreign to our story to add that

after Joe had been married a week he recollected to send to Miss Henrietta Larned, at the Menthaven Hospital, a newspaper containing the announcement of his marriage. When Netty read it, she exclaimed in a low voice : —

"Good! Good!"

"What is it?" said Sarah. "Who's married now?"

"What put it into your head it was a marriage?" said Netty.

"I don't know," said Sarah, "your tone, I suppose."

Netty read the notice aloud.

"The very girl!" cried Sarah. "What a queer thing!"

"It's perfectly splendid!" said Netty. "What a nice husband Joe Hale will make! And now we'll tell Clara Winthrop!"

SUSAN LAWTON'S ESCAPE.

I NEVER heard of a girl who had her own way so completely, so delightfully, and so respectably as Susan Sweetser did. She was an only child. Her mother died when she was a baby; her father, who had never married again, died when she was sixteen. He left a large fortune, the income of which was to be paid to Susan until she was twenty-one, and at that time the whole estate was to come into her hands as unreservedly as if she had been a man. Her guardian, whose function was simply a nominal one, was her uncle by marriage, Thomas Lawton, a man not more than a dozen years older than herself, — an easy going, indolent, rich fellow, who never gave himself any concern about Susan further than the depositing in the bank each quarter the thousands of dollars which she might spend as she liked. Mrs. Thomas Lawton was a girl only a few years older than Susan, and one after her own heart; and when, two years after the death of her father, Susan took up her abode in the Lawton

household, nothing could be jollier than the life
the two women led together. The death of her
father was no personal loss to Susan; she had
seen him only in her brief school vacations; he
was a reserved and silent man, wholly absorbed in
making a fortune. He had always had the theory
that when the fortune was big enough, and Susan
was old enough to leave school, he would take
some leisure, enjoy himself, and become acquainted
with his daughter. But Death had other plans for
Mr. Sweetser. He cut him down one night, before
that interval of leisure had arrived, and before Susan was old enough to leave school, but not before
the fortune had grown large enough to satisfy the
utmost wants of any reasonable being. More because of her own interest in study than from any
exercise of authority or even influence on her
guardian's part, Susan remained at school two
years after her father's death. During these two
years she held, by virtue of her independence and
her riches, a position in the school which was
hardly that of a scholar. A young lady who had
a carriage and horses at her command, and thousands of dollars every quarter for the expenditure
of which she was responsible to nobody but herself, was not likely to be held in much restraint by
her teachers. Madame Delancy was only too glad
to avail herself of Miss Sweetser's carriage on occasion; and Miss Sweetser's generosity, in count-
less ways, smoothed difficulties in the Delancy

household, which was like all boarding-school households, straitened at times, and forced to keep up
show at expense of comfort. If Susan had not
been of a singularly sweet nature, this abnormal
freedom and independence, at the age of sixteen,
would have hurt her sadly. As it was, the chief
fault developed in her by her situation was an im-
periousness of will, or impatience, if obstacles of
any sort hindered her in carrying out a project.
But as her projects were usually of a magnanimous
and generous kind, this impatience did not seem
unlovely ; and the imperious manner was often
charming. Her schemes could not be said to be
unselfish, because they usually were for pleasures
or profits which she desired for herself ; but on the
other hand they could not be said to be selfish, because she made them so wide in their scope, including everybody she could easily reach. If she wanted
to go to an entertainment of any sort, she took her
whole class, sometimes the whole school ; when she
went to drive in her pretty, blue-lined carriage,
somebody else always went too, — Madame Delancy herself, or some teacher, or some friend.
When she wanted strawberries, she ordered them
into the house by the dozen boxes, and had them
given to everybody at breakfast. And she did not
do this with the least air of patronage or condescen-
sion ; she did not think about its being any favor to
people, or that she laid them under an obligation ;
she simply liked to do it ; it was her way ; there was

no special friendliness in it; no exalted notion
either about conferring happiness ; why she liked to
do so, she never thought; and if she had thought
and questioned, would have been puzzled to tell;
she did it as little children gregariously by instinct
do, when they exclaim, "Oh, let's do" this, or that,
or the other — "it will be so nice!" That this was
a surface and sensuous view of life, cannot be denied ; but then, we are not drawing an ideal character ; we are merely telling the exact truth about
Susan Sweetser. She was not a saint by any manner of means, nor the stuff of which saints are made.
She got no end of preaching to from pastors and
from self-elected advisers, who saw in the free-
souled young heiress a great opportunity for that
obnoxious practice known as "doing good." But
against all their lectures and sermons Susan's light-
heartedness was a more effectual barrier than the
hardest-heartedness in the world could have been.
When they came, asking her for money, she pulled
out her purse and gave it to them; not always so
much as they asked for, because on some such
points Susan had her own ideas of proportion and
disproportion ; yet she always gave liberally. But
when they came preaching to her that she herself
should do this and that, should go here and there,
should be this and that, Susan smiled pleasantly,
said little, but went on her way undisturbed. The
odd thing was that she kept this undisturbed pla-
cidity of being comfortable in her own fashion, in

spite of the most dogged orthodoxy of religious belief.

Just before Susan was eighteen years old, and a few weeks before her graduation at Madame Delancy's, Mr. Thomas Lawton died. Mrs. Lawton was now left as free and independent, and nearly as rich, as Susan. Her love for her husband had been very sincere as far as it went, but it had not been of such a nature as to make his death a heart-breaking thing to her. Life looked very attractive to Mrs. Thomas Lawton as one morning, a few months after her husband had died, and six weeks after Susan had left school, she and Susan sat together in the handsome library, planning what they would do for themselves for the winter.

" Bell," said Susan, energetically," it 's perfectly splendid that you can *chaperon* me everywhere! I 've always had a terror of the time when I 'd have to hire some lay figure of respectability to live with me and go about with me, and all that. I know I should have hated her. I expect I should have changed her as often as poor papa had to change cooks. But now it 's all right. You and I can go all over the world together. You can do what you like, because you 're a widow."

"Oh, don't Susan!" exclaimed Mrs. Lawton, deprecatingly. "How can you run on so?"

"Why, Bell, dear, I did n't mean to hurt your feelings," said Susan; but it 's true — a widow can go anywhere. If you had n't been married, you could n't *chaperon* me, don't you know? And your being my aunt makes it all the better. You'd never do for my *chaperon* in the world if it wer'n't for that, you young-looking thing, you! I declare you don't look a day older than I do!"

Mrs. Bell Lawton did, indeed, look very young in her widow's cap, which lay in its graceful Marie Stuart triangle very lightly on her pretty blond hair, and made her look, as widow's caps always make young and pretty woman look, far less like a mourner than she would have looked without it.

"Now, Susan, don't talk nonsense," said Mrs. Lawton. "You know I 'm twenty-five next month, and I 'm sure that is antiquated. Oh, dear, if I were only eighteen, like you!"

"What then?" asked honest Susan. "Why is eighteen any better than twenty-five, Bell?"

"Oh, I don't know," replied Bell, confusedly. "I don't suppose it is any better?"

"I don't think it 's half so good," said Susan; "or, at any rate, half so good as twenty-one. I 'm dying to be twenty-one. I wan't all my money!"

"Why, Susan Sweetser!" exclaimed Bell. "What on earth would you do with any more money? You can 't spend all your income now."

"Can't I?" laughed Susan. "You just try me and see! I 'm overdrawn on this quarter already; and it 's so disagreeable to be told of it. Dear Uncle Tom never told me. He was a great deal nicer for a guardian than this old Mr. Clark is."

Mr. Clark was the family lawyer, who was to act as Susan's guardian and business agent for the next three years, and who had already made himself tiresome to her, by trying to instill into her mind some ideas of system and economy in expenditure.

"Overdrawn!" cried Bell. "You extravagant girl! What have you been doing?"

"I don't really know," laughed Susan. "I never keep accounts. I let poor Madame Delancy have a thousand; that was one thing. She'll pay me in the spring; and those riding parties were awfully dear. Mr. Clark says I must n't pay for my friends' horses any more; but I don't think it is any of his business. Lots of the girls I want to have go can't go any other way; their fathers can't afford it."

"You 're a dear generous soul," said Bell, admiringly.

"No I 'm not," said Susan. "There is n't any generosity in my sending Sally Sanford a horse, when I want her in my party, and know she can't come any other way. It 's to please myself I do it."

"Well, I think it 's generous for all that," said Bell, "and anybody in the world would say so."

"Anybody in the world will say anything," replied Susan, satirically; "there is one thing I made up my mind about long ago, and that is, never to mind what the world says, either for or against a thing or a person."

22

" You can 't afford to do that way, Sue," said Mrs. Bell, who was conservative by nature and training. " You 'll get talked about awfully, the first thing you know. "

" Let them talk ! " laughed Susan. " They 'll talk anyway. It might as well be about me."

" No, it might n't ! " persisted Bell, who had her own reasons for laying stress on this point with Susan. " No, it might n't. I tell you, Sue, a woman can't afford to be talked about."

" Can't afford ? What do you mean by that ? How much does it cost ? " said Susan, scornfully.

Mrs. Bell was not clever enough to answer Susan in her own phraseology, and say, " It costs loss of position, loss of the best regard of the best people, loss of absolute trust from men whose trust would be honor, and might be love ; " she only said, meekly : —

" You know as well as I do, Sue, that nobody really thinks so well of a woman who is much talked about. I don't think a woman can be too careful, for my part ; especially, Sue, women situated as you and I are ; we have got to be very careful indeed."

This was an opportunity Mrs. Bell had been anxiously awaiting for a long time. She had felt that it was necessary to define their positions and have some such matters thoroughly understood in the outset of her life with Susan, but she had lacked moral courage to open the discussion.

" I 'm never going to be careful, as you call it,

Bell," cried Susan. " Never ! and you 'll have to make up your mind to that. I hate it, the sneaking, time-serving, calculating thing. It is next door to lying and stealing. I 'm going always to say what I think, do what I like, have what friends I please, without the slightest reference to what the world says ; whether they call it strange or not, proper or not, right or not, it 's nothing to me. I don't care a straw for the whole world's opinion, so long as I am sure I am right."

" Then you 'll get into horrible scrapes ; that 's all ; I can tell you that," said Bell, hotly.

" Why, I 'm never going to do anything improper," retorted Susan ; "and how shall I get into horrible scrapes ? "

" Oh, millions of ways," replied Bell, despairingly. "When you 're as old as I am, you 'll know the world better. I tell you women can 't do that way ; and I don't think it 's womanly."

" What is n't womanly ? " said Susan, in a pettish tone.

" Why, not caring," said Bell ; " I think it 's a woman's place to care very much what people think of her, and to try not to offend anybody's prejudices , and above all things, not to go against custom."

Susan groaned.

" Oh, pshaw, Bell," she said, " what kind of a life would that be ? I 'd as soon be a cartridge in a cartridge case, numbered and packed. But don't et us quarrel over this. We shall never think alike about it."

"No, I suppose not," replied Bell, gravely. "But if we 're going to live together all our lives, it 's a great pity we should not, especially if, as you say, I 'm going to be your *chaperon.*"

"Oh, you motherly, grandmotherly old girl !" cried Susan, kissing her. "Don't you worry yourself ; I won't do anything you don't want me to. I believe in caring what one's friends say."

"You sweet, dear Sue !" cried Bell, kissing her warmly in turn ; "I know you won't."

From all which it is easy to see that Mrs. Thomas Lawton's chaperonage of Miss Susan Sweetser would not be a very rigid one.

Susan's phrase, "What friends I please," had not been a random one. For more than a year her intimacy with Professor Balloure had been such as to give rise to some ill-natured comment in the town, and to no little anxiety in the minds of her friends. Edward Balloure had been professor of belles-lettres in one of our large colleges in his youth, but marrying early a woman of fortune, he had at once relinquished his professorship, and had ever since led a life of indolent leisure, dabbling in literature in an dle fashion, now and then throwing off a creditable pamphlet or paper, but for the most part doing nothing except enjoy himself. He was a handsome man and a brilliant talker ; everybody liked him ; nobody loved him, not even his wife, who had soon found out that he had married her for her money and not from affection. This knowledge,

instead of crushing her, as it would a woman of
weaker nature, had turned her into a cold, hard,
bitter, ill-natured woman, whom it seemed, now,
nobody could like or live with; yet those who
knew both her and her husband when they were
young said that Martha Balloure, at the time of her
marriage, had been an impulsive, loving, lovable
girl. Be that as it may, she was now an unlovely,
cynical, sharp-tongued, heartless woman, without a
friend in the community, and the verdict of the
world was always, " Poor Professor Balloure!
What a sad fate it was that tied him to such a
woman!" Mrs. Balloure herself perpetually fed
this expression by her unconcealed contempt for
and dislike of her husband. She had a sad lack of
dignity of character, and could never forego an
opportunity of a fling at the man whose name she
bore. When people praised him to her, — said, for
instance, " How well Professor Balloure talks!"
Mrs. Balloure would reply, with a sneer, " Yes, outside his own house." Professor Balloure, on the
contrary, never spoke of his wife but with the utmost respect; always treated her with the utmost
courtesy, in the presence of others. Some close
observers noticed that his eye never rested on her
face — never met hers if it could be avoided ; and
when Mrs. Balloure replied bitterly, as she had been
more than once heard to, on his offering her some
small attentions, " Oh, pray don't trouble yourself ;
you know you wouldn't do it if there were no one

here!" these same close observers wondered
whether, after all, the brilliant Professor Balloure
might not be a hypocrite. But he talked so well
on high themes, he was so full of noble sentiments,
so sure to be on the right side of all questions, —
theoretical or practical, — it was hard to believe
the man hollow-hearted. And yet, hollow he was
to the very core, always excepting his sentiment
toward Susan Sweetser. This was the one true,
genuine thing he bore about him. He had been
irresistibly attracted toward her while she was a
mere child. Her frankness, her courage, her generosity, all allured him by the very greatness of the
contrast they bore to his own traits. Out of his
own meagerness was born his appreciation of her
nobility. He looked back at his own youth, — at
the time when he sold himself for money, — and
he wondered, with passionate admiration, at the
fearlessness, generosity, independence of this girl.
Susan had no beauty to thrill a man's senses ; but
she had the perpetually varying charm of overflowing life and activity, and fullness of thought.
When Professor Balloure was inquired of by
Madame Delancy if he would give a course of
lectures, accompanied by recitations, to the young
ladies of her senior class, he recollected instantly
that Mrs. Lawton had told him that this would be
Susan's last year at school, and he consented to
give the lectures for the sole and simple purpose
of thus bringing himself into relation with her.

"How kind of Professor Balloure!" everybody said. "Such a help to Madame Delancy! How kind of him!"

"Do you think so?" sneered Mrs. Balloure. She did not know what her husband's motive was, but that it was not kindness she was sure. She did not trouble herself to find out, for she did not care. She spoke of the lecture course as "one of Mr. Balloure's whims," and dismissed it from her mind.

She never went into society with him, and really knew nothing of his habitual manner of half-insidious, half-chivalrous gallantry toward young women. If she had she would not have cared; she despised him too thoroughly to be wounded by anything he might do; and the one great flaw in her nature — her lack of personal dignity — would have prevented her suffering as most women would from mortification. If anybody had gone to her and confided to her proofs of her husband's having had even an intrigue, she would most probably have said in her usual bitter tone, "You are surprised, then!" and have dropped the subject, as one of entire indifference to her.

It is an odd thing how very much franker a manner some types of hypocrites wear than a really frank person ever has. Edward Balloure had an off-hand, hilarious, half-confidential way with everybody. He seemed almost lacking in proper reticence and secretiveness, so familiarly did he talk with people whom he desired to please ; and he had a large, clear, light-blue eye, which looked full in everybody's face, and never wavered. It is only after a long and more or less sad experience of the world, that we learn to recognize such eyes as the eyes of traitors. I know to-day two women who are base and treacherous as if the very blood of Judas Iscariot filled their veins, and they both have sunny, clear, unflinching, light-blue eyes ; and I have known a man who could, on occasion, tell cowardly lies with as steady a gaze into your face as an honest man could give, — and he too had light-blue eyes, — sunny, clear, unflinching.

If anybody had said to Susan Sweetser, that Professor Balloure was not an upright, sincere man, she would have blazed with indignation. His beauty, his brilliancy, his seeming kindliness, impressed her in the outset ; and when by degrees he singled her out from all her class, and made evident and especial efforts to interest and instruct her, her admiration took on an affectionate and grateful quality which made her very attractive, and gave Edward Balloure great pleasure. Nothing was further from his intention than to have any flirtation with Susan. He was too cold-blooded and conscious ever to compromise himself for any woman ; and he really did care for Susan herself too truly and warmly to be willing to compromise her. But he did intend to enjoy himself ; and he did find a greater pleasure in teaching Susan Sweetser, in

watching her quick comprehension, her originality
of thought, her eager impulsiveness, than he had
found in anything for many a long year. The very
best of him came out to, and for, and with, Susan.
Gradually their intercourse dropped from the relation of pupil with teacher into that of friend with
friend. The technical instruction continued, but
its atmosphere was new; there was a partial re-
newal of the old bond. Edward Balloure could not
help reverencing this girl, whose belief in him, he
knew, had its foundation in her immovable belief
in honor and truth; whose affection for him in-
dividually was, he knew, also, based on her belief
that he was honorable and truthful. Probably
Susan was the only human being to whom he would
have found it difficult to lie. He said to himself
sometimes when he looked in her face : —

"Now, such a woman as that I never could have
had the heart tò deceive."

It soothed his uneasy consciousness of his hypo-
critical past to assume that, if his wife had been a
stronger person he might have been saved from his
deceit. But he was mistaken. If it had suited his
purposes, and the purposes had been strong enough,
he would have deceived Susan Sweetser as readily
to-day as he had deceived his wife fifteen years before. For a year and a half now the relation between Professor Balloure and Susan had gone steadily on, growing warmer and closer. When the lectures at Madame Delancy's ceased, and Susan had

left school, nothing was more natural than that she should continue some of her studies under Professor Balloure's guidance. And this was the ostensible pretext under shelter of which there continued an amount of intimacy which would have been otherwise inadmissible. But that it was partly a pretext, and that the intimacy was for Susan an undesirable one, Mrs. Lawton had come to feel most decidedly ; and there had been several earnest conversations between them on the subject. The most baffling thing to Mrs. Lawton in these conversations was the utter impossibility of making Susan comprehend what was objected to. She simply could not understand. Professor Balloure had been her teacher ; he was her teacher still ; he was forty and she was eighteen ; and above all he was a married man, and to Susan's mind there was something absurd as well as indelicate in any suggestion that there could be harm either to her or to him in their friendship.

"Why, I should as soon think of your objecting to an intimacy between me and papa, if he were alive," said Susan, vehemently ; "if I ever could have had an intimacy with papa," she added, sadly. " Papa was only forty when he died ; he would only be as much older than Professor Balloure, now, as you are than I ; there 's no real difference of age between you and me."

At such times as this, poor Mrs. Lawton always fell back hopelessly on the assertion that Susan did not know the world; to which Susan always retorted that she hoped she never should know it; and there matters rested, in no wise altered by the discussions, except that Susan was somewhat hurt by them, inasmuch as each one inevitably took away a little of her fresh innocence and inability to comprehend evil. Mrs. Lawton loved Susan better than she loved any one else in the world, and the purpose had been growing stronger and stronger for weeks to take Susan away from home and break up her intimacy with Edward Balloure. The purpose coincided also with her own wishes, for the great air-castle of her life had been to spend some years in Europe. The one short and hurried trip she had taken there with her husband, soon after their marriage, had been merely sufficient to make her long to go again. She had often spoken of this to Susan, so there seemed nothing abrupt or unreasonable when on the present morning, as they sat together in the library, discussing plans for the winter, she suddenly said : —

"Susan, we 'll go abroad."

Susan sprang to her feet, her face flushed with pleasure.

"You don 't mean it, Bell ? "

"But I do ! " said Mrs. Lawton; " I 've been meaning it all along."

"You blessed creature ! " cried Susan. " I 've been dying to go ever since I could recollect. I have had it on my tongue's end five hundred times

in the last three months to propose it to you ; but I
did not like to.   I was afraid you would not want
to go and would think you must go for my sake."

"Why should n't I want to go ? " exclaimed Mrs.
Lawton, wonderingly.

"Oh, I was afraid you might not feel like it,"
was Susan's evasive reply.   She did not like to be-
tray to Mrs. Lawton that she had doubted whether
she would be willing to leave her parents, now both
very old ; also whether her afflictions were not yet
too fresh in her mind to permit her full enjoyment
of travel.   Neither of these considerations having
entered into Mrs. Lawton's mind, she did not sus-
pect any hidden meaning in Susan's words, and
went eagerly on in the discussion of their plans.

Nothing is easier than for two women of large
fortunes and assured incomes to set off on a delightful tour of foreign travel.   All paths become
easy, thus smoothed by money, and so Mrs. Lawton and Susan Sweetser found.   Probably no two
women ever had a " better time " in the world than
did these two for the next three years.   I pass by
all details of these years spent abroad, because I
am not telling the story of Susan's life, only of two
days in her life — of an escape she had.   This two
days' story is worth telling, partly because each
hour of the two days was dramatic, partly because
there is in the story a lesson — a moral — which
any two who love may sometime come to need.

There are several years now of Susan's life to be

sketched in outline before we come to those days of danger and escape.

When she and Mrs. Lawton returned from Europe and settled themselves again in their old home, the event produced no small stir in all circles. The two richest women of the town, — each young, each enjoying absolute control of her property, each bright and individual, each gay and pleasure-loving, and keeping together a house of free and gracious hospitalities. What Susan Sweetser and Bell Lawton did, said, wore, afforded all the material that a whole town full of first-class gossips could need ; and what Susan Sweetser and Bell Lawton offered and provided and arranged for in way of hospitable entertainment was enough to keep social life going from one year's end to the other. It is not necessary to say that they became the leaders of the town ; that their house was its social centre. First and foremost among the men who sought the pleasure and the honor of familiar and friendly footing in the house was Professor Edward Balloure. He found his warm-hearted little pupil and friend changed into a brilliant woman of the world ; no less warm-hearted, no less impulsive, than of old, but educated, trained, developed, into such a woman as nothing but years of European travel and culture could have produced. It was not necessary now for Bell to explain social *convenances* to Susan. It was not necessary for her to point out to her the dangers of intimacies with men who had wives. Many men had loved, or had seemed to love, Susan during these years. She had been somewhat moved two or three times by their passion and devotion; but she had never really loved. It began to look as if she were obdurate of nature, in spite of all her warm-heartedness. Sometimes a fear came into Bell's mind that her old relation with Edward Balloure still stood between Susan and all other men; and when she saw the professor at his post again, handsome, brilliant, fascinating, as ever, devoted as ever, plausible as ever, in his assumption of the rôle of a privileged mentor, Bell Lawton groaned and said within herself, "How is such a man as this ever to be circumvented?" A sort of hate grew up in her heart toward him. Edward Balloure recognized it; he had the keenest of instincts, and knew on the instant the woman who trusted and admired him from the woman who unconsciously shrank away when he approached her. But he only laughed cynically when he saw poor Bell's desperate efforts to be civil to him, and said in his cold-blooded heart : —

"She's much mistaken, if she thinks she can come between Susan and me."

Bell had too much good sense to try. Beyond an occasional half laughing or satirical reference to Professor Balloure's devotion, she avoided the subject. She made no attempt to exclude him from the house. On the contrary, she endeavored to make it evident to the whole world that he was one of their established, intimate friends, — her own, as well as Susan's. And she absolutely compelled poor Mrs. Balloure's continual presence with her husband on all occasions of special festivity, until the poor woman relaxed a little from her rigid severity, and became, as Susan ungenerously remarked one day, " a little less like the death's head at the banquet."

Susan's own manner to the professor baffled Bell's utmost scrutiny ; it was always open as day ; always affectionate ; always reverential ; but there was a look now in her eyes when they rested on his face which made Bell uneasy. It was a groping, questioning look, as if she were feeling her way in the dark ; it was a great change from Susan's old child-like trust. Edward Balloure himself felt this, and was more disconcerted by it than he would have been by any form of direct and distrustful inquiry. It put him perpetually on his guard ; led him to be always discreet, even in his closest and most intimate moments with Susan : much more discreet than he would otherwise have been ; for day by day, Edward Balloure was learning to love Susan Sweetser more and more warmly. The vague remoteness in which she held herself ; the strange charm of mingled reverence and doubt, affection and withdrawal in her manner toward him, held him under a spell which no other woman could have woven. She was an endlessly interesting study to him, and that is the strongest fascination which one human being can possess for another.

Among all the men who visited at the house, and who were evident admirers of Susan, the only one whom Edward Balloure feared was Tom Lawton, a distant cousin of Bell's husband. If Professor Balloure had said to any one in the town that Tom Lawton was the one man he thought Susan Sweetser might possibly marry, the remark would have been greeted with exclamations of surprise, and possibly laughter.

Tom Lawton was a lawyer; a plodding, hard-working lawyer, not a pleader; there was not a trace of the rhetorician about Tom ; he could not have made a speech in court to have saved his life.

He made very few anywhere, for that matter. But for a good, sound, common-sense opinion ; for slow, sure, accurate working-up of a case ; for shrewd dealing with, and reading of, human nature, men went to Tom Lawton. When Susan and Bell returned from Europe, Tom, being the nearest relative Bell had at hand, drifted very naturally into the position of chief adviser in the affairs of the two women. He was a man of such habitual quiet of manner, that one grew almost immediately accustomed to his presence, and felt at home with him. All dogs and all children ran to him ; and his dark, blue-grey eye, which had usually a half stern look, twinkled instantly whenever he stooped to them. He was not good-looking. His face had nothing striking about it, except its expression of absolute honesty, good-will, and a certain sort of

indomitableness which came very near looking like
obstinacy, and no doubt did often take on that
shape. His figure was stout and ungraceful ; and
long years of solitary, hard work had given him the
manners of a recluse, and not of a man of the
world. Before Edward Balloure had seen Tom
Lawton one hour in Susan Sweetser's presence, he
knew that he loved her. Tom made no effort to
join the circle of gay talkers of which she was the
centre ; he did not pay her one of the most ordinary attentions of society ; but he watched her
with a steady, contented gaze, which to Edward
Balloure's sharpened instinct was unmistakable.

Professor Balloure had had occasion to know
some of Tom Lawton's traits very thoroughly.
They had encountered each other once, in some
business matters where trusts were involved, and
where the professor's interests and Tom's sense of
honor had been at variance. The calm immova-
bleness which Tom had opposed to every influence
brought to bear on him ; his entire superiority to all
considerations save the one of absolute right ; and
his dogged indifference to any amount of antagonism and resentment, had altogether made up an
aggregate of opposition such as the professor rarely
encountered. He chose to call it Quixotic obstinacy ; but in his heart he admired it, and respected
Tom Lawton more than any man he knew.

"If he makes up his mind to marry Susan he'll
win her sooner or later," said the professor to him-

self. "They 're made of the same stuff ; but she does n't care anything about him yet," and Edward Balloure groaned inwardly and cursed the fate which stood in shape of a poor helpless woman between him and this girl whom he so wilfully and sinfully loved.

It was quite true, as the professor had said, that Susan did not as yet care anything for Tom Lawton. In her girlhood she had been used to seeing him come and go in her uncle's house, quietly and familiarly ; his silent presence had produced no impression on her fancy ; in fact she hardly remembered him when she first met him after her return from Europe. But it was not many weeks before the quality in Tom's steady gaze, which had penetrated Edward Balloure's consciousness, penetrated Susan's also. She became afraid that Tom was beginning to love her too well.

"Dear Tom !" she thought to herself. "The dear fellow ! What shall I do ? Whatever put such a thought into his head ? How shall I stop him ? I don't want him to fall in love with me," and in the most right-minded way Susan set herself to work to prevent what had already happened. It had once been Susan's belief that any woman could save any man the pain of a direct refusal ; but the fallacy of this belief in individual cases she had been taught by some trying experiences. However, she still clung to her theory, and endeavored to carry it out in practice as conscientiously as if she had never discovered it fallible; and many a man had in his heart reverently thanked Susan Sweetser for having graciously and kindly made it clear to him that he must not love her. But this Tom was not on a footing to be dealt with by the subtle processes which told on a less familiar friend. If he had been Bell's own brother, Bell could not have trusted him or loved him more, or have given him more unqualifiedly the freedom of the house. That she never once thought of the possibility of his falling in love with Susan was owing partly to the quiet, middle-aged seriousness of his manner and ways, partly to her absorption in her anxiety about Professor Balloure's relation to Susan, and hers to him. And so the months went on, and the girls lived their gay and busy life, and every hour that could be spared from his business, Tom was with them, as unquestionedly and naturally as if he had been their legal protector. Indeed it was not infrequently supposed by strangers, that he was the head of the house.

Susan was uneasy. She was distressed. She had come to have so true an affection for Tom that the thought of having to inflict on him at some not very distant day so cruel a hurt as to refuse his love was terrible to her.

"If only he could know beforehand," she said, "he could leave off loving me just as well as not. He is one of those quiet, undemonstrative men 'hat can make up their mind to love any woman that they think best to love."

From which it is plainly to be seen that Susan did not yet know men analytically. She was yet too much under the influence of the presence of an idealist who could talk eloquently and mysteriously on the subject of unconquerable passions. Susan made several blundering attempts to make Tom see what she wanted him to see; but Tom was obtuse; he was basking in the sun of Susan's presence, and not acknowledging to himself distinctly that he wanted her for his wife. Susan was right in one respect: Tom was quite capable of leaving off loving her if he resolved to. But it would take more to make him resolve to than Susan supposed. At last, one day, in one of those sudden, unpremeditated, accidental moments which are always happening between men and women whose relations are not clear, there came a chance for Susan to say, — exactly what she never knew, and Tom never could tell her, but something which made Tom understand clearly that she wanted to save him from falling in love with her.

Tom looked at her for one second with a gaze which was stern in its intensity; then he said : —

" You 're a good, kind, true girl, Sue. Don't you worry about me. I 'm all right."

And poor Susan was seized with the most mortifying fear that she had spoken needlessly. " Oh, dear ! " she thought, " if it were anybody but Tom, how I should feel ! But he is so good, he 'd never misunderstand a woman nor laugh at her ! "

And everything went on the same as before. Tom's eyes told just as plainly as ever that he loved the very spot where Susan stood. Bell looked on unconscious. Edward Balloure looked on in sullen despair. The world began to say that Tom Lawton cared about Susan Sweetser, and how absurd it was! He might know that a brilliant girl like that was never going to marry a plodding, middle-aged fellow like him ; and Susan, meanwhile, — poor, perplexed Susan! — was perpetually asking herself whether, after all, Tom had really loved her or not. Weeks, months, a year went by, and to outside observers no change had come to any member of the little group. But the years write their records on human hearts as they do on trees, in hidden inner circles of growth, which no eye can see. When the tree falls, men may gather around and count the rings about its centre, and know how many times its sap has chilled in winter and glowed in spring. We wrap ourselves in the merciful veils of speech and behavior, and nobody can tell what a year has done to us. Luckily, even if we die, there is no sure sign which betrays us. As I said, at the end of a year no change which an outside observer would detect had come to any member of the little group. But if at any moment the hearts of Susan Sweetser, Tom Lawton, and Edward Balloure had been uncovered to the gaze of the world, there would have been revelations startling to all.

Tom loved Susan now with a calm, concentrated purpose of making her his wife. There was in his feeling for her none of the impatience of a fiery passion. He would not have rebelled had he been told that she would not be his for years, so that he had been sure of her at last. He had gradually taken his position with her as her constant attendant, protector, adviser. In a myriad of ways he had made himself part of her daily life, and this, too, without once coming on the ordinary lover's ground of gifts, attentions, compliments. He never even sent her flowers ; he never even said a flattering thing to, or of, her. He simply sat by her side, looked at her, and took care of her. How Edward Balloure chafed at all this is easy to imagine. When he met Tom in Sue's presence, — and he was seldom out of it except in business hours, — he eyed him sometimes fiercely, sometimes almost imploringly. Tom had for Edward Balloure but one look, but one tone, — that of concealed contempt ; the barest civility was all he could wrench from himself for the man whom he knew to be base, but whom Susan reverenced and loved. And Susan ! It must be a more skillful pen than mine which could analyze the conflicting emotions which filled Susan's heart now. Professor Balloure occupied her imagination to a greater degree than she knew. She idealized him, and then let her thoughts dwell on the ideal she had made. She was full of sentiment about him, she leaned on his intellect, sought his opinions, was stimulated by his society. She talked better to him, and before him, than under any other circumstances. She yielded to him in many matters, small and great, as she had yielded when he was her teacher. She knew, also, her great power over him. In the bottom of her heart she knew that he loved her, though never once had he said to her a word which could offend her delicate sense of right. But one day, in a sudden and irrepressible mood, he had poured out to Mrs. Lawton such passionate avowals of his long admiration and affection for Susan that Bell had been terrified, and had spoken to him with the utmost severity. He pleaded so persistently to be forgiven, and moreover argued so plausibly that she had totally misconceived the real meaning of all he had said, that he made Bell feel ashamed of having resented his words, and half guilty herself of having misinterpreted them. Wily Edward Balloure ! He thought that Bell would tell Susan of their conversation, and he watched the next day for some trace of its influence upon her. No trace was there. Her manner was as cordial as ever, — no more, no less so ; and the professor could never make up his mind whether she had been told or not.

One day when Tom had been taking unusual pains about some matters for Susan, she looked up at him and said with a sudden and shame-stricken sense of how much she was perpetually receiving at his hands : —

"Oh, Tom! how good you are! It is n't fair for you to be with me all the time, so —— "

"Is n't fair!" exclaimed Tom. "What do you mean?"

Susan colored, but did not speak. He understood.

"Do you dislike to have me with you all the time?" he asked, emphatically.

"Oh, no!" cried Susan; "no. You know it is n't that."

"Then I am content," replied he. "It is all right."

Susan made no reply. Her eyes were fixed on the ground. Something he saw in her face made Tom bolder than one moment before he would have dared to be.

"One of these years, Sue, you and I will be married," he said, quietly.

She started, turned red, then pale, and stammered: —

"Why, Tom, I told you long ago —— "

"Oh, yes," — he interrupted her in a placid tone, — "that 's all right. I understand it. It will be just as you say; but one of these years you 'll think it right," and Tom began to talk about something else as naturally and calmly as if no exciting topic had been broached.

When Susan thought over this extraordinary conversation, she laughed and she cried. At one moment she thought it the most audacious imperti-

nence a man ever committed ; the next instant she
thought it the sweetest daring that love ever dared,
and a strange surrender of herself to its prophecy
began in that very hour. No wonder. The prediction had almost a preternatural sound, as Tom said
it ; and while he spoke his eyes rested on hers with
an authoritative tenderness which was very compelling.

After this day, Susan never felt sure that Tom
was not right. After this day, Tom never felt a
doubt ; and from this day, Edward Balloure perceived in Susan a change which he could not define, but which made him uncomfortable. The
searching, probing, questioning look in her eyes
was gone. The affection remained, but the eager,
restless inquiry had ceased. Had she found out?
Or had she left off caring to know?

One day, in an impatient and ill-natured tone,
Professor Balloure said to Susan : —

"Does Mr. Lawton really live in this house ? I
confess it is something of a trial that none of your
friends can ever see you without having his company inflicted on them. He is a very stupid man."

Susan fixed her brown eyes steadily on Professor
Balloure's face.

" If any of our friends find Mr. Lawton's company an infliction, they know how to avoid it. We
do not think him a stupid person, and I trust him
more than any other man I know," and, with this
sudden and most unexpected shot, Susan walked
away and sat down at the piano.

Edward Balloure was, for once, dumb. When Susan stopped playing, he bent over her and said in a low tone : —

"I hope you will forgive me. I never dreamed that you had so strong a regard for Mr. Lawton. I thought he was Mrs. Lawton's friend, and somehow I had often fancied that he bored you."

"You were never more mistaken in your life, Professor Balloure," answered Susan, composedly. "Mr. Lawton is a person who makes you contented by his simple presence, — he is so quiet, and yet so full of vitality."

"She has studied Mr. Lawton then, feels a charm in his presence, and has reflected upon it enough to analyze it." All this passed through the professor's mind, and gave a peculiar bitterness to the coldly civil tone in which he replied, "Ah! I should not have thought that possible. It is only another of the many illustrations of the difference between the feminine and the masculine standards of judging men."

Susan colored, and was about to speak indignantly, changed her mind, closed her lips and smiled, and when Edward Balloure saw the smile, his heart sank within him. By that smile he knew that his reign, so far as it had been a reign, was over, and Tom Lawton's had begun.

Two weeks from that day Professor and Mrs. Balloure sailed for Europe. The sudden announcement of their plans caused no astonishment ; it had

always been the professor's way to set off at a
day's notice. He had been a restless and insatia-
ble traveler. But when it was known that his
house was offered for rent, furnished, for three
years, then people did wonder what was taking him
away for so long a time. Nobody but Edward Balloure knew. Bell Lawton suspected, but said nothing, and Susan did not so much as dream. She
was surprised at herself, and had a half-guilty feeling that she did not more keenly regret his going.
When she bade him good-by, she said, lightly : —

"Who knows where we shall meet next? Bell
and I may run over next summer. We have talked
of it."

"If I could think that, I should be very glad,
indeed," replied the professor, earnestly. " But
you will not come."

"What did he mean by that, Bell?" said Susan's
after he had gone. "How does he know what we
will do?"

Mrs. Lawton laughed, and skipping up to Susan's
side, kissed her on the forehead, and sang : —

"How does anybody know what anybody will
do?

> "'Wooed and married and a,'
> Kissed and carried awa',
> Is na the lassie well aff
> That 's wooed and married and a'?'"

This chorus of an old Scotch ballad had been
much on Mrs. Bell Lawton's lips of late.

"Bell!" exclaimed Susan; "are you going to be married?"

"Perhaps," said Bell. "And you, Miss Susan?"

"No," said Susan, stoutly. "No! And you sha n't be. I can't spare you."

At this moment Tom entered, and Bell ran out of the room, singing: —

> "'Wooed and married and a',
> Kissed and carried awa'!'"

"Who's married now?" asked Tom.

"Nobody," replied Susan. "But I'm afraid Bell will be."

"Why, Sue!" said Tom; "it is n't possible that you have not seen all along that Bell would surely marry Fred Ballister?"

Susan looked aghast.

"I never thought of such a thing," she exclaimed. "Why, what will become of me?"

Tom looked in her face without speaking. If he had been a less reticent, less obstinate man, he would have poured out a voluble torrent of words just then; but he did not open his lips. He knew that Susan knew what his look meant. Yet he might have made it less hard for her. What could she say? She flushed and lowered her eyes, and finally said: —

"Oh, Tom!"

There was a world of appeal in the exclamation,

if Tom would only have understood it; but he
would not, — would not or did not.

"All right, Sue! All right!" he said, cheerily.
"I shall never urge you. One of these days you'll
think it right to marry me. You'll know when the
time comes. All must be clear."

Susan could have cried with vexation. Did he
mean to punish her for having gratuitously refused
him before he had ever offered himself to her in
words? No, surely Tom was too noble for that.
Did he expect her to say to him in so many words,
"Dear Tom, I am ready to marry you now?" Did
she really and heartily want to marry him after all?
She was happier when he was with her than when
he was away. If a day passed without her seeing
him she was restless and ill at ease. She found
herself in all her plans and projects leaning on
him, including him as inevitably as if they belonged
to each other. But was this love? Susan was not
wholly sure. Altogether Susan was quite miserable, and none the less so, it must be acknowledged,
because Tom seemed so light-hearted, so content,
so thoroughly at rest and satisfied with the state of
things. Wise fellow! he had reason to be.

"I don't believe he really cares very much for
me," said Susan, pettishly, to Bell one day. "If I
were to tell him positively to-morrow that I would
never marry him, I don't believe that he would
mind it much."

"Oh, Sue, how can you say so?" cried Bell.

" Look at these last two years. Has Tom been
out of your presence one hour when he could be in
it ? "

" No," said Sue. " That 's one way he 's brought
me into this uncomfortable state about him. I 'm
so used to him, I never could do without him in
the world."

" Of course you can't," said Bell; " and when
I 'm married " — Bell's engagement to Mr. Ballister
was now formally acknowledged — " you can't go
on living here alone ; and as for your getting any
' lady companion ' to live with you, that 's out of
the question. You 'll never find another such
saint as I 've been to put up with your ways. My !
what I 've borne in these last five years ! No,
Miss, you 'd better take to yourself a husband, and
of all the good, true, sterling men in this world,
Tom 's the best, excepting Fred."

" I know it," said Sue, forlornly. " I told Professor Balloure not long ago that I trusted Tom
more than I trusted any other man in the world."

" Did you ? " cried Bell. " Did you say that to
Edward Balloure ? Oh, I 'm so glad. Oh, Sue,
you 'll never know how I 've worried about that
man's influence over you. I don't believe in him,
and I never did, and if his wife had died any time,
you 'd have married him as true as fate."

" I think not," said Susan, reflectively. " I am
afraid I don't believe in him either, and yet it seems
so horribly ungrateful after all he has done for
me."

"Well, he's safe out of the way now, thank heaven," said Bell. "That's one good thing. And you've got to make up your mind about Tom."

"Well, why does n't he make me?" said Susan.

"Susan Lawton," said Bell, "you ought to know Tom better. He knows that you know that he is ready and longing to make you his wife at any hour, and he will never urge you, — not if you keep him waiting on and on till you are both gray."

"I wonder," said Susan ——.

"No," replied Bell, "he never will. He's as obstinate as a rock, and more than that, he does n't want you for his wife till you want him for your husband. Tom is proud as Lucifer in his heart."

"But, Bell," pleaded Susan, "I can't go to Tom and say, 'please take me.' He had a good chance a few days ago when he first told me you were going to marry Fred, and all he said was: 'All right, Sue, all right,'" and Susan laughed in spite of herself at the recollection.

Bell laughed too, but she was vexed and anxious to see two people at such cross-purposes. Her own wooing and winning had been so smooth, so entirely in accordance with the conventional usages and customs, that she sympathized freely in Susan's position.

"I should n't like it myself," thought Bell. "I should never stand it if Fred treated me that way. But I know Fred would n't really do any more for

me than Tom would for Sue. I believe I 'll speak
to him."

"Speaking to him" was not so easy. Several
well-meant and carefully planned little speeches of
Bell's died away on her lips when she found herself
face to face with Tom. And time was slipping
away. Her own wedding was to come off in a few
months, and what could poor Sue do? Mrs. Bell
Lawton was much perplexed. At last one day she
took a desperate step. Tom had dined with them.
After dinner they were all sitting together in the
library. Bell rose, looked them both in the face
for a moment with a half comic, half severe glance,
and said : —

"Now, I tell you what it is ; it is high time you
two decided what you were going to do. Something
has got to be done. Now, I 'm going to leave you,
and if you don't straighten out things, I won't
speak to either of you again," and she marched
out of the room.

Tom looked at Susan, who said, nervously.

"Oh, how queer Bell is ! "

"She is right," said Tom. And then he looked
at Susan, and continued looking at her, and said
nothing.

Moments passed.

Susan could not bear the silence another moment.

"Tom ! " she cried, " tell me just once, would
you really mind very much if I did n't marry you ? '

Tom thought for a second that this must mean that after all, his hopes had been unfounded ; that Susan had at last decided that she ought not to marry him. He turned pale, and spoke very slowly.

"Yes, it would be a very great disappointment to me," he said. "But ——" He would probably have finished his sentence with his characteristic phrase, "It's all right, Sue, all right," if he had not just then looked up. Tears were in Sue's eyes, and her hands were stretched toward him.

"Oh, Tom!" she cried, "if you really have been so sure, why have n't you made me come to you before?"

"So there was never a day without a Mrs. Thomas Lawton in town, after all," wrote Bell, describing her own and Sue's wedding to a friend.

"We were married first, — Sue and Tom would have it so, — and as soon as the minister had made me into Mrs. Fred Ballister, he hurried on to make Sue into me. It is really very odd to hear her called Mrs. Lawton. I don't get used to it. But, my dear, if you want to see two happy people, you just ought to see Tom and Sue. I declare it is marvelous. You would n't think they were in the least suited to each other. You know, dear Tom is queer to the last degree. Much as I love him I never could live with him. I 've always said so. But Sue manages him most beautifully, and no won-

24

der, for she never even looks at him without such
love in her eyes — I did n't think Sue had it in her.
Fred is quite jealous. He says that the other Mrs.
Tom Lawton is the woman he ought to have married. She is a woman that knows how to appreciate a husband."

And now, where other stories end, this story
begins. For it was four years after Susan Lawton's
marriage that she had the " escape" which it is the
purpose of my story to tell, and all this which has
gone before has been merely what it was necessary
that one should know in order to understand the
rest.

The relation between Tom and Susan had grown
constantly closer and sweeter. It was a very peculiar one. People did not always understand it.
There were those who were shallow enough to say
that Tom Lawton did not appreciate his wife ; but
nobody would have laughed more heartily than Sue
herself at such an accusation against Tom. He
was still as reticent, undemonstrative, as he had
been in the days of his strange loverhood ; but he
was as sensitive yet to Susan's voice, look, touch,
as if he were still her lover, and not her husband.
What woman does not know how much this means !
How few women, alas, have had it given to them
to know the joy of it !

One day a letter came to Sue from Bell, who was
traveling in Europe with her husband.

"Only think," Bell wrote, "poor Mrs. Balloure

has died at last. We found her here, in this hotel. She had been ill for a day or two, but nobody thought anything of it. She had the Roman fever last winter and has never been well since. What makes it worse is that Professor Balloure is away. He has gone with a party of scientific men into Russia. They say he has not been with her half the time since they came abroad, and that the poor thing has been quite broken — has just sat still patiently wherever he left her till he saw fit to come back. Oh, I've no patience with that man! Well, she died last night, and nobody knows where to telegraph to him. Her maid is a stupid thing, and does n't seem to know anything. We can't find the professor's address anywhere among her papers, and so Fred is seeing to everything, and we've actually got to bury the poor soul to-morrow. Is n't it the strangest thing you ever heard of, that we should have come way out to this outlandish spot, to bury this townswoman of ours, — and, a woman we always hated so, too? Poor thing, what a life she has led of it. And oh, have n't you had an escape! I declare, the second thing I thought of was, how glad I am Sue's married all safe. I never could have stood your marrying Edward Balloure."

The letter ended abruptly, giving no more details, and, to Susan's great relief, no more comment on Professor Balloure. To Sue's loyal, loving, wedded heart there was something inexpressibly shocking

in Bell's light way of referring to him.   And it was
with a real sense of relief that she threw the letter
into the fire after having read Tom all of it except
the last paragraph.

"That's the first time in my life," thought Susan,
"that I ever had anything I did n't want Tom to
see."

The consciousness of it hurt her to the core, and
still more, she felt the hurt of it the next morning.
She had been talking with Tom about Mrs. Balloure's death, and saying that she hoped the professor would now marry a woman he could love.

"Well, he can't have you, Sue," said Tom,
dryly.

Susan gazed at him in wonder.

"Why, Tom Lawton!" she said, "what do you
mean?"

Tom looked at her with a grave face.

"I think you would have married him, Sue?"

"Never!" exclaimed Sue, "and it is horrid of
you to say such a thing.   I never trusted Professor
Balloure, and besides" — Sue stopped, colored —
"I think I always loved you, Tom."

This speech of Tom's rankled in Sue's mind all
day.   It troubled her by its reflected implication
as to the past.   During all those years had Tom
really believed that she loved Professor Balloure?
Was that the reason he had left her so free from
the urging with which men usually seek women to
marry them?   Had he — had her frank, open-

hearted Tom a secret capacity for jealousy? Ah! if he could only know how immeasurably higher she held him than she had ever held any other man ; how absolutely his strong integrity and loyalty of nature had won her trust and her love!

Later in the day Sue sat down to answer Bell's letter. When the letter was half finished, she was called away. She left the letter lying open on her desk.

When Tom came home at night and did not find Sue, he had a vague sense of discomfort, as he always did when she was not in the house. Roaming about the library, idly, he sat down at Sue's desk, saw the open letter, turned the sheet over to find out to whom it was written, saw Bell's name, and proceeded to read what Sue had written. Bell's letters to Sue and Sue's to her were always common property ; there was nothing in the least strange in Tom's reading that letter ; but this, alas! was what he read. After some comments on Mrs. Balloure's death and references to what Bell had said in regard to the professor's character, Sue had gone on to repeat what Tom had that morning said : —

"What do you suppose, Bell," she wrote, "ever put such an idea into his head? Bless him! Dear old fellow! How much happier, safer a woman I am, in every way, with him than I ever could have been with any other man! Now, Bell, do be careful what you write about Professor Balloure, for I never have a secret thing in the world from Tom,

and he might look over my shoulder any minute
and read your letter."

This was the way the thing had lain in Sue's
mind. Tom's speech in the morning had startled
her very much by its revelation that at some time
or other, if not now, he had felt a jealousy of Professor Balloure's regard for her. If he had that
feeling, nothing could so strengthen it as this sort
of light reference which Bell seemed to be inclined
to make to her old notion that Sue would have married the professor.

"I can't have Tom hurt by such things being
said," thought Sue. "Bell might know better than
to write so: she always was thoughtless. Why,
if he feels sensitive on the subject now, one such
speech as that of Bell's might make him believe all
his life that I had married him, loving some one
else better," and so Sue wrote that fatal sentence:
"Do be careful what you write."

Tom sat still a long time looking at the words.

"So there are secrets in connection with Edward Balloure," he thought, "which I am not to
know."

The blow was a more terrible one to Tom, from
the fact that one of Sue's greatest charms to him
was the frankness, the bold truthfulness, of her
character. Tom's long experience as a lawyer had
made him distrustful of average women. In Sue,
he had thought he had found one who was incapa-
ble of deceit ; and here she was not only concealing

something from him, but warning her accomplice to conceal it too.

"There was nothing which one of them knew that the other did not," thought Tom, as he sat glued to the chair, and gazing at the mute, terrible lines. Finally he sprang up and left the house.

Sue came home late, hoping to find Tom as usual in his big arm-chair, reading the evening newspaper. The library was dark; no one was there.

"Has not Mr. Lawton been in yet?"

"Yes, ma'am," replied the servant. "He has been in and gone out again."

"How very strange," thought Sue. "I wish he was here."

She sat down and finished her letter in few words; then went to the window and watched for Tom. It was long past the dinner hour when he came in. He seemed preoccupied and grave. After asking him tenderly if he were ill, and if anything troubled him, Susan became silent. She had learned, and it was one of the hardest lessons of her married life, that when Tom was tired or worried about business matters, it was better not to talk to him. After dinner, he sat down near Susan's table, and glanced over the columns of the newspaper. The letter to Bell lay on the table. Taking it up he said casually,

"May I read it, Sue?"

"Oh, I guess you don't care to read it, this time.

dear," she replied laughingly, and took it out of his hand. He made no answer, but turned back to his newspaper. Presently he said he must go down town; he had an engagement. He kissed her good-by in an absent sort of way and was gone.

"Poor dear Tom!" thought Susan. "He certainly is worried about something. It is too bad," and she set herself to work to make the best of a lonely evening. The evenings which Tom spent away from home were so rare, that it always seemed to Susan a fresh and surprising deprivation when one occurred. The loneliness of the house to her when Tom was out of it, could not be expressed; the very furniture seemed to take on a totally different expression. The clock struck ten, eleven, Tom did not return. Finally, Susan went to bed, and fell asleep, wondering what had become of him. The next morning his face wore the same grave and unnatural look. He hardly spoke, and when he did speak, the words were constrained. Susan was now thoroughly uneasy.

"Dear Tom," she said, "do tell me what is the matter."

"Nothing," was the only reply she could extract from him.

"Tom, I know something is the matter," she exclaimed, vehemently. "Are you ill?"

"Not in the least."

"Then something has gone wrong in business: something worries you."

"Nothing has gone wrong: nothing worries me '
Cool, curt replies : no relaxation of his face ; not
a smile; not a tender look in his eye. Was this
Tom? What did it mean? Susan was bewildered ;
she could do nothing but reiterate helplessly her
piteous cry, "Tom, what is the matter?"

He left her immediately after breakfast, with the
same strange formal kiss he had given her the
night before.

After he had gone, the impression of his altered
manner faded somewhat; it was all so new, so
strange, that as soon as he was out of her sight, she
thought she must have exaggerated it — imagined it.

"I dare say he really was ill without knowing it,"
she said. "It must be that. He is n't in the least
himself. Perhaps he will be better by noon."

Noon came ; Tom came. The same cool, reserved manner ; the same cool, distant tone ; the
same terrible silence ! Susan now grew seriously
alarmed. As soon as the servant had left them
alone, she exclaimed : —

"Tom, you shall not treat me in this manner any
longer. What have I done?"

"How do I treat you?" he asked coldly.

Susan could not keep the tears back.

"Why, Tom," she said, "you treat me as if I
had displeased you most seriously: as if you were
mortally offended with me for something. What
have I done? I do implore you to tell me."

"You have not done anything. I am not offended," he replied.

Susan was clinging to him, and looking up in his face with streaming tears.

"Tom," said she, you are not telling me the truth. You are as changed as a human being can be, and yet keep the same body. Something has happened; and you shall tell me. I have certainly displeased you, and I cannot imagine how."

He loosened her arms from his neck, and put her away, not ungently, but very firmly.

"There is nothing to tell," he said. "I am not displeased. I must go now."

Susan's arms fell, her whole figure drooped. She stopped weeping, and looked piteously into her husband's face.

"Tom," she said; you are very hard. I would not hurt you so for all the world," and she turned and left him.

All the long afternoon she sat like one in a dream of misery. It seemed to her as if the very sun had gone out. How helpless she was! How long could she live — she wondered over and over — if Tom continued like this!

When he came home at night, she studied his face timidly, and in silence. She tried to converse about indifferent subjects. There was no change in him; still the same frigid, distant civility; the glance, the tone of a stranger and not of a husband. By a great effort she kept back the tears. She was growing calmer now and more resolved. In a few minutes after tea was over, Tom said, with an attempt at ease : —

" I am going to leave you now. I must go down town."

Susan sprang up, closed the door, and standing with her back firmly against it, said, in a low tone, breathlessly, —

" You shall not go till you tell me what has so changed you in this one twenty-four hours. Why, Tom ! Do you know how you look at me ? How you speak to me ? Why, I should be dead in one week, if it kept on like this. What have I done ? What has come to you ? "

He looked at her curiously and observantly.

" How do I look at you ? How do I speak to you ? " he said.

Susan was crying hard, now. She could hardly speak.

" You look at me," she sobbed, " as if I were not your wife, and never had been. You speak to me as if you hated me ; all that is in your tone. Oh, you 'd know it quickly enough, if I looked at you even once with such an expression ! Tom, I shall go mad if you don't tell me ! You can't deceive me. You need n't think you can. I know every slightest intonation of your voice, every shade of your eye. I 've seen you vexed about little things, or out of patience, or tired — but this is different ; this is horrible. I know I must have offended you in some way, and it is cruel in you not to tell me, — cruel, cruel, cruel ! "

He still stood looking at her with a cool observant expression, and made no reply for a moment; then he said, taking hold of the door: —

"I must go now, I don't want to talk any more. I will be back soon."

"You shall not go," said Susan, more slowly, and in a voice of anguish. "I will follow you; you shall not leave me! Oh, Tom, Tom, tell me what I have done!" Suddenly, by what preternatural intuition I know not, — possibly, because, in her great excitement, she was lifted into a state of clairvoyant perception, — she stopped like one hearing a distant sound, leaned forward, and said in an altered tone, "Was it because I would not let you read my letter to Bell?"

As the words passed her lips, she saw his face change, — the first break which there had been in its fearful rigidity. She knew she had touched the truth at last.

"Tom, Tom!" she cried, "was that it? Was that it? I see it was. Why, how could you have minded that so much?" and she led him, half by main force, to a chair, and threw her arms around his neck.

"Ought I not to have minded it?" he asked, in a stern tone.

Susan was reflecting. How distinctly before her eyes at that moment, stood out the fatal sentence, "Be careful what you write."

"Tom," she said, "I will write this very night to Bell, and ask her to send back the letter, that you may read every word of it."

"I have no wish to read it," he said coldly.

Susan was in despair.

"Tom, what else can I do?" she said. "Oh, let me send for it? I never dreamed that you would mind not seeing it. Why, you don't see half my letters to Bell."

He made no reply. Susan sat silent for a moment. She seemed no nearer her husband than before. The same intangible icy barrier which had filled her with such anguish all day was there still. Suddenly, with one of those lightning impulses, by which men in desperate need have often been saved as by a miracle, Susan exclaimed: —

"Tom, I can tell you all there was in the letter. I mean all there was which I did not want you to see." She paused. Her husband fixed his eyes on her with as piercing a gaze as if she had been a witness in a case of life and death. "This was it," continued Susan. "It was about Professor Balloure. You know what you said to me the other morning, that at any rate he could n't have me."

Tom nodded.

"Well, I can't tell you how that shocked me. I never dreamed of your having had any feeling like jealousy about him, or any thought about him in any way in connection with me. Oh, Tom, Tom! how could you ever help knowing that with all the ove of my whole nature I have loved you! Well, you see, Bell had always talked to me about the professor's caring for me. She always thought he wished he could marry me, and in this letter telling about his wife's death she said several things that I did n't like; I did n't read them to you; and in my letter to her I told her how much safer and happier I was with you than I ever could have been with any other man in the world, and——"

Susan hesitated. How hard it was to quote that unfortunate sentence just as it stood! "and— there really was only one sentence in the letter I was un-willing you should see. I thought you would n't understand. I told Bell to be careful what she wrote to me about it, because I had n't any secrets from you, and you might look over my shoulder and read the letter."

While Susan was speaking these last words, Tom's eyes seemed to grow darker and darker, with the fixity of their gaze. As she finished, he put his arms around her, held her tight and kissed her. She felt that the ice was broken. Weeping, she kissed his cheek and nestled closer.

"Sue," said Tom, — it was his old voice, — "Sue, now I will tell you. I had read that letter."

Sue started, and exclaimed, "You! read that letter!"

"Yes," he said. "I came in and saw it lying there open, saw it was to Bell, and glanced down the pages till I came to that sentence which you have just repeated, and which, you will admit, I had cause to resent."

She was hardly listening to what he said. Her face was full of awe, almost of terror.

" Oh, Tom, Tom ! " she cried, was n't it like an inspiration, the impulse which made me tell you that sentence ?   Supposing I had not told you, you would never have believed in me again — never ! "

" No," said Tom.

" Don't you see, dear love," continued Susan, " just how I said that ? simply to save you pain ? — not in the least because there were any secrets in the past I was afraid of Bell's letting out, but because by your speech to me about the professor, I knew that you had had some feeling about him, and I thought, if Bell said any more of her light, jesting, thoughtless things in regard to him, they would only strengthen your feeling and give you annoyance.   Do you see ?   Oh, do say that you see just how it was ! "

" Yes, I do see," said Tom, kissing her.   " I do see, and I thank God that you told me yourself of the sentence.   That took the load off my heart."

Susan shuddered.

" Oh, suppose I had forgotten it ! " she said.   " I might have, though I don't believe I ever could, for the sentence hurt me when I wrote it."

Susan was weak from nervous exhaustion ; the twenty-four hour's strain had been a severe one. She laid her head on her husband's shoulder and closed her eyes.   Without a word, without a sound, without a motion, she knew that they were one again.

After a time she said softly : —

" Tom, what do you suppose put it into my head that it could possibly have been the letter which had troubled you? I never once thought of it at the time. I did not dream of your caring to see it. Don't you think it must have been an angel which made me think of it? "

" I don't know, dear," said Tom, solemnly. " It would have been worth while for an angel."

" Tom," continued Sue, " should you have seemed all the rest of our life as you did this day? "

" I can't tell," replied Tom.

" But you could never have trusted me again? " she said.

" Never," he answered.

After another long, peaceful silence, Susan lifted her head again and said : —

" Tom, will you promise me now one thing? Promise me that, as long as we live, you will never bury anything in your heart as you did this. Only think by what a narrow chance we have escaped terrible misery. Promise me that if ever again any act of mine seems to you wrong, you will come instantly to me and tell me. Will you? "

" Yes, Sue, I will," said Tom fervently.

And this was Susan Lawton's escape.